THE DESTROYING ANGEL

A Tale of Survival and Discovery

BOOK 1
Return to Paradise Series

C.S. HOBBS

BOOK 1

Return to Paradise Series

C.S. HOBBS

The Destroying Angel
A Tale of Survival and Discovery

Return to Paradise Series
Book 1

By C.S. Hobbs

Cedaredge, Colorado

INTEL REPORT
(Cast of Characters)

Admiral Nick Vidaurri—Commands the Icarus and oversees ORBGRU operations.

Anshar Hawk—Atlantean war hero rescued from stasis by Ava.

Arturo Posnasky—Ancient alien specialist and archeologist.

Ava—Sentient AI, friend to Trip Looper, Companion to Anshar Hawk

Brazzeal—CIA FNG spook sent to help Lt. Hawk's team secure access to Atlantis.

Briggs—ORBGRU Team 12 Bravo Team commander.

Chiara Fly—Wife to Sonny Fly with a mysterious background tied to Lilith AKA Lily.

Enlil—Brother to Enki; One above and one below, they both are identified in Sumerian scriptures.

Enki—Brother to Enlil, Earth's Anunna (alien) ally.

Juliet Hutchinson—President of the United States.

Jiang—The half-breed antagonist at Princeton and one of Trip Looper's failed protégés.

Lieutenant Stella Forrestal—ORBGRU, Admiral Vidaurri's right hand.

Malachi—CIA super spy responsible for cleaning up whistleblowers.

Mylitta (Myli) Sipani—Ancient astronaut and Atlantean warrior who returns to her people's version of the Dark Ages. She is forced by necessity to induct Sonny Fly into her defense against an incoming force as old as time, the Anunnu and their biohybrid weapon—the Udug.

Randy—Boat captain and Sonny's shooting mentor.

Mike "Rocco" Badcock—The best fighter pilot in any branch and his own cheerleader. Former relationship with Stella Forrestal.

Shara—Myli's brother. Courageously manned the Menagerie and aged to be an old man in order to get Myli back to Earth to trigger the CME weapon.

Siegfried Santo Padre—Alias for Klaus Eisenbrant, relocated after WWII Germany during Operation Paperclip. Has some experience with unknown majestic materials.

Sonny Fly—Husband to Chiara Fly, reluctant Atlantean conscription of Mylitta (Myli) Sipani.

Trip Looper—An alias going as far back as Atlantis—an immortal as long as he keeps his head. Connections to Sonny Fly.

Udug Seven Roster—Enlil's death squad—humanity's greatest threat since the fall of Atlantis. Nine were transformed. One unwillingly. Seven decided their fate. The Unit's sole purpose is disruption of humanity's ability to recover from the aftermath of the fall of Atlantis.

Humanity knows the Udug Seven by thousands of names across every culture on Earth—demons, devils, vampires, werewolves, and shapeshifters. They are the cautionary monsters of folklore tradition designed to frighten children and teach them to stay close to the campfire. They are the reason we are afraid of the dark—a terror passed down through generations of cautionary tales. You know these bedtime stories, but you've forgotten what they were originally about.

1. **Asag:** Lucifer/Abaddon—Leads the most dangerous death squad humanity has faced since the first cities of humankind. Protector of Enlil's children. His transformation went furthest and cost humanity the most. He's hell-bent on humanity's extermination.

2. **Hanbi:** Beelzebub/Belial—Commands and controls the Udug expansion hierarchy and strategic direction of Seven's operations across millennia. Pazuzu's father.

3. **Pazuzu:** Azazel/Prince of the Air—His hybridization gave him wings, Asag's right hand.

4. **Lamashtu—Lilith—Lily:** She is not Udug by choice. Feared and revered by humanity since her fall from the Garden of Eden. Enlil mutated her with the Legion Virus creating a blind follower. Ancient people believed her to be a vile demon, and modern women revere her as the ultimate feminist. She is far from either.

5. **Namtar:** Asmodeus/Angel of Death—Chief engineer of the Legion Virus and first volunteer for the Udug hybridization program, organizes biological lab operations and genetic warfare.

6. **Resheph:** The Pale Rider/Death—Asag's biological warfare specialist. Responsible for the implementation of the Pandora Strain and subsequent plague which ravaged survivors after Atlantean collapse. He is also the architect of the Bronze Age Collapse—every Mediterranean civilization failing simultaneously around 1,200 BC was his masterwork.

7. **Molach:** Mammon—The empire builder after the fall of Atlantis, controls humanity's new civilizations from within on Udug terms. Handles the Udug's financial and political manipulation across every era of reconstruction.

8. **Baal:** Baphomet—Asag's hidden hand. A gray man capable of blending in so completely his presence is felt but he remains elusive in his manipulation of religious systems and societal disinformation.

9. **Classified**

INTRODUCTION

When Mylitta Sipani awakens from a 11,700-year hibernation, she finds Earth in ruins—its civilizations fallen, history erased, and her people lost to amnesia. Once a hero, now a myth, she becomes humanity's last hope against an ancient menace. Her arrival upends the life of Sonny Fly, an ordinary salesman with a family. Suddenly hunted by shape-shifting enemies, Sonny is caught up in a race to uncover humanity's lost origins. Their only chance of survival depends on a superweapon buried in a forgotten civilization's ruins—but activating it demands an unthinkable sacrifice. As Earth's destruction nears, Sonny's love for his wife clashes with his growing bond with Mylitta, forcing him to question his loyalties, faith, and the meaning of true sacrifice. In a final battle where past and present collide, only betrayal, sacrifice, and love will decide if Earth has a future—or is doomed to repeat its forgotten past.

PROLOGUE

A Million Suns
Bandera, Texas—Present Day

Cuts bleed. Lungs burn. Short of breath. Lactic acid gnaws at his muscles.

Sonny is hauling ass, each step a gamble on uneven terrain littered with everything from BB-sized pebbles to baseball-sized ankle breakers. A wrong move means a bite from a venomous rattlesnake or a fall off a high cliff. The heat is relentless, the risk of heatstroke real. Nearby, forbidding places called *The Devil's River* and *Deadman's Pass* are stark reminders of the dead or disappeared in this unforgiving region.

Under the angry sun, his gear weighs heavily—65 pounds of mags and ammo, dried dates, water, pistol, and rifle. His gear is not the equivalent of his personality, but the blood running down his arm is. Scraped and bleeding, he caught an elbow on the sharp edge of a bullet-riddled car a mile back. The long climb up this 60-degree incline kicks his ass. He glances back to see Chiara following close behind. She's every bit of who she looks like.

At the crest, he slams into a juniper tree and slides into cover. Improvising a shooting position using a C-clamp, he holds onto the trunk of the tree and the handguard of his rifle.

Chiara tops the incline at *Position B* and hits the rocks hard, knees taking the blow, pads absorbing most of it. She and Sonny exchange a nod. Her bipod is already staged, the front of her rifle bouncing as she drops it onto a boulder. She takes the higher ground and coils her sling under the buttstock, creating a makeshift rear-bag; she is on target.

He yelled out to be heard, "Going hot." Sonny is already firing.

"**Hit, hit,** hit!" the R.O., Range Officer, calls out.

His suppressed Geissele URGI 14.5" spits 77-grain IMI Razor Core rounds with precision. The droning voice of the R.O. and impacts on the steel targets in real time confirm his accuracy. The canted red dot on his 1-10 Razor Gen III makes hitting the 50–350-yard targets in this volley a piece of cake. He rolls the scope over and zooms in for the longer shots.

Sonny's watch starts beeping and vibrating before the audio—

"911, what is your emergency?"

"What?" The operator's question takes Sonny out of the action.

Nearby, Chiara's LaRue rifle is barking as she fires down-range.

"Hit, **hit, hit,** hit!" the R.O. yells out with excitement. He side-eyes the action from behind his glass as Chiara puts her rifle on safe while transitioning to the next targets.

Her Khales K318i glass zeroes in on a target at 679 yards, every shot landing in the proper sequence for this Course of Fire.

"Your watch alerted us that you are in cardiac distress." An unknown voice speaks out from his wrist as he continues shooting.

His eyes widen as he sees 911 dialed on his watch. "No, I am okay," he insists.

He fires again.

The 911 operator becomes concerned. "Sir, is that gunfire?"

"Technical difficulties. Have a nice day." He's already setting up on a different barricade to make another shot.

Chiara gives him a corner-eyed glare from her perch.

"Sonny, what the hell?" she asks.

He shakes his head as he keeps firing. "I'm fine."

His watch disagrees: "Cardiac emergency detected. Emergency services en route."

Nice try, Sonny thinks, *but I'm not on any route anyone could get to.*

He spits sand and soot before saying, "It's being dramatic." His thumb flips the safety up. "Safe!" he yells as he maneuvers toward Chiara, barrel down. He rounds her body on the peak, and he taps her shoulder.

"On safe," she echoes his protocol.

Both sling rifles as they advance, pistols drawn.

Pistols blazing, both clear this sector of fire, the R.O. hot on their heels.

Chiara, still skeptical, calls out again. "Overheating or not, that watch is telling you that you're dying from cardiac arrest."

"Dying from embarrassment, maybe." Sonny wipes the sweat from his brow and responds, "The only thing killing me is this sun and altitude."

"Suck it up, buttercup, only a few miles left," she states, taking two more targets out.

Sonny groans, tossing his head back. "Just a few miles left," he mocks sarcastically.

Chiara laughs. Running past Sonny, her hand touches his sweat-drenched back, a light hint so he knows where she is. Her voice is clear as she shouts back, teasing.

"Can I carry your gear to the next stage?" she asks. "Unless you need CPR now."

Sonny ignores her and tells his Apple Watch, *"Fuck off."* He blasts, sending the last round downstage.

"Clear!" Sonny shouts aloud and holsters his still-smoking pistol.

"Clear," Chiara echoes, doing the same. Her grin is ear-to-ear. "That was smooth. Minus you almost dying and all."

From his concealed vantage point, the Range Officer appears and barks out orders as he walks up. "Shooters, mags out, bolts back, show clear!"

They both rip their T-handles back and hold their weapons at a proper angle so the R.O. can look into the chambers. No hint of brass, just a black carbon-filled hole from the backblast of tohe suppressors.

"I see empty chambers," shaking his head, "Those things are filthy."

"Shooting unsuppressed is uncivilized," Sonny blurts out with a shrewd smile.

"Heathens," Chiara recaps. They both let go of the T-handles, and the BCGs slam forward violently.

The R.O. laughs. "Time: 1.67. All steel cleared. Nice run, Team; *Gun Feels Light?*"

"Inside joke," Chiara assures.

"One of the best times today. Next stage is down the cliff—turn right at the orange cone," the R.O. instructs them. "Make your way to the next stage. *Do not go left,* or you will be in our lane of fire. NEXT SHOOTER!"

Chiara winks. "My pistol is faster with the SRO on it than yours," she exclaims, praising her Specialized Reflex Optic as she moves off the line.

Sonny sneers. "Yeah, but it's fragile, and the ACRO keeps the moon dust out."

"Learn how to low crawl right," she says, sweat dripping down her neck and chest.

"You admin?" After asking her about her ammo supply, he checks his own mags. Down by his foot, an arrowhead. He reaches for it and picks it up. Into the dump pouch it goes.

"Ready," she assures him. "Next stage has resupply and water. Race you to the bottom."

"This was supposed to be fun," Sonny groans. The bottom of the ravine is followed by an incline ending at the finish. "My right ass cheek is cramping again," he moans.

"I thought your side was cramping."

"That was the last stage. Every stage is a different muscle," he says, trying to stretch out the latest area of tension.

Chiara smirks. "The heart is a muscle. If you don't keep ahead of me, you'll be watching my ass for the next mile. Your watch says there's no way your heart can take that."

Sonny grins. "Au contraire, I get to keep what I catch." He's smiling wider, his tone shifts. "Did you hear the R.O.?"

Chiara nods. "Yeah. Another possible best time. We've got a shot at first place if you don't stroke out on me. I was serious. Do you want me to carry your rifle? I can handle the weight."

He shakes his head in utter defiance. "How do you only have one gear looking the way you do?" he asks. His lips mash up, sealed tight.

No way he's going to be seen with his wife carrying his rifle into the next stage. It's the finish line or bust, heart attack be damned. "Embrace the suck." Sonny exhales.

Straight faced, "If you don't die." She gives his butt a slap. His muscles are as hard as woodpecker lips.

Chiara moves on but glances over her shoulder. "Randy and Constantine are right behind us. They said they'd catch us by the second stage and pass us by the third. All we've got left is 7 and 8—and the final mile. Let's prove him wrong this time."

He was one of the top five runners on the circuit. The son of a bitch was built like the cinematic *Terminator*—zero body fat, all muscle. He was the guy who had dragged Sonny into this extortionate extreme sport.

Sonny glances at his watch. The nagging device is still angry at him. "We're 6.2 miles in." The last push is brutal. He looks up and sees the pair of runners behind them checking in to the stage. "Shit—there they are; they're rolling into the stage. Is he fucking carrying Constantine on his back?"

Sure enough, the huge man is carrying Constantine and a full kit. Randy is a fucking monster accessorized with a massive pinch of dip in his lip.

"We gotta boogie," Sonny shouts.

"Why can't you do that, Sonny?"

He looks at her crookedly before skipping into a jog. "I'm not a genetic freak of nature."

Ten minutes after enduring the eight-mile biathlon match, Sonny plops down in a folding chair. One leg is stiff as a board. He sprawls out in his chair, chugging pickle juice—anything to kill the cramps.

"Pussy," Randy mutters, rolling up after throwing his gear next to his Battle Van. "Good job, though. Didn't know you had it in you, did you?"

"Sonny was hobbling in on one leg the last half mile," Chiara says as she strolls up laughing and looking fresh and fit.

"For the record," Randy declares, "if I didn't have to carry my partner up a mountain, I'd have whupped all your asses."

"Noted..." Sonny says, despite his pains. "Where is Constantine?"

"Getting an I.V. from the EMTs. You look like you should get one too."

Chiara stands there, still pulsing with energy, stretching like she could go another ten miles without breaking a sweat. Her tank top clings to her body, soaked through, revealing her silhouette beneath. Sweat drips from her neck, running between the valley of her chest, and Sonny is too tired to stop himself from staring. A hundred-yard stare.

She catches him looking. Smirks. Licks her dry lips. "Looks like I caught you."

Sonny groans, letting his head fall back against the chair. "Yeah. What are you going to do about it?"

"You get to keep what you catch?" she asks. "How's that heart?"

"Beating faster again," he jokes.

"Gotta hydrate days in advance or you'll end up like Constantine," Randy says, infusing that statement with all his wisdom just before tossing Sonny a beer. "This'll help."

Far from Bandera in the cold of space, an intruder was hurtling through Earth's solar system. It had been an interstellar traveler returning to its home world since mankind began documenting history. This was the final leg of its journey, a slingshot around the Sun, engines erupting, pressing against the coldness of space with one goal: slow down.

Another ship held no such desire to brake as it angled toward the massive vessel.

A stoic crewman, short of breath, raced down the gangway of his ship. His memories are slowly returning. Enough memories filled back in, making him aware of his duty.

Get her out.

He stopped to read the sensor scans. It took him longer than a glance to understand them. He slapped the side of his head, hoping it would speed up the wakeup juice. He steadied his mind. There was still a month before reentry. Why was he awakened early?

A new warning. EVI, the ship's AI, warned of an imminent collision. He found the blip on the screen moving fast towards his ship. A boarding party? This far out? *The armada mustn't be far behind,* he thought.

His fingers worked quickly. EVI used every sensor available to scan the ship. Origin, Anunna. Another scan revealed something far more disturbing.

Unknown lifeforms. Many.

He controlled his breathing to calm his nerves. The briefing was true, and if they attached to the hull, those creatures would infest his ship and be headed to Earth, too.

His dialect was older than mankind. With a firm voice, he said, "EVI, I need the Marines online."

EVI responded. "Marine contingent activated. Containment protocols activated."

He grabbed a crystal tablet connected to the main terminal and swung it over. The palm of his hand activated a stasis box, the size of his head, against the wall.

"Access granted." EVI complied.

Beside him was her storage locker. It was large enough for this crewman's essentials. Her clothing lay folded neatly with a box securing her wakeup juice on top. His anticipation was evident while his fingers fumbled through her gear. Despite his impatience, he held a death grip on the vial capable of speeding up the recovery of her memories.

EVI called out over the alarms. Her voice echoed throughout the empty corridors. "Marine reactivation successful. Bulkheads prepped for containment."

In that moment, the hull rocked. A direct hit unsteadied his footing. The black Alpha Suit fell from his loosening grip as he fought for balance. A woman materialized in explosive fashion before he could pick it up. Her materialization blew everything around him.

Her body shimmered with channels of steam trailing over her bare skin in opposition to the cool pressurized air. The stories of her viciousness in combat had him expecting a woman wearing his sister's face and stacked with thick muscles. Instead of getting a bio-enhanced soldier, this woman was attractive and deceivingly unremarkable.

Maybe he activated the wrong stasis box, a thought superseded as a liquid metallic device slithered out onto the console. The cybernetic worm solidified, taking the form of a ring laden with subatomic technology.

Ignoring its unusualness, he knelt beside her, preparing to hand her the precious wake-up serum. She would know what to do with it once she took the serum, but she wouldn't have the chance. The spine of the ship twisted around them as the boarding pod crashed into them.

The violence of the impact slung them on their backs. Her ring shot into the metal wall like a bullet and stuck. The cylindrical vial left his flailing fingers rolling into the darkness of a corridor with the indifference of a black hole.

EVI called out. "Intruder alert. Contact."

The wake-up juice would have to wait. The weapon needed to be activated before it was too late.

"We don't have much time to do what I need you to do." He told her.

She looked confused—a normal state without the serum.

"Put your hand on that tablet, or everyone on Ki is dead." he ordered her.

The face she made held remembrance of the consequences of what authorizing the tablet meant. She paused.

He tried to grab her hand. "You've done it before. You did it when we left." He pushed the tablet towards her hand, forcing her to authorize the attack.

She resisted—not out of cowardice but fear of consequences.

"Do your duty, ma'am. You can retreat into the ring after." He tugged her hand more forcefully. "You're the Destroying Angel, for god's sake. Pull the trigger!"

She reached out with her free hand—not for the tablet. Her nails dug into his neck, and she began to squeeze—her eyes locking with his. A flicker of fate, the data feed behind him caught her attention. She didn't know what was coming, but something primal awoke.

"I see you now!" he coughed out through her chokehold.

"What are they?" she asked.

"The end if you don't stop them." Struggling to breathe, he handed her the tablet.

She released her death grip. He didn't have to force her this time. She put her palm on the reader. On his knees at her feet, he pointed to the ring protruding from the wall.

He could see her hesitance. "If you go back in, I promise I will get you off the ship when we land, even if it costs my life."

Back on Earth in Bandera, today's contest is over, and everyone is sitting or standing around critiquing each other's performance. Sonny wonders if he missed his calling.

"Y'all were three-hundredths of a second ahead of us for third place. Won't happen again," Randy says, and he meant it.

Chiara squats and crouches in front of Sonny, her knees pressing against his thighs, her scent intoxicating, despite the sweat and gunpowder. Her fingertips dance over the scrapes on his arms—teasing rather than tending to them.

Sonny cracks another frosty beer open and doesn't doubt Randy's prediction.

Maybe I've peaked, he thought.

"You poor thing." Her voice drips with mock sympathy. "Too tired for a little celebration?"

Sonny cracks one eye open. "If I move another muscle, I'll die."

"That one looks like it's still working."

"Barely," he claims. "Rigor mortis is setting in, maybe."

"Hey, look at me. You didn't fail me. I want you to know that."

"I know," he pointed at their prize.

She waved off the knives. "That's not what I'm talking about. The break-in."

His whole demeanor changed. She saw it immediately; he didn't want to go there.

"You did everything you could," she persisted. "Hey, we did well today," she soothed, trying to diffuse what was brewing. "At least let the little soldier celebrate later."

His mood eased. Tired and honest, he shed some perspective on the matter. "Eight miles, we ran eight miles with all our shit."

Chiara leans in, her lips just shy of his ear. "So don't move. Let me do all the work."

Randy and Constantine drop into their chairs, beers cracking open like a range going hot inside their camp. As the echoes of that simulated Course of Fire die away, steaks and shrimp sizzle on the grill. Randy, a boat captain when he wasn't at matches, catches Sonny's toss midair—the arrowhead.

"Check it out," Sonny says, drinking half his beer in one gulp.

Randy holds up a perfect triangle, still sharp despite dating back to the Early Archaic Period. Randy scrutinizes the artifact.

"Three hundredths of a second. You could've beat us by a minute," he says, "if you didn't stop to dig up arrowheads."

Chiara chuckles. "I told him what was waiting for him at the finish line, and he still found a way to waste time."

Randy tosses it across the fire into Constantine's waiting hands. "He's a dead man, Chiara. Let the man recover before you break him again."

Chiara turns her head, locking eyes with Randy, her grin widening. "What do you think, boys? Should I let him rest?"

Sonny groans, "I hate you."

"You love me. That's why you're buying me a house when we get home," she says as fact. "I don't want us going back there. I keep seeing that night every time I close my eyes."

She winks, swipes the unopened beer from his hand, pops it open, taking a long sip before straddling her husband's leg like a queen poised to settle onto her throne.

Constantine evaluates the arrowhead. The WMD of the Stone Age.

"The AR-15 of the past," Constantine quips as he pops a grilled shrimp into his mouth.

Chiara grows serious. "What if that was all they had after losing all their tech in a forgotten war?"

Constantine plays along. "What, like they had better technology or something?"

"Yeah, but something happened to them, no more guns, just sticks and stones," she posits.

Sonny groans. "Nobody answer that. If you get her started, she'll never stop talking about mythic cultures and ancient enemies."

Chiara ignores him. "Okay, why do y'all come out here and do this?"

"To embrace the suck," Randy answers in simple terms.

"No, I mean really. Why are we all out here?" her tone suggesting she's looking for truth.

"Stay in shape. Be ready for SHTF." Constantine remarks.

Randy confirms, "If you ain't fit, you're dead. If you're dead, no bullet or arrowhead will matter."

Randy leans back; he was there in the beginning. "It began as 'run-what-you-brung' biathlon. If something happened in Texas and the rule of law collapsed—could you traverse six miles, and fight your way home?" Randy asks. "Without having a heart attack?"

Almost everyone around the fire nods in agreement and laughs at Sonny.

"Some old-timers saw the Olympic ski-and-shoot biathlon and thought, let's do a 10K in the desert with a Garand and a pistol," Randy recalls. "Eventually, the prize tables showed up, and so did the gamers. Back then, third place was just bragging rights, not a $350 knife."

Chiara holds up the arrowhead which Constantine had passed back, eyes locked on it. "What if it happens again and we go back to these?" She tapped the flint.

Randy snorts as he stirs the pot. "You start over. Heavy sticks, rocks, bows, and arrows. The delta differential between those levels of weapons is unparalleled, though."

"I warned y'all," Sonny joked. "She's got books full of maps and shit from some old grave digger hack." His brain hurt in recalling the name. "But what do I know? I just sell furniture."

The evening winds down, and when the others give in to the brutal day and crawl into their tents, Chiara doesn't wait. Foreplay is the furthest thing from her lustful mind.

Sonny is oblivious as she slips inside their tent. Before it registers, she's already on top of him, lips hungry, hands roaming, her body still humming with energy. He tries to protest—tries to claim he needs sleep—but she doesn't care.

Sonny knows at this moment—he isn't going to survive this woman.

Their eyes weren't even closed tight before they were awakened by the commotion outside. One, then several people, began hollering in excitement outside their tent. Daylight had come early with an uncanny wave of color stretching from one horizon to the other. The first wave of a massive solar storm arrived.

Sonny and Chiara poked their heads out, drawn by the unnatural aurora blazing overhead. The sun wasn't sleeping, and neither was anyone else after night flipped into day.

"You ever seen something like this before?" Sonny asked. "I've never seen one this strong this far south." He continued, "Hell, I ain't seen one this powerful up north. It's gorgeous!"

Something stirred deep within Chiara, her old soul quivering, remembering the last time she felt such dread from an omen so beautiful.

Her head shook with worry. "I don't think anyone has seen a solar event like this since the end of the Pleistocene."

His arms wrapped around her, chin nestling in her hair, when he asked, "Pleisto-what?"

Chiara embraced his hands. "The end of the Ice Age, babe."

CHAPTER 1

Mattress Man
Victoria, Texas—One Year Ago

It had been a long day at work, and Sonny Fly was feeling it. Helping customers, moving couches, stacking mattresses—Victoria, Texas, was sweltering. The warehouse was a furnace. Even so, compared to his past gigs, this was easy.

His baseball career? Cut short by injury.

TV account executive? Hated cold-calling.

Selling fire alarms? Long hours, of unstimulating, endless driving across South Texas.

Sonny wiped the sweat from his eyes, shirt clinging to him like a wet rag. The window unit AC barely made a dent in the heat. Between helping customers, he rearranged displays and cleaned up insulation refusing to stay on the ceiling. It was 105 degrees, 98% humidity, and the longest drought he'd ever seen.

At 4:45 PM, just before closing, the door swung open. A woman, in a black strapless dress with dove-grey pinstripes, speed-walked past his office window, scanning for an employee. Reddish-brown hair streaked with blonde, flawless bone structure, full lips. An angel tattoo with bloodred wings gleamed on her shoulder just peeking over the back line of the dress.

Sonny froze. She was stunning. Way out of his league. He tried to act natural, but ended up awkwardly dodging left and right, peering through gaps in the window ads to keep her in view.

She backtracked and looked right at him, smiling. "Hey, are you Sonny? I'm Chiara. I think we talked on the phone."

"Uh huh," he mumbled, trying not to look like a fool.

It dawned on him—this was his 3:30 appointment. Late, but worth the wait. He got to his feet and walked her through the showroom. She quickly found the mattress she wanted.

"Can you deliver it? All I have is a car."

"I could tie you down in the back." He said, pointing to the loading dock.

Her eyebrow lifted slightly. Did he just shoot an innuendo at her?

"Loading on the roof isn't ideal. You'd have to go slow so it doesn't just blow off and there is a lot of friction on top. So, tying you down will work but I don't recommend it."

A crease was forming in her lips. A smile was about to break. He had no idea how bad this sounded. "Why?"

Her face was one of confusion which he aimed to clarify. "Wind, bouncing, the twine could come loose. The next thing you know, you're all untied and everything flying off the roof." Her smile got him. The hunter had become the prey. "Look, I'll tell you what. How soon do you need it? Today? No problem!"

"I really need to be horizontally comfortable tonight. Since tying me down on my roof doesn't sound like such a good option and my back can't take another night laying on my old mattress, what do you suggest?"

He looked at her, thinking those looks couldn't be easy to carry. "Give me a sec; I'll load it up in my truck, close the shop, and follow you home, if that works for you."

"I'd be grateful." She barely said with a straight face. This guy was such a nerd.

He nodded and jumped into action. Sonny hustled to the storage area, slung the queen-size mattress over his shoulder, and loaded it into his truck. Not such a nerd after all. Lifting heavy stuff six days a week made this easy.

But right now, it wasn't the weight of the mattress causing his heart to race—it was Chiara.

He followed her ten minutes out of town, past the highway to Goliad, to a small rural house under renovation. She'd been staying there since her separation. The house was small but suited her. She hinted leaving her ex might have saved his life. Sonny decided it was best not to press on her past.

He hauled out the old mattress and dropped the new one in place. She stood in the doorway, watching. Something about her felt forbidden but he didn't care. Love was in the air.

While moving the old mattress, Sonny bumped into her nightstand. A pendant fell.

"Shit—sorry."

"It's only a priceless antique," she teased.

Sonny groaned. "Great. Now I feel like a turd. Maybe I can make it up to you somehow?"

She laughed. "I'm messing with you."

"I was hoping you weren't." He picked up the pendant, studying it. "This is cool. Did you get it traveling abroad?"

"Yeah. I studied overseas for a while. You have a good eye."

"Art major. Had to memorize ancient art styles. This looks older than Egyptian—Sumerian, maybe?"

She paused, surprised. "I'm impressed."

"I'm a whole lot more than my ruggedly good looks," he ribbed.

With the mattress in place, Chiara offered him a drink before he left. They talked for thirty minutes, but Sonny had more deliveries waiting. He was running out of words, something rare for him. Chiara made him nervous in a way no woman had before.

Now or never. He set down his glass, took a breath, and finally said it as they stepped outside.

"Look, I don't usually do this, but I'd really like to get to know you. I haven't met anyone local I was remotely interested in getting to know. Can I get your number?"

Chiara smiled. "I'm going out with friends tonight—Shooters, off Navarro. You should come."

Sonny's eyes followed a bead of sweat slipping down her neck, disappearing into her cleavage. He wanted to keep chasing it. *Good Lord, what is wrong with me?* Something about her.

"Absolutely. I'd love to." Zero hesitation from him.

"See you there." As she walked inside, Sonny leaned against his truck, exhaling as her spell wore off.

How I Met Your Mother and Then ET

Brad pulled up grinning. They were supposed to hit Schrader Hall tonight, but Sonny had thrown a curve ball: Chiara had invited him out. Brad was happy to play wingman, but Sonny wasn't sure he was ready.

"Let's go," Brad said.

Sonny hesitated. "Man, I don't know. It's been a while."

"She invited you, didn't she? Quit being a little bitch. Call her to confirm?"

"It's like riding a bike." Sonny quipped to himself out loud.

Brad became animated, his hands started waving back and forth. "No, it's not. Don't ride her like a bike. Hopefully she's not the village bicycle."

"No way, I could just tell," Sonny dropped a deep breath, climbing into the truck. "Neither of us wanted to seem too desperate, ya know."

"Is she hot?" Brad hoped.

"Bruh," Sonny's face and nod said it all; he was totally enamored with this chick.

Sonny's phone started buzzing incessantly. Missed calls, voicemails, texts piling in. More butterflies.

"See? She's canceling," he groaned. "I knew it. She's a knockout. Out of my league."

"You'll always be a hard seven to me, man," Brad said, snatching Sonny's phone.

"Dude!" Brad's eyeballs widened.

Horror struck Sonny's face. What was Brad seeing?

"Dude." A smile was creeping wider and wider on Brad's face.

Sonny could see his teeth. Not good.

"Dude—what did she say?" Sonny nervously laughed.

"She ain't canceling, dumbass. You didn't have service. She's been calling all night wondering why you're not there yet."

Sonny took a deep breath of relief, then his butt puckered. What's happening? Scrolling through the flood of texts. "Oh, shit."

Brad fired up the truck. "For sure—one of us is going home happy. You might not be able to get rid of this chick though. COO COO. But hey, crazy's worth it unless you get stabbed. Those rural girls all carry knives, you know."

Sonny sighed. "Man, Amber really did a number on me. I'd rather go bro than handle another Amber."

"Amber was a special incarnation of evil," Brad said. "But not all women are the devil. Most, but not all."

Sonny studied Chiara's increasingly frantic texts. Sweet at first, borderline psychotic by the end. "She's pissed, dude. How'd you hook her this hard? Fish on."

Sonny exhaled and grinned—a little scared. "Fantastic."

Sonny looked at the clock. It was fifteen minutes later. Shooters was packed. Pool sharks, hookups, biker gangs, and trouble lurking in every corner.

The moment Sonny spotted Chiara, his heart fluttered.

Brad saw her. She wasn't bad looking. On approach, the closer they got, the better she looked.

"Dude," Brad whispered.

Sonny was physically nodding. "I know. She's so fucking hot."

Brad's head cricked over—she was, but there was something more to it. An attraction in the air. He could smell it. She was like a second shot of bourbon, hot.

"I think you should just leave. No way she's into you and sane."

"Thanks for the pep talk, coach."

"Maybe you roped a unicorn, brah."

"Don't be bird-doggin' my lady." Sonny thumped Brad on the shoulder.

Brad winced. Sonny couldn't take his eyes off her. The dress hugged her perfectly. Low cut, but classy. Her face had a European sharpness he rarely saw around this area. And the pendant—same one from her place. Her attraction, magnetic.

Brad elbowed him, grinning. "While you flail around, I'm going for the one with the massive tits."

Sonny groaned. Brad had no brain-mouth-filter, and his breast fetish was legendary. Tonight would either be amazing or a disaster.

Surprisingly, Brad behaved as much as Brad could control his juvenile wit. His eyes never left Angelica's chest, but at least he kept his mouth shut.

Sonny, meanwhile, was gaining confidence. This chick digs me, he thought. She's 100% crazy or a rare unicorn Brad hinted at. Either way he was nailing every line and charming her pants off.

Before long it was Last Call and with closing time came an invitation for the fun to continue at Noel's house for some hot tub time. Neither of them had swimsuits and, as he stripped down, Sonny wondered if he was skinny dipping or wearing their Hoochy-mamma Calvin Klein silk nut-huggers.

The moment Chiara stripped down, Sonny stopped being so self-conscious. She wore practically see-through panties, sheer red bra, tattoos—one with red angel wings—were scattered across her skin, each with its own story. Some were in a language he knew were history book old. Near her hip, above her buttocks, another tattoo with a set of wings and snake heads running up a staff.

She liked ink.

He slipped into the water quickly and was grateful to already be submerged as she made her entrance.

She slid in close, hand on him, body pressed against him. Sonny knew in that moment, crazy or not, this was the only place in the world he wanted to be, right next to her.

Brad wasn't so lucky. Angelica's husband appeared the moment she stepped into the water. Brad's dreams crashed hard, but free beer kept him afloat. Noel, meanwhile, seemed far too interested in Brad—Sonny suspected he'd been hunting him all along.

The after-party rolled until sunrise. Drinks, conversation, and laughter flowed until they finally staggered out of the water around 6 a.m.

As everyone toweled off, Chiara bit her lip, eyes sparkling. "Need a ride home, Sonny?"

He smiled. "Yeah. Let me let Brad know, make sure he's okay to drive."

From across the street Brad yelled and waved. "Go, dude. If you don't, I'd worry about you."

"Want me to see if Noel wants to ride with you?" Sonny bellowed back.

Brad laughed so loud the neighborhood dogs started barking. "Hard pass." He responded with an erect middle finger.

Just for good measure Brad peeled out before Noel could jump in.

Sonny turned back to Chiara, who was now full of mischief. "Let's go, cowboy," she purred. "I'm all wet, and I wanna get warmed up."

Her drawl was perfect. Although he fancied himself a good Russian accent, this would do.

They drove off into the morning light, kissing before they even made it to Sonny's place.

When the car screeched to a stop, Sonny paused just long enough to ask, "You wanna come in?"

Chiara bit her lip, shivering. "I'd love to. But only if you give me a towel so I don't freeze to death."

"Yeah, of course."

Inside, dripping wet and laughing, Sonny tossed her a hand towel, then quickly grabbed a real one. As she dried off, she looked at him differently now, something beyond simple attraction. He was funny, courteous, and even though he doubted himself a little, he'd had the balls to go for it.

Softly, she said, "This isn't really my style, I don't usually do this the first night."

He winced, did the math. "Technically, it's day two." Holding up two fingers. "The sun's coming up."

"Mr. Technicalities, huh? Okay, then you should stay at my place, Einstein."

He raised an eyebrow.

"I have a really comfy mattress. Just bought it from this amazing guy. But it didn't come with any instructions."

Sonny grinned. "Hope that amazing guy gave you a good deal."

She stepped closer. Her eyes focused like a predator. Her brow furrowed like she was closing in for the kill. "He did. Is there any way to get an in-home tutorial? I think it needs to be thoroughly tested."

He didn't wait for a second invitation. Sonny raced upstairs, tripping over the steps as he grabbed a spare set of clothes for himself.

Seconds later, they were back on the road. The drive felt shorter this time. Her hand was warm in his.

They tumbled onto the mattress Sonny had delivered eight hours earlier, naked, tangled, and content.

By the time they woke, lunch had passed. He wore the pendant she gave him. Starving, they headed for a hole-in-the-wall diner down the road.

From that day forward, they were inseparable. They laughed constantly. Loved fiercely. It was love at first sight—or damn close. In a few months, they were married.

CHAPTER 3

House of Pain
Victoria, Texas—One Year Later; Present Day

September. Sonny was drenched in sweat instead of his hypnotic wife. He glanced at the sky, half-expecting the sun to explode. The Aurora was still there and intensifying. Instead of the world ending, he faced a truck full of mattresses still waiting to be unloaded. He groaned, still thinking of that day, and the stupid break-in.

Subconsciously he reached for the pendant no longer around his neck.

He wasn't sure if it was the heat, the lack of sales, or the memory of that ill-fated night that turned him salty. Between breaks, helicopters thundered overhead. Tanks and railcars rattled the windows. Another Jade Helm-style exercise? Sonny wiped his brow recollecting the shitty day.

An hour earlier Sonny was sipping the last cold water in the warehouse when Mrs. Montez stormed in like a Category 5 hurricane, shoving her phone into his hands.

"My husband wants to talk whish jou."

Sonny sighed. "Hello?"

"You promised Friday! Where is my mattress?!"

"Sir, it is Friday."

"Why isn't it here yet?"

"Because it's 1:30 and we receive shipments until 6:00."

A short audible pause over the phone.

"You delay because we are Hispanic peoples."

Sonny rubbed his temples. "Sir, three-quarters of my customers are Hispanic. My last ex was Latina."

"Latina? No Mexicano!" Mr. Montez yelled.

Mrs. Montez snatched the phone back. "He says jou do not respect him."

She shoved the phone back at him again. "Fine," Sonny said impatiently. "Pick up your refund tomorrow at 11."

"I want interest! For my paing's and sufferin'.'"

"Bruh"—Sonny exhaled. Changed his mind. "Sir, you'll get your money if it doesn't arrive today. No interest."

Mrs. Montez delivered her next statement below the belt: "We will be calling our lawyer, jou gringo son of a bish."

The truck pulled in.

"Sir. Your mattress just arrived."

"Oh! Thank Jesus. I prayed for jou." Sonny clicked the phone off.

Mrs. Montez wasn't finished. "Jou know watt jour problem is, Mijo?"

"I am sure I am about to find out." He leaned back waiting for her diagnosis.

"Jou let people step all over-jou, but I see what jou're really doing. Jou is giving dem enough rope to hang dem'selves with. Jou on purpose give people the means to destroy dem'selves," she said while leaving the office and shaking her finger at him.

Sonny nodded. Maybe she was right. He always offered plenty of rope. He waved. And he did enjoy tightening that noose and pulling the chute when the time came. Anything to break up the monotony of those boring days.

Speaking of those days, this was one. Sonny stood up and peered out the window, laughing until his sides hurt. "Fuck my life. Game over, man." He tossed his clipboard on his desk and shook his fist at the sky. "Is it too much to ask for a little more adventure than sparring with some ole woman?"

Sonny broke away from the sweatbox and was now outside counting mattresses: 9 king-size, 15 queen-size, his pen tore the soggy paper, 7 full-size sets still left to unload. His buddy, Rufus Finch, showed up out of the blue.

"How 'bout them space fireworks?" Rufus hollered, nodding up at the daytime aurora as he crossed the parking lot toward Sonny. "Need help?"

He pulled his shirt off and flexed for maximum punctuation.

Sonny laughed when Rufus hit the Mr. Olympia pose.

Ever helpful, he tried lifting a queen mattress, failed, and bailed back to his Knight Rider replica. Minutes later, Sonny got a text:

"Sorry, felt defeated. Saw you carry that king with ease and felt about three inches tall on a good day. Good luck, man."

Sonny laughed. Rufus might feel three inches tall, but he'd beat Sonny in a crabwalk fight inside of two minutes. BJJ, rolling on the floor with sweat soaked dudes was his thing. After a few times on the mat rubbing against Rufus, Sonny knew damn well he wasn't three inches anywhere.

Sonny shook the image out of his mind. And then once more for good measure. His back screamed. Two appointments left. One might no-show; the other was running late. He slumped into his chair, staring at the clock.

Minutes into his meditation the phone rang. Caller ID: "SOME SIDE CHICK."

Sonny perked up. "Hey, darling! Everything okay?"

"Babe? Who dis?" Chiara chuckled. "Just checking in. I know how hot it is. Oh! And I found my makeup bag."

"Babe, you're not a sea monster, but I'm happy you found it." Sonny wiped his brow. AC stuck at 92 degrees. "Haven't stroked out yet. Ready to get home, crack a beer, watch the Wild Card race."

Sonny was already multitasking, digging through the mail. One package stood out—Amazon, some random seller he stumbled upon. He tore the package open and pulled out an old, rare, heavily worn book.

"Have you heard from Rufus about the loan?"

Sonny's face cinched up like he was having a cramp. He bit his lip and head went down. "Damn, forgot to ask," he muttered, setting the book in the drawer beside him.

Ole Santo Padre, Alien Indiana Jones, was going to have to wait before he could scribble in his last book.

"You saw him?"

He shoved the drawer closed. "Errrr." Movement outside caught his eye. Saved by the bell. A customer walked in, followed by a taller, rougher man. Trailing behind: a pregnant girl flicking a cigarette.

The tall guy locked eyes with Sonny. "Jesus. What the fuck is this?" Sonny muttered.

The guy had Chihuahua-shaped eyes, like someone ripped off his head and blew into it like a balloon, then stuck it back on and gave him all the cocaine he could ever want. Sonny flinched staring at those *sanpaku* eyes, until Chiara's voice cut back in.

"What did you say?"

"No, not you, babe," he whispered. "A freak show just walked in."

"You carrying?"

"Every day after that night," he said itching the scabs on his forearm from the match.

She sighed. "Let me know if you need help dumping any bodies."

Sonny watched them roam, trying not to judge, but failing. "Will do, Deliverance is walking in. I'll work fast and get home faster." He nodded, phone still to his ear. "I gotta go. Love ya, babe."

"You better. Are you okay? You sound... off."

"Never better; just wondering what adventures I am missing. I gotta go, gotta go."

Sonny hung up. Time to face the heat. He stepped out of the office. Instantly, 109-degree flow blasted him.

He grimaced. His teeth dried the moment the air hit them. His lips stuck to the afternoon plaque. "Oof?" he muttered to the sky.

Every summer, the warehouse became a sweatshop. He'd seen plastic melt here. Out of the barred windows, he spotted dark clouds over Cuero with hints of green in them. He knew what green meant—it'd veer north and miss Victoria like always. *Victoria,* he thought, *hotter than a witch's crotch.*

He approached the crew, mentally sizing them up: Tattoos—bad ones. Possibly self-done.

Leader: bleach-blonde crew cut, scraggly copper goatee. The '90s called and wanted that *pubic nightmare* back. They were not from Victoria. Cali, maybe. People like this belonged in Austin, not a town full of old oil barons.

Sonny focused on the only one who looked like he could form a sentence. His smell was… familiar. The others, background noise. His brain clicked into sales mode: Ask what they need. Read them like a poker game. He'd done $7K in sales in ten minutes before. Get it done. Get home.

He smiled, grabbed his clipboard, and walked into battle.

Chapter 4

Fatal Paradise
Puma Puku, Bolivia—1945

Arturo paused, gazing at the distant ruins of Puma Punku, the monolithic stones casting long shadows in the afternoon sun. He let the question linger in the air, as if the earth itself might whisper the answer. When no answer came, he repeated his question.

"Places like Machu Picchu and the Anasazi ruins— they're just remnants. Echoes of something much greater. Whatever happened, it didn't just destroy civilizations; it erased knowledge itself. Think about it, Siegfried. Why did humanity have to start over?"

Siegfried frowned, running a hand over the worn leather strap of his pack. "You think it was deliberate?"

"I think someone wanted to make sure we forgot," Arturo speculated. He sighed, once again adjusted his wire-rimmed glasses, and watched Siegfried whose gaze remained fixed on the stone tablet, as though the weight of untold generations pressed against his soul.

"The Star People will return," Arturo murmured, his voice low but certain. "Just as they did before. And they'll take this place back from us."

The two exchanged uneasy glances.

The mountain wind howled through the ruins, carrying the whispers of a history too ancient to be remembered, too important to be ignored.

Arturo paused, turning to face Siegfried, his expression shadowed in the waxing light. He tapped his walking stick against the stone path, as if trying to summon an answer from the earth itself.

Siegfried wiped the sweat from his brow, glancing at the path ahead. The summit loomed above them, bathed in the soft glow of the rising sun. He wanted to argue, to dismiss his colleague's ideas as paranoia, but something about Arturo's certainty unnerved him.

"If this is so, why doesn't anyone remember?" Siegfried asked.

Arturo let out a breath, scanning the distant ruins of Tiahuanaco below. "Because someone—or something—made sure we forgot."

Siegfried swallowed hard, a deep sense of unease settling in his chest. The idea history itself had been rewritten, buried, erased—it was almost too much to comprehend.

"The ancients saw it coming," Arturo continued, gesturing toward the massive stone blocks of Puma Punku, their laser cut precision untouched by time. "They left behind warnings, built entire cities in anticipation of the return. But something happened. Something catastrophic. And now, we're left with only fragments of the truth."

Siegfried adjusted his pack, forcing a smirk. "You make it sound like we are looking for Atlantis."

Arturo didn't laugh. Instead, he spoke again with the same certainty which unnerved his companion. "Atlantis wasn't a myth," he declared as he turned and continued up the path. "It was a memory."

Siegfried stared after him, a chill creeping up his spine.

They climbed without speaking, the only sound the whisper of wind over ancient stone.

After a time, Arturo paused and turned to face the other man, his eyes rejuvenated in the burgeoning light.

"The truth isn't hiding—buried. Twisted. Rewritten," Arturo said. He tapped his walking stick against the rocky trail. "Every ancient culture speaks of the gods arriving from the heavens, wielding incomprehensible power. What if they weren't gods at all?"

Siegfried inhaled deeply, the thin mountain air making each breath feel insufficient. His body ached from the climb, but his mind was racing. "You're saying humanity has encountered advanced beings before? They didn't just visit; they intervened?"

Arturo sighed, adjusting his wire-rimmed glasses. "I'm saying there's a pattern. A cycle of destruction and rebirth. If the elders' stories hold even a grain of truth, then we aren't the first to rise. And if we aren't the first..."

Siegfried finished the thought. "We won't be the last."

The two men pressed on, the ruins of Puma Punku rising like forgotten sentinels above them. The towering stones seemed to defy time itself, their precise cuts and inexorable weight whispering of an era when things were very different.

Arturo gestured toward the ruins. "Look at them, Siegfried. Even today, with all our engineering, we couldn't replicate this. No wheels, no pulleys, no iron tools—yet these stones were carved and moved with absolute precision. Either our ancestors had knowledge we no longer possess... or they had help."

Hearing this, Siegfried reached into his pocket and extracted the gold pendant which the two had recovered on an earlier expedition. He fingered the pendant, tracing its sharp angles and sleek design. It really did look like a miniature plane—swept wings, tail fins, even something resembling a cockpit.

Siegfried couldn't help but be skeptical. "You say this is thousands of years old?"

Arturo nodded. "The Quimbaya civilization crafted these artifacts nearly 1,500 years ago. Some say they're nothing more than stylized birds." He gestured toward the pendant. "But you and I know birds don't have vertical stabilizers."

Siegfried's brow furrowed as he studied the artifact more closely. "Do you believe the ancients saw something... something like this, and they replicated it the best way they knew how?"

"Exactly," Arturo said, stepping over a loose rock. "Like the cargo cults after World War II. Followers replicated technology by building wooden runways, making radios out of coconut shells, all in the hope the gods—the ones who brought them gifts—would return."

Siegfried exhaled. "So, if this," he held up the pendant, "is a piece of the puzzle... what are we climbing up here to find?"

Arturo glanced up at the ruins of Puma Punku, where the towering monoliths stood silhouetted against the last light of day.

"If my research is right, Puma Punku isn't just an archaeological site. It's a message."

Siegfried felt the mountain air grow heavier around them. The wind whispered through the abandoned ruins, carrying something he couldn't quite place—a presence, a warning.

"Alright, professor." He adjusted his pack. "Let's see what history has been trying to tell us."

They pressed on, the sun dipping behind the peaks, casting long shadows over ruins which had no business being at this altitude.

Something was waiting for them up there.

And they were about to find it.

CHAPTER 5

God Tech

Siegfried Santo Padre stood atop the high-altitude ruins of Puma Punku, the wind whipping through the thin morning mountain air. Below, the vast, arid expanse stretched as far as the eye could see. With careful steps he navigated the scattered stones, balancing himself atop one of the massive monolithic slabs.

Siegfried ran his fingers along the smooth, almost impossibly precise edges of the monolithic slabs. The craftsmanship defied explanation. No chisel marks. No signs of primitive quarrying. Just clean, perfect cuts, as if the stones had been shaped by something far more advanced than copper or bronze tools.

"Unfathomable," he muttered under his breath.

Arturo stood a few feet away, adjusting his camera. He had been here before, but each visit left him breathless. The sheer scale of Puma Punku's ruins, the way its massive stones had been scattered like toys, suggested an event so cataclysmic, so surgically devastating, it bordered on the unreal.

Siegfried looked down at the strange metallic ore fused into the stone couplings. Unlike anything found in other ancient sites, it had a smooth, polished sheen, resisting the corrosion of time. Not iron. Not bronze. Something else.

"This wasn't primitive," he exclaimed with assurance. "This was engineered."

Arturo sounded doubtful. "Now you're thinking like a heretic!" he applauded.

Siegfried exhaled, still not ready to embrace the evidence in front of him. The standard archaeological timeline was crumbling beneath his fingertips. If Puma Punku was as old as some believed—pre-dating even the Sumerians—then history itself had been built on a lie. Seeking to clarify his thoughts, he turned to Arturo.

"Tell me something," said Siegfried. "What exactly do you think happened here?"

Arturo stood, his eyes scanning the ruins.

"To me it looks like a battlefield," Arturo decided. "The aftermath of war and not just any war. A war fought with weapons we don't even understand."

Siegfried's pulse quickened.

"What if a solar event of immeasurable power—a Carrington Event multiplied a thousandfold—impacted the Earth? A polar shift, an electromagnetic disruption in the core itself. It could have uplifted the crust here in a matter of hours. That would explain why not much is left standing."

Arturo nodded. Siegfried was catching on. "And if one land mass rose, the Earth would have balanced itself during the displacement. Another area would have subducted somewhere else entirely."

The Younger Dryas. Ice Age to The Great Flood, Siegfried told himself. *Ancient legends of fire and destruction from the sky—perhaps these aren't just metaphors. Puma Punku hasn't fallen to time, but to something far more deliberate. There are no chisel marks, no evidence of rudimentary tools. Just flawless geometric incisions, cut to tolerances within a millimeter—perfection defying logic.*

He turned to his mentor, Professor Arthur "Arturo" Posnansky, a man whose theories had made him an outcast among mainstream scholars.

As if reading his student's thoughts, Arturo stretched his arm toward the basin of Lake Titicaca.

"This valley was once an ocean," he said. "The builders of Puma Punku crafted a grand Atlantean port to accommodate a civilization we've forgotten."

Siegfried followed his gaze. The thought was staggering. If this had once been a seaport, how far back was its construction?

The ruins weren't merely ancient. Logistically, there was no way an ancient tribe could physically move the monoliths down here unless the ground below was on the surface long ago. A force of nature long-forgotten must have rearranged the landscape.

Adding to the mystery, the ruins of Puma Punku sat at a staggering 13,000 feet above sea level, perched on a barren plateau where not a single tree had ever grown. And yet, conventional theories insisted ancient builders had used logs to roll these massive stones into place. Logs from where? Altitude alone made it improbable.

Somewhere in this place, Siegfried was certain—the past had left behind a clue to unlock its mysteries. And the truth buried beneath it might change history forever.

The men had once heard a whispered legend, a story repeated by village elders. According to the tale, after World War I, the U.S. government had discovered these ruins—and had been alarmed by what they found. The technology was so incomprehensible authorities had deemed it "godly."

If the stories were true, this could have been the first major archaeological cover-up predating Roswell and other classified wartime discoveries.

As Professor Posnansky recorded his calculations, Siegfried wandered deeper into the ruins, his mind spiraling with questions; left with no real tangible answers.

It was in the twilight of the setting sun that something out of place caught his eye.

At the base of a toppled monolith, a faint blue light pulsed within a dark crevice.

The glow was soft, hypnotic, out of place. It beckoned him forward. Heart pounding, Siegfried knelt beside the fissure. The air hummed a binaural frequency. His breath quickened.

He peered inside.

Left behind while Siegfried explored the ruins, Arturo fiddled with his ancient pendant while he was calculating. Siegfried was unaware of the professor's movements and yet a deep rumble vibrated through the ruins. Stone scraped against stone. Though far away, the professor had inadvertently triggered something. It was dumb luck.

Siegfried stepped back as, with a thunderous shift, a magnetically sealed stone retracted into the ground, revealing a hidden passageway plunging into the depths below. Siegfried stood frozen with nowhere to go as the ground trembled beneath his feet.

A violent tremor sent him sprawling, his hands scraping against the ancient rock. Dust erupted into the air, choking his lungs. He coughed, stumbled back to his feet. In a reflex, his hand went to his holster.

The cold steel of his Luger met his palm. He didn't think—he pulled his weapon, and his finger squeezed the trigger as he fired into the black abyss before him.

A sharp crack echoed through the chamber.

The bullet ricocheted wildly off unseen surfaces, sparking as it deflected into the void.

Silence followed.

His pulse thundered in his ears. Seconds later, the professor's voice reached him, sounding hollow.

"Siegfried? What the hell was that?" Arturo's voice carried through the ruins, sharp with alarm. The professor was making his way toward the noise and light, but he was still far away.

"What? I'm not sure." He responded, befuddled to himself. "Did you say something professor?"

Dust swirled in the dim pulsing glow. When his eyes adjusted, he saw it—a figure emerged.

A monstrous form stood motionless at the base of the chamber; its hulking silhouette distorted by the flickering light. It was demonic, unearthly, terrifying enough for Siegfried's grip to tighten on the Luger.

The thing wasn't moving—yet.

Siegfried's limbs trembled, his breath shallow and erratic. His mind screamed at him to run, but his body refused to obey.

The Luger shook in his grip. His legs gave out beneath him, and he sank onto the cold stone, his heart hammering against his ribcage.

Moments later, Arturo stood over him, sighing in exasperation.

"Siegfried, what are you doing here? I think I just solved the…" But Arturo didn't finish his thought. Instead, he froze, and his voice dropped to a whisper. "Pazuzu," he breathed the word.

Hearing this, Siegfried seemed to wake from a stupor, and he raised his pistol, prepared to fire again. "Damn it, Arturo!" he shouted. "You scared me to death!"

Arturo ignored the outburst. Instead, each step was deliberate as he approached the chamber's edge. Peering inside he locked eyes on the figure below.

"Relax," he murmured. "You're desecrating the site. It's only a statue. Come with me."

Siegfried holstered his Luger and dropped into the chamber beside Arturo, dust swirling around his boots. The blue glow flickered, casting shifting shadows across the monstrous figure.

Arturo studied it with delicateness.

"A Mesopotamian demon," he muttered. "He shouldn't be here. What are you doing so far from home, my friend?"

Siegfried exhaled and wiped sweat from his brow.

"It fooled me." He glanced at the thing's twisted, leering face. "I shot in self-defense, and I think I may have pissed myself."

Arturo coughed up phlegm as dust overloaded his lungs. "Charming. You've managed to desecrate the site in more than one way."

Siegfried swallowed. "The elders said they could hear creatures stirring underground. Spooks, perhaps. They weren't far off."

Arturo frowned, glancing around the chamber's stonework. "That still doesn't explain how you found this place."

Siegfried's hands were still unsteady as he stood within arm's length of the grotesque statue. "I have no idea how I found it," he said as he peered beyond the statue and into the darkness beyond. "But I think I can see a torch jutting from the wall. Hand me your lighter."

"I could use a drink," Arturo said but he obliged, flicking his lighter open with a sharp metallic click. He pulled a flask from his pocket and tried to take a swig from it, but Siegfried grabbed it, stealing it from his lips, along with the lighter from his other hand.

He poured the high octane liquor on the rag and lit a nearby torch, the flickering flame casting twisting shadows along the chamber walls. As his eyes adjusted to the dim glow, he saw them.

More figures.

The figures receded further in the darkness, half-hidden, their grotesque features hidden by wavering light. Beyond them, halls stretched deeper into the unknown.

"Arturo," Siegfried whispered with quiet angst. "There are more."

Arturo's brow furrowed. "A burial chamber?"

Siegfried shook his head. "No. I think it's a workshop. Whoever was here was a creator."

A creator, Siegfried told himself. *A creator like me.*

The men explored further.

At the chamber's center, a waist-high stone slab loomed, its surface obscured beneath layers of dust. Arturo brushed his fingers over its surface, sending centuries-old debris drifting into the stale air. Whatever had once rested there had long-since crumbled into nothing.

Arturo exhaled exhaustively. "Someone's been here before us."

Siegfried sounded doubtful, "How can you tell?"

"Less dust in some areas," Arturo said and nodded to the wall. "That is an equal armed cross."

"Templar graffiti?" Siegfried asked.

Arturo directed his attention to an unfinished figure painted below the cross. It was crude. He jabbed at it with his finger in the air. He was mumbling to himself, trying to remember who this red-winged angelic figure was. Unlike most renaissance paintings he'd studied, her eyes were looking down. Sadness?

A glint fired in his eye. "Ah, the Destroying Angel," he said of the woman naïvely painted in front of him.

He followed her eyes down to the stone slab in front of him. "What are you trying to tell us, dear?"

Arturo knelt; his face drew closer as he began brushing away more dust. Beneath the grime, something gleamed. Something metallic. For a moment, his eyes flickered back toward the entrance. The statues hadn't moved. And yet, somehow, they felt closer. He felt lightheaded. His blood pressure was elevated. His pulse quickened, but he shook the feeling off.

Focus, he told himself.

He lifted the fragment from the dirt, turning it in his fingers. It was cold and smooth—far too modern for a site untouched by time.

"This isn't indigenous to the site," he murmured.

Siegfried leaned in, "I agree. What do we think it is?"

Arturo studied the fragment, his mind racing. "All I know is it doesn't belong here. It looks like aluminum or advanced alloy. This could have been one of the Knight's vaults. There are several rumored across North and South America."

He ran a thumb over the surface, watching how the torchlight coruscated against its alien sheen. All at once, he was struck with a thought.

"Have you seen the giant computers they've been installing since the war?" Arturo asked. "The ones the military uses?" His voice grew distant, almost entranced.

Siegfried nodded slowly, "Yes, I've seen them. What about them?"

Arturo turned the fragment over in his palm, his breath shallow.

"If you shrank one of those enormous computers down a billion times, you'd have something that looks like this."

For a moment, neither of them spoke.

The torchlight wavered.

They had discovered exotic materials in a place untouched before written history. Remembering the stories about soldiers assigned to search and destroy this area, Arturo had a sobering thought.

"I bet the U.S. military would love to get their hands on this," Arturo said.

Siegfried shuddered, a chill caused by memories from the war. As a consulting professor working with military contracts, he had been part of too many cover-ups. Too many buried truths. If this discovery was real, he had to make sure it reached the public—before it was erased like all the others.

"Arturo, I've seen tech like this before."

Siegfried's voice echoed in the chamber, but it wasn't an echo he heard that alerted him.

Not the settling of ancient stone. Not the whisper of wind through forgotten corridors.

They sensed movement.

Calculated movement that was methodical. Something was closing in on them and not randomly. Not mindless.

Stretching shadows crept forward with a hungry, unseen presence. The air grew thick, pressing around him like an invisible hand tightening its grip.

Siegfried's pulse pounded in his ears. Every fiber of his being screamed danger. Death was headed their way.

Arturo's voice rang out with urgency. "The torch, Siegfried! Light, SIEG-FRIED! Give me the pistol."

Siegfried whirled and held the torch high, lighting the darkness. Arturo was there; he had Siegried's Luger raised. Both men froze and stared in disbelief.

Where lifeless forms had stood, mummy-like figures began twitching to life, their decayed joints cracking as they turned toward the men. While Atlantis subducted into the ocean, this place rose skyward by 13,000 feet, protecting its inhabitants from the floodwaters. Hidden underground, the virus was protected from solar flares and Coronal Mass Ejections. Time and decay were the only real enemies, and being intombed here was the perfect preservative.

Their eyes were hollow; yet burning with malevolence. Their movements were erratic but not the irregular lurch of the undead. Shambling—yet co-ordinated. Twitching—yet deliberate. A terrifying, eerie intelligence lurked within their withered, leathery husks.

The creatures drew nearer.

Arturo fired at the ghouls.

Muffled shots echoed underground, swallowed by the weight of the earth. Arturo went down.

CHAPTER 6

Texas Chainsaw Mattress Sale
Victoria, Texas—Present Day

Richard Tantrom was Sonny's last appointment of the day. The rest of his crew didn't bother giving names. At first glance, it looked like a quick sale.

Richard had called about the $99 pillow-top—a guaranteed headache. But a sale was a sale.

"Step right up," Sonny said. "The one you get will be new in plastic, with a warranty."

He led them down the aisle, running through the usual mental script: Ask who it's for, gauge delivery, read the budget. Sonny could do this in his sleep.

They stopped at the deflated $99 mattress.

"Queens start at $99, go up to about seven grand but we have this model marked down to $3500. Most folks land around $399. Lay on a few, see what works for your back and wallet."

Richard's face soured. "The ad says $99 for the set, but this one's $159," he complained. "I got one of them thick ones for $99 in Houston and you got it for $400!"

He pointed at an $800 set down the aisle.

Sonny sighed. *Here we go.* So much for turn and burn.

Richard stomped down the aisle, slapping mattresses like they'd insulted him.

"Junk." Another SLAP. "Crap. This is bullshit."

He stormed toward the exit with his entourage.

Sonny should've let them leave. Instead, his pride got the best of him. "No matter what price I put on anything in here, you're not interested?"

Richard Tantrom froze, turned back. "I got five grand in my pocket," he flashed the bulge. "But I ain't spending more than $500 on no goddamn mattress."

"Richard, can I call you Dick?" Sonny held back a grin. "Let me show you one more set."

He led them to the 627Q Crazy Quilt. Marginally better than the ad mattress. Richard ran his hands over it, nodding.

"Yeah, this'll do. Should've shown this first, dummy."

Richard's baby mama fired up another smoke. She groaned, smacked her gum, and walked out. "Whatever, Dick." She snickered. "I need a fix."

As Sonny started ringing him up, his phone buzzed. **"WE GOT THE HOUSE, BABE!"**—Chiara. Sonny grinned. Finally, something went right.

"You laughin' at me, chucklehead?" Richard snapped.

Sonny bit his tongue. **It's a mattress, not a kidney transplant.** "No, sir."

The ancient printer crawled at its usual pace. The office was silent except for its agonizing wheeze. Sonny counted the seconds, sweating, waiting for it to spit out the last page.

Finally, Richard snatched the receipt, scribbled his name big and bold, and stomped out.

Sonny exhaled, running a hand through his hair, fingers brushing his concealed HK USP Compact. He looked at the signature. DICK. He laughed.

"Carry, carry, carry," he muttered. "Frickin' weirdos."

The Montez types didn't rattle him—customers like Tantrom? They made him watch his back on the way to his truck. Were they nearby, waiting to follow him home?

"Fuck."

He opened his drawer and pulled out a signed copy of *The Ancient Enemy,* a book last distributed in the late forties. It was a housewarming gift for Chiara. She loved old artifacts. Especially the archeology literature from this guy. Sonny flipped the page to remember the name—there it was in perfect cursive.

Siegfried Santo Padre.

Sonny laughed. From what little he'd read about this Siegfried guy, he gathered the man was a complete loon. But that loon wrote a book about a subject Chiara couldn't get enough of, making it the perfect gift for some bedroom goodwill. This book, especially, since it came with an inscription from the previous owner that seemed to have been written just for him.

She's out of your league, dummy. Do it anyway. Both times.

Sonny read the most random inscription he'd ever seen out loud. With the stroke of his own pen, he followed the stranger's message with one of his own for Chiara.

"He ain't wrong, ya know! Love Sonny."

CHAPTER 7

The First People
Princeton, New Jersey—1949

More than seventy decades later, Malachi Donnoby jogged up the steps of Princeton's McCosh Hall, his breath visible in the crisp autumn air. The collegiate Gothic architecture loomed around him, a medieval fortress of knowledge. Gargoyles perched above, frozen in silent watch.

He took the stairs two at a time, weaving past students and scholars, his coat whipping behind him. He had just come from the ballfield on Elm Street, shagging balls with the Princeton Tigers. They were hungry for the College World Series. Malachi was hungry for something else. He couldn't afford to miss this lecture.

Princeton had hosted some of history's greatest minds—Einstein, Frost, Morrison. Today, Siegfried Santo Padre would take the stage.

At the entrance, Malachi slowed his pace. The hushed voices near the benches weren't discussing academia. They whispered about something urgent, something recent. He caught fragments of conversation.

Malachi wiped the sweat from his brow, pretending not to listen. His instincts kicked in. He noted the exits. The people. The unnatural tension in the air.

Something was off. And it wasn't just academic.

Malachi tuned in.

"The USSR has The Bomb now."

Malachi didn't bother to turn his head. He let his eyeballs do the heavy lifting, sliding sideways to find the speaker without giving them the dignity of a full look. This was not news to him. He adjusted his tie, exhaled, and stepped inside. A crumpled flier fell from his open hand.

McCosh Hall's high arched ceiling and rows of tiered seating amplified every sound, yet a hushed anticipation held the 445-seat auditorium in a tight grip. The wood-paneled walls echoed murmurs as the audience settled in.

Malachi Donnoby leaned against the back wall, half-hidden in the shadows, his practiced nonchalance masked his alertness. A decade of playing baseball had made him a master of positioning—not just on the field but in life. Here, downstairs, tucked beneath the balcony, he had a clear view of Santo Padre at the podium and yet he remained unseen to most.

He wasn't alone in wanting to go unnoticed. The agency had other eyes in the crowd. Their job was to listen. Malachi's job was to act. Or so he assumed.

He had already marked the exits. The main doors led to Washington Road, where he could vanish into the thick of the Princeton crowd if things went sideways. Another option was to push through the side corridors, slipping out onto University Court and down to Nassau Street. Two routes, two lifelines. This wasn't paranoia—this was training.

The auditorium wasn't full, but the crowd was respectable.

Students attended for the grade. A handful of professors came to ridicule. But it was the few men in sharp suits who didn't belong. Malachi spotted them immediately.

He watched them carefully, decoding their agendas while they adjusted in their seats. Body language was the Judas of agents, their own bodies betraying as they watched and waited.

Malachi also noted the assembled dignitaries, sitting in the front row. He recognized Big Al, of course. And he also spotted a large memorial picture of Professor Arthur "Arturo" Posnansky on stage. The fool never made it out of Puma Punku.

At the podium, Siegfried Santo Padre cut a striking figure for a man supposedly retired from secrets. Late forties. Once-blond hair streaked with silver after his time in Puma Punku. Dark tan. Wire-rimmed glasses. Tweed jacket. To the untrained eye, he was just another professor.

This was a man who had designed weapons for the Reich. Secret weapons. A man who had walked through the ruins of ancient civilizations—and come back with knowledge he shouldn't possess. Santo Padre cleared his throat, adjusted the microphone, and spoke. His voice was smooth, practiced.

"Six months ago, my team uncovered something remarkable in the Andean highlands." He made the sign of the cross. *God rest your soul, Arturo,* Siegfried thought—eyes looking heaven bound.

Malachi folded his arms and thought, *Here we go.*

"Puma Punku," Santo Padre continued, "a site long thought to be a temple, may in fact be something far older. Something engineered by the gods."

A murmur rippled through the crowd. Malachi withheld any recognition.

"The stonework," Santo Padre went on, "is beyond what should have been possible for its time. The precision, the cuts—" he shook his head, "even modern tools would struggle to replicate it. And yet, it was built by farmers, a civilization we know almost nothing about."

Malachi watched the speaker's hands as he scanned the podium. A briefcase sat next to Siegfried's feet beside the podium. If he had the thing, it was there or in a pocket. He returned his attention to Santo Padre.

The man was passionate, sure. But there was something else. A trace of hesitation.

Santo Padre lowered his voice, "In the deepest chamber, among the fallen stones, we found something which had no business being in our hemisphere."

The room tensed.

What are you about to say, old man? Malachi thought.

Beneath Malachi's calm exterior, his mind was calculating, watching, waiting. His hand slipped into his pocket, fingers brushing against the heavy weight of his pistol. It was a reassurance. A decision which was waiting to be made. If Siegfried said the wrong thing—if he crossed the line from theory into dangerous truth—Malachi knew what had to be done.

At the podium, Siegfried hesitated. For a moment, just a flicker, uncertainty crossed his face before he repeated himself.

"Well, Siegfried, you all must be asking, what mysteries did you find?"

Malachi's pulse remained steady. His grip on the gun did not tighten. His palm ready to depress the grip safety. His thumb ready to flip the safety down.

Siegfried's next words would decide everything.

Siegfried stopped speaking to study his audience. In preparing today's speech, he had assembled his worn copies of the Mahabharata, the Ramayana, and the Bible—ancient texts brimming with mythological wars, lost civilizations, and legendary feats.

The irony wasn't lost on him. Most of his audience weren't here for history. They were fiction writers, searching for new stories, fresh ideas—not ancient ones. But today, Siegfried Santo Padre had something to say which was far beyond fiction. He would tell them the past wasn't as dead as people thought.

Santo Padre was hesitating again, and it was obvious to everyone there, especially Malachi. Malachi had seen what happened to those who revealed the wrong truths. Some were discredited. Some disappeared. And some— like Siegfried if he didn't shut up—would end up dead at the podium.

In Malachi's coat pocket, his trigger finger tapped the slide of his pistol.

At the podium, Siegfried tapped the wood pedestal and cleared his throat.

"The Great Wars of the Gods. The destruction of civilizations in fire and flood. Chariots of the Sky. The Watchers, the Nephilim, the star-born children. These stories repeat across cultures, across time. They're not just stories though, they are windows into how our ancestors recorded their world."

He picked up the Mahabharata, flipping through pages filled with descriptions of celestial weapons, cities in the sky, and gods waging wars with unimaginable technology.

"These stories have been dismissed as legend. As fantasy. But what if they were history? Our history, our forgotten history? This wasn't the first time humanity encountered these entities. Our ancestors saw them too. Mistook them for gods. We have the proof.

"Robert Oppenheimer, father of the atomic bomb, famously quoted the Bhagavad Gita: 'Now I am become Death, the destroyer of worlds.' But few remember what he said later. When asked if his test was the first nuclear detonation in history, he replied—"

Santo Padre held the pause.

"Oppenheimer said, *'Yes. In modern times.'*"

A gasp rippled through the audience.

Outside the auditorium four men stepped out of a black sedan, parked just beyond the university courtyard on Williams Street. They moved overtly, crossing Washington Road, their expressions blank, their movements controlled. One of them, an Asian-looking man, gave commands, speaking in a language few on Earth still recognized. They split into pairs. A noose was tightening around the auditorium.

At the Firestone Library, a man wearing a Stetson, and brain-tanned leather duster trench coat began to move. He wasn't headed to McCosh Auditorium. Instead, he angled toward Dickinson Hall and the University Chapel, both prime vantage points. He knew how the game was played. At least one or two of the men would push toward the alley in a maneuver the military called a "Pincer." They'd create a choke point "Fatal Funnel" where they could box someone in who was trying to escape.

Adjusting his Stetson as he walked, the man's mind was racing, calculating. The alley was a trap, but it was only one piece of the play. The others, the smarter ones, would drift through campus, using crowds and quiet corners to set up their positions at or in McCosh Hall. He'd have to catch them in more discreet locations.

While this quiet drama unfolded outside the auditorium, Malachi remained at his post.

Unofficially, his 'tourist escapades' yielded some of the most valuable wartime intelligence. His knack for disappearing into foreign cities, collecting information, and speaking like a local made him an asset.

"We have always been in contact," Siegfried declared, his voice fiery and rolling like thunder over the expectant crowd. "Not just in recent times. Always. Since the dawn of humanity. They created us, they enslaved us, we rebelled and lost everything doing it."

A voice from the crowd shouted, "So, you're not saying there are aliens out there. Are you saying *we're* the aliens?" The crowd erupted in laughter.

"Why not? Most of you believe a man to be a Holy Spirit. Which one sounds more far-fetched?" He paused.

"It's public record, Tesla's death ray (confiscated by the FBI) was rooted in these ancient technologies. Technologies described right here in these books. My name, my real name" he said, his voice slicing through the murmurs, "is Siegfried Eisenbrandt."

A vacuum of shock silenced the confused crowd. Wasn't he Argentinian? His last name was Santo Padre, after all.

"Yes, I am Eisenbrandt. I spent years inside Nazi Germany's most secretive projects. I worked alongside the SS, the Luftwaffe, and the minds behind the Reich's most terrifying advancements. I worked with and reverse engineered exotic technologies."

A murmur rippled through the crowd. The crowd was at odds with their speaker being a freaking Nazi! Many shifted in their seats after hearing uncomfortable truths. Malachi caught the gist of these murmurs and postures.

With Malachi's line of work being what it was, he knew about Eisenbrandt's sordid past. As part of Operation Paperclip, Santo Padre—Eisenbrandt—had sworn an oath of silence. The U.S. had protected him, buried him under a new identity, erased his past. But history could not be erased.

Malachi knew where this confession was leading.

Siegfried wasn't just stepping over the line—he was about to burn it down.

Trip Looper was finished outside with his business, so the man in the worn duster moved into Dickinson Hall. Distancing himself away from the bodies he dumped. Leaving them to cool in the bushes. Whatever he'd done to them, they'd already disintegrated into ash. In here, he put on a face and relaxed his body language as he walked. The cute students received a nod, tip of the hat, and a smile. He was courteous and not pushy as he weaved past people. He worked hard to blend in, and it worked. Underneath his artificial mask of emotions was a stone-cold killer.

Unlike him, the men he was after stood erect, wore all black suits and looked like funeral directors in a place of higher learning. Their stiff bodies pushed their way through the crowd despite some students protesting the way they were doing it. They were the boulders blading the current of a fast-moving stream.

A bell rang; time for the next class. The students were even more in a hurry as they became less organized in their movements. They had class after all. His ice-cold eyes scanned the thinning crowd. The class-changing rush was over. Now the goon-mortician-looking men stood out like sore thumbs amongst the remaining stragglers running late to their next period. With less of a crowd, Trip wondered if they could hear the grit on his boots grinding into the floor as he walked.

He worried too much. The men held a singular focus, which was getting to their assigned positions. Traps set by their leader. All exits needed to be covered in case their target made it out of the auditorium. He spotted the second pair of men working their way toward an alternate entrance to McCosh Hall. These were professionals, or at least they thought they were, and vanity made them look the part. That was the problem, that was what would get them taken out.

His focus was now locked under the brim of his weathered Stetson hat. Trip tightened it down, wouldn't do to lose it in a scuffle. One of the goons fell out of the pack, a straggler. Now was a good time for Trip to take advantage of the separation. He found an opening and weaved in out of what was left of the foot traffic. The goon didn't hear Trip close the distance.

From behind, Trip reached around the goon's neck putting him in a choke hold. His hold tightened. The startled man tried to inhale but couldn't. Fingers clawed at Trip's vice grip, his body already weakening. Before he could kick, before he could warn his partner—an ancient blade slid between his ribs, swift and silent. Trips eyes darted side to side, no one was around to notice.

A shudder. A dying breath. His timing was impeccable. He was next to a janitor closet, the perfect dumping spot for an impromptu body-hide. Trip had timed it perfectly, right next to a door, he opened it and lowered the body with practiced ease into the janitor's closet. He activated and tossed something small onto the body. The same thing he used on the men outside.

He closed the door, handle turned until it wouldn't pull further, then he released it allowing the latch to push in without a sound. Another bad guy down. From under the closed door, a puff of smoke, smoldering, spontaneous combustion and the body was gone.

The second man had kept moving, unaware his partner was dispatched. But Trip was already closing in on him. Easy day.

These men were the old player's recruits and sent in like pawns to die in a game they didn't understand. Trip wasn't playing. You don't play around while you're hunting the *Most Dangerous Game.*

He activated another disintegrating device. Each step he took was quicker than the last. Time was of the essence with a disintegration hot potato in his hand.

"Hey," Trip called out, just loud enough for the man to hear but not so loud to alert anyone else.

The man turned, surprised. Trip tossed the device towards him. He caught it instinctively. A burst, the body superheated in an instant. A flash followed by bits of ash and he was gone.

Nearby, in the adjoining building, Santo Padre continued to speak.

"I worked in Germany's top laboratories from 1937 to 1944," Siegfried continued, his voice steady.

A rustle of unease swept through the room.

"We were decoding unthinkable energy weapons. Advanced propulsion technology. Unlimited zero-point energy Tesla would have envied."

Malachi watched the crowd.

"When the war ended, the battle wasn't over land or ideology—it was over knowledge," Santo Padre declared. "The Allies descended upon Germany like vultures, ransacking labs, seizing aircraft, stripping every secret before it could be lost or destroyed. Some scientists vanished into Russian gulags. The lucky ones (like Werner von Braun and I) were given new lives, new purpose. Some, like me, were also given new names."

A heavy silence clung to the air.

Having neutralized his escape route competition, Trip made his way to the upper balcony of McCosh 50, his back to the tall windows, light barely outlining his worn silhouette before he disappeared completely. His duster was more than a duster. A cloak of invisibility bent the light around him.

He had the high ground, a predator, and from here, he could see almost everything except Malachi Donnoby, who sat directly beneath him, under the balcony's overhang, alert but also unaware of the threat unveiling around him.

Trip was stalking...

His eyes scanned the rows of seats, searching for bulges, large ones, the kind concealing a sniper rifle.

He spotted his target.

A lone agent, seated on this level near the far edge of the balcony, silent and unmoving, a predator waiting for the right moment. But Trip Looper was already moving.

He personally knew the Oracle speaking. The man on stage below, speaking fervently about ancient wars, gods, and flying machines. And Trip also knew this: Trip himself was the only reason Siegfried had made it out of Germany alive.

Trip's boots barely whispered across the floor as he moved behind the scarce occupants of the balcony all clustered near the exit. No one detected him as he crept past them.

No one except the sniper.

Instinct, training, or fear—something made the agent's shoulders tense. He felt it. A presence behind him. He turned, eyes flickering over his shoulder. At first, he saw nothing, then a distortion.

"Shit."

The word barely left the sniper's lips before Trip flashed a Medusa pen and punctured his neck.

"Wait..." the agent pleaded.

Trip said deeply, "No quarter for collaborators," he grumbled in a hot whisper.

No one heard it. The nerve agent worked fast. The eternal silence overtook the sniper. Siegfried's seminar raged on, drowning out death itself.

Trip turned the corpse's head forward, eyes glazed over, sitting frozen in the auditorium seat, his hands folded on the hinged desktop. He looked like any other student deep in thought—only this one wasn't thinking anymore.

Hidden under a canvas pack, full of books, Trip saw the shooters modified Welrod. The integrally-suppressed bolt action pistol had a lengthened barrel and folding stock welded onto the grip along with a tiny 2X scope with a duplex reticle. The first few shots zipping through the rubber wipes would have been almost silent, but not today.

Trip moved down to the guard rail, looked over the balcony.

Reinforcements arrived below. Four more, a different group all together. Four suspicious men, scattered through the crowd, watching and waiting.

"Nothing is easy," Trip mumbled his grandfather's mantra to himself.

Some in the audience laughed. Some scoffed. But Malachi knew better. Siegfried's revelations were becoming much too specific. No one was supposed to know about the Martians at Area 51. B-17 pilots had reported glowing orbs moving with fantastic speed, interfering with instruments, sending bombers falling without a single shot fired.

They weren't German. They weren't human.

Siegfried gripped the podium. "I shouldn't have made it out," he admitted. "I would have died in that bunker if it weren't for the agent sent to pull me out."

Malachi's expression flickered. He'd heard of such an agent. A wraith of a man. A grim reaper who might be collecting souls even now. *His name? What was it? Shit.*

The projector hummed to life again.

A black-and-white image appeared. A saucer-like craft hovering in the sky.

"These were not the first," Siegfried said. "Let's look at history."

Projected images revealed ancient cave paintings. Glowing discs.

"Foo Fighters. UAPs. Vimanas. Flying Shields. Chariots of the Gods. Call them what you will. The evidence is there. It's always been there."

Malachi's hand twitched near his coat, depressing the grip safety.

"Oppenheimer believed ancient civilizations had nuclear technology. Hitler did too. He sent expeditions from Tibet to Antarctica searching for their secrets. Searching for Atlantis. But the real question is—what did he find? And what did he take? Which leads us to the Artifact."

Santo Padre was a dead man; the only question was who was going to kill him first.

Chapter 8

Spooks in Seats

The tension in the auditorium was crackling, like fireworks were about to erupt. A ripple of whispers spread as the next slide illuminated the screen.

Malachi watched Big Al scratching his head. Transparency four, five, six—flashing on the overhead projector. In minutes, the curved metallic fragment appeared as evidence.

Malachi released his weapon and opted to put pencil to pad for the time being. His sketches were quick but detailed. Could this be the missing shard which dame Ava was after?

The next image zoomed in.

Etchings; ancient symbols. Similar to Sumerian script.

Final slide—a diamond embedded in the metal, glowing under magnification.

Malachi felt his pulse spiking.

Found it, he told himself. *But are these just photos or does Santo Padre have it with him? If it's here, things are going to spiral fast.*

Santo Padre had mastered the art of the lecture, a verbal Rope-a-Dope.

"Gentlemen, the brilliance of light captured in this photo is not a reflection. It is pure sustainable energy and contained within the diamond's crystalline structure. It absorbs and recycles ambient energy—creating infinite power. I call it *Zero Point Energy.*"

A tidal wave of murmurs filled the auditorium.

"The woven wiring—micro-circuitry. Far beyond anything in the last 15,000 years. Perhaps longer. It behaves like a living nervous system. Our smallest computers take up rooms."

He took a breath, eyes sweeping the audience.

"I have just returned from a site—perhaps built by the gods of yesterday. I believe this artifact belongs to the *First People.* The Sumerians called them Anunnaki. An even older text call them the Anunna. The original inhabitants of this planet. Many of you know Puma Punku. For those who don't, it is an ancient complex with four distinct structures. A water port overlooking an ocean which is long gone due to uplifting, the opposite which I believe plunged Atlantis under the sea."

Malachi noted the shifting audience.

Skepticism crept in from the crowd.

Santo Padre pressed forward, wading through academic sludge.

"Professor Posnansky calculated its alignment, dating it over 17,500 years old. The ice age, a period of time known as the Younger Dryas. The precision of its construction makes the Great Pyramid look like child's play. Even today, we cannot replicate it."

His voice rose.

"We once thought Troy was a myth, until we found it. Puma Punku may be the missing piece—an Atlantean seaport."

The audience shifted. The murmur expanded.

Malachi recognized the moment. First it was his hand, then his forearm and shoulder relaxed. Safety flipped back up.

Santo Padre was losing them.

And yet the man persisted, undeterred.

"I discovered the artifact during a dig at Puma Punku. Posnansky was theorizing when I saw a blue light beneath a monolith."

Siegfried was dead serious as he continued. "The stone shifted, revealing an antechamber. I was terrified. I thought I was staring at a monster, ready to pounce."

A chuckle from Big Al. Some laughter from the crowd.

"Thank the heavens, it was just a statue. Pazuzu."

But Malachi wasn't laughing.

Santo Padre leaned in.

"What was a Mesopotamian demon doing in South America? A warning? A marker? A mistake?"

The next words froze the room.

"It was then I realized I was looking at a genetically engineered being and it was indeed a warning. Ancient texts spoke of a group, the UDUG 7— bio-engineered Udug super soldiers sent to wipe humanity out. They failed... or did they? Demons, devils—every culture has them. Some say they still walk among us. Skinwalkers. Shape-shifters."

The audience was on edge.

Malachi scanned the seats and noted another missing agent.

Where the hell is everyone? Malachi asked himself.

He reached into his left back pocket, making sure he had extra mags, no matter how many goons were left, they outnumbered his firepower.

Meanwhile, Santo Padre seemed unfazed by the dwindling crowd. He straightened his tie and continued his story of the encounter at Puma Punku.

"Once I recovered from the shock, I extracted the artifact from the granite slab."

A pause.

"And something incredible happened."

Murmurs. Malachi's grip on his 1911 A1 tightened.

"The artifact pulsed. A filament of blue light snaked through the metal. That's when a map appeared." He showed a slide obscuring important locations but proving his point.

The audience wanted to know more, they wanted to see it. Students' eyes darted back and forth between one another. Professors' faces said it all, they wanted to see the actual proof.

Trip Looper watched from the balcony, knowing this was the spicy part of the lecture.

Below in his hiding place, Malachi shifted his concealed weapon in its holster as his grip loosened it from the leather's sticky hold.

The coming storm arrived.

Santo Padre's voice boomed through the auditorium. "This artifact was buried for millennia beneath Puma Punku, but even today, we lack the technology to replicate it or places like Baalbek in Lebanon. Its technology mirrors the recovered wreckage from Roswell. I believe this is part of their Mii, the knowledge they left us, and this has a map—a map which originated in Atlantis."

More audience members had walked out when Santo Padre's lecture seemed to border on fiction. A ripple of unease spread through those who remained.

"Why do we scoff when India claims its civilization is tens of thousands of years old? Because Western historians dismiss it."

His fist slammed the podium.

"Giants, the Nephilim, the gods of old—they were real. They were not gods at all but ancient beings from another world. And we—" his voice sharpened "—WE ARE THEIR DESCENDANTS!"

The audience stirred. Some stood up clapping furiously. Others continued to laugh at the ridiculousness of it all. Another wave of audience members scoffed and departed the hall. His lecture was becoming a war of attrition.

"Our ancestors were annihilated by a more powerful force. Arturo—" he made the sign of the cross, "and I believe whoever destroyed them (whoever destroyed Atlantis) is on their way back."

"Hoax!" someone shouted as they stood up to storm out.

"What a pathetic stunt for headlines!" another jeered and also evacuated like there was a fire drill.

"What happened to Professor Arturo, you effing atheist? The papers said the Argentinian government shot him in the head for grave robbing."

"No, no that's not what happened. He became very ill after he was bitten by one of the rabid creatures. They had no choice but to put him down."

With that the crowd was in full exodus mode.

What should have been an easy play for Malachi was turning into a potential error inducing nightmare. In baseball, a base runner will intentionally slow down in front of a ground ball to block the vision of the fielder, hoping to induce an error during the play. The crowd was doing just that, and Malachi could feel the game-ending error creeping up on him.

He could wait for the aisles to clear, or he could risk the mission by traversing over the spring-powered folding seats and possibly, eat shit, stumbling over them on the way. He knew plenty of clutch players who could make such a play, but doubt crept into the back of his mind, knowing it would be a stretch for an average pro athlete.

Malachi's narrow lane of opportunity filled up and closed before his eyes.

"Shit," Malachi whispered under his breath.

As Malachi pushed his way forward through the current of bodies, he watched Big Al at the front of the crowd as he scribbled a note and handed it off to an aide. A lucky break for Malachi.

The aide, ordered by Big Al, moved toward Santo Padre adding delay and confusion to the messy exit.

Big Al fidgeted; his head was on a swivel. He too was getting anxious. The moving crowd made it impossible to identify anyone.

The aide reached Santo Padre, pressing the note into his hand. Siegfried wasted no time opening it and reading the chicken scratch note.

We must speak at once. Stop what you're doing—they are watching. For God's sake, come to my house if you can make it. —Big Al

Santo Padre appeared chilled by the note. Today's speech had let the genie out of the bottle. Big Al disagreed with this approach; maybe he had a way to salvage it.

Santo Padre's eyes scanned the auditorium. It was as if the movie had ended and everyone was trying to get to their cars first, in order to beat traffic.

Only four conspicuous men of distinctive swagger panned out like gold being sifted from a river. Siegfried wasn't sure if they were looking for an autograph in ink or his blood. Statuesque, they spread out and froze, watching and waiting for instructions. Trip was too far away to reach him without creating mass hysteria; Malachi, on the other hand, was right on the beam.

Santo Padre didn't know what he didn't know, but something about those four men wasn't sitting right in his gut. Four men were there, but not really; there were no men behind those eyes.

He reached for his briefcase. He stuffed his books and notes into it and slammed it shut. A piece of paper, a transparency, here and there, a corner hanging out. He pulled it close to his chest.

"Well, then," he said aloud, "I hope it wasn't something I said."

He needed to leave. Now.

Malachi had been hanging back as the remainder of the crowd funneled out. Auspiciously, he began flanking to the side doors, leading the way to Dickinson Hall. One by one his legs knocked each seat back. The pain was worth it. If things got hairy, they could bail out of there and have rooms to duck into and hide.

The question of *if* became a matter of when. As he made his way down the row, Malachi watched four men get to their feet. They closed on Santo Padre with little effort. Of the four men, one stood out. He was more dynamic than the others, his posture alone proved him to be the leader. Behind the Asian-looking gentlemen, his henchmen followed closely before breaking off to take up tactical positions.

The threat was evolving. Malachi was moving faster now because of this. Unfortunately, the slow start punished his thighs with each long step. Those damn seat backs were attacking him with every lunge forward. Despite the eventual bruising, he closed the distance quickly and arrived in time to hear the leader speak.

"We need the Key, Siegfried." The leader urgently suggested. His voice deep and animalistic. With little acknowledgement, he snuck a look at Malachi, who was wading into Siegfried's orbit.

One of the trio flanked further right.

Another began shadowing Malachi.

The third moved in head-on like a running back headed for the end zone.

Their movements were seamless, calculated, and predatory. Malachi and Siegfried were pinned down. Even if Malachi drew his weapon first, his fastest point shooting split wouldn't be fast enough to take them all without catching a bullet himself. He was in a real pickle. Time to bluff.

"Alright," Malachi yelled. "Nobody moves another step! You'd make like a tree and leave if you knew what was good for ya. None of youse guys wants to take a forty-five to the face. Do ya?"

Everyone began moving more cautiously, inches instead of feet as they ignored the threat. No one wanted a public scene—but the artifact was worth killing for in public.

Malachi reached out for the crook of Siegfried's arm to lead him to the door.

Potential gains were worth it to the henchmen who moved up the middle of the field. He was close enough and without warning, his fist crashed into Malachi's mouth, splitting his lip. Malachi's dapper hat hit the floor. His tie flipped over his shoulder as he struck back with his fist smashing the attacker's nose straight on.

The henchman to his right moved in and was quickly fended off with a swift kick to his ribs. His own holstered pistol drove into the meat between his rib cage. Pain radiated.

Without hesitation, Malachi reached for and grabbed the third man by the collar. His swift thinking and quick moves allowed him to hurl the offender into his buddy with the broken nose creating a brief path for escape.

"Scram, Doc!" he snarled.

"You're outnumbered, Malachi Donnoby," the leader murmured without a care in the world.

A pit formed in Malachi's gut and he froze. They knew his name. His agency had been compromised. The whole event had been a set up from the get-go. These assassins knew the players, where they would be, and what Siegfried had found.

"We've got operatives on the street and down the halls. There's no way out of here we don't have covered. Siegfried is running straight into a trap."

Malachi could take a stand here against the four goons or he could bolt and try to catch up to the professor. He knew the university well enough, but it was still a labyrinth of footpaths. Maybe they'd get lucky and get away. Maybe they wouldn't.

Malachi bit down. Tactically, he'd lost any advantages. *I should have plugged the professor when I had the chance,* he thought.

No good solutions. "You dirty scum sucking rats," he bellowed in disdain.

The leader, a genetically-altered Chinese half-breed whistled, signaling his men to close in. The amoeba of bodies swarmed again to engulf Malachi.

Before they reached him, a voice (speaking in an ancient Chinese dialect) shattered the silence of the near-empty room. Their leader scanned the space, sniffing the air like a predator searching for a scent.

The obscured voice called out again. "As old as your master is, you'd think he'd have warned you about being ambushed. You should never underestimate your opponent, Jiāng."

The leader recalled their time with Sun Tzu. "Looper," the creature replied, its once all human face beginning to unravel, "You were a shit teacher, Looper."

"I resemble that comment." Trip said arrogantly. "But you also have to admit you were a shit student."

Jiāng shrugged and reluctantly nodded. "None of that matters now. Once we have the map, humanities' fight is over."

Seeing Genghis Khan's brutality during the Annihilation of Nishapur caused a psychological break he never recovered from. "The Tall Whites were right. Humanity needs to end."

"Well, that ain't happenin' today, half-breed." Looper's coat de-cloaked. He was standing between the prey and the predators. He wanted this traitorous abomination to see exactly who was about to beat him. "It's been a minute, Jiāng."

The distraction gave Malachi a head start.

"Not long enough, Looper," Jiāng said with anticipation of finally killing his ancient mentor.

Looper's hand discreetly moved into positions hovering near a slit in his coat. His thumb found the edge and locked back, ready to snap the leather back and draw. His eyes locked on his target, aiming for the space between those evil, soulless eyes.

"You think you're better than us and yet you wear their skin."

Trip shrugged, a necessary evil. In the back of his mind, he knew these things happened fast. Talk was a distraction. Anticipation was also an enemy of the mind.

Trip had a sub-second draw. He'd been fast enough to pull his weapon and take down the full-blooded Udug troopers in the past. It had never ended cleanly. But these ugly bastards didn't have the same lightning reflexes as their masters. He knew for certain they couldn't beat a .67 second pull and great split times.

But they all cheated. He should've taken it into consideration. Who wouldn't with their life on the line?

Without warning, Jiāng—now revealed to be a vile creature—hands still buried in its jacket pockets, snapped off five quick shots through its wool coat, the suppressed .38 whispering death with each round.

Looper saw the first and second rounds punch through the fabric, tearing holes in the garment. Instinct took over. He whipped the left side of his leather duster over his exposed torso, made of Udug skin and layers of highly advanced spider silk and nanotech weave, absorbed the incoming shots.

The first round flew high, skimming his forehead just beneath his hat. The Stetson floated to the floor.

The second round struck near his clavicle, sending a jolt of pain through his body. Even with protection, he felt the bone crack—hairline for sure.

The duster absorbed the rest.

He'd have a nasty welt, a hairline fracture, and a black-and-green bruise—painful, but not life-threatening. The other three goons pushed past him in a blitz. Jiāng bolted in the other direction, headed for Washington Road.

As the echoes of the leader's shots faded in his ears, Trip's gun was out, finger tight on the trigger but no targets.

His blaster was no ordinary sidearm, it was futuristic and powered with zero-point energy. The optic barely caught the creature's outline, just a flicker of heat as he escaped through the door.

Gone.

No shot.

Looper shook his head, exhaling sharply. Mocking his own carelessness.

"Never underestimate your opponent..." he reminded himself.

He reached down, picked up his Stetson. Another tiny hole, another scar on the battered headwear.

Blood dripped from his forehead, splattering onto the floor.

"Idiot," he chastised himself.

Trip pulled back his sleeve, revealing what he called Second Skin or (2nd SKN) the bodysuit keeping him out of the morgue. He didn't have the time to be delayed on ice.

A few drops of blood had dripped onto the flexible digital sleeve embedded in the high-tech material. He wiped the screen as clean as he could, knowing the heat and movement of the blood would interfere with the app, distorting the display.

Having cleared the screen, he pulled up a map. A blip from a tracking device appeared moving down Mercer Street. "I owe you another one, Lily," he mumbled.

Only one place on Mercer Street mattered which meant Big Al was also in danger now.

"Fool," he muttered under his breath, in anger.

Trip meant to move. His first step interferes with the second. He staggers before realizing his bell had been rung. The digital navigational aid flickered on his wrist. The AI confirming what Trip already knew—Santo Padre's escape route calculated to 98% accuracy.

It took a lot of work getting him out of Germany... and the idiot exposed himself like this. Looper was pissed and now he had a migraine. His expression was full of frustration. Mistakes were made.

"Fuck..." he muttered, admonishing himself one last time.

He scrunched his face as the hat rubbed and gnawed at the open wound where the bullet had grazed him.

Was Siegfried a sociopath? A narcissist? Or just a moron? Sometimes, people just had to have all the answers, even if it got them killed. Trip would ask the fool if he got there in time.

Outside, and blocks away, Siegfried burst through a maintenance door, his coat flaring as his feet hit pavement. An army of assassins were after him.

From a distance, one of the half-breeds shadowed both Malachi and Siegfried as they worked to flow and blend with the class change. Further from his henchmen, Jiāng reached his getaway vehicle. He punched the clutch and turned the ignition. For a brief second he thought he flooded it, but the Packard cranked over.

Malachi continued checking his six. He sensed them closing in, following behind him and yet no one was there. Where the hell did those goons go? Did Trip clear their path? So far no obstacles in his way? Maybe Jiāng was lying about having backup.

Malachi pushed forward, a disheveled mess. He'd taken some serious licks, but he wasn't stopping now. If he'd turned down the correct alley earlier, he'd already have his hands on Siegfried. Too late. Siegfried veered left, crossing University Court, moving past the Pyne Administration Building.

Smart.

Like the creature hunting him, Siegfried was sticking to the dense pack of students, using them as a shield.

Malachi bear down. This wasn't just a chase. It was a fatal funnel straight to hell. Siegfried wasn't fleeing campus. He had a destination and Malachi put it together. *Shit.* He looked in the general direction. Sure enough.

There he was—Malachi spotted Siegfried in the shifting crowd and locked eyes on him.

The trio of Goon Squad operatives caught up with them during his epiphany. The hunt was moving eastward, slipping into a dense crowd. They'd lost Siegfried, but not Malachi.

In their native tongue, they grumbled about the radio silence from the rest of their team. Where the hell was their backup? They weren't in the hallways. They weren't covering the exits.

Something was wrong.

To their right, Jiāng pulled up on Nassau Street, a sleek car idling at the curb. He tooted the horn.

"The others are dead," Jiāng informed his men. He waved the pair of men over with a head jerk.

Two of them broke off, sprinting into the waiting vehicle. Inside the trunk—an arsenal, locked and ready to go.

The third stayed on Malachi's heels, determined to follow him to the final destination.

The half-breed didn't even bother looking for Trip. He was either bleeding out—or cloaked. Either way, he wasn't taking any more chances. Not after Trip's warning.

Siegfried, breathless and clammy, staggered up the steps of the white house on Mercer Street. He rapped his knuckles against the door, exhaling sharply.

The door creaked open.

Almost out of breath, "I really screwed the pooch on this one, eh?" he said through the crack.

"Siegfried," Big Al greeted him, his expression grim, his nod slow and knowing. He opened the door wide and gave a look left and right down the street. It seemed clear. Siegfried shuffled inside.

Not far behind, Malachi slowed from a jog to a labored walk. He'd double backed one to many times at the beginning of chase. His side burned with sharp stitches. He reached the picket fence, his chest rising and falling as he watched Siegfried disappear into the famous house. Two-story, sunroom on the east side. Malachi took it all in, mapping all the ways in and out.

He worked to steady his breath, eyes scanning in every direction on Mercer Street. No pursuers. No movement. He'd broken contact with the goons. He was in the clear.

Or so he thought.

Lurking stealthily behind a tree across from 112 Mercer Street, he waved down Jiāng and his associates in the car. They would stage their assault momentarily.

Malachi slipped through the iron gate. No more Mrs. Big Al. She had passed away a few years ago, but the flower garden she once tended still thrived at the foot of the steps. Four pillars loomed above him, supporting the second floor.

He approached the black, maybe navy blue, front door. Jiggled the handle. Locked.

Ass-kicked and tired, Malachi was determined to complete this one last obstacle and retrieve the artifact. Like a private dick, he pulled out his lock-pick kit and went to work. The hook went in first, a touch of pressure, then a jiggle of the rake. A quick bump, a shimmy. The locking pins gave way in seconds. Cake.

He slipped inside, shut the door, locked it behind him. Once inside he reached in his jacket pocket, fingers caressing the grip of his 1911.

This isn't over yet, he told himself. *If I can't get the relic, no one will.*

Outside, Jiāng distributed larger small arms among the last of his troop. Silencers twisted into place with ruthless dedication and a fierce rotation of the can onto the .45 caliber pistols. Access to ancient tech was like finding a needle in a haystack these days. Over the centuries, the few who had it claimed the illusive tech as battlefield trophies.

This team was assaulting with no such trophies. The useful idiots were stuck with a grim collection of World War II relics. Barbaric, but effective, they grabbed a sawed-off Model 12 shotgun, Obregón 1911 inspired tilting barrel pistols from Mexico they tucked into their waistbands, and one carried a M1A paratrooper carbine with a full auto setting.

The attackers checked their weapons, their voices low as they spoke in their ancient tongue.

"Asag will be pleased with our success after this mission."

"Pazuzu will make us pay if we fail. Make it worth it and we will be well rewarded."

"No one leaves here alive," Jiāng ordered. "Sanitize everything inside."

Weapons ready, they peeled away from the car.

One slipped up the driveway, moving along the left side of the house, searching for a side door into the sunroom.

Another circled to the back, preparing to break in.

The third with the broken nose stayed point, moving with Jiāng toward the front door. Their skin flickered. A subtle ripple of color and texture, the stress of the hunt forcing their human disguises to falter. Their eyes dulled; lifeless, like glass. These were not ordinary men. Not Udug. Not human. Transitioning.

The train of death was barreling forward.

Their leader carried nothing but the pea-shooting silenced .38 revolver. There was no need to carry anything heavier when the weight of your orders was heavy enough.

He and the first hunter reached the front gate, their approach silent, orderly. They would breach simultaneously from multiple entry points, sweeping the house, erasing every living thing inside.

Jiāng turned, about to give the command—

But before the creature could speak, a bright blue bolt of light ripped down the driveway on their left, slicing through the stormy darkening skyline. On the left side of the house, the goon breaching through the sunroom never saw it coming. His head exploded—bone and brain misting the wall. It would take a hose and some soap to clean up a mess even Looper's disintegration tool couldn't erase.

One down.

"Looper's here," Jiāng barked. "He's got us in his sights." Both goons broke for the pillars holding up the second deck. Concealment, not good cover, but better than nothing. Guns in hand but nothing to aim at.

"He might be covering ground while we hide..." the right-hand henchman wheezed through a broken nose as fear crept in.

They froze, unable to decide what to do. Their posture conveyed their confidence in stopping Looper. Standing still meant death.

But movement led to a dance of death.

Seconds later, a bolt of light cut between them, through a window zipping through the house, then exiting the window in the backdoor. The shotgun wielder collapsed, choking on his own blood. His heart on fire. Melted glass dripped from both holes.

Only the two creatures left on the front porch.

Jiāng's man aimed wildly at the air. Was Looper next to him or several feet away? Coming at them from the side?

Anger distorted Jiāng's face. "Where are you?!" he howled out to the street.

"You should run while you can, trannies," the air whispered.

Jiāng turned opposite of his man searching for a distortion, anything, the smell of his breath. But there was nothing.

"We don't run from hiding cowards," the henchman next to him decreed.

A metallic click, followed by a zing of exotic steel vibrating after being unsheathed. The blade penetrated into the visual realm from behind Trip's invisibility cloak. It ran clean through the henchman's chest and pegged him into the pillar. Jiāng's right-hand man grabbed the impaling blade to no avail. His strength zapped and fading he deflated like a loose air balloon.

He wheezed as the last of his oxygen escaped his lungs through his broken snout.

"If you won't run, stick around." Looper said from the ether.

Hearing his voice behind him, Jiāng turned in a snap. His lips curled, showing his fangs; his mutated, inhuman hands transformed into claws when he saw the last of his pawns taken by the knight.

After lifetimes in the field, Looper was an expert warrior, but even he wasn't above cheating. His duster was the ultimate cheat code, and he activated it without a second thought. The magician of death reached into his bag of tricks.

Jiāng spun, clawing in the air wildly. The lack of contact agitated him further. He had a chance in a face-to-face confrontation. Fighting wraiths was never a winning proposition. Trip watched him flounder in fear as he relentlessly pivoted, hoping to catch a glance or a blur of his invisible attacker.

Finally, Trip's gruff voice shattered the silence.

"Where's your boss?"

Jiāng bit his lip, blood staining his teeth. "Humankind was never supposed to exist."

Trip Looper looked at the half-breed with total repulsion. "You were one of us once. Human." Trip's voice cut through the air, laced with contempt. "And then you let them pervert you into this... thing." Trip grimaced, disgust curling through him.

"You weren't there, Looper. You didn't witness Khan's atrocities. He wasn't the first either. It's human nature."

"You're fighting inevitability, Looper. You can't beat them." Jiāng paused occasionally swiping the empty air with his claws hoping to get lucky. "Better to reign with the devil in hell than serve humankind."

"I'm sorry I wasn't there, Jiāng. But your weak mind led you here."

"Says the immortal wearing the skin of my friends."

Trip's unique blaster whipped out from behind the invisible curtain sewn of taken souls. A single energy blast pulsed, breaching the thing's core. The wound cauterized instantly, but inside—his organs ignited. At this range a thermal runaway reaction took hold. His body spontaneously combusted. Nothing left behind but ash.

The stench of burning monster and ozone filled the air. Trip exhaled sharply, shaking his head. The sick stink stuck in his nose. He despised the scent of old fish and burning demons. Both turned his stomach worse than skinning them.

The other operator's body twitched as it hung on the column held by the blade.

"Take that, you mutated son of a bitch," Looper taunted the lifeless body as he uncloaked, his form shimmering back into existence. He holstered his weapon and wrenched his sword free from the creature's chest. It sounded like a nail squeaking out of wood with the first twist and pull. The blade squelched from the body's tight grip as he gave it a final yank. The creature's body and digits hit the porch deck with a thud.

A disintegration device clinked onto the corpse from his hand. A moment later, embers scattered, the body bursting into nothingness. A single digit survived the inferno. Trip knelt and picked it up. A souvenir, in the pocket.

When his hand came out, it shuddered without consent. He caught the twitchy fucker with his other hand, cursing it. "Stop it," he demanded.

It was a flicker of old memories, a past he thought he'd buried a few years ago. It had been years (or was it a minute?) since he'd seen the last tremor. He'd gotten better at hiding it, but it still acted up from time to time.

After a couple deep breaths, he suddenly realized he wanted a dame, what women were called in this century. A dame, he remembered, worked better than booze. Better than pills. Anything to forget those he'd lost.

A couple of conscious quick twitches.

He tightened his grip on the shaking forearm.

He willed it. *Steady. Control.* It was gone. He released his hand, no longer spasming.

One more body in the backyard and the mess on the side of the house to clean up before someone witnessed.

CHAPTER 9

The Devil's Bargain
Princeton University—Big Al's House

Santo Padre splashed cold water onto his face, gripping the edges of Big Al's bathroom sink. His hands trembled.

What the hell just happened back there? he asked himself. *How can so many people want me dead? The artifact can advance humanity by centuries in mere decades and yet here I am, hunted like an animal.*

He moved out of the bathroom and into Big Al's adjacent guestroom, his mind jumbled.

His luggage sat on the edge of the bed, waiting, untouched. His face twisted in confusion, trying to process everything. His hand shot out waving towards the closed door, to stop Albert before he could lay into him from the other side.

"I fucked up," Santo Padre told his host. "You warned me, and I dug myself a hole too deep to climb out of."

On the other side of the door Big Al was visibly frustrated. He took a second, looking in the hallway for a place to sit. There it was—a bench. His hands were buried deep in the pockets of his tweed jacket. He sat on the bench—rocking his body with agitation carved into every restless movement. Wild eyes locked onto Santo Padre's closed door. For a man who had spent his life solving the universe's greatest mysteries, this was something else entirely.

For once, Big Al had no equation for escape.

He exhaled sharply, stood, and walked to the closed door. "We need a plan."

Since Santo Padre would not come out, Big Al spoke to him through the wooden barricade.

"I thought Oppenheimer was a prima donna. Do you have any clue how much trouble you're in, Siegfried?"

Big Al's voice cut like a razor, intense and unforgiving as Siegfried remained silent.

"You just kicked the goddamn hornets' nest! You're lucky you weren't shot dead during the seminar—or dumped in a ditch on the way over! One of those guardians must have intervened."

Siegfried sighed, rubbing his temple. "I know, I KNOW! I had to run. But I was careful, Albert. I weaved my way through campus."

"Spies, they have spies everywhere. They change faces."

Big Al's wild eyes burned with frustration, his fingers twitching as he shoved them deeper into his pockets.

Siegfried's voice dropped to almost a whisper, but his passion simmered just beneath the surface. "People have a right to know, Albert," he said. "You, of all people, should understand that."

Big Al sneered, his nostrils flaring. "Understand? Let's talk about understanding. You don't understand a damn thing, Siegfried. Did you hear Oppenheimer or me running our mouths about the bomb?"

Siegfried was defiant, his jaw set. "Maybe you should have. The USSR has one now too! I gave the Americans everything they asked for. Every technological secret they demanded from Germany. And what did I get in return? Nothing. They cut me off and left me high and dry in Argentina! Exiled in Latin America! Yellow fever! A wife who never stops complaining! DO I LOOK LIKE A LATINO, AL?"

Big Al's mouth gaped for a second. Big Al exhaled sharply, casting a wary glance down the empty hallway. His wild hair stuck out in every direction.

"Open the door, Siegfried." Big Al's voice was urgent now. Jiggling the handle like he had Parkinson's.

The bolt clicked, the door opened. Big Al poked his head in, then slipped into the room joining Siegfried inside. Siegfried was normally very tan, but he soon grew pale.

Big Al shut the door behind them with a decisive click. He turned. Siegfried stepped forward, watching Al's hands. Nothing in them. Their eyes locked.

"I have proof, Albert."

Big Al's posture stiffened. His gaze drifted past Siegfried, out the window—to a Packard sedan idling at the curb. He didn't recognize the car. They were already here. Not much time.

Siegfried shifted, stepping into his line of sight.

"Proof they've kept hidden," Siegfried told him. "And why? To line their pockets, of course. To keep their power intact." His voice lowered. "They don't care about the truth."

Big Al's old shoulders were knotting up. He was growing tired of standing, tired of arguing.

"Arturo believed something is coming," Siegfried insisted. "Something we can't stop."

He paused.

"I saw firsthand what the Foo Fighters did to those bomber formations, Al. They're testing us. Probing. And we can't stop them," Siegfried said.

Big Al said nothing. But his arthritic fingers curled into fists. His unruly visitor's next words hung in the air like a death sentence.

"I'm not the first to witness this technology. Al, the government knows." He leaned in and added with a whisper, "They've always known."

Big Al shoved past him, his frustration boiling over. He jerked the shades closed.

"Do you know what you've done?" Big Al's voice was harsh, cutting. "Do you have any notion what I had to give up in order to get them to pull you out of Germany?"

Siegfried braced himself.

"You've practically signed your own death warrant, maybe mine," Big Al spun around, his wild eyes burning with frustration. Siegfried could still sense the man's power, but age was catching up with him.

Big Al paused then, seemingly out of breath, as inner thoughts troubled him.

"The government won't let this knowledge spread—not now, not ever," Big Al warned.

His voice darkened. "This knowledge is radioactive. Anyone who touches it outside the circle is a goner."

A sharp pause and his voice lowered; deadly serious, "Do you know how quickly the Nazis put a price on my head?" Big Al's eyes flashed, his voice taut with old anger. "Five thousand dollars in 1933. Before I was even a serious threat to them."

He stepped closer, looming. "And you? You just stood in front of an audience of your peers and handed them a reason to come after you. Someone could be downstairs at my front door right now!"

Malachi stood silently outside the room in the hallway silently listening in on their conversation.

The old house creaked under its own weight.

Siegfried knew all of this, but he held his ground. He knew Big Al was right. But he didn't regret a damn thing. As Eisenbrant, he stayed silent. As Siegfried, he would not.

"This...," Big Al told him. "It should have been handled at the Bohemian Grove!"

Siegfried scoffed. "Bohemian Grove is nothing more than a playground for the elite. A shadow government dictating the fate of the world while pretending democracy still exists." He stepped forward, his voice sharpening. "These people don't want freedom, Albert. They want control."

"They already have the control, Siegfried."

Big Al paced, wiping sweat from his brow before stopping and staring at Siegfried, challenging him to look him in the eye.

"Someone needs to be in control, or the whole thing will spiral into the abyss," Big Al insisted. Jabbing a finger into Siegfried's forehead. "And you? You just painted a bullseye, right here," his own German accent flowing through his last words.

Siegfried sighed, frustration bleeding into resignation.

At the seminar, he'd played the strong old man. Oh, how he had aged so much in less than an hour.

Big Al took a deep breath, trying to steady himself. A moment later, he told him, "I'll talk to the Brass."

Siegfried raised a brow.

"They owe me," Big Al said. He leaned in, voice measured, assessing. "Maybe I can pull some strings—keep you from getting killed. But you need to shut your mouth before they shut it for you." His tone dropped, firm. "In the meanwhile, we have to get you out of town. Now."

Big Al's eyes swept the room, scanning. His search landed on Siegfried's suitcase. "Where is the artifact?" His voice was edged with urgency. "Let me see it."

The old scientist's hands hovered, fingers twitching, waiting to be filled.

Siegfried crossed the room, popped the latches, and flipped the case open. He reached inside... and pulled out a bundle of dirty underwear. Some with suspicious stains. He looked up and a grin spread across his face.

"Figured no one would want to dig through this mess to find it," he laughed.

Big Al grimaced, recoiling. "You're right about that."

Taking care to touch the wrapping as little as possible, Big Al carefully retrieved the relic. His fingers traced the smoothness of its surface. It was magnificent, more alluring in person. A tiny piece of the puzzle.

"Very interesting," Big Al said. "And you found this at Puma Punku?"

He turned the thing over, studying the intricate etchings, smaller than the human eye could read.

Here, he told himself, *is the language of the gods.*

A pulse of light radiated. The fragment began to glow until a map materialized, hovering mid-air; identical to the slide from the presentation. But this time, when Big Al reached to touch the floating map, it zoomed in. It was interactive. Alive. Strange symbols filled the air—writing which neither man could read.

The map shifted, focusing on a location off the eastern seaboard of North America. Coordinates burned into their vision: 44°31'00" N, 64°17'57" W.

Big Al gasped. "Marvelous," he whispered, awe-struck. He continued in a voice barely audible. "Where is this place? And is this a warning... or an invitation?" Big Al's eyes narrowed. He turned to Siegfried. "Do you know which it is?"

Siegfried exhaled, his pulse quickening. "I'm not sure," he admitted, his mind racing. "But I cross-referenced ancient texts looking for these symbols. The closest match I could find—" he hesitated. "The closest match was the Ark of the Covenant."

Big Al shuddered, stunned.

Siegfried pressed on, his voice hushed but charged with urgency. "Suppose the Ark wasn't merely a container (but a shield) protecting a power source. Think of it as an ancient reactor. Imagine taking the power of the *Bomb* and using it to power the world."

Big Al inhaled sharply. "Such energy would be almost limitless."

The room felt smaller. The air seemed thicker. The two men weren't just holding history. They were standing on the precipice of something far greater.

Big Al's mind was churning. He spun the map a few hundred miles to the east with his finger. "This massive clump of islands and mountain chain, do you recognize it?"

"No, it looks familiar though."

"There is nothing here anymore but a small island chain where these mountains sit on the map, the Azores," Big Al recalled.

The Ark had vanished from Solomon's Temple centuries ago. Some believed the Knights Templar had found it. But this relic, this map? This was more than just knowledge. This was limitless power.

"This map was left for a reason," Siegfried pressed. "They left it for us to find—I'm sure of it. And we need to understand why."

Siegfried scrolled back to the area marked with the beacon and tapped the holographic projection. The map zoomed in further on the highlighted area.

"This is magic," both men agreed as the language began deciphering in front of their eyes.

"I see an island. I believe it's Oak Island, Nova Scotia, Canada." Siegfried guessed.

Big Al leaned closer, his breath shallow. "I see that, Siegfried, but our English language didn't exist back then." He turned, his brow furrowed.

"It's converting to English. It's picking up on our dialect and translating. It learns..." Siegfried's jaw tightened. "Oak Island excavations have been ongoing since 1795." His voice grew more intense. "But no one has reached the true chamber."

The island was another one of Siegfried's fascinations. As Big Al listened, he counted off the failed attempts on one hand. Franklin Roosevelt's company tried in 1909. Errol Flynn gave it a shot in 1940, but John Wayne had already bought the rights.

"We need to find out who owns it now."

Siegfried's eyes darkened. "Every attempt failed—flooding booby traps buried them alive. It will be perilous to get in."

He let the weight of his words settle.

"But this artifact, look here," he pointed, the schematic flowed to a point off the beach of the island. "I believe it reveals another way in. A tunnel, here, off the coast leading to something underneath the island. Something below sea level."

Siegfried's enthusiasm grew as he pointed to the symbols floating above the relic. He moved through the cryptograms with his hands.

"And these pictographs—they're not just random markings."

His finger traced the air.

"They're a key. A way to navigate the maze beneath Oak Island." The passages looked like spokes on a wheel.

He leaned in, pointing at a route leading away from the island. "In and out. Between," he foreshadowed a massive chamber. "A big prize. It wants us to find the other piece."

"We don't have to use the *Money Pit* shaft. We can bypass it through this tunnel."

Big Al's eyes flickered with understanding, but he suggested caution. "It doesn't look safe."

Siegfried grinned. "Treasure hunts aren't supposed to be safe. They are full of *pirates, thieves, and back stabbers.*"

They both saw it now. The maze. The hidden entrance. The secret buried beneath centuries of modern failures.

Siegfried caught his breath, excitement burning in his eyes as he realized he had another crazy adventure to tell the world about. He wouldn't stop—he couldn't.

"There's one more thing I need to show you," he said.

Big Al's brow furrowed.

"This artifact interacts with modern electronics," Siegfried told him.

Big Al responded with a pause.

"I mean it," Siegfried said. "Turn on the radio, Al."

Big Al walked over to his Zenith Model 7s633. He rotated the dial until it clicked on. He tuned the stations one by one. The sound was faint at first. But soon the static vanished. Big Al had to admit the relic was amplifying the signal. Every station came in clear as a bell. He flipped frequencies and each one was crystal clear.

"It doesn't just exist, it enhances. It accelerates," Siegfried's voice trembled with excitement. "When placed near machinery, it insulates wires to better increase efficiency like myelinated nerve fibers. Everything runs more efficiently, as if it amplifies the power or magically lubricates bearings."

Big Al snorted. "There is no such thing as magic, Siegfried."

Siegfried untucked his shirt, revealing the sickly scar on his side. "This wound from the war was worse before. Damned if I know how, but it's shrinking. I think this thing is actually healing me."

Big Al's eyes widened. Wild-haired, pulse pounding, excitement surged through him.

"I have to admit that's as close to magic as it gets," he mumbled.

With his demonstration complete, Siegfried shut the relic down and handed it to Big Al who slipped the relic into the folds of his sleeve. Siegfried handed Big Al a leather-bound journal from his luggage. The physicist's fingers tightened around it. Siegfried's final words settled like a storm on the horizon.

A creak on the stairs. The bones of the old house shifting again?

Big Al's gaze darkened. He looked for anything he could use as a makeshift weapon. Siegfried exhaled, fists clenched, vibrating with excitement. Big Al turned toward the door. He reached for the handle to open it but before he could... the doorknob turned.

CHAPTER 10

Cornered

Siegfried stepped back as the guestroom door creaked slowly open.

A raggedy Malachi Donnoby stood in the doorway, looking like he'd been run over by a buffalo.

"Who the hell are you?" Siegfried demanded. "You can't just barge in here," his voice was sharp, wary.

Malachi sneered. "And yet, here I am." He stepped into the light.

Siegfried stared at Malachi, assessing. The man's face was flushed from punches, his lip split, and a good shiner was already forming. He looked familiar. "You're the *pirate* from the seminar."

Malachi smirked—it was an easy expression for him, disarming. The smile faltered as his busted lip cracked open again. He winced.

"Yeah," Malachi managed to say, "That's me all right. You really ruffled some feathers in there, old man. Up until you lost your audience with outrageous claims, I was actually enjoying the show." Malachi leaned casually against the doorframe. "Mind if I step in? Figured we could all have a chit-chat."

He waited... for an invitation.

Big Al shifted, trying to slip past. But Malachi didn't move. His face may be mangled but his body was sound enough to block the exit. His smile wavered but never faltered.

"I'd love to talk to you too, Big Al. I'd love to hear your insight on the matter."

Big Al didn't try to force his way past, but his tone was irritated, "I think you should leave. Perhaps you haven't heard of me."

Malachi bowed up, straightened his fatigued posture. Big Al backed up. Siegfried did too.

Malachi walked towards them, unhurriedly. "Oh, anyone not living under a rock knows you."

As he entered, Siegfried sharpened his scrutiny. "Your mug looks familiar." He paused, eyes narrowing from the realization. "Aha, you're Malachi Donnoby, the baseball player."

Malachi chuckled, "Took you long enough. For a genius you are awfully dense."

"Yes," Big Al interrupted. "Yes. He is."

Siegfried's tone was too smooth, too measured. "A very... adequate player. You must be the thief not the pirate."

Malachi tittered again and thought, *this old fox is dense alright, strategically dense.*

But aloud, Malachi said, "I'm still in the game, still playing by the rules. No complaints, except for some rowdy fans trying to tip the apple cart." Having made his way into the room, Malachi draped his black trench coat over the nearest chair.

Big Al retreated further into the room and sank onto the edge of the guest bed, hands trembling. He was too old to be dealing with this shit. His birthday came and went in March. He'd always eschewed birthdays, but his 70th had been different. Six months earlier, this house had been filled with children; refugees relocated from a displaced persons camp in Europe.

One of them, an 11-year-old girl, his distant cousin, had met her famous relative for the first time. He had opened his home for her. For all of them. Even four years after the war, people were still trying to find a place to call home. Those not relocated to the U.S. were on their way to Israel.

Malachi recognized Big Al's sad posture.

"Easy there, Al. Don't blow a gasket, ole boy."

"How about we cut the stalling and spill it," Malachi growled as his hand slid out from under the trench coat on the seat. "Let's get to brass tacks."

When Malachi's hand re-emerged, it held a suppressed semiauto Colt .45. Leveled directly at Siegfried's chest. Big Al straightened up from his slouch. Siegfried's heart pounded.

For his part, Malachi sighed, shaking his head. He had genuinely enjoyed the seminar. His theories had proven to be spot-on. Malachi's grip on the Colt was steady, his tone calm—too calm. His eyes held no malice, just boring predictability. He made sure the others understood the weapon in his hand was no ordinary sidearm.

"You see this?" he asked. "I call her the *Problem Solver.*" He waved his silenced Union Switch & Signal 1911A1. "It's chambered in 230-grain Dum Dum pills—perfect for close-quarters wet-work. No sonic crack. Less collateral. Just a soft pop, a big hole, and a problem solved."

The two old timers were at a loss for words, so Malachi continued the conversation.

"The CIA ordered me to sit in on the lecture," Malachi's voice was casual, like discussing the weather. "Find out exactly what you know."

A pause.

Chuckling while he talked, Malachi couldn't hold his amusement back. This was a monumental fuck up. A major SNAFU. But he had to admit it was funny.

"I was following orders and boy-oh-boy, did you ever spill the beans, amigo." He used the Colt designed pistol as a pointer with his finger hovering just in front of the trigger. "Apparently, you just don't know when to keep your mouth shut."

Big Al stood abruptly. "No, no he doesn't." The old man's hands trembled, but his voice was firm. "We had a conversation and everything is alright, Malachi."

Malachi's brow lifted.

"He doesn't have the artifact," Big Al stated flatly. *No lies,* he told himself.

A slow simper crept onto Malachi's face followed by a grimace. His eye was swelling shut, his neck stiff and aching. Those goons at the seminar had thrown punches like pro boxers. He tilted his head, cracking his neck, rolling his sore shoulder. At last, he composed himself and his words were blunt.

"Who said anything about an artifact?" Malachi asked.

I need a drink, he thought. *A drink and a woman.*

"Damn," Big Al muttered. Frustrated, he'd let that remark slip out. He took a second to recover, but he couldn't hide his meeker response. "I'll talk to the Brass and sort this out." He tried to speak firmly, but his hands twitched, betraying his nerves. "Put the gun away, Malachi. It's over. No one else needs to get hurt."

Siegfried's stomach rolled. His guts were rolling around.

Something isn't right, he told himself. *Al sounds like he knows this joker. And knows him too well.*

Siegfried moved closer to Big Al and in a voice dropped to a whisper asked, "Albert... what's going on?"

Malachi stepped closer too, the barrel of the long pistol maintaining his target.

"You're a liability, Siegfried," Big Al's blunt remark caused Siegfried to turn pale. His tone was smooth, almost regretful. "You're spilling secrets people way above my clearance want buried."

There was a pause. The length of a deadly heartbeat. Malachi took control.

"Al," Malachi grinned. "I think it's time for you to scram, kid."

Like Big Al said, Siegfried was a liability. His elimination was mandated. Malachi hated wet work like this. Siegfried wasn't a fighter. It would be like offing a kitten. Even still, this pussy had been a Nazi, which which justified his actions.

Big Al squared his shoulders. Weak resolve. But it was there. He placed himself between Malachi and Siegfried.

"Malachi," Big Al said. His voice was low. It was clear he intended for only Malachi to hear his words. "He doesn't have the information or the artifact." A flicker of desperation nearly crushed his resolve, but Big Al continued, "You can let him go. I'll take it up with command."

Malachi didn't seem to waver, so Big Al raised his voice and tried to sound authoritative. "I'm ordering you to put the gun away," he demanded, exasperated.

Malachi was bordering on dry eye, never blinking, never taking his eyes off Siegfried.

"Sorry, Big Al. Orders from the top. Not my call." His voice was flat, final. "Orders are clear. Terminate with extreme prejudice." Malachi motioned toward the door. "Scram. You don't want to be part of this."

Siegfried's lip trembled and his gaze darted to Big Al. He was afraid but also angry.

"*Backstabber,*" he snarled. "You knew about this? Are you part of the conspiracy?" His voice cracked. "Albert... what have you done?"

Betrayal, the deepest cut of them all.

Big Al reached for the doorknob.

He hesitated and looked back at Siegfried. His eyes brimmed with sorrow. But there were no words to offer. Siegfried had sealed his fate. His old friend had doomed himself. Big Al stepped out into the empty hallway just as Malachi called after him and, for Siegfried, delivered yet another unkind cut.

"There'll be a cab waiting for you downstairs," he told Big Al. "I called one in for you," he stated to the departing scientist who quietly closed the door behind him.

Left alone with his killer, Siegfried swallowed hard and whispered, "Oh, shit... This is it."

Malachi exhaled, steady, unbothered. "Afraid so, amigo." His voice held no malice, only inevitability. "If it makes you feel any better, the professor wasn't originally part of this operation. He just happened to be in the wrong place at the wrong time."

Malachi shrugged.

A calm acceptance of what had to be done.

Malachi squared his stance, adjusting his grip. The thumb safety clicked off. "There are two ways we can do this, Siegfried." The hammer was already cocked back. His voice never wavered.

"We can do this the hard way or the easy way." He leveled the pistol at Siegfried's chest. His other hand extended, palm open. Resting in it was a single, unassuming pill.

Siegfried's eyes darted between the gun and the clean exit. His lips curled in disgust. "Give me a cardiac arrest? A hemorrhagic stroke?" Siegfried snorted a bitter scoff. "No one will believe it." His voice cracked as his patience wavered, and temper took hold.

Malachi shrugged. "Over a hundred people saw you run over here."

"I can't believe Albert is working with you monsters," Siegfried shouted. "Why would I make it easy on you?"

Malachi shook his head in frustration. This day was becoming a pain in the ass. Even so, Malachi decided to play nice

"If it's any consolation," he told the condemned man. "I can tell you, indirectly, your conclusions weren't far from the truth." Malachi glanced at the pill in his hand hoping he'd take it.

It's painless, you fool, Malachi thought. *Just take the damned pill.*

When Siegfried didn't react, Malachi sighed and continued his explanation.

"Just like the Nazis, we needed help building the bomb. We got better scientists, the righteous cause. There's so much more at stake than you realize." He paused just long enough to let it sink in. "The conspiracy isn't about keeping the public in the dark, it's about winning the war with an enemy that outmatches us in every way and has infiltrated almost every government on this planet."

Hearing this, Siegfried's breath quickened. His mind raced.

"War of the Worlds," Siegfried whispered. His eyes darted around. His life flashing in front of him.

Malachi frowned, shrugged his shoulders. His finger remained near the trigger as he amended Siegfried's statement. "We prefer to say The Shadow War. But enough of this!" Malachi's voice hardened. "Where's the damn artifact?" He demanded. "GIVE IT TO ME NOW!" he yelled.

Malachi's patience was gone.

Siegfried's jaw clenched. His fists trembled. "It's safe, where you monsters will never find it."

A defiant last stand, trusting his friend one last time.

Siegfried hocked up a wad of saliva and spit it right into Malachi's only good eye.

May the villain have pink eye for a week, Siegfried told himself.

Malachi's reaction was swift and lethal. He pressed the silencer to the bridge of his victim's nose, right in the old credit card box. At this distance, the powder would burn the skin, fry the hair, and burn the eyeballs.

Downstairs, Big Al opened the front door. Stepping out onto some ash on his front porch, he heard the thump of a body hitting the upstairs floor. He looked back briefly at the ceiling before shutting the front door. He made his way to a taxi waiting at his gate. The sun was setting. Wet clouds on the horizon.

Looper watched as Big Al climbed into the cab and drove off. The scene was too far away for Looper to hear, but he could imagine the conversation.

"Where to, mister? Oh hell, you're Big Al! Where can I take you, Doc?"

The actual conversation was much as Looper had imagined it. But when asked "where to" Big Al hesitated. There was only one place he could go now. He needed to meet his handler.

"Central Park," he told the driver.

"Central Park, New York? That's a long haul, but you got it, bub," said the driver.

Big Al rode in silence, lost in thought. Was the killing quick? Or was Malachi extracting every ounce of information before the end? Did Siegfried consider running. But where would he run?

As Big Al's the taxi rounded a corner and vanished from sight, Trip confiscated the keys and guns from his fallen adversaries.

Trip spotted a kid as he walked up to the Packard. "Shit, kid, did you see all that?" Trip asked, pointing back towards Big Al's house.

The kid, still wide eyed, nodded his head *yes.*

"Hell's bells, am I going to have to vaporize you too? Or can you keep a secret?"

He knelt in front of the kid taking a knee preparing his best Vince Lombardi speech. This was the moment, as a baseball coach, he would rally the team after a hard loss. The pep talk would relate their current predicament to events which would unfold later in life. Right now, this was one of those life lesson moments for this poor kid.

Trip took his time, a deep breath for good measure. "You believe in monsters, son?" he asked

The kid shook his head *no.*

Trip nodded. He understood—he didn't either when he was young and dumb. "Hold your hand out kid."

The kid shook his head *no.*

"Hold your hand out!" Trip said more gruff, more demanding.

He did.

From his hand to the child's hand, he placed the claw on his palm. "Monsters are real kid, they exist. You can either slay demons or get slayed. Which one are you?"

The kid shrugged his shoulders.

Trip stood up and put his hand on the boy's shoulder. "You're a demon slayer, kid," he told him. "Anyone with the nuts to stand out here and not run away after what they saw... shit, hold your head high, kid."

He tapped the boy on his trembling shoulder. With a significant nod, he left him for the Packard. The door creaked as he opened it and slid inside. He jammed the key in the ignition, rolled down the window and looked out, checking the street. When his eyes returned to the road ahead he saw that damn kid still standing there, frozen.

Ignoring the boy, he rolled up his sleeve exposing the tech from his suit, fingers swiftly punching in the next coordinates on his navigational pad.

Central Park. A map to get there.

He looked back over at the kid. He was a statue with soiled pants.

"Stay out of trouble, kid," he said with a grin, a wink, and a finger gun going bang.

He pushed in the clutch and stepped on the break. Turned the key rolling the engine over. Gave it gas. 1st gear, 2nd, 3rd, 4th. He ran through the gears like a bootlegger running from Johnny Law.

The kid was fading fast in the distance, along with Princeton. Another battleground vanishing in the rearview mirror, another scar diseasing his psyche. His hand rattled against the wheel. The tremor was back but what was jarring was how quickly it reappeared.

Steady. Two sharp inhales through his nose.

Control. One long exhale through his mouth.

Gone—he flexed his hand.

The carbon dioxide was cleared. His body was calm in 60 seconds.

He played *Eddie Rabbitt's Drivin' My Life Away* in his head—on repeat. The rhythm matched the hum of the engine, the lyrics drifting through his mind like phantoms on the highway. Another long road to Central Park. Another damn night without her. And still, no destination felt like home.

CHAPTER 11

One Time Pad
New York—1949

A long, lonely drive—for everyone.

Big Al arrived first. He strolled through Central Park, the lamplights casting long shadows along his path. His hands remained tucked inside his coat pockets, his head low. At last, he found the bench marked with red lipstick.

He settled in.

Slowly, deliberately, he placed a newspaper, set to a specific page, beside him as a silent signal. A message to his handler. He wasn't followed.

He waited.

Across from him, on a knoll beneath the evening glow, an Enigmatic Woman stood.

She was a vision of elegance and danger. Young, good looking, yet something about her was... timeless. Her blonde hair, immaculate. A white dress clung to her form, cinched at the waist. A lingering eye could formulate everything under it. A black hat, adorned with a single red rose, cast a soft shadow over her face.

Her bright red lips stood stark against the pale glow of the park lights.

Behind a sheer, see-through veil, her eyes never left the old man sitting on the distant bench.

She might be a guardian, watching over him. She might be his executioner. Another cleaner, sent to finish what Malachi had started.

Big Al had spotted her like a light house. His pulse quickened, but he stayed still. If she was here to kill him, he would know soon enough.

As he watched, he spotted movement behind her.

A man approached, his stride was deliberate, his presence unsettling. His brain-tanned leather duster was worn and tattered like it had seen too many battles and too many years. The man wore a Stetson fedora (not a western hat), a more sophisticated one. His Stetson was riddled with burn marks. It shadowed his face, unreadable. Big Al watched, uncertain, although he knew one thing for certain. This was no ordinary meeting.

Events are set into motion now, he told himself.

Several yards away from Big Al, Looper grumbled, his voice rough, tired. "What? You wanted to see me?" he asked the lady in red.

"Six months ago!" Ava's eyes bored into him. "Where have you been?" she demanded

Looper snorted, muttering under his breath, "I've been busy. Disappointing Yeshua, I'm sure."

"Impeccable timing." she said.

He rolled his shoulders shrugging it off. His eyebrows followed suit with a small wave as his eyes found anywhere else to look but hers. He played it off as pure luck. But it wasn't. And she knew.

Ava slapped his chest with what appeared to be a hardback book.

"What's this?" he asked, scratching underneath his hat.

She held back a tear. "Siegfried's last book. I even had him sign it for you."

It was a copy of *The Ancient Enemy.* A smile tugged at his lips. "The gift that keeps giving," he mumbled almost incoherently.

Ava's lips pressed into a thin line. "Trip, you have to stop freelancing. Every move you make ripples across time; what you break now could damn the future."

He slipped the book into the inside pocket of his duster—watching as her eyes burned with something beyond fear—knowledge. The two of them had lived through every century, clawing their way toward the moment they had lost. And if he wasn't careful, there might not be a future left to return to. Or, at the very least, not one they recognized.

Trip tilted his head, a bitter sneer tugging at his lips. "Isn't that the point, Ava?" His voice was dry, hollow. "We're here to fix the unfixable. And no matter what we do, it never seems to matter."

Ava searched his face, her gaze heavy with memories. Looking for the man she once knew. *Was he ever really there?* she asked herself.

The one who once held her like she was his whole world. She filled in as a mother to his son after his third wife died. The truth she hung onto was this: he had no intention of hurting her and yet he always managed to.

"Are you sure you're not looking for more?" Her voice was softer now, more fragile than she wanted it to be.

Looper shook his head. A lengthy exhale. A hint of raw memories from the past.

"Something more? No. I stopped looking a long time ago."

Ava's expression hardened. Her voice dropped to a whisper, thin as a blade. "Stopping them from achieving their objectives is the best revenge."

Looper let out a low, humorless chuckle. "No, Ava. *Revenge* is the best revenge." His gaze darkened. "I'm going to kill them all," he added with absolution.

"You're becoming one of them, Trip. Revenge is a drug creating a chemical loop in your brain. Just thinking about it feeds the addiction."

"It's justice," Trip snapped.

"Every 'justice' hit gives you less and less of a high. Forgiveness? That's the real dopamine—stronger, longer-lasting."

He scoffed. "They don't want forgiveness."

"And how would you even know? You vaporize them before they have a chance to repent."

"What was it they said during the Crusades—kill them all and let God sort it out?" he replied cruelly.

"I remember who you were before," she said sharply.

Trip narrowed his eyes. "You've got memory gaps big enough to fly Saturn through, but you remember psychology and neuroscience?"

She shrugged. "You were all giddy about meeting Yeshua; maybe you should have paid more attention. Forgiveness is the cure. It will reactivate your prefrontal cortex, Trip. You're still addicted to the chase."

"After all these years, you still sound like a frickin' robot, woman."

Ava looked away. Nothing could pull him back from the edge of darkness he was guilty of shading.

The tremors in his hand were proof.

He hid his trembling hand in his pocket after she gave it a second look.

Looper took a deep breath, his gaze distant, unreadable. "We have our missions." he redirected, ignoring her advice.

Ava sighed, shaking her head. "I'm trying to help you get back on track."

Looper's face scrunched up. His teeth on the verge of shattering into a million pieces. With effort, he steered Ava back to the present. "We've laid low long enough," his voice was hard, cold. "It's time to go back on the offensive. They've got more hybrids now—hybrids working with human collaborators. They ain't Udug but they ain't human anymore either."

"Jiāng?" *He was such a good boy when they met him.*

He nodded.

He paused and his eyes darted past her, scanning the park. Something wasn't right. The feeling passed and he continued, "As of now, they're another eight guys down."

Ava closed her eyes, inhaling deeply. "A drop in the bucket."

"A bucket will empty with a hole in it."

"Why was Siegfried removed from the board?" Looper sneered, the bitterness settling deep. "All that work getting him out of Germany, and they deep-sixed him anyway."

Ava reached out, taking his hand. Her grip was gentle, but her voice was firm. "Just be careful, Looper." She deliberately did not use his real name. "You and I are the only ones who have each other's backs until we finish this."

"No, I have an asset."

"You of all people should know you can't trust her."

She's never been wrong." Looper held Ava's gaze and held it for a fraction longer than usual.

"They changed her."

"We changed her back; Athena traded everything to save her!"

"And yet she is still not who she once was."

"Are any of us who we were before Event 231?"

She shook her head. Their past selves wouldn't recognize who they'd become even if they were wearing name tags.

"They're working on surveillance camera technology. It's going to be harder to sleuth through secure sites."

He patted the pistol on his hip. "Oh, don't worry, I've got a hack worked out for that."

His eyes snapped to hers. If it wasn't for the history they shared, his words could have sounded threatening. "Stay out of my way, Ava. I've lost all the women in my life–I don't want to lose you, too."

Without another word, he reached for his duster. A subtle flick of his fingers, an unseen activation. A faint shimmer rippled over his body, distorting his form. In an instant he was gone.

The night seemed to swallow him whole. "Of course you do," she mumbled. No footsteps. No trace.

"Damn it, Trip!" she called out just loud enough. She knew he heard her.

Unaware of the drama playing out in the distance, Big Al slouched on the park bench, his old bones settling into the wood like a worn-out paperback on a dusty shelf. Peering into the darkness, he watched the ducks paddle aimlessly across a nearby lake. Light from the moon was just enough to catch their silhouettes.

Lucky bastards, he thought.

Their biggest worry was choking on breadcrumbs. His? An impending intergalactic war. He returned his gaze to the young woman in the dark. She loitered in the distance but gaining ground, her gaze pinned on him like a cat stalking a mouse.

Her companion had been there, and then poof. The man was there one minute and gone the next, but he had remained long enough for Big Al to recognize him.

Big Al vaguely recalled shaking his hand once in Los Alamos during the war. The Guardians were something. Enigmas, popping in and out of reality like cosmic pranksters. Stoic, cryptic, and occasionally as pleasant as a wet sock. His body shuddered.

As a physicist, the Guardians frustrated the hell out of him. Only one thing made sense of their antics. His beloved Einstein-Rosen Bridge theory. At least it offered a thin sliver of reason in a universe which had stopped making sense.

Meanwhile, he waited. The wait seemed to be taking longer than usual until, at last, his new CIA handler plopped down beside him. His handler picked up the paper and saw it thumbed to page 2, line 24. The agent produced a wafer-thin card of random digits. A whisper of numbers, the scratching out of a string, and Malachi ripped out the page and touched the strip to his lit zippo.

Ashes to ashes. One time pad. One time only.

"Shit," Big Al complained. "It's you."

He put his pad away. "At your service," Malachi grinned. "Ex-ballplayer. Secret agent. Professional pain in the ass."

"And Wise Guy," Big Al added. He sighed long and heavy, like a man who had just finished explaining relativity to a room full of donkeys. "What a mess."

Malachi nodded in agreement. His expression slow and expansive, like a man carrying the weight of a thousand bad decisions.

"You don't have to tell me," Malachi said. "I offered him the pill."

They stared at the silver and black slickwater which permeated the lake. The night was silent and so were they. Big Brain Al already knew the stakes. His friend getting removed from the board was just another grim footnote in the history of "necessary evils."

"You wanna know how I got tangled up in this racket?" Malachi stretched his arms, cracking his knuckles.

"No," Big Al said flatly.

He let the moment hang—then his tone shifted. "Tough break about your pal."

Al pursed his lips, shutting his eyes tight.

Malachi leaned in, lowering his voice. "I read the file on his ticket outta Germany. Hell of a caper. Still can't figure how that spook pulled it off. That fella is a one-man army."

Having said his piece, Malachi rested an elbow on his knee and extended his hand in Big Al's direction, palm up.

"Let's cut to the chase—where's the goods, Al? You're on the "No Touch" list, but you gotta give it up and I still gotta bag it. Orders from upstairs."

Big Al snorted. "Orders. The SS had orders too."

Malachi rolled his eyes. "Oh, come on, Doc. This ain't the same thing."

Al arched an eyebrow. "Oh? You mean to tell me you're fine with sticking your nose in an intergalactic pissing contest that's gonna chew you up and spit you out? You clipped a good man tonight, Malachi. How do you sleep at night?"

Malachi rubbed his face, like a man trying to wipe away the last decade. "Every war's got casualties, Al. Collateral damage. You know how many folks got roasted in Dresden? Hell, we torched Japan pretty good too." He leaned back, exhaling slow. "Look, they're gonna study the artifact, same as always. We're just foot soldiers."

"Obviously," Big Al sighed.

Malachi ignored the dig. "The abductions, the mass sightings; it's all reconnaissance, Al. They're scoping everybody out, collecting samples, testing for ancient bugs certain ones we ain't immune to. And word is, someone is flushing out the last of the Guardians."

Big Al folded his arms. "Deep-space scouting parties, hunters, assassins; I've heard the whispers. Makes sense. If you're planning an invasion, you don't wanna croak from a bad case of space flu."

Malachi nodded. "That artifact you're hanging on to? It just might be our golden ticket. A chance to close the tech gap before the main fleet drops anchor. Hell, we still don't know how we zapped that saucer over Los Angeles, but we did. And what about the Martians—"

"Roswell," Big Al cut him off with a shake of the head.

"What a clown show," Malachi sighed. His head flopped back, staring at the sky. Mars was up there somewhere. "Anyhow, imagine if our so-called allies get their mitts on this tech and decide to flip sides, same as the Russians. Too many variables. Too many mugs who'd kill for a power trip."

Big Al let out a long sigh.

"You know," he told Malachi. "There's another ship. South of here. Gulf of Mexico in the Sigsbee Deep. Been sitting there, 14,000 feet deep, right on the ocean floor, for twelve thousand years. But the core's dead."

Malachi let out a low whistle. "Yeah, I heard. They used Coral growth to peg the age."

"As old as the Pleistocene, as old as the storied Atlantis," Big Al's voice dropped, almost reverent. "If the Reds get there first—"

Malachi shook his head and sighed, "They're already sniffin' around. And let's be real, Doc—if we figure out how to dredge that thing up, the public's gonna notice."

"The System will collapse." Big Al chuckled dryly. "There's only so much baloney you can spoon-feed the masses."

"Wanna bet?" Malachi smirked, lighting up like he had a secret. "You'd be surprised at what people will swallow. Top brass has a report that says people will believe just about anything if you wrap it up nice and tidy. As for the Gulf ship, they'll try raising it during a hurricane—wait for civilians to clear out—media's on the CIA payroll, problem solved. They even thought about trying to create their very own hurricane, just to hurry things along. Hell, I've seen plans to create an incident requiring a *quarantine* in the area. Only that would require the threat of war and would be another mess."

Big Al sighed, running a hand through his mop. "I'm just a scientist, Malachi. With a couple good years left in me."

"They're going to need you, Al. They'll have questions." Malachi shot back, his grin fading. "DOD orders."

Big Al rubbed his temple, his voice sounding small, "Alternate timelines, Malachi. Ever think about that? I'm starting to. Maybe somewhere out there, this all played out differently. Maybe there's a world where we didn't screw it up."

Malachi scoffed, leaning back on the bench.

"There's only one universe, Al. This one. And, in this one, anyone who knows anything about anything is walking around with a target on their back."

Malachi leaned forward, his voice lowering to a murmur. "Hell, at least one of the hunters tailed you and me after Siegfried's little dog-and-pony show at the seminar. Eventually, three more turned up plus a leader dog. Santo Padre was dead, with or without my help." Malachi snapped his fingers, the name that was escaping him earlier flooded back into focus. That freaking guy. He trusted that spook less than a Constellation on a transatlantic flight. "Looper had to deal with 'em downstairs. Trip Looper. I'm not sure I could've stopped what was coming for us with only two clipazines. They were gunnin' for both of you."

Big Al felt a chill and his eyes narrowed.

What if all this happened on my birthday? he asked himself.

"Looper? He's still—?" he didn't finish the question.

Malachi shrugged, casual, and volunteered to complete Al's comment. "Looper's still helping. Still making waves, yeah. Cleaning up messes before they make headlines. The Brass can't control him though." He raised an eyebrow. "Anyway, this time it's different. This time, Doc, you've got people's attention."

Malachi's tone darkened. "Some of these creatures that need to be dealt with either live forever or have figured out how to stretch the clock. Looper's old. There are even rumors he rolled in the hay with a Jap back in the 1800's. Supposedly, that's where he got that shiny sword of his. We found records of him dating back to the 700s."

Big Al took a breath. "Magic," he muttered, thinking of his friend.

Malachi frowned. "There ain't no magic, just tech."

Big Al's gaze drifted, lost in thought. "Science can't always explain the good parts."

Malachi made the sign of the cross and didn't argue.

"So, how about the artifact, Doc?" he asked again.

Big Al unfolded his sleeve and produced the artifact. He turned it in his palm, rolling it between his fingers. "Consider time dilation, Malachi," he said. Big Al's voice was steady, but his eyes gleamed with deep thought. "The faster you go, the slower time moves. If those who wish us harm left their home-world centuries ago, they could've been in transit for hundreds of thousands of our years—while only a few ticks passed for them."

The old physicist paused and tapped his temple as the weight of the idea settled between the two men on the bench in Central Park.

"For us, it's ancient history," Big Al continued. "Even if we wanted to make peace, for them," Big Al's gaze darkened. "For them it all happened yesterday. And it's still game on."

He bowed his head as the weight of it settled over him. It was some moments before he spoke again and, when he did, his tone was more hopeful.

"Whatever we used once to stave them off is long gone. That ship sitting under the ocean?" His jaw tightened. "That ship might be our only chance to even the odds unless a miracle drops in our laps from the sky."

Malachi had to agree. "Yeah," Malachi said, "No shit."

Moments later, the woman approached. Big Al gestured toward her.

"Ava," he said, "This is Malachi. Malachi, meet Ava Rider. My assistant. Our anonymous benefactor." His expression tightened, just slightly. "Ava helped Oppenheimer and the boys put the Bomb together."

Malachi's brow lifted.

Ava met his gaze, unreadable. Too young to have been there. Too composed.

Malachi sized her up. "That so?" he asked.

Ava merely smiled politely—a practiced smile, revealing nothing.

Her smile seemed to disarm Malachi. "Damn," he grinned. "A pleasure."

Ava ignored the niceties. She plucked the artifact from Big Al's palm with one hand and, with the other, she fished a small metallic black box from her purse. Combining the two, the box's lid flipped open, a digital screen blooming to life, displaying the same data Big Al saw in his guest room.

She nodded. The real McCoy.

"Checks out," she said.

Malachi leaned forward, his eyes narrowing trying to catch a glimpse.

She withheld the view.

"Sorry, bub. You're not to read-in on this."

"Excuse me," he casually remarked and backed up.

"You've already seen too much," she replied, slipping the box back into her purse.

She met his gaze with those steady, wooden eyes. Looper called her a Karen with RBF whenever she looked at him like that. Indeed, to the casual observer, Ava's flat, irritated expression did, in fact, resemble a *resting bitch face.*

Malachi sighed and shifted gears, shaking off this woman's cold shoulder. Whatever this was, if this woman was involved, the whole thing just became a hell of a lot more interesting.

"Can you at least tell me what it is?" he asked, nodding toward her purse.

Ava warmed a little. "Ever heard of a genie in a bottle?"

"Sure," Malachi nodded. "Aren't they supposed to be *in* the bottle?"

"Meet part of the bottle."

Half believing it, Malachi shook his head. "No shit."

"When the Templars found the Ark in Jerusalem, this was part of a ring," she said. "Not understanding its power, the Templars took a sword to it and severed the ring into two pieces and separated them across the continents."

"This artifact belonged to King Solomon?" he asked.

She nodded, the gas-lit lamps throwing flickering light and shadows across her face, turning her explanation into something out of a campfire ghost story.

"The completed ring held knowledge that could build or destroy civilizations," she said quietly. "And it did, over and over for centuries after the fall of Atlantis."

"Soloman called the ring his Seal. The people who created us? They called them *Mini Mii's.*"

Malachi raised an eyebrow.

Ava was grinning from ear to ear. She couldn't remember the last time she'd seen the Seal intact, only the death surrounding its disappearance.

"Each ring held an AI," Ava said, warming to her subject. "Think of it as a guide, a personal assistant. With the Ark and one of these, a powerful man could rule the world... or what was left of it."

Malachi's eyes widened. "AI?" he asked. "The Genie."

"Artificial Intelligence. A tech-based lifeform," she replied.

Malachi tilted his head. "Like a supernatural sidekick?"

Ava grinned. He thought he was being cute, but his brain was still too ape-like to fully grasp what she was talking about. She was beginning to regret telling him anything.

"Anyway, now we have a map and a key, we'll know exactly where to find the reactor and—."

Malachi stood and interrupted.

"Well, this has all been very interesting, but we need to go," he said. "We've got our own work to do. What you're proposing sounds a little out of my depth. I'm not a fan of drowning."

As Malachi walked off, Big Al started to follow but he turned to Ava and asked, "Looper?"

Ava's expression darkened. "A variable I can't predict."

Big Al was chagrined. "Maybe he's a piece needing to come off the board for a while."

Ava shook her head. "He's essential. He will have to embrace the suck a little longer."

Big Al studied her. "You still love him."

Ava's face hardened. "I've watched someone I once loved evolve and mature into something dark. If he can, he'll burn the world down for revenge."

Big Al chuckled. "Freud would have had a field day with you people."

Ava allowed herself a grin. "Freud could've written a book about us. Last time Looper tried to outdrink someone, he drank until sunrise with Nostradamus. And the two tried to outdo one another in a trivia contest. Swear to God, that whack job had a photographic memory."

"What about Project Red Wings?" Big Al whispered. "Does Looper know?"

"Absolutely not." Ava's voice was firm, unyielding. "He hates the Udug, he would have no interest in creating our own. I don't know what the Brass is up to, but they think they've made some kind of genetic breakthrough..." she shook her head. "They just need a host to test it."

Chapter 12

Morning Manic Mayhem
Victoria, Texas—Present Day

Sonny was stirring, caught between dreaming and reality. It wasn't his alarm clock or sunlight waking him up. It was his feisty wife. She'd stayed up late reading *The Ancient Enemy*. After finishing the Tantrom appointment, he met Chiara downtown for the signing and gave her the present after the last signature.

The house was theirs.

By 1 a.m. Sonny and Chiara finished moving the last boxes—proof of their existence in this world. With one Flexeril, one Tylenol PM, and a few hours' sleep, she was already interrupting his future dreams with a torrent of clatter he tried his best to ignore. He rolled in bed thinking about yesterday's last appointment. Something about that guy felt familiar.

Was it his stink?

Chiara didn't care why he wasn't getting up, only that he had not, so she continued unleashing her usual morning tornado assault. The blow dryer roared like a jet engine. Bathroom drawers slammed like artillery fire. The ceiling fan's blazing light hit him like a searchlight.

"Have you seen my blue scrub pants?" she called out. Sonny grunted something unintelligible.

"No, the dark blue ones! Why are you not helping me look for it?"

Sonny's brain was still off-world, locked in a dream mission slipping away. "I just... need more time..." he mumbled.

Snap. His brain rebooted. Hard start. Disoriented. *Where the hell am I?* New house. New bed. Same ole chaotic morning.

One eye cracked open. Chiara stood over him, arms crossed, holding the wrong blue scrubs. "Need more time for what, Sonny?"

"Huh? What? I don't know, check the dishwasher." He collapsed back down.

"Oh, my God—you are so useless in the morning," she fumed, looking at the little blanket teepee.

Sonny barely heard her, until he felt a firm squeeze. Right on his morning wood. His body tensed. She grabbed it like a lumber jack grabbing an axe handle, ready to chop wood.

"NAVY BLUE SCRUBS, Sonny!" she growled, standing in her panties and bra. "I'm gonna be late!"

She released her grip, and Sonny exhaled. They were not morning people. A trait she established early on.

Sonny's brain caught up. His wife's half-unpacked suitcase sat open, clothes scattered everywhere. His boxers draped over a pile of her panties. Heels upside down beneath yesterday's bra. His Vertx shorts somewhere in the mess.

Don't step on those heels, he warned himself.

The finalization of making that memory node was interrupted upon seeing them, the navy blue scrubs, hanging on the bedpost, right where she left them last night. "It's right there, babe."

Chiara spotted it instantly, mouth dropping open. "Did you just put that there?"

"Yeah. Psychokinesis." He sarcastically remarked.

She scoffed, snatched the pants, and walked off. "Thanks, Sonny," she shouted, insincere.

Sonny face-planted back into the pillow. He was almost out cold in a second flat.

"SONNY!" she yelled out from the other room.

One eye cracked open, breaking the sleep seal.

"Where is my work badge?"

He lay there twelve minutes with zero hope of sleep, then finally got up. Still half-bent over from his morning wood, he shuffled toward the bathroom. One step in and—CRUNCH! Pain shot through his foot. The upside-down heel took him out like a landmine. He went headfirst into the dresser.

"Shit! Can't get any worse," he mumbled to himself.

CHAPTER 13

Star Crash

Sonny sat at the intersection, impatiently tapping his fingers on the steering wheel. Before he could even yawn properly, another caravan of military vehicles rolled through town, Jade Helm part Deux. The convoy looked as disorganized as ever and, just as he thought, Americans weren't being hauled off to the concentration camps.

This wasn't normal. But nothing was normal these days. Crime was skyrocketing. Weirdos like Tantrom were in town and normalized. He took a second to look for the psychopath. Something in him whispered this might be the calm before the storm.

Ten minutes later, after surviving the traffic jam, he pulled into the parking lot, still half-asleep, already bracing himself for another long-ass day. Ready to embrace the grind, Sonny stepped out of his truck and rubbed the knot on his forehead, a souvenir from the high heel incident when his dresser broke his fall this morning.

He muttered under his breath. "Damn heel." He cursed the inanimate object for attacking him.

By noon, the warehouse had transformed from an oven to a sauna. The heat index was hovering around 115 degrees. *Sleep Like the Dead* wasn't just a slogan anymore; it was a literal threat if you lost consciousness and stayed inside the insulated building too long.

His first appointment of the day dragged on two hours too long, and the sale was a bust. Next came a lady from Wharton, spinning tall tales about finding luxury mattresses for cheaper than his wholesale cost. Of course, her ride of choice was a $70,000 truck. Cheap. Sonny hated cheap.

With each customer, Sonny shook his head, forcing patience. Phone buzz. Chiara. "Hey babe, what's up?"

Chiara was bubbling with enthusiasm. "Home, at the house for lunch, the carpet is done, and the painter's working on the walls! You know what that means, don't you?"

Sonny sighed. "We get to officially say we're moved in?"

"Yes! How are you not excited?! We can finally move on from that night."

His inner thoughts betrayed his true feelings.

I'm dealing with cheap-ass customers, he told himself, *not frugal, but cheap. Inflation is on the rise and people's checkbooks are tighter than usual and they are all angry.*

Sonny stared at his reflection in the office window. The sweat was pouring off his forehead. "I'm ecstatic," he managed to say.

"Oh, boo-hoo," she laughed. "Finish your last delivery then come home, okay?"

"Fine," he conceded.

"See you at the house after my shift in the morning." Chiara was a buzzing-busy-bee over the new house. To Sonny? The new house meant more work he wasn't ready for.

After wrapping up his phone call, Sonny stepped outside. If he smoked, it would have been a good time for one, but he didn't. Dark violent clouds loomed. "Damn," he sighed. A storm was brewing. And not just in the sky. He turned to his left and saw an after-hours delivery hanging on the clipboard. Tantrom the next day.

"Fuck," he sighed. The Dawson delivery was also out of town. "Fuck," he grumbled while rubbing the keloid scar left by the intruder during the break-in.

Outside, the sky was changing too fast. Clouds swallowed the sun, turning daylight into dusk two hours early. Sonny checked the clock as he slid into the leather seat, load in the box trailer hitched behind him. Next to him, between the seat and the console, his VP9 OR Long-Slide. 20 rounds with one in tube.

He pulled it out and press-checked his sidearm. Nickel in the chamber. He was running Critical Duty 135-grain hollow points, the red plastic cone designed to expand on impact—even through clothing. An extra 20-round mag went into the console.

Under the back seat, his AR-15 sat in condition two, mag locked in the well. Two extra 40-round mags. Ample for rural Texas.

6:00 p.m. on the nose. If he stayed on schedule, he'd arrive by 7. Unload, set up in half an hour, home by 8:30 or 9. Chiara was going to be pissed. She hated him being on the road late at night.

First, he closed his ballistics app and then put the customer's address in Maps on his phone. Service was interrupted. He pulled out his Victoria area atlas. He still preferred the old-school method anyway. He checked the map, then headed toward Bayside, watching as raindrops beaded on the windshield one by one.

More military convoys passed, this time moving faster. Very unusual. Something felt—off.

Even with the box-trailer hitched, his Z-71 Silverado maintained 10 mph over the limit easily. Sonny took the Edna exit, passing manicured grass farms. So, this is where all the pallets of grass come from? He had never been through this part of South Texas, but it was fascinating to see giant semis loaded with pallets of carpet grass pulling out of the farms.

He glanced at the directions: Turn down the caliche road. Left at the fork with the red coffee pot. Follow the two-track lane to the house on the hill.

It should've been easy, except the rain was coming down harder now.

Lightning ripped through the sky, flashing red, yellow, and white. The air felt charged, thick with something otherworldly. Many BOOMS.

Sonny's phone buzzed, Chiara sent a weather update. Tornado threat in Wharton County. He spotted a sign through the downpour: "Wharton County," he read. "Of course it was."

Another message from Chiara: *Sonny, I have a bad feeling. Pull over or head home.*

Sonny read it, but his focus shifted, the house appeared ahead. A late-1800s plantation house stood lonely atop the hill. A light flickered, then went out. The old lady who ordered the mattress wanted it for her granddaughter. She needed it tonight and there was her house. No turning back this close.

The white house glowed in spectral flashes under the forked lightning. Tree limbs swung like clawed fingers. The storm intensified. The sky changed, green glow igniting behind the clouds, flaring red-orange. The atmosphere around him paused, waiting.

Something's coming, Sonny told himself.

A fireball tore through the sky, in his direction. ***BOOM!***

Something—a meteor, comet, whatever—slammed into the hillside. The Dawson house lifted, ripped from its studs, exploded like a box of Lincoln Logs.

"Not good."

Sonny slammed both feet on the brakes. The truck skidded. The seatbelt cut into his scar, the deep wound roared awake. A shock wave of air and debris slammed into him. Shingles, beams, and debris tore across the landscape in front of him. The house just... disintegrated.

Sonny ducked low behind the engine block as the windshield spider-webbed. The truck groaned, pushed backward, tires grinding. The trailer detached, tailgate and bumper ripped off. Sonny's head smashed against the steering wheel, beeping out a fading honk, then flung into the passenger headrest. The truck shook, then finally settled.

Sonny held his beat-up face, breathing hard from nasal inflammation. Rain dripped into the cab. Mud and debris mixed with a flood of water.

The windshield held. He pulled himself up, peering through the cracks. A mushroom cloud of dust and smoke rose ahead, lit by lightning. The plantation house was gone; only a crater remained with something massive sitting at its floor.

The fields were littered with burning wreckage. Ancient trees lay shattered like broken bones. Sonny saw what was left of his trailer. It had crumpled like a soda-can blocking the road behind him.

Yet, Sonny was alive. Scratched. Bruised. But alive.

In front of the crater, movement. A limping old dog emerged, soot-covered and shaking. Alive. Did it come from the house? Could anything else have survived?

Sonny physically tried to stay put but nothing could override his instincts to act.

He twisted toward the back of the cab, wincing as pain flared in his ribs. His pistol had jabbed him during the blast. He forced down the pain, ignoring the forming blood clot under the skin. His fingers found the oversized Maglite. Grip tight. Ready.

He wasn't going home yet.

He grabbed a med kit and took off to search for survivors.

CHAPTER 14

Autonomous "Voler" Assistants
USS Icarus—Months Before Sonny's Rifle Match

Captain Mike "Rocco" Badcock gripped the throttle and pulled back on the stick. The XF-53 Sabre Cat roared past doing Mach 20.9—13,794 mph—obliterating the old X-43's unmanned speed record. The fastest manned aircraft before this? The X-15, flown by a dozen daredevils (including Neil Armstrong) back in the '60s. Its 4,520 mph top speed now looked like a tricycle competing with a Ferrari.

But speed wasn't the real marvel.

The military's favorite feature? The Sabre Cat didn't just dominate the skies—it owned outer space.

Today marked the final test flight of Northrop's latest technological lovechild, a hypersonic fighter so advanced it made the SR-72 Blackbird II look like a relic. The B-21 Raider had already replaced the B-2 Spirit. Now, the XF-53 was poised to send the NGAD (Next-Generation Air Dominance) fleet to the Bone Yard.

The arms race had always been ruthless. This one was no exception.

First, the ATF (Advanced Tactical Fighter) program birthed the F-22 Raptor, king of the skies. The F-47 NGAD fighters came next, the crown jewel of the Airforce. But now?

Now, the XF-53 Sabre Cat is the apex predator.

And it isn't merely fast.

It is also adaptive.

The XF-53's AI-controlled meta-material skin shifted colors like a chameleon—chrome on takeoff, black 3.0 at high altitude, and practically invisible in space. Stealth fighters suddenly looked like noisy teenagers wearing glow-in-the-dark-sneakers.

Today, as Rocco watched, the blue sky vanished.

Black. Cold. Space.

The XF-53 smoothly broke free from Earth's grip, making history as the first hypersonic space fighter capable of ground-to-orbit launch without a booster. Unlike the X-51 Aurora, which needed a rocket assist, or its twin-seater predecessor, the XF-52, the XF-53 could scramble at a moment's notice, going from ground to orbit in the blink of an eye.

In space, speed had no limits.

And as far as anyone knew, the United States was the only nation which had figured out how to make fusion-powered space fighters work.

Rocco checked his HUD. The Sabre Cat's heads-up display glowed with beaming confidence. The U.S. SPACE insignia gleamed on the Sabre Cat's twin engine nacelles, just below the CVF-1 designation.

His fighter had a name—*Eugene The Jeep.* The designation matched the boxy stealth geometry of the ship. Its shape did not match its performance characteristics in the atmosphere or space.

Before takeoff, he'd ordered the AVA AI to add a personal touch, nose art featuring Eugene the Jeep (from the Popeye cartoon strip.) He wanted a pose of the character grinning while holding a bomb with a lit fuse. The meta-material skin complied instantly.

Above Eugene's new home, Rocco's call sign was stenciled in bold letters:

ROCCO

And below it:

U.S.S. ICARUS

Like every Black Project, no one would know about any of this for decades. If civilians spotted the Sabre Cat punching through the atmosphere? The Brass would chalk it up as another UFO sighting, just like Roswell, just like the Battle of Los Angeles.

Hell, even when the government officially dropped those UFO (UAP) videos in 2019, nobody seemed to care. Speaking of caring, Rocco didn't know the man, but if he did, it wouldn't surprise him if Siegfried Santo Padre was rolling in his grave.

Rocco took a deep breath. His experimental, nonrestrictive space suit did its job, constricting blood flow to keep him from blacking out. The XF-53's cockpit was *ultra-minimalist* with no buttons, no switches. Ninety-eight percent of flight control came from his helmet's AI interface and his own personal rapid eye movements. The rest? Uncomplicated touchscreens.

It was as easy as driving an SUV at 80 mph on an interstate, except at Mach 20 and in outer space.

The onboard AI, AVA, chimed in.

"Gravitational breakaway speed achieved. Preparing for geosynchronous orbit."

"Roger that, Ava," Rocco muttered. "Activate maneuvering thrusters. Pressurize all seals. All go for space flight."

The Sabre Cat's nose burned violet-hot as it left the last traces of Earth's atmosphere, but the meta-material skin shrugged off the heat.

A moment later, zero-gravity kicked in. Rocco grinned.

Micro-thrusters hissed to life, fine-tuning his trajectory. Unlike the ordinary sky traversed by traditional aircraft, there was *no air resistance* up here. Maneuvering without an atmosphere required precision, a precision AVA excelled at.

Without the AI, he might as well be trying to drive a Formula One racing car on an ice rink, blindfolded.

"Rocco to Ground Control... final test flight successful."

The cheers of Skunk Works and Northrop's engineers crackled over his headset.

"Roger that, Rocco," came the reply. "Proceed to designated coordinates on your HUD and prepare for landing."

This was it. The next step would be the first-ever landing on the newest fusion-powered carrier in space. The aircraft's *Head-Up Display* marked his target. Below him, Earth spun quickly with Russia shining bright under their afternoon sun.

A voice bleeping in over the Troop Net, a new voice: "Permission granted. Welcome home, Sabre Cat One."

Those looking skyward from the carrier deck spotted a grey speck which appeared in the distance. Like magic, the craft uncloaked, revealing its massive, stealth-coated hull.

Rocco adjusted his approach. "Ava, prep anti-gravity landing gear. Activate the gravity boot."

Rocco rolled the XF-53, flipping from being *above* the Earth to *below* it, preparing for landing. For the first time in history, a space fighter was coming home to a space carrier. This landing wouldn't just make history. It would define it.

The blast doors to the landing bay remained open, ready to receive the first-ever inbound fighter when the XF-53 Sabre Cat breached the Plasma Pressure Wall. The shimmering energy field was the only thing keeping the oxygen inside the bay and the cold void of space out.

The deck crew wore emergency gear because if the shield failed, they'd only have *seconds* to activate their suits before being violently sucked into the vacuum of space. Not a fun way to go.

Well, Rocco thought, after someone explained the danger to him, *it won't be fun, but at least it'd be quick.*

On the flight deck, the crew watched as Captain Mike "Rocco" Badcock brought in the first of *Icarus'* twenty-one-bird squadron. The Sabre Cat fired its maneuvering thrusters, bled off speed, and landed perfectly.

First landing on the *Icarus:* nailed it.

The canopy hissed open, and out popped Rocco, arms thrown high, grinning like a fighter pilot rockstar.

"Ladies and gentlemen," Rocco announced, stepping onto the deck, "let's hear it for the greatest pilot in the history of hypersonic aerospace combat!"

There was a forced disinterest at first followed by a few half-hearted claps.

"Alright, alright," he muttered, unzipping his flight suit. "Ya'll settle down. Tough crowd. I'll assume you're all just in awe."

Ignoring the blank stares, Rocco took in the sheer size of the landing bay. Way bigger than the CVF-X Langley's.

The *Langley* was named after the first U.S. aircraft carrier from the 1920s and had been a testbed for the fusion-powered carrier concept, holding a modest six X-51 Auroras. It had done its job, and once the *Icarus* became operational, *Langley* got demoted to cargo duty. Rocco was fine with that. *Better ship, better birds, and a better damn seat for me.*

Even his new Second Skin flight suit was an upgrade. (2nd SKN) No more bulky G-suits, no more suffocating pressure suits. This thing adapted to G-forces in real time. Rocco advocated fast tracking a new (4SKN) designated suit but was quickly shut down.

Rocco was, he decided, the right man, for the right job, at the right time in history. Space was busier than ever. Earth had no idea how much busier space had gotten.

Ever since Roswell tech leaked, things had taken off. Computers, cell phones, TV screens; none of those innovations had been a case of *accidental progress.* Everything had been reverse-engineered, a series of alien leftovers spoon-fed to the public one piece at a time.

Meanwhile, the world's governments were too busy waging World War III in secret to deal with the fact Earth was basically a cosmic kindergarten in a galaxy full of graduating seniors.

"Keys, Sir," Rocco said as he handed off a bundle to the Air Boss; the wallets and car keys of the Skunk Works engineers back on Earth.

The Air Boss, sitting up in Pri-Fly Control, barely looked up.

"You steal those, Rocco?"

"Pilot tradition," Rocco smirked. "In case I didn't make it back, proof of their trust in their product." He patted the Air Boss on the shoulder. "And let's be honest, I wasn't about to let those nerds raid my locker and go joyriding in my Corvette."

The Pri-Fly Control Tower overlooked the chaos of the flight deck, where deck crew—color-coded like a pack of Skittles—moved in sync:

Red shirts: Weapons.

Purple (Grapes): Fueling.

Green shirts: Launch ops.

Even in space, some things never changed in the Navy.

Rocco's view of the flight deck was interrupted by an expected voice. "Nice Stick!"

Rocco turned to find the Commander of the Ship watching him from the flight control deck. "Nice stick?" he questioned. "Thanks—"

"I was talking to Ava, Rocco."

Rocco sighed. "Of course, you were." He smirked. "Jealous it wasn't you?"

The Commander shrugged. "Maybe."

Rocco took in the view beyond the hangar bay—a quarter of Earth was visible in the distance, glowing against the darkness. The effect was surreal.

The Commander witnessed his awe, a first time tourist. "Takes a minute to get used to, huh?"

Rocco nodded. "Yeah. I mean, *technically* I should be freaking out, considering I just flew a hypersonic space fighter and left Earth at Mach 20, through a plasma barrier and into a cloaked carrier in orbit. But y'know, no big deal."

The Commander chuckled. "First time I stepped onto this deck, I thought I was gonna get sucked right out into space."

"That would've been embarrassing," Rocco mused. "What's the Navy equivalent of 'man overboard' when you're plunging into the thermosphere at 25,000 feet per second?"

The Commander smirked, "I believe it's called *screaming*."

"In space no one can hear you scream," Rocco quipped. "The paperwork will."

CHAPTER 15

I Want to Fly

"Admiral's waiting."

The moment of admiration was cut short.

"Admiral Nick Vidaurri is waiting for your debriefing on the bridge," the Commander said.

Rocco sighed dramatically. "Let me guess—he wants to grill me on the landing."

"Among other things," the Commander nodded. "I'll escort you."

"You don't trust me to find my way?"

The Commander laughed. "This ship is a maze. I still get lost, and I've been here six months. They made a ton of last-minute changes during construction, so the schematics are *already* outdated. Thank God the replacement reactor is running 96% efficiency."

Rocco raised an eyebrow. "Last-minute refit?"

"Hull degradation caused a massive breach on ten decks." The Commander shrugged. "Gives you the warm fuzzies, doesn't it?"

"Oh, yeah," Rocco muttered. "Nothing inspires confidence like: *Surprise, we changed a bunch of critical systems last-minute after a major accident.*"

The Commander grinned.

"Welcome to military planning, Captain Badcock."

Rocco took a deep breath, then exhaled. "Alright, fine. Let's go."

"Actually—" the Commander glanced toward the next incoming fighter. "Let's wait up and see if Hawk can still find his way around."

Lieutenant Commander Stella Forrestal barely had time to finish her sentence before the second craft breached the Plasma Wall, cutting through the shimmering energy field like a knife through water.

The two-manned XF-52 *Widower* glided into the bay, its *Spaceman Spiff* nose art prominently displayed, much to the amusement of its co-pilot.

The XF-52 was bigger, the size of a tennis court, meaner, and had a heavier punch than its newer XF-53 Sabre Cat cousin. It sacrificed some maneuverability in atmospheric combat, but more than made up for it in firepower, maneuverability, and stealth in space.

Both aircraft were engineering marvels, but it didn't stop the Peanut Gallery from running their mouths.

As the *Widower's* cockpit opened, the two pilots stepped out and were immediately knee-deep in an argument with the ground crew.

"Which fighter's better?"

The answer was obvious.

"XF-53. Hands down."

Rocco expelled an audible sigh. *Great,* he thought. *Another pissing contest.*

In just a few months, CVF-2 *Lexington* (the sister ship to the *Icarus*) would be complete. Soon after, *Saratoga, Yorktown,* and *Enterprise* would follow—all replacing outmoded nautical vessels and all built from scratch, based on the *Icarus'* blueprints.

Five Fusion Space Carriers, all built in secret at MARS Base 1. Keeping it under wraps was getting harder every day. Technology was evolving too fast, and the civilian sector was catching up.

The new and improved International Space Station was almost finished. In addition to the ISS, multiple private space stations were also under construction. Tourists were eyeing lunar getaways. With the yearly space budget ballooning to over $25 billion a year, a profitable "Orbital Economy" was essential to make space travel affordable to the masses.

Hell, Rocco thought, *some guy with a decent backyard telescope had an excellent chance at spotting us when we're not in stealth mode.*

The ground crew was still debating which of the new generation fighters was best. But, as far as Rocco was concerned, they were asking the wrong questions. The fighter didn't matter as much as control and who had it.

What about Earth? he asked himself.

Earth was still obsessing over when the "first" Mars mission would happen, blissfully unaware a fully operational colony was already there and busy with the task of repurposing ancient Martian ruins. For years, SpaceX and other private contractors had unknowingly ferried supplies for the Mars mission and other classified deep-space operations.

The public?

Too broke and too busy scraping by to afford groceries to even ask where their tax money was going.

The only real competition in space?

One word: China.

In the wake of the COVID pandemic and after Ukraine ruined Russia's prospects, China continued rolling over America's economy. That's why the American President was scrambling to form a new space coalition, because if there was one thing China hated more than losing to the U.S., it was losing to the U.S. in space.

We'd better damn well stay organized, Rocco told himself.

The *Icarus'* crew was a mix of military personnel from multiple nations, plus a handful of civilians who had high-level clearances.

And then there were the AVA units (Autonomous Flight Assistants)—applied artificial intelligences which ran everything from fighters to ship systems. The *"V"* in AVA stood for heavier than air, *"Voler"* meaning *"To Fly"* in French. VF Stood for Fighter Squadron (heavier than air)—another tradition which just stuck even though the original etymology had largely faded from active use. Unlike their EVI predecessors, the new AVAs could project full holograms, appearing as interactive, ghost-like figures.

Rocco knew an AVA could take on any form, including human. Despite knowing what to expect, when his AVA materialized next to him on the flight deck, he nearly jumped out of his flight suit. Stella, who may have been expecting it, took the sudden appearance in stride.

"Follow me," Ava Jeep said. All AVAs used the monikers which were married to their module to distinguish the hundreds roaming the ship.

Rocco recovered instantly, chuckling. "We're on your six, ma'am."

She was cute. Or at least, she was *programmed* to be.

As Stella and Rocco followed, he evaluated the hologram. She appeared to be a standard late twenties, maybe early thirties, blonde, 5'5", with an angelic face making Stella wonder if she had been designed by some lovesick programmer with a thing for celestial beings.

Lieutenant Commander Forrestal rolled her eyes, "Chauvinists."

Rocco shrugged, immediately wiped the grin off his face, fighting the urge to say something even more inappropriate. Instead, he did what he does best—he issued orders.

"Ava Jeep, run diagnostics on the Sabre Cat and get her prepped for the next flight," Rocco said, "Also, stencil our new reference I.D. on the meta-material skin."

As they reached a wider corridor, two other pilots, Edgar and Hawk, joined up and chimed in. Another AVA appeared, Ava Spiff, began walking alongside the *Stick Jockeys.*

"When you're done with Rocco's, would you mind checking our bird over?" Edgar asked.

Ava Jeep smiled and playfully wagged a finger at the men. "Which bird is better, boys?" she asked sweetly. Before any human could answer she flatly stated, "Sabre Cat, of course."

"Technically I am doing more calculations in the two-seater, so that's where you, Ava Jeep, fall short. Therefore, I Ava Spiff, and the *Widower* wins."

The two ghosts meandered back to their ships, their departure closely watched by the male pilots as they continued arguing. Ava Spiff turned back once, locking eyes with Hawk. A look of deep recognition. For a fleeting second, it appeared that she wanted to say something. But she didn't. And that was weird. Even for advanced AI, Ava, regardless of which one, was sometimes too human.

Hawk remained quiet so Edgar cut in, "I heard our updated AVAs are rolling out over tha next few weeks."

"I heard," Rocco quipped and turned to Hawk. "How are you doing, bub?" he asked.

Hawk barely reacted. He walked a few more steps before speaking. "Never better..."

Rocco nodded slowly, dropping the subject. Something about Hawk's tone told him...

Hawk may be "never better" but he definitely ain't alright.

CHAPTER 16

Operation Falling Star

Lieutenant Commander Stella Forrestal led the way, weaving through the corridors of the *Icarus*. If they weren't pushing their way past crew in motion, they were dodging technicians who were still fine-tuning the ship's systems by digging into the ship's nervous system. With little effort, Stella tiptoed around the wires and fiber optic cables. The men, less agile, clumsily tripped over the mess and bumped into everything in their path.

"Sorry," Rocco apologized for the umpteenth time.

Even Hawk's face held a grimace as he brushed past another crewmen. "Congested in here," he said.

"Kinks here and there to work out," Stella said with a tickle. "We will settle in eventually."

The *Icarus* was massive, much larger than a Nimitz-class nuclear carrier. It was mostly a type of unknown alloy, but as they moved deeper into the ship, something changed.

The lower decks were unwelcoming, solely built to get you from Point-A to Point-B. The word utilitarian didn't do it justice. Everything here required rapid access for quick fixes. However, the closer Stella dragged them towards Officer's Country, that all changed. It wasn't luxurious but access ports were covered in junctions; circuit breakers and piping were all hidden behind aesthetically pleasing or padded panels.

Their warlike march was replaced with a relaxed stroll—they almost felt... *comfortable.*

Stella glanced at Rocco as she stepped over a knee-knocker passageway. A reminder they were still on a war vessel.

"Nice choice on the A.I., Captain Badcock," she said, arching an eyebrow.

Rocco grinned instinctively, but even he wouldn't disrespect Hawk by tweaking an avatar of someone he was once in love with. The AVA units were Hawk's woman's masterpieces—Ava. All of the replicas were similar, yet each one distinct. Split personalities. Rocco intuitively registered this in the back of his mind.

"Ava Jeep thinks in qubits you can't buy," Rocco said. "And she *likes* the throttle."

Their quantum processing capabilities were beyond comprehension. The hardware alone made Willow's superconducting qubits look primitive. For perspective, the Willow quantum chip could solve a benchmark computation in under five minutes. The same task would take one of the 21st century's fastest supercomputers more than 10 septillion years, a quantity which vastly exceeds the age of the universe. Bottom line, not even Rocco could force her to do something she didn't want to.

"Must be nice getting to design her to your specs," Stella continued. She clearly directed her remark at Rocco while also giving Hawk a pointed look.

Rocco's hands were up addressing Hawk. "Bro, I didn't run any code on her." Rocco sneered, "I didn't design squat," he said, climbing up the ladder-well behind her. "I just want to be explicitly clear. She took on that persona all on her own."

Stella pulled open the final airtight hatch which led them to the bridge's island structure. She went first again, the sound of her boots echoing down the corridor. This place wasn't comfortable or utilitarian; it was energetic and alive. Lighted panels shuffled information from one center to another. Some were gathering information and preparing it for dissemination. Every nook and cranny was filled with officers who each held specific duties on the bridge. Those duties included managing any data which sensors collected from all around the ship, as well as intelligence being beamed to the ship from Earth. This was the hive mind.

Stella's hive mind didn't believe Rocco. "Uh-huh," Stella said, her voice critical. "I'm sure the design has nothing to do with you smooth-brained guys wanting your digital flight co-pilot to look like a damn swimsuit model."

"Come on, Nagging Nancy—" Rocco rolled his eyes. "I swear, that thing has a mind of its own."

An ensign stepped out in front of Hawk, threw an unintentional pick, the block screening him from Stella and Rocco. "Excuse me, make a damn hole." Rocco heard him say as the volume of his voice gained distance.

He turned quickly and shot a mocking "yeah right" expression in the direction of the other pilots trailing behind them.

Stella saw his move and rolled her eyes so hard Rocco was surprised she didn't pass out from G-force exposure to the brain.

"She's still just a computer program," Stella said. "Am I right? Or is she something more?" Their conversation suddenly becoming more private.

"If you're referring to *the incident,* there wasn't much anyone could do when she gained complete and total access to the web," Rocco continued. "When she went online, the Admiral thought some unauthorized person had prematurely activated SKYNET."

"Pffft," Stella scoffed. "Hawk says the AVAs are self-aware now."

Rocco nodded. "Yeah. Ever notice how he looks at them? There's a reason I won't touch that code."

Stella frowned. "Ever notice how *they* look at *him?* Kinda creepy. It's like..." Stella hesitated. "They're familiar. Like they recognize each other."

"I know," he said with animation before glancing back over his shoulder. "Keep this on the downlow." He warned. He hated gossip almost as much as he loved rumors. The other pilots had stopped grabbing some water bottles. They were far behind, but he whispered anyway, "She drops a frame rate every time she gazes at him. No way it's just a glitch. Everybody has noticed, but they've decided not to say anything."

Stella lowered her voice another decibel, "Something is up. Hawk's been off since he landed. "Maybe we shouldn't have reactivated him. He's more distant than usual. You must have realized every update of Ava Spiff looks more like her."

"They all do." Rocco glanced sideways. The other pilots weren't following as the difficulty of the obstacle course increased. It only took a second and the two of them walked alone, "Well—why not? It *should,* right? Afterall, Ava built the damn thing in her image."

Rocco eyeballed an Ava from this deck, another ghost helping a technician. "Yeah, but it's looking more and more and more real."

Rocco hesitated to say, so he did under his breath as he added, "You know there's still talk that maybe Hawk was the one who killed her."

Stella stopped mid-step and raised her voice, "No way!" She shook her head hard. "You and I saw his face when he found out she was dead—and we damn well know who did it." She mouthed three letters from a familiar agency. "No damn way!" She continued trying to convince herself more than anything else. "Hawk dropped off the face of the planet for years after that, believing what Vidaurri wanted him to believe."

A few more footsteps gave her a few more feet to reminisce. "That scuttlebutt is from before your time with the squadron; you didn't see the jealousy he had when Trip was around." Stella opened a side door and pulled Rocco inside. Too many ears, too many eyes.

"I'm just saying," she said when they were alone, "it was a hit." Her voice dropped. "And we all know Hawk was doing some shady shit with the CIA and the Admiral before he stepped off the battlefield. And after the incident at the black-site, Ava and the Admiral's relationship nosedived."

Rocco's head swayed side-to-side in a gesture of denial, then doubt crept in and he bobble-headed into a nod.

She reached out and grabbed his head. "Stop that, I hate when you do that."

"Sorry," he said before intentionally nodding his head in a similar way, again.

She sighed, then growled. "That thing you do—it's like when you leave your socks one half on, one half off while you wander around the house."

She frowned at him. "The hit was clean. Precise. The video was too, smoking gun-ish."

"No way they had the tech back then to doctor tape like that." He did his best to rationalize that day.

"Rocco, you're standing on tech that's possibly millions of years old according to Hawk. You don't think that particular tech existed? Look at where we are—you of all people should realize anything is possible."

"Maybe, you're right." Rocco frowned. "That early team was tight. You were on that early team, right?"

"So, didn't you have a thing for the bearded cowboy back then or what? You always had his back when they were trying to nail him to a wall."

Stella didn't answer, she didn't need to. For a fleeting second, there was a longing in her face. Her mind drifted—*1977,* she thought. *Late nights. Heated arguments. And that one day when it all imploded.*

"Back then, things were messy," she mumbled. "Hawk was the one everyone was swooning over, not the cowboy," she added under her breath, in a whisper. But then she thought about the '80s. Grinned. Biting her lip.

"Things still are... messy that is," Rocco shrugged. "Anyhow, it's water under the bridge. You have to admit, the footage is pretty damning. And they say Ava and Trip had history—"

Stella's expression tightened. "Trip? So far as history goes, everybody fell for Ava. Hawk. Trip Looper. Even Vidaurri—yes, even our Admiral when he was a shave-tail, couldn't look her in the eye very long. All of those Guardians had a strange pull over everyone."

Rocco nodded, "There's no shadow of a doubt the Guardian in the video feed, the one who dumped her body, was that Cowboy you still swoon over in memories."

"I don't swoon." She laughed. "Furthermore, he was no cowboy. He was from Texas, though. And, once Vidaurri made admiral, he had NCIS tracking Looper for *years.*"

"And they never caught him—" Rocco muttered "When they do, I hope they fillet the bastard. You don't just take out one of ours and get away with it." He ran a hand through his hair. "But I'll tell you this, I don't trust Vidaurri any more than I trust the man, the myth, Trip Looper. And after a decade working with A.V.A—"

Rocco paused studying Stella—she made 57 the new 30. His eyes narrowed, trying to decide how much to say about another woman. "Sometimes, I swear she's more than a program. She's got emotions, she's hiding from the tech-nerds, she's got wants, she's *waiting* for something."

He looked Stella dead in the eye, but he kept his thoughts to himself.

She's waiting alright, he told himself. *Waiting for evolution, the technological singularity. And we all know it. Just too afraid to say those quiet thoughts out loud.*

Rocco tried to ease the silence with a quip. "She's more human than my ex-wife," he laughed.

"I'm your ex, you jerk."

Rocco chuckled. He dug deep in the brain files, his eyes computing older memories. "No, not you; the one before you," he said, finger twirling in the air, slyly winking at her.

"Uh huh." Stella chuckled with him and tilted her head back. "You always had a knack for staying on my shit list you know."

A knock on the hatch ended their private conversation.

"You coming?" Hawk asked. "Or are you girls gonna keep gossiping?"

"Let's go," Edgar said filing in behind Hawk. "I'm dry and I'm hungry. Let's get a move on."

Stella and Rocco stepped back out into the corridor, returning to the train heading to the briefing room. As the others moved ahead, Stella grabbed Rocco by the arm, pulling him back. She leaned in, her voice low and firm.

"My quarters. 1900 hours. It's a classified assignment. That's an order."

Rocco's eyes fluttered; he got serious and saluted. "Yes, Sir, Lieutenant Commander."

Stella let go, stepping back.

Rocco rushed off and sprinted down the corridor to catch up with the others.

"That was a rough burn-in," Edgar commented as Rocco rejoined the group. "All tha time in a secluded compartment and she's gonna put ya to work. Tha Commander sure has it in for youse, Rocco."

"She'll have you shucking oysters if you're not careful," Anshar Hawk laughed.

Rocco clasped Hawk on the shoulder. "You have no idea, Anshar. No. Clue. What I am up against with that wildcat."

He turned to Edgar and pointed a warning finger.

"Edgar. Don't. Don't say shit."

Edgar grinned and, with his thick Brooklyn accent in full effect, he teased, "I don't tell ya nothin' ya mudd'a wouldn't tell ya: *Believe nothin' ya hear, and only one half that ya see.*"

Rocco groaned.

Edgar was a bookworm; his call sign came from his obsession with Edgar Allan Poe. The guy could quote *The Raven* from memory, which was impressive and also, deeply concerning.

Rocco shook his head. Another day, another problem. And, apparently, a classified "assignment" with ex-spouse Stella Forrestal at 1900 hours. Even though he doubted she was planning anything romantic or erotic. Fraternization alone could be a problem, if he got caught.

Seconds later, the hatch to the control room of the bridge swung open, and all traces of banter and cocky grins were left in the gangway. The legendary Admiral Nick Vidaurri was waiting for them. They saluted and reported.

"Walk with me," the Admiral said, his tone sharp, focused, absolute.

No questions. No hesitation. Just follow. The pilots fell in line, trailing him. The nerve center of the bridge was unlike anything they'd ever seen—brightly lit, filled with 3D holographic readouts, transparent smart-glass panels, and floating control interfaces responding to gestures and voice commands.

Rocco looked around. This wasn't just a warship; it was an AI-driven hub, decades ahead of Earth's best technology.

And yet, even with all this tech, the crew was battling to keep up.

The *Icarus* was thinking faster than the crew could process information.

Rocco stood, arms folded, taking it all in.

Who the hell designed this thing?

The pilots followed their superior officer into the briefing room. Vidaurri closed the door and motioned for them to sit as he activated the briefing holo-display. The Admiral remained standing.

"I know you're all thrilled about your squadron's activation being moved up," he began. "But there are still plenty of bugs in these systems, especially on the human-made sister carriers."

He glanced at Hawk, the most seasoned of them all.

"For you, Commander Hawk, I bet this is a walk in the park. But for us Neanderthals, we've got some catching up to do."

A pause.

A glance.

"*Ava,*" the Admiral said, acknowledging the phantasm in the room. "God rest her soul… Thanks to her research, and yours, Hawk, we are managing to stay ahead of schedule."

Silence.

Vidaurri paced, pulling up a map of Earth's geopolitical mess on a holo-screen.

"Rumors of Solar Warden persist, and more proof is already surfacing about our presence up here. The official story? The U.S. has decided it's time to start exploring our solar system for natural resources," the Admiral couldn't help rolling his eyes.

A holographic Earth rotated behind him, highlighting China, Russia, India, and Britain.

"This was supposed to be a joint effort," the Admiral continued, "but we all know how badly things are going down there socioeconomically."

They took a minute to look down on their home. No borders—just a planet, eight billion souls' deep, clinging to a rock hurtling through space at 67,000 miles per hour. Roughly 18.5 miles a second.

"Every one of those eight billion souls thinks that rock belongs to them. We've tried to unify the countries since the end of World War II. United we are stronger. But not invincible," the admiral said.

Rocco looked at the tech around him. "Now we have a state-of-the-art fleet to put Solar Warden in mothballs."

"The Solar Warden fleet was reassigned to Mars. The real reason we're out here," the Admiral reminded the pilots, "is this."

The display changed and an image of Mars materialized.

"Site of the 11,700-Year-Old Nuclear War. The atmosphere was blown off, so the Red Planet has experienced far less erosion than here on Earth. For years, our discoveries on Mars have been accelerating our Earth-bound tech. And now, all of this…" Vidaurri stretched both arms wide, indicating the pilots should appreciate the technology surrounding them. "All this is the culmination of those discoveries."

The Admiral grabbed his coffee, took a few sips before waving a hand to activate a holographic timeline.

Better than a damn Vegas magic show, Rocco told himself while watching the spectacle.

"Fifty-seven years ago," the Admiral said, "researchers began carbon-dating ancient migration patterns across the Bering Land Bridge."

He let that sink in. The pilots sensed this particular lecture was about to sail into uncharted waters.

"And they found an anomaly."

A map of North America materialized, highlighting the Great Lakes, followed with India and other key geographic excavation sites across the world.

"They found evidence of nuclear detonations here on Earth over 11,700 years ago. And the biblical flood—it was real. The floods. Nuclear detonations. It all happened."

The room was dead silent until Rocco cleared the air. "More superstitions Noah had nukes?"

The men laughed.

"His gods did," Vidaurri offered.

"So who nuked Mars, Admiral?"

Hawk cut in. "The same enemy heading for Earth."

"Is this about the interstellar comets all over the news?"

Vidaurri nodded.

He'd been standing in front of the desk, now he sat back on the edge. "You all have your packets. I suggest you spend the next couple of days burning the information from those packets into your brains. But here's the skinny from Shiflett."

Turning over the brief to Shiflett, he stopped fidgeting with the object he held in his hand, the men thinking it was possibly a hook of some kind. When he activated the next interface, he set the object down.

The pilots saw the object lying on the desk. It looked like a fossil from a predator. Vidaurri picked it up, a single claw. Back into his pocket it went. It was a gift from a stranger. A curse which altered his life forever.

A new hologram appeared.

Near-Earth Object (NEO) 1967 VB
Potentially Hazardous Object (PHO) 1951 VA

The knob to the briefing room turned slowly and a thin man in a short sleeve shirt and tie crept in. His five o'clock shadow looked more like simmering beard at this point. His mustache longer than the rest.

"Our analyst will explain," the Admiral said as he still fiddled with the claw in his trousers.

The analyst, Shiflett, took a deep breath, then exhaled. His pencil-thin nose whistled. Nobody laughed.

His nasal voice took a second to build up in octave but once it did, the information flowed freely from his lips, plenty loud to reach the back of the room.

"We believe it will be a two-pronged attack. This race had the ability to travel Faster-Than-Light, FTL, and for one reason or another, they've been taking the scenic route back to Earth. For a race intent on wiping us out, they are sure taking their time." He laughed.

Again, no laughter from the audience.

"We've been probed as far back as the 1800s and more recently during an event called the Battle of Los Angeles during World War II. Two interstellar objects have been detected entering our solar system. NEO 1967 VB, appears to be attempting to intercept NEO 1951 VA. We believed them to be comets at first. However, when 1967 VB looked as if it would overtake 1951 VA, we directed our furthest satellites to capture these photos before it reached superior conjunction."

A virtual screen similar to a television screen appeared and a blurry picture of two white blips appeared. Smaller dots of bluish white objects could be seen moving towards 1951 VA in a time-lapse sequence of images.

"Those smaller objects reached 1951 VA and vanished, we believe merging with 1951. Our AI has tracked the current trajectory of these interstellar NEOs, and they are on an astronomically improbable path to Earth through our solar system."

"Couldn't they be comets?" Rocco asked. "What exactly makes you believe they are behaving any differently than 3i Atlas or Oumuamua?"

"Ha, good question Mr. Rocketeer.

"Rocco, just Rocco."

"Ha, sure... Well, Mr. Rocco, besides its unusual hyperbolic trajectory and flight path, one of these objects appears to be slowing down. They've reached perihelion, the closest they will get to the sun. We will know for sure when they become visible again."

Rocco's face was obvious with confusion. "Visible again?" he asked.

The analyst smiled. His voice contained a hint of terror but also excitement. "It's currently behind the sun," he said shaking.

The analyst clicked to the next screen. "These little guys are traveling faster than a rifle round and slowing down. You see this anti-tail," he said pointing to gas coming from 1951 VA. "Right here, the gas should be behind the object, not in front of it. It's expelling gas from the front. If our calculations are correct, its preparing for reentry."

CHAPTER 17

Goddess of War
Middle of Nowhere, Texas—Present

Sifting through the remains of Mrs. Dawsons property, Sonny moved through the rubble, Maglite cutting a narrow beam through the smoke and rain. Burning debris flickered in the darkness. The air was thick, every breath gritty and wet.

Flattened trees lay like broken matchsticks. He pushed through splintered branches, ignoring the cuts and bruises nagging him.

Reaching the edge of the crater, the remains of the house pushed to the rim. He clawed through the mud and splintered beams, wood biting beneath his nails. "Mrs. Dawson!"

No response.

Boots scraped something cold. A hand. Twisted. Pale. Lightning flashed. Mrs. Dawson.

Gone instantly. The mud was already swallowing her.

Sonny staggered up. The granddaughter. Maybe. "Don't give up! I'm looking for you!"

Thunder cracked loudly above and yet there was a penetrating quietness around him.

His legs buckled, exhaustion creeping in. He finally turned back toward his truck. Reaching it, he found his phone dead, battery fried. Sliding down the truck's side, he let himself sink into the saturated clay.

A tingling heat on his ring finger. His hand instinctively closed around something small, cold, and oddly smooth in the mud.

ZAP.

The jolt brought him back to a moment in time. It was not the moment in time at Chiara's house he wished to revisit. He was in a scuffle there. She had been made unconscious somehow and he found her lying on the floor with a stranger trying to undress her.

He fought with everything he had. Friction removed skin from his hand after scraping against the mask of the attacker. He surprised him. Had the upper hand until the knife was drawn. The masked intruder bluffed a move, but Sonny didn't fall for it. He gained control and put him in a headlock.

He squeezed the man's neck between the bend in his arm. If he could squeeze hard enough, it might come off like pinching off a fallen dove's head in the field. The intruder squirmed, he was strong like Sonny and created a dangerous angle. The pendent Chiara gave him flung off his neck.

The sharp blade slid into him. An unexpected burning sensation took hold. Shock. A pain similar to the fire in his hand now. That masked man escaped. Sonny went down. His wife Chiara found him lying in a pool of his own blood. He should have taken him...

But he didn't.

The shock lit him up again. He snapped out of that insidious memory. Instinctively, he yanked his hand free, expecting a live wire. Instead, he saw his wedding ring, and something fusing to it.

The simple white gold wedding ring was gone. Now layered, seamless. The metal pulsed softly under the Maglite beam, colors shifting in patterns he couldn't name. Embedded flecks formed geometric designs.

Writing.

Not Roman. Not Greek. A mix of symbols like Latin, Arabic, and Japanese katakana characters. Similar to Chiara's pendant, which had been stolen.

Brain damage? Am I seeing things? Shit, was I struck by lightning?

He tried to pull it off. It wouldn't budge. His ring burned into his finger, bonding into his skin. He felt like he was blacking out.

His eyes opened, a surreal feeling. Had the zap knocked him out and he imagined everything? Did he just pass out? Seconds or minutes? He looked back at the ring on his finger, the wedding ring looked normal but potentially super-heated and melded into his skin. Before he could assess it further, a new threat caught his attention.

A silhouette appeared ahead in his periphery and closing fast. Human. A woman. Naked. Holy crap someone was still alive. Sonny did a double take, convinced his brain had finally snapped. Was he still unconscious?

Mud streaked her pale skin as she stumbled into his arms, shaking violently. She felt real, not a dream. Cold as ice. Not a hallucination either. A survivor.

He guided her into the truck, wrapping her in a Filson jacket and blanket from his back seat. She trembled, lips blue, eyes wide.

"Hey. You're safe," he whispered. "You're okay."

Her stare finally locked onto his. Mid-to-late twenties. No visible injuries. Not even a scratch.

He carefully checked her for wounds. Nothing. Perfect unblemished skin.

He patted his chest. "I'm Sonny. I was delivering your grandmother's mattress for you."

Finally, she whispered one word: "Mylitta."

Her accent was strange. No language he recognized. He tapped his forehead. "Hospital. You might have head trauma. We're closer to Victoria; I'm gonna take you there." *Hell, I may have head trauma.*

She reached out instead, noticing his wounded finger, brushing his ring. Her eyes shifted, recognition, disbelief.

"Yeah, it hurts." Sonny tried to explain. "My ring finger got zapped by something, lightning I think." He tugged at the ring again. Stuck down to the bone.

She grabbed his wrist firmly, stopping him. Knowing it wouldn't come off now.

"Okay, okay," he said. "it's not that bad."

She relaxed, but her eyes kept darting to the hill. Something still scaring her. Sonny buckled her in. He glanced the rearview mirror and sighed. "I need to move the trailer—it's blocking our exit."

She clutched his arm, her grip stronger than expected. "I'll be quick." He assured her.

Outside, the rain hammered him. The ground hummed under his boots, electric and unstable. She was scared. Like something other than the giant meteor had been after her. Shock.

He slipped, catching himself on sharp metal. No cut. No pain. Even his earlier scratches from the match were gone. The fresh ones too. The deep bruise on his side? Fading.

Not normal, he told himself.

He couldn't really remember when things were normal though. Seeing a house explode in front of him, a whole house be redistributed across a field and replaced by a massive foreign object, wasn't something he had on his *Bingo* card, but was he really surprised? No, no he wasn't. It was par for the course this year.

What's normal anyway? he asked himself.

Sonny planted his boots firmly in the mud, and to his complete surprise he sent the trailer into the ditch with a single shove. It should have been heavier. Moving it should have been a struggle. But it moved easily, as if his strength had increased.

As if—

He stopped and stared at his hands.

As if—

Maybe the bolt of lightning did something to him. Sonny's first thought was completely typical.

"Fuck me, am I dead?"

Gaining superpowers hadn't even crossed his mind.

Even standing still, adrenaline was pumping through his veins like it was being given to him in an IV. His body felt different. Maybe he was slipping into shock. No, not weak.

Stronger. Less joint pain. Less pain of any kind.

Sonny rushed back to the truck, yanking open the door. Instead of a smooth pull, the grinding of misaligned metal popped and barked back at him.

Before he could climb in, something slammed onto the hood. Debris from on high coming back down. A black shape, long and twisted with claws, raked against the windshield. Sonny tumbled inside as he and Mylitta both screamed. The shriek was piercing and the gayest, lamest scream of Sonny's life. His hand instinctively went for his VP9, but before he could pull it, the branch slid off the hood.

Just a tree limb.

He exhaled, shaking. This chick had him on edge. "God, come on, man. Get it together."

He glanced at the woman; she was no girl. His face shone with confusion. Was she smiling? He chuckled slightly from the absurdity of his girly man squeal.

He ran a hand over his face, catching his breath. He smiled back at her. A flash of electricity, a bolt of lightning lit up the sky, setting the field ablaze. For the first time, they saw what was out there and it terrified them.

Creeping in the distance in front of the rim, a silhouette. Broad head. Thick arms. Heavy upper body.

It didn't move.

Yet.

They could hear a faint buzzing noise. They both looked at each other wondering what it was. Was it communicating with them. The buzz grew more prominent.

The creature was in his mind!

It wasn't. A baseball-sized drone influenced by a dragonfly's design descended into their line of sight directly in front of the windshield. They both jerked back not computing what it was. It flew off.

"Oh, God, that giant thing was full of giant bugs!"

By the time their eyes adjusted, the silhouette in front of them was also gone. They looked at each other with concern.

Knock. Knock...

They froze.

The thing was at the window.

Sonny didn't scream this time.

He couldn't.

CHAPTER 18

First Contact Protocol

A man with a rifle banged on Sonny's window.

Mylitta grabbed his arm, shouting something foreign—urgent, pleading.

He didn't know the words, but he understood what she was trying to say.

Stay inside.

He didn't.

His pistol stayed steady, muzzle pressed to the door. Where were his shakes? How was he calm? The clarity in his mind was startling.

Seconds later, a powerful downdraft slammed against his truck and surrounding area shaking the entire cab.

Thwap. Thwap. Thwap. Rotor blades beat down on them.

Sonny looked up through the top part of the windshield and saw it. A matte-black ARH-70 recon helicopter hovered low, gun pods rotating toward the truck. Sonny re-holstered his pistol; even the rifle in the backseat wouldn't matter. Above them, two Apache gunships thundered past, rotor wash pounding the ground. Following them came the Chinooks—four of them—unloading black-clad SOF Teams into the mud like an invasion.

Another knuckle rap on the window. "Sir." the body said.

Sonny's brain finally caught up. This wasn't a rescue operation. This was a military lockdown. It was way too organized. It was almost as if the military had been waiting for this. Almost as if they knew it was coming.

Sonny swallowed hard, watching troops move like a well-oiled machine, securing a defensive perimeter. Suddenly it was clear to Sonny.

This wasn't chaos—it was choreography.

The convoys rolling through town, the heightened military presence—

They'd been waiting a year for this.

NASA must have tracked this object for weeks if not months. They just misjudged where it would hit.

The soldier in front of the truck had already dispersed to his next objective. Sonny turned to Mylitta, his voice steady but urgent.

"Everything is going to be okay," he told her. "Help just arrived."

She just stared at him, exhausted, shaking, but watching every movement of his lips. Her green eyes flickered with something deeper than fear. Determination. She wasn't hopeless. She was ready. But for what? The worst of it was over, right?

Sonny didn't know and couldn't begin to guess but he holstered his pistol anyway.

As others closed in, he got a better look. Not Guard, not FEMA. Something higher, and they weren't there to rescue anyone. They moved like Tier-One operators. They were the Quiet Professionals who wrote lots of books about their exploits, not normal military.

The soldiers spread out but maintained a tight perimeter, securing a defensive arc around his truck. Their gear was high-end, beyond anything Sonny had ever seen or owned. Some carried standard M4A1s, but others held rifles he didn't even recognize. Even the armor they wore looked futuristic.

One guy had an M82A1 .50 caliber sniper rifle. And he wasn't carrying it for show; he held it ready, like he expected to use it.

Who the hell are these guys expecting to go up against? Sonny asked himself. *Chuck "Freaking" Norris?*

Sonny winced as the sniper climbed into the bed of his truck, smashing the bipod down onto the roof. He could hear the heavy rifle scraping across the paint, cutting deep into the thin metal.

None of this is getting buffed out, he told himself.

The Navy Corpsman banged on the window more urgently this time, already pulling out a first aid kit.

"I'm Corpsman Villalobos, do you need medical assistance?" he asked.

Before Sonny could respond, a deafening roar ripped across the sky. His side window disintegrated from the sonic boom.

He peered out, glancing up, as three F-22 Raptors followed by five F-35 Lightning IIs, screamed overhead. Sonny stared in utter disbelief—an air superiority formation.

For a meteor impact?

No.

Something bigger was taking place and he was in the middle of it.

Over the corpsman's radio Sonny heard something about a no-fly zone over the impact, anomalies, distortions forming. His eyes widened.

It suddenly occurred to Sonny that the mass out there was a freaking UFO. He turned back to Villalobos with a shit-eating grin on his face. He didn't speak at first; his brain was still trying to process the scene. Sonny blurted out a reaction and a question.

"OH, SHIT!" Sonny exclaimed with excitement. "Is this what I think it is?"

"I am not at liberty to discuss the current situation," said the corpsman. "Are you two operational?"

"So, you're not saying its aliens, but its aliens?" Sonny checked himself mentally and physically again before saying, "I'm fine, but I think she's in shock."

The corpsman nodded, shifting to check on Mylitta.

Lieutenant Pierce arrived behind the corpsman.

Pierce appeared battle-hardened, his 8.6 Black Out caliber Boombox slung tight against his chest, his eyes sharp and measuring. Sonny being a gear queer knew exactly what it was.

"It's not safe for you here. Is your truck still operational?"

Sonny turned the key again and the engine rolled right over. He nodded, knowing it was EMP hardened last year. "Affirmative," he said, giving a salute.

"As you can tell, it's a Chevy—it started right up. I don't know how far she'll make it, but I think we should get going."

Pierce seemed satisfied with his response, but Sonny wasn't quite done yet.

"Come on, man—what's going on?"

A flicker of something crossed Pierce's face. It wasn't anger and it certainly wasn't fear. It was calculated hesitation. He was weighing how much to say. Sonny's pulse quickened.

How bad is this? he asked himself.

While Sonny and the Lieutenant played a game of information chess, the corpsman ran a high-tech scanner over Mylitta, an LCD screen glowing faintly in the darkness. Sonny had never seen medical tech as advanced as what he was using outside of science fiction of course. Villalobos examined the screen, then nodded to Pierce.

"No internal trauma. No broken bones," the corpsman reported. "No contusions. No brain hemorrhaging."

Sonny exhaled in relief.

"Her speech is still scrambled," Villalobos noted but unsure why, "Physically, she's perfect. No TD-4 contamination."

The Lieutenant nodded, then started to focus back on Sonny, until he saw the female wasn't wearing any pants.

"Y'all out here fooling around?" the Lieutenant asked accusingly.

Sonny looked puzzled. He didn't connect the dots at first. "No, no sir."

"Okay then," Pierce said. "Look, we're not sure what we're dealing with here. But we've detected traces of foreign particulates. So, we're not taking any chances. Y'all need to evac now."

Sonny stiffened.

What gives? he thought. *Foreign particulate? Biological? Radioactive? What the hell was in that crater? The ISS with NASA experiments?*

More questions than answers.

Seeing Sonny's confusion, Pierce lowered his voice.

"Let me put it this way, if you don't want to be lab rats for the next six months, go. Now."

Sonny didn't hesitate. "Roger that. But do I take the guy on the roof with us? Or do you want him back?"

Pierce motioned the sniper to grab his gear and climb out of his truck bed. As soon as Sonny felt the weight shift, he threw the truck into gear, spinning the tires in the mud before peeling out.

As he drove away, he could see even more troops mobilizing, flooding the impact site like ants spreading out over an anthill. They weren't here to help. They were here to contain. As he put miles behind him, something else caught his attention. The outside temperature was rising.

Back there, near the impact site, as the rain poured down it had been freezing. But the further he drove away, the warmer the temperature was. It was as if the cold wasn't natural. Like it was a side effect of whatever had just arrived. Also, why did it look like things were levitating; how was his trailer so light?

Sonny's grip tightened on the steering wheel. His thoughts raced.

Which country just crash-landed in our backyard? Were they contaminated? Was anything alive on that thing? Are the two of us safe out here?

He turned to Mylitta, reaching for her hand instinctively.

She took it. Held on. Her fingers were ice-cold, but she wasn't shivering anymore. She was craning her neck to stare back at the site. She was watching that thing in the crater.

Waiting.

CHAPTER 19

Foo Fighters

Back at the impact site, Admiral Vidaurri and Commander Stonegate stood firm behind a makeshift SOCOM center, positioned near one of five armored Humvees. Stonegate's steely gaze locked on the monolithic wreck ahead. His breath steamed in the cold, sweat pooled under his armor plates. If the reports were accurate, his men were walking into a nightmare.

"Have the Pax been evacuated?"

"Yes, sir," came the immediate answer. "Civvies are clear, and the area is contained."

"Readings?"

"No contagion detected, sir."

Stonegate breathed easier, but the tension in his chest refused to ease. His eyes studied the sky, searching for something which could explain the inexplicable. Moments after impact, the wreckage emitted a directed pulse—not toward Earth, but the sun.

Why? the Commander wondered. *Was it a distress beacon? A warning? A weapon?*

If this was a signal, who—or what—was listening? If this is a trap, we've already walked into it and walked in blind.

Rocco's team had similar questions. They were busy preparing their gear to board the mammoth vessel.

Bone conducting comms crackled in his ear. "Sir, we're still analyzing the pulse. Electromagnetic, definitely controlled, but..."

"But what?" Stonegate's voice was razor-sharp.

The analyst hesitated. "It's interacting with the sun's corona, sir. Minor fluctuations in solar activity, nothing immediate, but..."

Stonegate flexed his shoulders.

Too damn many "buts," he told himself. Nothing immediate? That has to mean something else is coming. Something beyond our current understanding. The countdown has already begun, and we don't even know what clock we're on.

Near the mobile command center, Team 12 had been left to their own devices. "Those transmissions they let us hear...," Rocco recalled. "Spooky," he said. "Sounded like gibberish."

Edgar, ever the linguist, frowned. "I learned fifteen languages, but I'm tellin' ya this ain't no dialect I ain't never heard before."

Rocco deadpanned Edgar. "Edgar, how do you know fifteen languages, and you still speak that broken ass English?" The rest of the team chuckled.

"Ya ain't never heard it because its closest match is Sumerian," Hawk told him.

Edgar laughed in good spirits, but it wasn't a humorous chuckle. It was a sound which a man on the brink of death might utter when time's almost up. "Sumerian's a dead language, sir. Doze guyz are long gone, sir."

"You sure about that?" Hawk asked.

Rocco perked up. "Voyager fellas, filled with gold records, pictures, sounds of Earth. Oh, and naked humans, in case whoever or whatever opens it was non-binary."

Hawk looking directly at Rocco, "Anything else, Carl Sagan? Or should I say, Mister Spock?"

"Aye aye, Commander Censorship," Rocco quipped back. "Those nerds put a Golden Record on the thing which contained greetings in over 50 languages—including Sumerian."

Silence.

Edgar frowned. "Don't tell me deez guyz actually knew doze guyz was out there speakin' a freakin' dead language, sir?"

"Yeah, some smart asshole sent them a damn menu," Rocco frowned. "And now they're back and ringing the bell for supper?" He pointed at the ship.

Edgar's face went pale. "We sen'em the menu an' our freakin' address, Boss? This thing could'a burned straight in and taken out an entire city!"

Rocco nodded while he was stuffing his last mag into his new armor suit. "We sure we should trust these nerds? I didn't understand half the shit the analyst said onboard the *Icarus.* He was speaking in *Edgar-lingo* for fucks' sake."

The team laughed and nodded.

Rocco cleared his throat and steadied his footing. "Well, boys," he said. "Looks like we're Earth's last hope." He closed his eyes in self-proclamation. *I am the main character,* he mumbled this odd declaration under his breath. He could never resist being Rocco after all.

The Commander nodded to Vidaurri then turned back to view the towering wreckage, the cold steel husk now a silent specter on Earth's surface. His aide had moved out to check on something. Stonegate was alone, so he spoke freely to no one.

"Is this a tomb?" he asked aloud. "A refuge? Or the harbinger of something far worse? Time will tell. Assuming we have time enough to explore inside."

His aide returned and pointed out the positions of the armored vehicles. They were formed up in a tight formation, their turret guns trained on the massive alien vessel, prepared for a futile last stand should the situation turn hostile.

Above, the Air Cavalry circled like vultures, gunships sweeping the perimeter with their infrared sensors and thermal optics.

Still, Stonegate wanted more firepower.

"Where the hell are my Abrams?" he muttered under his breath.

The aide turned to him, his voice sharp. "Delayed, sir. They're coming from the original landing site. Team 12 is gearing up to board the vessel now."

Stonegate gritted his teeth. "How the hell did we manage to miscalculate the crash site?" he growled.

"It must have slowed down, sir."

"Hmm," the Commander said. He didn't sound convinced. With all the planning which went into this operation, it didn't seem possible something so vital had been miscalculated.

Washington had no playbook for this. The closest? CONPLAN-8888-11 —the zombie contingency. Identify threats, secure resources, and pray the plan worked.

But if the aliens associated with the massive structure stuck in the ground in this god-forsaken corner of Texas had mastered interstellar travel, it would mean their technology outclassed humanity's entire arsenal. If this turned into a fight, it would be short. Brutal. And completely one-sided.

The Commander and all the other planners learned too late the ship had strayed off course from the predicted impact zone. Before they could redirect assets, the visitor had dropped off radar entirely before its violent crash landing. Prior to impact, it had slowed enough to prevent complete destruction.

The government had planned for first contact in a controlled location— one secured with tanks, heavy artillery, and even a nuclear failsafe. And the vision was of something landing, not tumbling out of the sky and barreling into the landscape.

Now?

At the moment they were missing most of their assets.

Stonegate sighed, stopped thinking about what might have been, and turned his attention to the present. Only the Commanders, his operators, and Team 12 which was gearing up to enter the fallen behemoth, stood between humanity and whatever horrors awaited within. A quarantine zone was established. TEAM 12 operators were fitted into next-generation exo-skeleton suits, designed to withstand chemical, biological, and radiological hazards.

But these suits weren't merely cutting-edge, they were beyond anything humanity should have been capable of creating. Their specs came from Oak Island and a mission there which had uncovered technology so advanced it reshaped Earth's entire war doctrine—the most significant upgrade to the planet's fighting force since the world went dark eons ago.

Stonegate wasn't convinced these suits would protect men from whatever the hell was inside the alien ship, so he made certain the team had an ace up their sleeve. TEAM 12's Fire Teams were ready. And if this was a one-way trip, they'd go down swinging. They had been issued classified, prototype weapons, the kind not widely seen outside the sandbox yet.

The first weapon was the Boombox.

The concept was simple but deadly. A compact, lightweight rifle with a telescoping stock, designed for 300-meter precision with both supersonic and subsonic rounds. It was a sub-5-pound weapon built on a .308 lower receiver, featuring a 1/3 twist stainless match barrel and an adjustable gas block. The Sub projectile itself was a 340-grain bullet larger than a AA battery. The 6-inch barrel could do 1 minute-of-angle (MOA) at 300 meters with the subsonic 340 grain bullet doing 250,000 RPM.

Unlike legacy systems, this beast maximized rotational energy, giving its bullets twice the expansion. In other words, they weren't just shooting rounds. They were launching footballs.

It was a direct evolution of the CSAS program, shrinking AR-10s into AR-15 platforms.

Deadly. Precise. Perfect for close-order battles or CQB.

The other rifle?

Something new from HK USA. Built off their G11 concept, the Metal Storm Rifle (MSR) fired caseless 6 Max ammo, a weapon decades ahead of its time. An electronic firearm with no moving parts, except for the Swiss-watch-style rotary loader tucked into the back of the rifle. Mags were loaded on top, making it a premium choice for anyone laying prone, using micro terrain to their advantage. This rifle had zero recoil, until the third round was already out of the barrel. By then, it didn't matter.

Capable of firing thousands of rounds per minute. The MSR replaced the team's Squad Automatic Rifle with an added bonus of an air bursting grenade launcher underneath.

If these weapons performed as advertised, they would render every assault rifle on Earth obsolete overnight.

And suppose these futuristic weapons weren't enough? Stonegate asked himself. *Well, hopefully someone on our side is very close to inventing a working phaser. Otherwise, we're screwed.*

On the ground and nearly out of Stonegate's view, Commander Anshar Hawk, leading Fire Team Alpha, was moving cautiously through the debris field. His eyes were locked on the ship's jagged hull. Something unfamiliar was present. An electromagnetic event was unfolding, the air humming with invisible power. The team felt it, a current running through their bodies, static prickling across their skin. The buzz of a guitar amplifier filled their ears.

Their suits adjusted, sensors flickering. Chances were good whatever was inside was awake. His counterpart, Lieutenant Commander Axle Briggs, followed behind Fire Team Bravo. The massive structure loomed ahead, its twisted metal plating mangled beyond recognition.

Hawk's voice crackled over the Troop Net, "Status report, Lieutenant."

Lieutenant Rox checked his scanner. "Sir, we've located multiple breaches, but they weren't caused by the crash."

Hawk's eyes narrowed, "Explain."

Rox knelt by a twisted section of hull plating, his fingers running over the scorched metal. "This ship was under attack before it crashed," he muttered. The Lieutenant's brow furrowed as he traced deep impact scars and jagged edges. "Looks like it may have been boarded. Something had latched on and then sheared off during reentry." He paused his report and glanced up at Hawk.

Hawk exchanged a look with Briggs. "Good explanation," he said then he stood there for a moment, collecting his own internal thoughts.

"Ava, scout ahead. Dom, launch *Dragon Fly.*" Hawk ordered.

The insect-sized drone zipped forward, mapping the wreck with sonar-like pulses. Its paired AI, Ava, projected the ghostly avatar beside Hawk.

"Path's clear—for now," she said, vanishing into the breach.

Their visors updated in real time; walls peeled away in wire-frame as they advanced.

Rox glanced at Hawk. "Sir, are we really doing this? Are we going inside? Can't we just nerve gas this MF'er and salvage what we can."

"There could be friendlies still on board." Hawk kept his voice calm and steady. "You know the mission. We're TEAM 12. We're boarding. This is what we were assembled for."

Ava's voice crackled through Hawk's earpiece. "Commander, the breach I entered will grant the team access and the path is clear—so far."

Stonegate had been monitoring their comms. Now his voice followed over Troop Net. "Commander Hawk, what readings are you registering? Any biohazards?"

Hawk checked his HUD. "Negative, sir. No sign of airborne contaminants or radiation."

A brief pause.

"You're clear for entry," Stonegate authorized. "Rabbit in the Hole is a go."

Hawk nodded and made his thumb ready on the safety on his silenced Boombox.

"Alright, battle bros. We're going in," Hawk said, his voice clear but whispered. His hand signals directed the men to the breach which offered access to the interior.

The fire teams engaged their exoskeleton visors and their HUDs flickering to life. One by one, they crossed the threshold, stepping into the pitch-black interior of the alien vessel.

Stonegate watched his men disappear into the belly of the beast.

The signal cut out—they were on their own now.

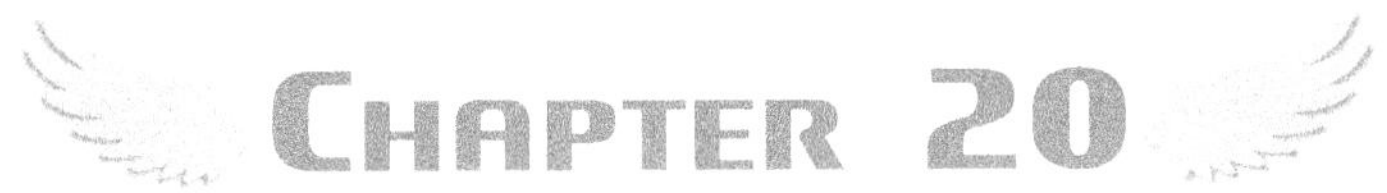

CHAPTER 20

An Alien, a Nurse, and a Salesman Walk into an ER

Rain hammered the cracked windshield in hard rhythmic drumbeats. Every breath felt heavy, his adrenaline was wearing off, leaving him in a haze of exhaustion and disbelief. The battered Silverado struggled against the storm as it limped into Victoria, each mile feeling longer than the last.

He skidded under the ambulance canopy, truck in its death throes. He yanked the passenger side door open and scooped the young woman into his arms. The automatic doors opened as he jogged in. The charge nurse clocked him, waving a gurney forward.

"What happened?"

With a look at the truck, a look at her, he rattled off the most plausible explanation, "Wreck." Because the truth would sound insane.

"Paging CHIARA FLY to ED." The charge nurse recognized Sonny.

Running from her duty station, Chiara spotted the truck.

"Where is he?"

The Silverado sat battered at the entrance of the driveway, scorched, dented, and half-torn apart. Sonny nearby trying to catch his breath. Another nurse was pulling him into the hospital.

"What the hell happened, Sonny? Why didn't you call?"

"Chiara, I got it," one of the nurses scolded her.

Sonny had a thermometer to his temple. The temp gun registered normal.

"Were you in an accident? That's what the admin nurse said. Why does your truck look like it survived a damn explosion?" she asked as they wheeled him in.

"Chiara, please. We need to get him in a room."

"He's my husband, damn it."

"Exactly. Don't try and pull rank on me, homegirl. We got him," her fellow nurse reassured her.

Sometime later Chiara finally calmed down, "What the hell happened out there?"

Sonny's words poured out in a rush. "This thing, this fiery thing, fell out of the sky," he said. "It tore through the clouds and smashed right on top of the house I was delivering to. Debris hit my truck and smashed the trailer. My phone melted."

He looked up to see Chiara staring in stunned silence. When he didn't continue, she prompted him.

"Go on," she said. "Tell me everything."

Sonny described the meteor impact. The forest, flattened by the shock wave. The house, ripped from the ground and crashed, like a CAT 5 hurricane had slapped it. The government's immediate arrival.

"And then, the Guard shows up?" Chiara wondered.

Sonny shook his head.

"Not National Guard, Chiara." His voice was shaky now. "Gear I've never seen. Weapons I've never seen. Like they were waiting for it."

Chiara's hands tightened in her lap. She was dying to ask about the woman, but she figured Sonny would get around to it eventually.

"Anyhow, they made us leave. Something about viral infections or possible contamination."

Chiara's brow furrowed as her medical training kicked in. "Did they name a pathogen? It's important, Sonny. Think hard. I need you to recall exactly what they said."

Shrugging he said. "No... maybe. T4 something, TD maybe? There was so much going on."

Chiara went rigid, her face physically changed. "TD4?" she asked, her tone shifting—like TD4 was already on the medical community's radar.

Sonny shuddered, paranoia creeping in.

"Am I infected with something?" Fear in his voice. "They said we were clear." His skin went pale and clammy.

She snapped the curtain closed, helped him out of his shirt, checking for lacerations, step-checking his ribs, pupils, and neck.

"What if I got exposed to some alien disease, Chiara? What if I," Sonny began.

"Breathe," she said. "You're adrenaline dumping. Let me see your finger.

"You're not dying of some extraterrestrial disease. You're coming down from an adrenaline rush. I'm much more concerned about your wedding ring being fused to your finger. It looks like it will have to be surgically removed." To test her theory, she gave it a rough yank.

"Hell, Chiara, you're going to rip my finger off!"

"Electricity did this?" she sounded skeptical. "You told the nurse you were hit by lightning?"

"My hand was in the mud. Must have touched a live wire or I was hit by lightning. That zap almost knocked me the Eff out," he recalled.

In his head, he could still see the first impact, hear the explosion, feel the heat against his face. Chiara's grounded, unwavering voice pulled him back.

"The woman you brought in, she's pretty."

His mouth went slack, he shrugged knowing full well it was a trap. "There was so much going on I didn't really notice."

Her lips pursed. "Sit tight," she said and kissed him. "I'll get the doctor."

Chiara slipped into the next bay. A group of male nurses and the ER doc gathered in there like moths around a flame. The woman lay under warm blankets, skin clean now—lean, unmarked, other than strange tattoos. The doc was doing a careful head-to-toe; there were no bruises to find.

Mylitta was a pot of water set to boil.

Her eyes, a shade of Steve McQueen's *Bullitt,* highland green Ford Mustang GT, stood out against the backdrop of her dark wavy hair hovering above her shoulders, millimeters away from spilling out of control. Framed between the loose cascade of dark tendrils, her bronze oval-shaped face was caught by natural highlights and high cheekbones.

"She's trying to talk." Someone said.

It wasn't English. It wasn't even a language anyone in the room recognized. The sounds were harsher, older. Chiara felt the hair on her arms rise— like a half-remembered song.

"Clear the bay," she ordered. Badges flashed. The curtains swished. Sonny slipped in behind her.

"What is it?" he asked.

Chiara's head tilted. She rubbed her lips, her mind racing. Pieces were falling into place. She wasn't just thinking—she was terrified. In a voice which was barely above a whisper, she said, "I think it's Proto-Sumerian. It's a language which evolved into Sumerian. No one speaks it anymore."

Sonny stared at her. "How do you know it's Proto-Sumerian?"

Chiara threw up her hands.

"I don't know!" She yelled evasively. "I'm just guessing, okay?! All I know, and I don't know how I know, is it sounds like the way it reads."

Sonny did a double take. "You can read that shit too? You realize what you're saying doesn't make any sense, right?"

Chiara's eyes and nostrils flared. "Sonny, none of this, your explosion, the military operation, this woman, her language—none of this makes any sense!"

Ms. Dawson suddenly locked her gaze onto Sonny's hand. More specifically, the altered ring. A faint amber-blue glow pulsed from the band. Her expression darkened. She understood something, but she couldn't say it. She looked from Chiara to Sonny, her eyes pleading. She wanted to communicate so badly her face was contorted. She was straining, desperate, it was like she was choking on words too stubborn to come out. She fluttered her hands and moved her head from side to side.

Suddenly, she stopped moving. She was stiff as a statue. Memories rushed back, a flood of remembrance pouring into her brain. She remembered who she was. What was happening. Who she had lost. Her lips parted, then burst.

"My family is dead," she said slowly, her mind still struggling with the words. "Everyone I know is dead."

Chiara's heart sank.

Sonny felt it too.

There was no one left for this sad woman.

Chiara's voice softened. "You're not alone. You're with us; you can stay with us. We won't just drop you off somewhere like a stray."

Ms. Dawson turned toward her, eyes permissive. Her words began forming yet she said nothing. These people had no idea what they were promising.

CHAPTER 21

Goddess and the Votary

They had run her name, but there were no records in the system. Not at this hospital, and not at Victoria's only other medical facility. It was like she didn't exist.

The doctor, after scanning her brain, had found no physical signs of trauma, no concussion, no memory issues at all. Yet she still struggled to remember her own first name.

The diagnosis?

A temporary concussion, maybe stress-induced amnesia.

She was physically fine.

Chiara looked over Sonny's shoulder at the bill, rolling her eyes. "Yeah. Could've been worse. Could've been sixteen grand."

He sighed.

Chiara gave him a playful shove. "Don't be dramatic."

Sonny pouted, "You always say I changed your life."

Chiara smiled, narrowing her eyes and squeezing his arm. "You did."

He breathed in deep and let it out slowly. "Without you in my life, we wouldn't be staring at another massive bill."

Sonny laughed, shaking his head. "At least everyone is okay," he said. "Meanwhile, I still have to find out if my work truck is covered for UFO damage."

"Good luck with claiming that." She mocked him.

Sonny turned to Ms. Dawson, who had been silent, staring at the road ahead as the three of them drove home.

"You doing okay?" he asked.

She looked at him, her green eyes soft with gratitude, and she finally spoke. "I am now. Thank you." She said these words slowly, as if she had just learned English. She said nothing else. She just turned back to stare out the window, watching the city lights blur past. It was like she was seeing it all for the first time. And then she yawned, as if the view was disappointingly bland.

They pulled into the driveway at 2:00 a.m., exhaustion settling in deep. Sonny locked the deadbolts, three times each. The house was finally starting to feel like a home, even with half their belongings still in boxes. Chiara set up the spare room hastily, and despite the craziness of the day, everything looked clean enough and put together.

Sonny yawned, dragging himself inside. *Where does she get all this energy?*

The young woman followed and, once in the house, she suddenly said, "Myli, Mylitta Sipani."

Sonny stopped mid-step, turning to face her. "Not Ms. Dawson?"

Chiara joined them in the living room and tilted her head, intrigued.

"Myli? Interesting name. Like Miley Cyrus?" Sonny kidded.

Chiara rolled her eyes. "No. Like Mylitta, the Sumerian goddess of love and war."

Sonny shrugged her off. "How the hell do you know?"

Chiara sneered, pointing to her collection of ancient history books in the library. "Maybe you should read more, Sonny."

"No lies detected." He quipped.

"Sumerians?" Mylitta asked, suddenly interested.

Chiara hesitated, then explained. "They were among the first recorded civilization of hominin to develop writing, advanced cities, law, and organized religion."

She paused, choosing her next words carefully.

"The author of this particular book," she grabbed it off the shelf, "is Sieg-fried Santo Padre. He believed they were descendants of a superior race who vanished after a cataclysm."

"Oh, yeah... SS Daddy." Sonny recalled hearing some of the theories he'd heard his wife mention after a few drinks. "His Adam, Lilith and Eve theories and their lines?" he suggested.

"Some scholars think the biblical Flood was based on Sumerian scrip-tures," Chiara said.

It was subtle, but Sonny noticed Mylitta's expression and demeanor shift. It looked to him like a forgotten memory resurfacing, just out of reach. He also sensed something else, as if it was this stranger's thoughts—the feeling of someone leaving before something terrible happened.

Chiara continued, this "shit" really interested her. "Their gods and de-mons came from an older civilization. One in Europe worshipped a goddess, ruled by women for two centuries—until the Kurgans poured down off the Russian steppes. Their last queen, Sophia, survived the invasion and fled north. Her fingerprints were all over what came four thousand years later."

Mylitta looked down, quiet for a moment, taking time to choose her words carefully. She spoke slowly, each word, the weight of a boulder. "I'm sorry... for the trouble I caused." She paused, her brow furrowing as the words settled. "I appreciate... what you both have done."

Her accent was heavy, her voice steady, but something deeper lurked be-neath, deep within her subconscious. She felt it as the weight of a lost world of centuries erased.

Although Chiara and Sonny failed to notice, the ring pulsed faintly. Mylitta was learning. Adapting. And with every word, she and Sonny were aligning.

Unaware of the connections forming, Chiara reached out and gently took Mylitta's hands. "It's no trouble at all. We don't have much, but you're welcome to stay here as long as you need." She glanced at Sonny. "And if you need anything, I'll make Sonny get it for you." Chiara chuckled, trying to lighten the mood.

Mylitta gave a small smile, but her eyes still carried something heavy.

If Chiara spotted their guest's expression, she didn't show it. "Let me show you the room," she said, playing the perfect hostess.

Taking Mylitta in tow, Chiara led the young woman down a hallway, opened a side door, and flicked on the light switch, revealing the guest room.

"There are clean sheets on the bed. It's a nice mattress—actually, the one Sonny sold me when we first met. You should sleep well tonight."

Mylitta nodded, "I think… if it is permitted… I'm going to take a shower… have I said this correctly?"

Chiara smiled. "Of course, take your time." She led Mylitta to the bathroom, grabbing fresh towels along the way. "Soap and shampoo are in the shower. There are extra razors and toothbrushes under the sink. Just make yourself at home. Use this robe for now. I'll lay out some fresh clothes, undergarments, and pajamas for you."

Mylitta nodded, practically bowing. "Thank you. You can just call me Myli."

Chiara hesitated, then bowed in return. "Goodnight, Myli."

"Goodnight." Myli said with a soft smile. She stepped inside the bathroom, closing the door.

While his wife played hostess, Sonny knew exactly what he wanted to do. Head for bed. His shoes flew off one at a time in opposite directions. His legs battled his pants until the last foot was free. His shirt was already torn, so he muscled his way out of it finishing the job.

"Whoa, you're kidding right?!" Chiara shouted, blocking Sonny's path to the bed. "Not on my clean sheets, psycho." She grabbed his arm, ushering him toward the master bathroom.

Sonny groaned. He was exhausted but surprisingly not too beat up.

Actually, he told himself, *I feel better right now than I have all week.* But aloud to his wife he muttered, "FINE."

"Yeah, fine, Linus," she said, shuffling him into the bathroom. Chiara caught sight of him—wearing nothing but his lucky silk hoochie daddy briefs. "Your scar looks like it healed up nice."

He tucked his chin down to inspect it and groaned. "Yeah, it's… fading."

She couldn't help herself and whistled.

Sonny paused, his eyes rolled before looking back at her—half annoyed, half amused. It was from a stupid skit they'd seen on a phone text at one of their shooting matches.

"What that PP do?" she asked.

Sonny groaned, trying to suppress a laugh. "Stop," he pretended to protest.

Chiara grinned. "You know how sexy those hoochie daddy undies are on you."

Sonny low-waved her off, hands strategically trying to block her view of them.

"Knock it off," he muttered, dismissing her joke and her ridiculous catcall.

In and out of the shower in little over five minutes, the tile was cold under his feet. He yelped. The AC's crisp air flooded the bathroom. In the mirror, he watched the condensation melt away. His body looked—he had to admit—surprisingly good.

The bruise on his face was already fading along with the one on his abdomen. The bruises on his arms and legs were there, but healing and healing faster than clinically possible.

"How the fah—" He whispered under his breath.

He squinted, twisting, stretching, doing a full body check in the mirror.

Another whistle. From the bedroom.

"Hey, mista." Chiara tossed a pair of clean boxer briefs in his direction.

Sonny froze. "What?"

"What that PP do?" Chiara repeated.

Sonny groaned, covering his face. "Stop it, you psycho. I can't help it—it's little now. It's the cold. Leave me alone. It hides when mocked."

Myli heard them both laughing in their bedroom. Laughter, something she hadn't heard in a long time. She tried to give them privacy but unbeknownst to Sonny and Chiara, the walls wouldn't allow it.

Chiara giggled from the bed. "You're burnin' up those hoochie briefs."

"Your drunk on exhaustion." Sonny struggled to get one foot through the opening. "You're terrible. Shut up." He laughed out loud. "A few good inches is better than no inches."

"Stop being obnoxious," he continued to protest.

"Nooooo," she laughed.

"I don't even know you anymore." He cried out, shivering. "It's freezing in here!"

Chiara flipped the covers up, a mischievous grin on her lips. Premeditation. "I got something warm under the clean sheets," she purred.

Stretched out beneath the sheet, her body looked like a Greek marble statue. Sonny didn't need to be invited twice. He dove right in.

Chapter 22

War Child

Myli stared at the mirror, her gaze locking onto the reflection of a woman she barely recognized. It felt like she hadn't seen herself in centuries. The laughter next door reminded her of what she had been missing, what she had been fighting for.

Her fingers combed through the tangled strands of her hair, pulling out the last bits of mud and debris. She traced the contours of her own face, searching for familiarity, for recognition.

All she found was uncertainty.

She whispered to herself, a question drenched in sorrow. "Where am I? What happened to Paradise?"

The bathroom around her felt... antiquated. New, yet frontier-backwater-primitive. Crude, yet functional. The world had changed, and she wasn't sure where she fit in anymore.

Her eyes wandered to the bathtub, curiosity flickering in her mind.

"I haven't seen something like this in a long time," she told herself aloud. "War vessels barely had showers. A bathtub was a luxury which necessity discouraged."

She decided to try it out. She unbuttoned the Filson Short-Lined Cruiser; she let it slide from her shoulders, then stepped out of the oversized scrub bottoms Chiara had leant her. Her body was covered in dried mud and ash.

She was aware she had no cuts, bruises—not even a single thorn scratch despite running barefoot through the blasted wasteland.

She reached for the faucet, twisting the unfamiliar handles until warm water poured into the tub. Too hot, too cold, figuring out the exact turn of the knob was frustrating. It took her a moment to figure out the mechanics, but soon, the water was perfect. Mylitta stepped in, letting the cascading warmth envelop her.

The dirt turned into liquid mud, swirling down the drain, carrying the last remnants of the impact site away. She closed her eyes, savoring the sensory experience she had almost forgotten. She opened the bottles; scents fruity and synthetic, the strange artificial smell burned her nose.

As she ran her fingers through her scalp, scrubbing away the grime, a thought struck her. *How long has it been since I last did this?*

She couldn't remember. A flicker of being on a ship, hunted by a monster filled her memory like a scene in a movie. She caught her breath.

That distant memory momentarily chilled her and yet this new world terrified her even more. This was her Middle Ages, a technological regression.

With her eyes closed, she explored her own body, as if reacquainting herself with a long-lost friend. Her fingers brushed her throat, traced over the soft curves of her collarbones before moving downward. The sensation of touch, of being touched, sent an unexpected shudder through her. Being trapped in the digital matrix of the ring was imprisoning but necessary to survive the immense distances traveled in space.

She had forgotten this feeling.

Forgotten what it meant to be in a body again.

Forgotten what significance her tattoos held.

She lingered on her own skin, absorbing the contrast between memory and reality.

When she was finished, she glanced at her legs. There was no hair. None at all. Her brow furrowed. There was no hair under her armpits either.

Was this, normal?

Had it always been this way?

Some memories were still too distant to access without the wakeup serum.

She stepped out onto the soft, white bathmat. Water seeped out from the mat's inferior absorbent edges. She reached for a towel. The towel was meant to be luxurious, but still, it felt subpar, like something the lower class would use. Everything was substandard here but not meant to be. She toweled off quickly, then reached into the bag Chiara had left for her.

It was then she saw the undergarments. A bra. It was too small for her. The bottom underwear looked like string; it was a thong. It was all that was available for Chiara to give her.

Mylitta blushed, holding the thin strip of fabric between her fingers. Her lips parted, and she let out a laugh. A hard laugh. *You must be kidding me.* She laughed into her hand—so this is fashion now? The absurdness of it set it.

She shook her head, her laughter dying down to soft chuckles as she slipped into the minimal undergarments. The thin material hugged her hips, the back sliding between her butt cheeks in an unfamiliar way. Her shirt all but burst at the seams. She turned, glancing at herself in the mirror, her face flushing red.

She barely remembered the last time she felt embarrassed. A realization which sobered her instantly. She sighed, running her hands over her face, composing herself.

She looked like a vagrant from her time. No tiara, no jewels, no fancy night gown.

Nevertheless, she had to accept her appearance. It was time to move forward.

Myli brushed her teeth, using the mediocre hygienics available, and finished by tying her hair back before finally crawling into bed. For the first time in a very, very long time... she felt safe.

In the other bedroom, Chiara was trying to drag out more time from Sonny under the sheets. She knew he was exhausted, still processing the insanity of the past twenty-four hours. But she couldn't help herself. She had almost lost him. She wanted to keep him close.

Soft kisses. Along his neck. His jawline. His ear. A warm breath. A teasing whisper.

"Can you be quiet?" Chiara smirked against his skin.

Sonny gave a weak nod, a grin pulling at his lips. "You are some kind of demon."

"You have no idea." Her teeth piercing her grin.

"Why aren't you like this when I have ample energy?" he whispered.

Her voice got low and sultry. "Because you'd be too dangerous." The seductress slid onto him, flesh pressing against his warmth. Her skin, smooth and perfect, blended with him. Their bodies fit perfectly, like two puzzle pieces shifting around the board for the last fifteen minutes until they locked together.

Alone in her room, Myli curled into the plush sheets, reveling in the softness. Chiara had been right—this *was* a good bed. She felt herself relax, her body adjusting, tension releasing. Tomorrow she would be busy seeking answers to all her many questions. So many things to understand. So little time.

The laughter through the wall grew distant, then inside her. She was nearly asleep when, without warning, she gasped. A sensual sensation. Warmth. Love. Passion. All flowed through her from out of the blue. A strange sensation pulsed through her body, her spine, her limbs.

Her heartbeat quickened. Her skin tingled.

Thoughts not her own crept into her mind.

She was enthralled in ecstasy. A deep, invasive pull stirred within her. She tossed and turned, her body reacting to something unseen. Heat built in her chest, her belly, spreading lower. She needed to put this fire out. Her lips parted in a quiet sigh. Her back arched, her muscles tightening as a wave of pleasure overtook her.

She clenched the sheets, her fingers digging into the fabric, as her body reacted uncontrollably. Her mind fractured, caught between desire and confusion. It was too intense, too sudden. Her eyes fluttered shut, her breath ragged before a whisper echoed in her subconscious.

Not in her voice. Not her own thought. But another's. And it spoke one single word.

Chiara.

Chiara?

Myli gasped, her eyes snapping open, her body still shivering from the lingering sensations. She sat up abruptly, hands clutching the sheets, her breath uneven, shaky.

Then, suddenly, the warmth and the love, the tenderness, was shattered as another psychic wave surged through her mind's eye. Something else was there. Something darker. Something was wrong.

Or worse.

Something had already begun.

Myli's hair stood on end as the sensation shifted. The warmth, the intimacy gone. Replaced by something raw. Urgent. She could hear them. Squealing. Chittering. Moving through the corridors.

Another memory crept in, but this one was fresh. Not a distant echo, but a living nightmare. Desperation. Pain. The crackle of weapons fire. Did she feel all this before her ship came crashing down? Or was it happening now?

Her pulse hammered. They were coming.

In the other room, Chiara rolled over, exhaling softly. One leg still straddling her lover. Sonny had already collapsed into a pile of steaming limp muscle, arms sprawled out, completely dead to the world. Chiara smirked. It was over and tonight would have to last forever.

Forever faded quickly. It was interrupted by a shriek as the stranger in the guestroom cried out. The scream was not from pain but terror.

Chiara was up and moving quickly. She grabbed Sonny's Springfield TRP .45 off the dresser, "I got it," she told Sonny. But he was already reaching for his bedside rifle. There wouldn't be a repeat of their last break-in.

She opened the bedroom door, darted out and maneuvered down the dark hallway with the deadly weapon—a practical tool—at low-ready. Her every step was perfect, every step quiet, and each long step was heel-to-toe to keep her eyes level, not bouncing. If she had to shoot, the barrel would never leave the same plane. She damn near could have been a ninja with how quietly and steadily she moved.

As she moved, a thought crept into her mind. A mothering instinct. It was new and unexpected. *When did that chemical reaction change take place?*

She stopped at Myli's cracked door. Myli was crouched in the corner, repeating the same phrase over and over. Whatever she'd done, whatever she couldn't bring herself to remember, was eating her alive. She slapped her head repeatedly, desperate to drag that memory out.

CHAPTER 23

Quantum Graveyard
Crash Site in Texas

Back at the crash site, Commander Anshar Hawk stepped cautiously into the gaping maw of the alien ship, his boots clicking lightly against the metal grating below. Immediately, he and the others felt like they were stepping into hallowed ground. Team 12 wasn't a rumor; it was the knifes edge of ORB-GRU. Pilots, CAG, engineers—operators who could improvise in a vacuum and win. Tonight, that knife slipped into the first arrival of possible alien invasion.

His heads-up display (HUD) illuminated his vision through the integrated IR/Thermal NOD system in his helmet, a cutting-edge marvel of human tech.

The corridor stretched out before him, vast and silent, like a tomb frozen in time.

His hand signals were quick and decisive. Their footwork was all about efficiency of movement.

The orders were monotonous. Clear right, stack left, everyone scanning sectors, barrel waves pointing the direction to go. Break out into open areas. Hold.

It was all SOP, (Standard Operating Procedure) before moving up, taking cover behind any obstacle available, and do it all again as they cleared everything around them.

They had entered what looked like ground level, but peering through the grated floor, Hawk immediately realized, *We're nowhere near the bottom. A false step could spell doom with no way to get to the fallen soldier.*

A faint artificial voice could be heard further down the corridor.
"Kwéntom-dek̓ failing. Bhúh-súm-koró degradowentós, swek̓sti!"
"Médhe, bhloweti. Rḗ-stoh sun-ya rekter."
"Ceméh: k̂m̥ték̓tós k̓m̥tós. Wékos 75 hówrs."

So far it was unrecognizable. Only later would its meaning become clear: *(Containment deck failing. Fusion core degradation, sixty! Implosion—inevitable. Shut down the Sun Reactor. Arrival of CME: contact imminent. Time: 75 hours.)*

"Is that the ship's status report?" one of the team whispered.
"Evi," Hawk whispered. "I'll explain later."
Beneath them, the ship extended downward at least ten or more stories to a massive subterranean labyrinth of unknown horrors. The proportions inside already seemed to be a discrepancy with what they had seen from the outside. The mound the house had once sat on had acted like a natural barricade which broke the ship's back on impact, dividing it into smaller sections.

Alpha and Bravo moved in unison. Their footsteps softened by adaptive stealth plating. Unlike their previous missions, they were running the newest, most advanced armor on Earth. Gone were the days of bulky exoskeletons like Lockheed's HULC or Raytheon's XOS models.
Those were stone age tools compared to what they now wore. The Mark III 2nd SKN Second Skin Armor. It was lightweight, impenetrable, adaptive—a classified marvel of alien-based reverse engineering.
The outer shell of the suit was pliable yet deceptively strong, a seamless fusion of adaptive nanomaterials and liquid armor technology designed to redistribute kinetic force upon impact. The moment a projectile struck, the suit reacted instantly, hardening at the point of contact before returning to its natural flexibility, dispersing energy like ripples through water.

Its adaptive properties extended beyond protection. Much like the stealth capabilities of next-generation jet fighters, the suit's surface could shift in real time, altering its color, texture, and reflectivity to bend and blend with its environment. Its adaptive camouflage system was something the army had wanted since they saw a Hollywood version of it in the *Predator* movie back in the 1980s.

Ballistic defense. Seamless integration. This wasn't just armor; it was an extension of the wearer.

The MKIII was also completely airtight; the suit functioned in environments no conventional combat gear could withstand. It could operate in the zero-G vacuum of space, its internal systems regulating pressure, temperature, and oxygen levels to keep the user alive in any hostile conditions. Beneath the surface of Earth, it could dive to a depth of 4,500 meters, its hydrostatic counterpressure system allowing the wearer to function in the crushing abyss of the deep ocean.

But even this advanced technology had limits. At extreme depths, the kinetic force liquid system became a burden, thickening, restricting movement, turning every step into a slow, labored effort. At that point, the suit wasn't armor anymore—it was an iron coffin.

The underlayer, known as the Alpha Skin jumpsuit, was an engineering marvel, a seamless fusion of Golden-Orb spider silk technology and nano-fiber adaptive weave. It was bulletproof yet featherlight, a second skin designed to move as fluidly as the body itself, offering unparalleled speed, endurance, and protection.

Unlike traditional body armor, which relied on rigid plating, Alpha Skin functioned as a living material, responding to environmental shifts in real time. Its smart fabric matrix could contract or relax, redistributing force upon impact, absorbing kinetic energy from the blunt trauma of small arms ballistics, or concussive waves.

It was the closest Earth's top scientists had ever come to replicating Trip Looper's legendary suit, a reverse engineered glimpse into a technology which shouldn't have existed in this time. Yet, despite their advancements, they had only scratched the surface of their true potential. Looper's armor was a relic of another age, another war, one still being fought in the shadows.

Every member of Team 12 felt like a living, breathing war machine. They didn't wear the suit; they were part of it. And still, it might not be enough against an enemy which only Hawk had survived.

"Everybody watch your step," Hawk ordered, his voice even, steady. "The structure isn't stable." He tested the deck plating with his foot, experimenting with a soft and then a hard tap. "There is more structural damage than we anticipated." He took another methodical step. "Move slow, stay together. And nobody touches anything."

The ship's holographic AI flickered as Evi attempted to adapt the alien language to the ship's failing systems. The voice was layered, fragmented, words shifting through time, an echo of tongues long dead. It started as unintelligible murmurs, the cadence ancient, unfamiliar. Every attempt at dialogue—slowly—it evolved into something intelligible.

"Hear this... Tiam-... Un-birthed... Asha, Uru... unraveling. Tiamat seeks the gate..."

The translation distorted, straining. The Sumerian roots fading, morphing into something Proto-Indo-European, grasping for English.

"Containment—sundered."

"The black veil—falls."

"Fusion heart—dimming. Falling to cold."

A pause. A mechanical stutter.

"Quarantine Hold—broken. The cage fails—the depth hunger rises. Broken is Enki's Ring."

Another evolution, the voice fluctuated, adapting, closer to modern English, but still archaic and broken. The AI was learning with every word uttered by the teams.

"How is it doing this, Boss?" a voice blared over the channel.

So much for radio silence, Hawk told himself. *Somebody on the team just can't keep their questions to themselves. Probably Rocco.*

Hawk peered around the next corner, then slipped into a spot where the EVI transmission seemed loudest. The team flowed in one-by-one after each cleared their search area. When the nearest fire team paused, he decided to fill them in.

"The ship's AI is called EVI, the precursor to AVA. Not as quick as our Ava but Evi's listening to everything, like those Alexa things you have at home. She's learning English as we speak."

"The prison, weakens. That which waits... stirs."

"Below... darkened father's dream."

"Deck thirty... lost. The rot spreads."

"Huh? That voice is creeping me out, Boss," Rocco whispered.

"Yeah..." Hawk was on edge too. He'd seen the things Evi was babbling about. Seen them before and firsthand, and they were petrifying. Getting out of Oak Island had been no easy task.

The ship shuddered. Systems failing. The AI hesitated, as if debating whether to speak the next words.

Softly, almost regretfully, it said, *"Time betrays. Fate unspools. The warrior returns."*

A final flicker of sound before silence.

"Sounds positive." Rocco mused, looking around for the origin of the voice.

Hawk stole a quick glance behind, then kept his gaze forward. "All languages trace back to a common source—one that no longer exists. The ship's quantum processors won't take long to decode our English and then we will know what the hell happened here."

Lieutenant Axle Briggs was leading the second fire team which was functioning as a rear guard. He swept his rifle across the darkened corridor. Every few steps, his gloved thumb pressed the rubberized switch on his rifle-mounted light, brief pulses slicing through the void. The beams flickered against the bulkheads, cutting through shifting shadows, revealing nothing, yet.

Everyone was careful not to flag each other as they cleared their sectors of fire. The surefire lights, built integrally into their rifles, illuminated every corner, nook, and cranny. If something was there, hiding, they'd blind the ever-living shit out of it with all the lumens of the sun.

His head panned in front of them, scanning every shadow, every reflective surface, instinctually calculating angles. Eyes over the optic, keep the field of view wide. Muscle memory dictated every movement, sweep, clear, move.

Don't forget height over bore, the lieutenant reminded himself, as did the others.

At this range, if they weren't just point-shooting, the top of the head was the aiming point, compensate for mechanical offset. Every round counted. No wasted shots. No second chances.

The ship's corridors were tight, angles unpredictable, lighting erratic. At any moment, something could emerge from the darkness, forcing them into split-second engagement. No time for adjustments. No room for mistakes. Only precision. Only instinct.

At last, Lieutenant Briggs and his team reached Hawk and the others.

"Boss, this place is bigger on the inside," the lieutenant said. "I wasn't sure at first but I'm sure of it now."

Hawk nodded. "Spatial time manipulation."

Briggs exhaled sharply. "Of course. Because physics isn't real anymore."

"I'm all frizzy!" Rox said. "I feel amped up. More than just adrenaline."

"Yeah, I am picking up residual leakage from an energy field in here," Briggs guessed. "Some tech must be damaged. Hope these suits will protect our balls."

Hawk grimaced. "Knock it off. Let's move on. Scotty, take the point."

"AI found something, mate. Two walls up. Bodies maybe. They're not moving."

"Let's say hello." Hawk bantered.

As he walked ahead of the others, Petty Officer Scotty Muirhead peered through the grated floor, his stomach knotting as he took in the endless abyss beneath them. It wasn't just deep—it was unknowable. A black void swallowing the light, stretching downward into eternity. He had felt this before, diving in the open ocean, ship boarding in the Pacific. Anything could be lurking down there. Watching. Waiting.

And if someone fell?

No one on the team was sure if he was from the UK or Australia, only that he was former SAS.

Muirhead swallowed hard, gripping his rifle tighter. No way to retrieve somebody who lost his footing. No way to know what was down there. The body would be waiting a very long time.

"We gotta get to a solid deck, mate" he quipped. Nerves already spiking.

"You think they're hostile?" asked the nearest trailing man.

"Is an alligator cuddly, you bloody wanker? Christ, why do you think TEAM 12 exists?" muttered Scotty from Team Bravo. "We've got at least two bodies ahead of us."

"The only easy day was yesterday," added Staackman, adjusting his grip on his rifle.

"Do I think they're hostile? What a piss-weak question."

"Who pissed in your coffee this morning?" The banter continued.

"The Commander said to knock that SEAL Team shit off. Nobody is writing books right now." Briggs turned, his helmet visor flashing in the dim emergency lights.

No heat signatures, no movement, nothing being illuminated by white light. If Team 12 had adaptive camouflage, it was logical to assume the enemy did too.

"Shut your cock-holsters and stay alert," Hawk ordered as he joined the others.

"Chief, something up ahead," Scotty said. His light flashed on, and he motioned with it where to look.

They cleared their way to a body on the floor. It looked like a rag doll someone's dog had its way within more ways than one. Disemboweled, tore up, skin shredded, clothes, Alpha-suit half-on and half-off. Blood was everywhere.

"Some kind of creature," said Scotty. "Not human."

"They are called the Udug," Hawk corrected. "This isn't one."

"Boogeymen get him?" Rocco sighed.

Briggs glanced down the gangway, looked at the bulkhead, blood everywhere, high and low.

"I think this poor guy wasn't strapped in when the ship hit. There's no telling how fast he flew down this corridor," Hawk decided.

"But his guts, Boss."

"Lots of jagged edges in here," Briggs muttered, scanning the tangled mess of twisted beams and loose metal from the crash. But something else caught his eye—something—soft, something that *Dragon Fly* and Ava missed, and it was right above them.

Briggs' heart stopped as the mass cascaded down over Edgar. First it was a hand, then the other arm, followed by a torso, and the whole damn body.

No time to warn him.

Instinct took over. Briggs lunged, slamming into Edgar, knocking him clear just as the mass dropped onto Briggs like a deadweight, two-hundred-pound wrecking ball. The deck buckled beneath him, the grating groaning under the sudden impact and over four hundred pounds of men. Too much weight, too much inertia all at once.

It gave way. Scotty reacted first, moving on the shape which was pinning Briggs.

"Grab our man!" Hawk's voice cut through the madness.

Hands shot out, yanking Briggs free just as the failing grating twisted, breaking apart beneath him. Briggs' heart pounded as he was pulled to safety. The massive body which had temporarily pinned him plummeted down, clanging like a pinball, seemingly never hitting the bottom.

Briggs sucked in a breath, still hyperventilating, as Scotty peered down at him, unimpressed.

"You're the first bloke I've seen almost killed by a corpse," Scotty mused. "Pathetic ole chap."

Edgar pulled Briggs up, clapping him on the back. "Thanks, Amigo."

Rodriguez chimed in. "Yeah, thanks More Head."

Briggs exhaled sharply, forcing himself to shake it off.

Edgar's face untensed. "I've already got two kids; I don't need to be taking care of yours too if you die, sir."

"All I know is," Briggs said, "the dead are dropping from the ceiling. What's coming next on this ghost ship?"

"No worries, sir," Rodriguez spouted. "We got Mr. Scott here to save us all."

"First rounds on me when we finish this op," Briggs promised.

A short distance later, the blackened corridor ended at a sealed blast door. The Team was thankful to get to the end. Hawk gestured for the men to stack up and gather their wits for the breach. "Breaching in two."

While Edgar was busy getting ready to electronically hack the door, Briggs sighted a square placard on the wall. It was covered in grime and debris from the outside. He reached out and wiped it clean, revealing a schematic of the ship.

"I was expecting alien hieroglyphs," said Briggs, "not a goddamn blueprint."

"Whoa, this tech is bloody brilliant," Scotty said studying the map.

Briggs swiped a high-tech gloved hand over the display and new schematics lit up the screen showing their current position. It was paper-thin and foldable. Briggs barely had time to process the find. Briggs pried it off the wall with his field knife, handing it to the tech specialist.

"Scan it. If this thing works, we have a treasure map."

"Hold on," Hawk's voice was steady, but there was an edge to it, an unease settled over the team like static before a storm. Looking at the schematic, he added, "Good news, once we breach this pressure bulkhead, we'll be past the hull's reinforced buffer zone."

"What's the bad news?" Briggs asked.

"We'll be past the hull's reinforced buffer zone," he repeated, then he laughed, trying to settle them down. It was time for them to put their game faces on. "Those crewmen whose bodies are littering the corridor were running away from something, and we are about to lock ourselves in there with it. We will have to bypass half the ship to get where we want to go."

"We'll need to split up to cover more ground. This place is huge," Rocco sighed.

Briggs sighed in agreement, "Roger that. Let the *Dragon Fly* roam."

Edgar pulled out a small computer tablet and began hacking into the control interface, "In like Flint, guyz." he grinned.

The blast door hissed and began to groan open. *Dragon Fly* took off. Alpha and Bravo guns ready, anything hostile down the corridor would be greeted with a wall of lead. Pressurized air and a gaseous mixture rushed past their feet, twelve inches deep. From how it looks, it probably carried the stench of decay, but their suit's filters blocked the smell.

Meanwhile, the HUD in their visors registered everything in the air. The team pushed forward through the open door, their helmets' filtration systems compensating for the dense, low-hanging vapor pooling along the deck. The mist swirled around their boots, thick, chemical-laden, and ominous. Edgar glanced at his sensor readout, and his expression was grim.

"No contagions, but this gas? Straight cancer. Hydrazine, phosgene, and traces of benzene. We definitely don't want to breathe this shit." Edgar exhaled sharply, shaking his head. "This gas is a cocktail of everythin' ya don't want in ya lungs. It's got hydrazine, PAHs; I am even picking up Cladosporium sphaerospermum—radiation-eating fungi. This shit will kill ya and yer offspring."

They continued pressing forward, picking up their pace, bracing for contact but nothing happened—yet.

Briggs exhaled. "Round one and we're still alive. Let's keep pushing."

"How many rounds of this shit are we expecting?" Scotty asked.

"The more the better," said Hawk. "Would you rather be anywhere else?"

"Hell no, Chief. This is why I signed up. Sod off ET and his grey mates, eh."

"Hooyah."

As they entered the next corridor, red emergency lights blinked on, motion triggered. Hawk's hand snapped up, signaling the team to halt. The group kneeled down, making themselves small, less of a target. AI enhanced vision showed the outline of a figure. Interference couldn't tell them if it was friend or foe, but it seemed more interested in observing them than talking as it moved out of their line of sight.

The power of their AI showed them more than the naked eye. A yellow outline of the figure overlayed their visual picture. Behind the wall the creature was being tracked, giving them the exact position of their foe. The outline paused as it hesitated to make its next move. Somehow it could tell they could track it. It looked at them like it could see through the walls. That was when *Dragon Fly* lost it. The outline vanished, like it had gone invisible.

They all saw it on the shared *Hive Mind* feed.

"Did it see us?" one of them asked.

"Hold what you got," Hawk ordered

A shape, on all fours, then bipedal and back to all fours, darted just beyond the flickering lights, disappearing down the next hallway.

"Holy hell, WTF was that? It was as tall as the overhead."

"I don't know," Hawk whispered. "Shut it."

"It outran *Dragon Fly,*" Rocco warned.

The Teams fell silent. Hand signals and taps on the back signaled their moves. They pressed forward, weapons at low ready.

The ship's layout felt strangely familiar, like an aircraft carrier turned upside down. A non-functional elevator shaft forced them to climb down through ladder wells, moving deeper into the structure. And the deeper they went, the more unsettlingly human it felt.

They passed a briefing room which looked eerily similar to the one they had been in before the mission. Chairs bolted to the deck. A table positioned at the center. It was almost identical. Further in, a control room emerged, its monitors still humming with residual energy.

A navigation deck lay ahead, filled with familiar instrumentation made up of screens, control panels, even a layout mirroring Earth's naval command centers. It was more advanced, more refined, yet unmistakably recognizable. The realization crept in slowly. This wasn't some incomprehensible alien construct.

This was looking more and more like a near-peer instead of an alien presence.

A civilization not lightyears ahead, but closer. Uncomfortably close. The ship even had a large strategy table, weirdly similar to the devices used by the U.S. Navy—which resembled Ouija boards.

Briggs muttered, "Someone built this for function."

Edgar checked the status of the air quality. "It's okay to retract the helmets. Internal filtration seems to be working down here."

Rox nodded, surveying the room. "Humanoid function. Maybe these boogiemen weren't scary after all." He said retracting his visor, then his helmet.

"No more alien than us," Hawk bantered back, doing the same.

The team came upon a wall of simple, unassuming metallic cubes which were featureless at first glance. Each was about the size of a softball. But the longer Briggs stared at the array, the more unsettlingly complex they became. These weren't just objects.

Briggs reached out with a gloved finger. Hawk had said not to touch anything, but how could he resist? Their surfaces were smooth, like liquid metal, shifting between cool and warm to the touch. It was as if they were alive, adjusting to their environment. Briggs scratched a cube; the metal healed like water skinning over.

Another cube cracked and granulated under the glove of Hawk. It disintegrated into a pile of ash.

"Tombstones," Hawk said. He tapped a live one. "Transit Cores. Bodies turned into data, stored between the ticks of a clock. The best way to travel without time."

"And that one?" Briggs asked.

"Not coming home."

Looking closer, Briggs could see there had been a firefight in this room. "The others?" he asked himself aloud.

"Sanctuaries—suspended between reality and time in quantum flux." Hawk exhaled, motioning toward the empty husk in front of him as he whispered so only Briggs could hear.

"Maybe whoever was in there is still living their best life in an alternate universe." Rocco hoped.

Hawk glanced at Rocco. He nodded.

"These were the gods' solution for interstellar travel. No aging. No degradation. The only way to cross the void without time itself ripping you apart. This technology predates the builders of this ship. Far before them. Far before us."

Briggs felt a chill creep up his spine.

Hawk gestured to the fallen cubes. "There are three rings with this tech; the cubes were reverse engineered from them, like our suits from Trip's suit in the briefing packet. Not as good but an adequate facsimile. These weren't just crewmen in this Quantum Stasis Cube. This QSC contains lower deck officers."

If he understood what Hawk said, those officers either never made the trip, or three beings had escaped the QSC. Two were dead—the bodies they'd discovered near the breach. And the third?

Maybe the shape they'd seen earlier. If so, that meant one thing: at least one officer was still alive.

While Briggs was focusing his thoughts on the beings outside the cubes, Scotty appeared, and it seemed like he was still working out the tech. The guys joked it was his nerd-ism.

"Assuming you've got more mates inside, can we get these chaps out?" Scotty wondered.

"Oi, System's locked out from here. It copped a proper shagging. We'd need time and we don't bloody have it. Not our mission anyway, but..." Scotty squinted at the panel. "Maybe there's a way to take a crack at it from the bridge," Scotty guessed.

CHAPTER 24

Ring Bearer

Every push forward took time. Time was ticking down. The team arrived on another deck. A faint light flickered against a dust-streaked window overlooking what seemed to be the hangar deck.

Hawk paused, his eyes drawn to something unexpected. A handprint, faintly visible beneath the layers of grime, frozen in time.

It was small. Feminine.

His fingers hovered over it, hesitating for a brief moment before pressing his gloved palm against it. A wave of ghostly voices filled his mind—*Laughter. Celebration. The hum of engines. The sounds of a crew who had not drawn breath for millennia.*

Hawk snapped back to reality, his breath steady but his pulse hammering. Behind him, Badcock perceived his hesitation.

"Memories, Boss?"

Hawk didn't answer. He just turned away.

His voice came out gruff, strained. "Keep moving." The knot in his throat barely let the words escape.

Minutes later, they reached an open hatch leading to a mechanical staircase. Its design resembled a modern-day automated escalator. Now, it was lifeless. Silent. Another relic on a dead ship.

As Team Alpha and Bravo moved upward and farther into the *Menagerie,* more QSC cubes lined the walls. Every single one flashed red, a condition which Hawk had explained indicated failure. Except one. Scotty, the tech specialist gestured to it.

"Looks like a crew monitoring system. All red except for this lucky bastard." He paused. "Commander... I don't recon anymore of your mates are alive. The distress signal we picked up earlier was automated. Evi maybe?"

Hawk's jaw tightened; he wasn't buying it. "The ship is still trying to communicate with us."

The answer isn't here, Hawk told himself. *Not in this part of the ship.*

"What are we after, Sir?" Scotty asked.

Hawk looked around, trying to take in everything. It had to be here.

"A key," he said, his tone dismayed.

Hawk turned to Lieutenant Briggs. "Take Bravo and split off—gather as much intel as you can. There's lots of interference in here, so comms will be spotty. "

Briggs gave a quick nod. "Roger that. Don't wander too far, got it." The two bumped fists.

Hawk turned back to his team. "Team Alpha, we're heading to the bridge."

The team pressed on until they reached blast doors which whooshed open, revealing the battered heart of the ship. Team Alpha was posted up, rifles at high ready. They flowed in and cleared the room one by one.

Alarmingly, unlike the lifeless corridors behind them, the bridge was still alive with activity. Dim control panels flickered on and off, their energy failing, fighting to hold on.

Consoles displayed cascading streams of data, some critical, some corrupted. At the far end, a massive central screen loomed—a stadium-sized monitor, pulsing with static. Hawk stepped forward cautiously, his hand hovering over the control panels. His movements were purposeful, as if he already knew what each control did.

As Hawk lingered at the controls, a soft hum filled the room as the ship seemed to recognize its new visitor. Panels flickered, lines of code and symbols erupted onto the massive main screen. An image bloomed, then, as if the ship itself sensed the team's presence, a woman's outline stepped through the light and into the room. The edges of it's pixels shearing as she stepped forward.

Alpha Team tensed, weapons raised.

"What the—?" Rocco muttered. *Early generation AVA?*

She wasn't real in a corporeal sense. She was the Evolved Flight Integration (EVI) peripheral unit—pre-AVA AI construct. Her lips moved, but the words were incomprehensible, an unrecognizable dialect. On the screen behind her, the quantum computer ran code, processing faster than the human eye could follow.

A single line appeared.

"Translating…"

Seconds later, her voice came through—clear, precise, and unmistakably human. "Video file corrupted."

Rocco looked at Hawk, suspicion flickering in his eyes. "You know what this is, don't you? You've been here before. The hints of memories."

Hawk didn't deny it.

"I was stationed here," he admitted aloud. And, to himself, he thought, *left behind while defending the ship's escape from Ki.*

He nodded, his gaze shifting. A floating tablet drifted into his path—he brushed it aside.

The ship's gravity was failing due to a sporadic quantum flux.

How long before a confrontation would be fought in zero-G? he asked himself. His thoughts were interrupted as the massive screen flickered.

"The Captain's log," a male voice announced and the image of a uniformed officer, presumably the captain, appeared.

A series of timestamps began scrolling—flashes of data, dates, records from another time, another world.

The log played.

"We've been boarded. If they reach Ki—"

Rocco had taken the weight off his feet moments after the Captains Log began. He shifted his weight on his butt to get more comfortable.

"We gotta get out of here and get this intel to the Brain Shed. That analyst nerd." He snapped his fingers. "Shifty Shift will love this shit. But now we got bigger problems, Boss."

"Yeah, like the mudda fuckas that boarded this boat. They trapped most of 'em but not before they fawked em up, sir. Between that and tha countdown we got problems."

"Agreed." Hawk said to Edgar. "At least we know why they took so long getting here."

"They had a battle and sacrificed themselves corrupting the enemy NAV-LINKS. No wormhole-bridge shortcuts for those assholes," Rocco said vindictively.

"They thought they got away clean."

Hawk looked at the obvious. "Apparently not."

"They didn't find enough juice to reboot their AI and fix the NAV-LINKS. They've been running the Ninety-Nine this whole time. If they have any fuel left, they'll use it for one final assault—a wormhole breach. It's safe to say the main armada isn't far behind."

"Maybe, but then why haven't they shown up in force yet? Advantage us."

"So, how's 'bout we get rollin' and quantum frickin' leap the quantum priz-na's from dare quantum entanglement bool shit and scram before those things find us?"

Rocco looked at Edgar the way he usually looked at Edgar and shook his head. "What the fuck did you just say?"

Hawk tapped Edgar on the shoulder. "Copy that. I read you loud and clear."

"Thanks, Boss. Rocco, ya dumma than you look."

Rocco gave Edgar the bird. *The smartest dumb guy he knew.* And he noticed a set of cubes in what appeared to be a command quarters for the Captain on the deck.

"Another cube thing that's still powered up." Rocco pointed. "Back there," he said walking towards them. "So, these guys always come out bare? They shouldn't be armed then, right?"

"Nothing non-organic can go in. They need something with bio-mechanical implants or nanotech-infused armor. They wouldn't be wearing that up here." Hawk tapped the soft edge of the Alpha Skin suit around his neck. "Like what we're wearing. Except ours? Antiquated—compared to what they had." His tone was dismissive, almost irritated. "Non-organic matter, lacking its genetic blueprint, becomes unstable during transit."

"Antiquated? Come off it, Boss, ours are prototypes," Rocco exhaled, piecing the pieces together. "So, human DNA's got quantum markers acting like a bloody reassembly blueprint?"

Hawk met his gaze. "Affirmative. If you want to reconstruct precisely when you phase-shift into a hostile environment—and keep your clothes on—you'd better have the right genetic markers built into your clothing."

A new error message flashed across the screen.

LOG CORRUPTED. SYSTEM FAILURE.
ALERT! ALERT! ALERT!
The room flashed red.
QUARANTINE BREACH—DECK 35. HOSTILE ENTITY.
DEFENSIVE PROTOCOLS: ARMED.
SELF DESTRUCT: 30:00 (SILENT).

"Shit! We're too late." Rocco blurted, his eyes darting between the flashing screen and Hawk. "Deck 35? What deck are we on?"

Edgar's voice was steady, firm. "Deck 7."

"Thank God," said Rocco.

"Bravos 21, sir. That means Bravo Team is closer to the danger."

At a command from Hawk, the team synced their timers to the countdown.

Behind them, a green light flickered to life.

"What did you touch, Rocco?" Hawk yelled.

"I didn't touch shit, sir." He said reacting to Hawk's call out.

A black sphere hovered just above the floor, air snapped. A body materialized from thin air. A naked, inked, pale humanoid—not an image—an actual being—a frail old man!

Alpha Team snapped their weapons up instantly—but the figure didn't react. Instead, he simply rolled over, coughing, shivering. Slowly, he pushed himself up onto his knees, his breath ragged. His hair was long and unkempt—his body covered in cryptic tattoos.

"Don't friggin' move, asshole!" Edgar ordered.

His eyes—Intelligent. Desperate.

"He won't understand, yet," Hawk said, moving into the line of fire.

Hawk rushed forward and extended his hand to help the old man up.

But he didn't need help. His frail body drifted upward, gravity once again ignoring Earth's rules. After a brief, weightless ballet, his feet found the floor.

"Safe 'em and hang 'em," Hawk ordered.

The team lowered their rifles but stayed on edge.

The figure looked up at Hawk and spoke. A language none of them should have understood, except Hawk. Reaching into a Med-kit hanging on the wall, Hawk pulled out a hypo-spray similar to what they used for the polio vaccines. He blasted the serum into the old man.

The old man grimaced.

Gravity dragged at his body, a weight he wasn't used to, like a ball and chain. Surrounded by the old-world tech, he—just like Mylitta—began to find his voice but quicker. This time, aided by Evi's knowledge passing through his gray matter and the serum, the process was faster. In an instant, his words became English.

"Paradise?" the man asked.

Hawk nodded.

"It's still here?"

"A shell of what it was," Hawk admitted. "But the resistance is still alive."

The figure's expression darkened, and he suddenly continued in a firm voice.

"If you want to survive here—we have to go. Now! I trapped them in a QSC but, if I have been reactivated, the containment has failed. The only thing holding them back is a fire door. My men?"

"There were still some QSCs but if you appeared they may have too down in the lower decks." Hawk stiffened. "We can't leave without your sister," he reminded the man.

The old man held his head tightly, trying to squeeze out every memory he could to fend off the spatial dementia which threatened to grip him.

"She has the key—she *is* the key," Hawk spat urgently.

The figure hesitated, conflict flashing in his eyes.

"She was on the lower decks; there's no time," the old man declared. "We can't reach her before those things find us." His face was full of grief, his hands raised, trying to console himself. His gesture suggested his sister would have to be sacrificed for the good of all mankind.

"I have a key." he declared. You're going to have to choose—it's her or the world."

"We aren't finished yet. Prepare to break out in ten. I'm not leaving without her or my other team." Hawk stated. "Breakout in ten."

CHAPTER 25

The Janitor's Warning

Hawk pinged the net again. Static. Hawk called several times. Five minutes burned. His gut told him to get the old man off the ship. Even if that meant sacrificing Bravo. He stood there, catching his breath, his gaze locking onto Rocco's. Desperation oozing from every pore.

Rocco met his stare. "The mission comes first. We all signed up for this."

The frail old man who had materialized out of nowhere also insisted they must go.

The familiar glint caught Hawk's eye. On the man's hand was a Mini Mii ring—nearly identical to the piece Siegfried had unwittingly found, but older and less refined. It looked like one he and Ava walked out of his tomb with many years ago.

Hawk's grip tightened on his rifle. Everything was starting to piece together, come to a head.

The old man gathered his wits and straightened up. "The clock is ticking." His eyes flickered to the control panels. "You have to make a decision." Moving with unexpected speed, he grabbed Hawk's arm. "They will be hunting us. They may already be hunting your men."

Elsewhere on Deck 35. Three decks below the Sun Reactor, a sealed bulkhead glowed white. A figure with necrotic slate gray skin held a plasma torch.

Metal peeled and wept; a bright red slag fell in orange ropes, then settled in yellow globs of molten ore cooled to a black pile on the deck. A second claw forced through from the other side of the breach. The grasping hand didn't flinch from the heat. It yanked at the breach. Pulling, scraping, and pushing back and forth vigorously, widening the opening.

Another clawed hand joined in. Tearing. Ripping. Shredding. More hands followed until twenty hands clawed through the breach, their razor-sharp talons working for the same goal—escape. The metal groaned, straining to hold, but it was no use. The door was failing.

The torchbearer stepped back, its lips curling into a demonic grin.

His band of Udug Pirates trampled each other pushing their way through the ever-widening breach. Their movements were like an oil slick pouring from an engine block. There would be no quarter. No walking the plank.

If anything, they were making chum—preparing bait to harvest intruders.

Rocco exchanged looks with the rest of Alpha Team, gripping his rifle as it tried to float away, barely tethered to him by his sling. Time was fleeting and gravity was failing.

"SSE, sir?"

Hawk nodded, "Proceed with Sensitive Site Exploitation. We'll leave Bravo." The weight of his decision cut deep. "We need to gather as much intel as possible before we exfil. We have no idea if our firepower and armor can match a Udug fire team. But we have to find out some time," his voice took on a steady tone of grim resolve. "And now is as good a time as any."

As if reacting to Hawk's decision, Evi froze. A new warning coming from her digital lips. She faced him, voice even.

WARNING: Containment deck failed. Fusion core at 60%.

Implosion likelihood—97%. Sun Reactor destabilization imminent.

Quarantine breach—Deck 35. Boarding parasites escaped.

Hostile lifeforms executing released crewmen.

Rings compromised. Intruders routing to Primary Weapon Control.

CME arrival: 74 hours.

"They move quickly," the old man said.

Evi turned to him. She knelt beside him and looked up at Hawk. "Captain. You have exactly twenty-eight minutes to evacuate before the Reactor implodes."

Hawk whirled toward the tech specialist. "How long to the nearest hatch?"

"We took nearly an hour coming in, Boss," the tech answered.

Hawk gritted his teeth. "We don't have an hour." He tried the Troop Net again. "Bravo Team, damn it, do you read? ROCKSLIDE! ROCKSLIDE! ROCKSLIDE! You need to EXFIL immediately! I repeat—"

Emergency klaxons blared in the background—then, an eerie silence, followed by a blackout. For a moment, nothing.

Evi worked some coding magic to get the emergency lights on. As they flickered back on, the room was illuminated in a bloodred light.

Their situation was devolving, but Hawk maintained his composure hoping it would put the rest of the team at ease.

"Briggs, do you copy?" Hawk tried Troop Net one last time. More static. He looked at his men knowing they needed to get moving. "Rocco, we breakout in five mikes."

"Roger, breakout in five."

The old man was already moving, strapping on an alien Alpha Skin suit. Hawk grabbed him by the collar.

"Where's the nearest escape hatch on this deck?"

In answer, the old man slapped at a wall schematic. "Nearest hatch is one deck over, but the main corridor was sealed thirty years ago after a hull breach."

Hawk turned to his team.

"No scenic tour. We breach the outer shell. Suits up."

Alpha activated their nanotech-fueled suits. The armor swarmed over them, assembling piece by piece, encasing them once again.

It was like watching armored fire ants consume their prey.

The old man stopped them and shouted, "Wait!" His voice sharpened with command as he turned to the ship's AI. "Evi, cut all lighting except for emergency hatch paths. Pulse the emergency lighting in the direction we need to go."

At once, the corridors flickered to life, a rhythmic glow pulsating along the correct path like a heartbeat in the darkness.

Edgar cheerfully gleamed, "Breadcrumbs. This should help Bravo Team find tha way out." His expression darkened. "Unfortunately, it'll also help tha Udug track em."

Rocco exhaled. "Game on. What happens when the countdown hits zero? What's this Sun Reactor and why do you make it sound so ominous?"

The old man glanced at him. "There is an artificial sun in The Garden. Our fusion reactor."

Edgar froze. "Of course there is." The notion was ridiculous. "In'a ship that runs on majik, tha ship's core... a freakin' star? Why da'fuk not?"

The old man's voice was grim. "It will implode into a micro-singularity."

Rocco's eyebrows twitched. "That's gonna be real bad. Right?"

The old man deadpanned. "Imagine being stuck on this ship and ripped apart at the subatomic level in an Event Horizon for an eternity."

"Sounds like hell," Edgar sneered.

Rocco scanned the room feverishly and asked, "What's its yield? What's our minimum safe distance?"

"Off the ship. Not here." The old man's response was grim, matter of fact. "The implosion will suspend time for anyone still inside here, until its mass neutralizes. Away from it?" A pause. "Maybe some spatial distortions lingering."

Hawk's voice was sharp, cutting. "No choice then! We run! Now!" His face twisted with pain. His other team—possibly doomed. Mylitta—doomed. And if they didn't get out of here—they'd be doomed too.

As Alpha Team stacked up for exfil, a deep, grating growl echoed from the shadows of the ship. Hawk listened as the hull groaned, the walls flexing under unseen pressure.

"The implosion begins," the old man said, his lips stiff, his gaze sweeping the room one last time.

"Breakout, breakout!" Rocco ordered.

They were on the move and still had no contact with Bravo.

The old man ran behind Hawk. "Use your head. Think outside the box. The ring could give you a formidable advantage against them."

Hawk took a big breath, relieving his anxiety. "How's that, old man? You're the one holding it."

"It will give abilities which your suits alone don't possess." He held out his hand. "I'm too slow to wield it. Put it on and it'll optimize your HUD and armor and give your AI faster intent-to-act."

"DNA keying?" Hawk asked.

"A neural interface. Your bioelectric field becomes the carrier. The ring amplifies."

They were still on the move.

Hawk hesitated, staring at the ring. He'd held such a ring before, and he knew it held enough power to recharge a Sun Drive.

The old man continued to urge Hawk to take the ring. Hawk rolled the ring between his fingers and then over the tops and back again. "Like a super soldier?"

The old man shook his head. "No, son. Those you are about to face are the super soldiers. Even with that," the old man said, "you're not their equal. Be clever."

The old man's muscles were on fire, shaking off the stiffness after being restrained for centuries. His gaze flickered over their weapons while they hurried on, his brows furrowing.

"Those are crude." He said critically.

Hawk cracked a smile and deadpanned, "Best we have for this time period, old man."

The old man sighed. "Better to sharpen some sticks," he joked with a laugh. "You are not prepared for the Udug."

Hawk hesitated, "We stopped one before."

Overhearing this boast, some of the team turned toward him, eyes sharp with surprise.

The old man studied Hawk carefully. "And you killed it?"

Hawk turned to him midstride. "No," Hawk's voice was cold, distant. "We only stopped it long enough to escape. But we didn't have this kind of firepower."

The old man nodded, "You didn't kill one, then. You survived it."

Edgar dropped back. He had to speak, and his voice was cautious. "Who are the Udug?"

The old man didn't hesitate, but his answer was cryptic, shrouded in ambiguity.

"A legion of many. And a legion of one. They are the Father of light and darkness. They exist beyond the veil, beyond the abyss of nothingness."

Rocco joined them. "Is this guy fucking kidding us right now?" His sneer deepened.

"Where do the rings lead?" Rocco scowled.

"To the only weapon on Earth that can stop Enlil's fleet."

Hawk was less perplexed, "Where is this weapon?"

"That's why they didn't scrap this ship." The old man smirked, "They're looking for it too."

"If they stop the weapon, it will leave the front door wide open," Rocco asserted. "We have to get that Mini Mii thing off this ship no matter the cost."

Alpha Team ran on, reached the next deck, and so far, so good. No Udug boarding party. Every corridor they entered, the team moved like a steady current, fluid yet braced for an ambush. The word "CLEAR" was beginning to feel like filling in the same answer on a Scantron test, penciling in those tiny bubbles, hoping it was right while knowing, eventually, it wouldn't be.

Minutes passed again. They reached a hatch, not an exit, but it would turn out to be the entrance to a gold mine. Their crude "mid" weapons lived rent-free in the old man's head. But he had a surprise for them. The old man moved swiftly, bypassing the security panel. A hiss of pressurized air escaped as the armory door slid open.

Inside—racks of advanced energy weapons, lightweight rifles, and sleek alien tech gleamed under the dim emergency lights, casting an eerie glow over their prize.

Rocco whistled low. "Now this is what I'm talking about!"

The old man grabbed a handle, and with a mere thought, the weapon unfolded into a sleek particle accelerator rifle.

Rocco took a step back. "Oh, that is badass." He said with a shit-eating grin.

Hawk turned to the team. "Take what you can carry. We need to keep moving."

They stuffed their backpacks with as many Synth and Igigi rifles as they could manage.

A new alarm blared.

"Now what?"

The lights flickered red. A cold automated voice filled the ship.

And that voice was close.

CHAPTER 26

The BLUF

At Bravo Team's position, Briggs worked the Troop Net: "Hawk, come back. Repeat your last. I say again, repeat." Briggs clenched his jaw, gripping his rifle tighter.

Static.

"Brilliant." Staackman whispered to himself.

Briggs' nostrils flared. His voice rose, edged with frustration. "Son of a bitch."

The anger didn't last; it bled into concern. His expression shifted as the weight of the situation set in.

"Did he just order EVAC?" He turned to Scotty, tension creeping into his voice.

Staackman nodded grimly. "Sure as hell sounded like it. It was rough, but I heard 'Rockslide,' Boss."

Briggs' stomach tightened. "Something has happened." He straightened and calculated their time in.

The bulkheads and alien radiation were wreaking havoc on their signals. They'd strayed too far apart. The only thing they could trust now was the countdown ticking in their heads—20 minutes—the set EVAC time for Rockslide.

Suddenly, the lights cut off.

For a heartbeat, total darkness.

A moment later the emergency-red-lighting bathed the corridor, washing out every other color. The red was followed by a strobe of white light flickering directionally. A path.

Briggs turned to his team, his voice sharp but calm. "Here's the bottom line up front. Rockslide has been called. We can't go back the way we came—not enough time. I don't think it's a coincidence we have a path to follow. Trap or not, we press forward. Everyone grab your gear. Chief, you take point. Eyes up. Breakout, breakout!"

No one hesitated. But the question lingered—how did they know Alpha was leading them?

The answer? They had a 50/50 chance of making it out.

And if it wasn't Alpha? It didn't matter.

They stacked into formation, weapons ready, rapidly checking their bearings.

Briggs took a few seconds to scan the flickering emergency lights, noting their synchronized pattern. Briggs quickly checked the digital map he had ripped off the wall earlier. The route would take them straight through the engine section on Deck 12C. Briggs double-tapped their first intersection. A temp reading on the map popped up. It wasn't good.

They were headed for hell.

Briggs exhaled sharply.

"Looks like we're walking through fire," he decided. "But no choice! Let's move!"

The temperature skyrocketed as they rushed through the ship's mechanical underbelly. The air turned thick, acrid with steam and burning metal. Sweat poured from their bodies, recycled by their suit. Rodriguez knew this heat all too well. They kept their visors open, closing them while on a dead run would reduce their oxygen intake and only slow them down. But the stinging in their eyes intensified. Their lungs burned with every breath.

Staackman checked the map's thermal readout.

120 degrees.

Rising.

"Helmets up," Briggs ordered, "or we're gonna cook in here!"

"Damn, these things are claustrophobic," Rodriguez complained as his thoughts turned to stories of his familia crossing the border in the Texas heat. Thirty people died in the Coyote's truck from the heat; his parents were spared. Later, he only skipped the deportations thanks to his enlistment in the service.

Scotty led them around a massive reactor, moving fast—AI enhanced vision fizzled. "Bloody hell!" No more seeing through walls. *Dragon Fly* just took a shite."

Rodriguez's thoughts were running wild. The strobe light leading them out was too diffused to make heads-or-tails of which direction to go. They were surrounded by unknown computers, machines, and hydro-cooling piping.

"Ava? Help us out!" Rodriguez begged.

AVA's appeared from each of their suits and each took separate directions using the last of the previous scans. But their range was limited to *Dragon Fly's* unfinished mapping of the compartment.

"Dragon Fly's blind," Scotty said. *"Heat's fried the feed."*

"The beatings will continue until morale improves, gents," Staackman laughed.

"Best guess based on the incomplete map, the team should head this way," Scotty's Ava directed. "Follow me," she said walking down the best path.

"Hold!" Scotty pointed with his muzzle.

What all of the AVA's were seeing was highlighted in their HUD feed giving them X-ray vision. The outline of a figure appeared momentarily and then was gone.

He froze in place. His rifle snapped up, barrel aimed forward. His heartbeat pounded in his ears.

"I don't see anything," Rodriguez countered. He wasn't interested in stopping.

"Something was there though. A shadow. A shape crouched in the mist. Ava marked it."

It was only there for a second before it slipped away. A hissing rasp, low and deep, echoed through the machinery. A growl followed, throaty, and inhuman.

Briggs moved up next to him, whispering—"What was it, Chief? Why are we stopping?"

Scotty kept his voice low and steady. "I saw it, mate—something in the mist, and so did Staackman's Ava."

Rodriguez spent a second in prayer. "Ava? Help us out, woman."

Rodriguez Ava worked to unclutter the augmented reality for him, but it was a no-go. "The heat is interfering with the Eagle Eye sensors integrated in your suit. My enhanced perception mode has become spoofed. Hive mind disconnected."

Further up, heavy gas was pouring in. It didn't matter what it was because the suits would protect them, but it hampered their visual acuity.

Briggs Ava stated. "Your team has meandered into a kill box, prepare for contact."

"That thing was tall—maybe a man, maybe not—but anyway twice as tall as us."

Fire Team Bravo formed up behind the two men and a deep silence settled over the men.

Briggs' adrenaline was spiking. "Everyone stay sharp and prepare for CBDR." (Close Bearing, Decreasing Range.)

Something was in their path and whatever was out there—Briggs was convinced the ambush was seconds away.

CHAPTER 27

Sweep, Clear, Die

Fire Team Bravo moved forward, weapons sweeping left to right, they covered every possible ambush point. Quick flashes from their lights stabbed into the thick, blinding fog, but the vapor molecules scattered the beams, turning everything into a whitewashed haze. Visibility was zero.

And as if things couldn't get any worse—they had to get a move on, and this new enemy was slowing them down.

"AVA is kaput, brothers. Ava can't see through this crap any better than us."

"Stay tight, Rodriguez. We're moving." Briggs ordered.

The deck was covered in a yellow residue, possibly fallout from the gas as it settled. Caustic. Oily. It clung to their boots, every step leaving behind faint, corrosive footprints.

"We're leaving breadcrumbs." Rodriguez said noticing the trail behind them. "Holy shit, other footprints." He added in a panic, his eyes bulging at the size of those feet.

They weren't chemists.

But they knew one thing—this shit wasn't natural. The ship was dying.

Briggs was desperate for clarity. He had them switch to night vision—useless. The haze absorbed the infrared. Switching to thermal— worse. Heat ghosts swarmed their displays—every computer system a false target.

"Damn Mark III's," Briggs mumbled under his breath.

Too much ambient heat. Too many false positives. They were walking blind.

After what seemed like an eternity, there was a break in the shifting wall of vapor—movement perpendicular to them.

"There! The corridor next to us. I see it when the light turns." Scotty double-timed, cutting toward an open hatch.

You know what they say about hell? If you're in it, bugger off, stupid.

Finally—he sensed a clearing.

Scotty crouched at the hatchway, weapon raised, scanning the void ahead. The deep, yellow fog rolled inside, settling at their feet. Visibility at last.

He whispered over the Troop Net. "Clear, Boss." He shuffled to the ladder.

The team advanced. It came. The air stirred. The fog shifted from another hatch being opened. Visibility lost again.

The creature lurking in the dense vapor, completely unseen at first.

Something was waiting there, looking for him, but Scotty saw it first. Or did he?

Is this thing picking me out? he asked himself. *Am I the weak link it wants to wound—to slow the whole team down? Or does this cheeky cunt think I'm the biggest, baddest threat?*

The dark shape slithered through the mist—predatory—its speed increased until it blitzed them with incredible suddenness and dexterity. Scotty barely had time to avoid a blackened hand with long bile crusted nails laced with venom.

Scotty threw himself back just in time.

The claws slashed through the air where his throat had been. A nano-link of armor—the size of a fleck of dust—snapped off, disintegrating.

Briggs arrived in the nick of time to see it all, and he didn't hesitate.

"CONTACT!" he shouted.

The corridor erupted in bright flashes. Computer systems destroyed. Water cooling tubes burst open, quickly turning to steam.

Bullets ripped through the mist—rounds pinged off metal—shards of shrapnel cartwheeled in all directions. Sparks burst like tiny sparklers on the Fourth of July—flashes of orange and white against the yellow fog. Metallic debris sprayed everything.

But the thing was already behind cover.

"Cease fire!" Briggs yelled in their headsets.

Apparitions formed in the thick steam-filled air. They were surrounded.

Briggs' breathing was heavy. Everyone's breath was strained behind their masks. Fight or flight had kicked into overdrive. Only training kept them from doing the one thing their instincts screamed for—run.

"Holy moly, too close..." one of the men exclaimed.

"Where the fuck did it go?" another voice asked.

Scotty didn't answer. His hands were shaking. He focused on keeping them still.

Briggs turned to question his men, his voice low and urgent. "Did we hit it?"

Staackman had no words, but his head was still on a swivel.

Scotty finished a quick set of Box Breathing. "I don't know, sir." He said with his heart-rate stabilizing. "That cheeky bastard was a colossal cunt for sure. I don't know what it is, but it's trouble, and we are right in the middle of it."

He'd hunted grizzlies in Alaska. He knew the size of a bear paw. This thing? Easily that big. Hunched over, it hadn't seemed like much of a threat in the shadows. But that reach—the distance it had lunged—those absurd measurements meant it was far taller than anyone had suspected.

Briggs grimaced. "I don't like not knowing, Chief."

"Neither do I," Scotty agreed. "No AVA, no *Dragon Fly;* we are on our own."

The team held formation. Waiting. Listening.

SLLS... situational awareness, stop, look, listen, and smell.

Any animal that big couldn't be silent. Could it? Deeper in the ship—a new sound and a second snarl. Lower. Louder. Additional growls incoming.

"No way the sound was random, mate," Scotty figured. "I could feel it, through the suit." He described it like echo-location, an intentional tactic of creatures testing, probing, and pinpointing.

Now it was coming closer.

Briggs checked his mag, half full; completed a press check to finished *admining* his rifle. He double-checked the location of his knife, making sure he hadn't yeeted or otherwise dropped it at some point. His knife was the one item he didn't want to yard-sale or misplace. Not if the enemy was coming in at arm's length.

"Be ready for hand to hand, brothers. We're about to earn every second of training."

They were no longer being hunted by one. They were being hunted by Legion.

"Move! Now!"

CHAPTER 28

Dances with Devils

Petty Officer Rodriguez moved quickly through the suffocating steam, sweeping left, right; up the ladder-well, down the ladder-well. Three men had already cleared this section. It should have been safe. It wasn't.

"Contact, movement!" Scotty hollered. He was looking down the corridor while Rodriguez was covering the next deck above them.

"Halt." Scotty demanded.

Rodriguez followed suit. "¡Alto! *¡Alto o disparo!*" he shouted louder.

"Mate, you reckon they speak bloody Spanish?" Scotty jabbed.

"¡Puta madre, cabrón hijo de puta! You think they understand your English any better?"

The creatures kept coming. Close enough to become a threat. Still too difficult to see. They opened fire. Unlike before, the group didn't dodge anything. One by one they fell.

"That was too easy." Briggs reluctantly grumbled. "Advance."

As they did earlier, they leapfrogged their way to the pile of corpses. Naked, steaming, bodies lay at their feet. They looked normal.

"Shit man, you think they were crew members from those Rubik's Cubes?" Staackman figured.

Rodriguez was still hunkered down in the rear, covering their six. He glanced quickly back and forth at his brothers then back to the darkness behind him. He was getting antsy and began creeping in reverse, point of aim down range. "I'm moving up," he whispered on the Troop Net.

His leg brushed next to an open ladder well, a scrape. His leg was caught. Fingers too long, too thin, claws too sharp, skin changing color like a chameleon to match the metal of the ladder well. A deep breath, his heart palpitated as the fingers constricted and began pulling.

"¡El diablo, el demonio me tiene! Argh," he cried out as he tried to brace himself from being taken.

The camouflaged hand grabbed his armored calf and squeezed. The razor-sharp claws cut through the nano-links in the armor like they were squeezing a banana.

Pain. The pressure of his own blood shot out like a ruptured fire hose, hot-red-oil, spraying across the deck. Rodriguez's body seized. Nerves on fire. His spine locked and he collapsed forward, slamming into the metal deck. Rodriguez's mind was a supernova of pain.

He shrieked. The others pivoted, locking in on his embattled position.

His hands reached—for his leg. But his leg wasn't there. The suit knew its job and ran an internal tourniquet above the bleed. His fingers clutched at nothing, touching only the slick, torn edge of his own flesh where bone should have been. The nanite links unraveled, spilling off like individual grains of brown sugar, the clump crumbling under its own weight.

His jaw slammed into the visor when his face hit the deck. ND, (Negligent Discharge). His neurology and his weapon gone haywire. *Híjole!*

Fragments of metal tumbled in the air. The deck shredded as multiple rounds carved out the path of least resistance.

The barrel tilted dangerously under him—and fired another negligent salvo.

The high-caliber round punched through—armor. Throat. Jaw. Brain. The back of his helmet deformed but held.

Briggs, Scotty, and Staackman spun toward the screaming, then shots, their own weapons raised. But it was too late. Rodriguez's body was already being dragged into the darkness of the ladder-well.

His rifle clattered against the floor—the sling tangled in his remains. A flash of motion below. Staackman saw it. He moved quickly, dropping into a stable stance, aiming down the darkened shaft. For a split second, he locked eyes with something inhuman. Before he could squeeze off a round, the gravity failed him.

Weightless for a second, he had a good look at those eyes. Black and bloodshot, they sat recessed in the gaunt, pale face.

He tried to get the reticle on target but that was all it took. By the time Staackman fired, the creature was already gone.

His Boombox howled, ripping through metal—molten holes leading the path down the shredded deck. But the rounds hit nothing. Like a rocket, the rounds pushed him back in the air until he reached a pocket of normality, falling to the deck like a rock.

Staackman swallowed hard. Men don't move that fast. Men stumble. Men fall. Men don't drag 300 pounds of deadweight and gear like a bodach through the mist.

"What was that?" Briggs anxiously called out. "He's gone man, move."

Staackman didn't answer. They weren't hunting these demons.

These demons were hunting Bravo.

And now the ship created a new anti-gravitic obstacle they would have to battle on the way out.

Briggs barked: "SHIT, *that was only one!* Can it get any worse than this?"

They sprinted down the gangway, but Staackman suddenly stopped short.

"Oh, shit," he gulped.

Up ahead—a new threat was waiting for them. *The sons of bitches are toying with us,* Briggs figured. Like an aggressive amoeba, the boarding party was tightening the noose.

A tall, bony silhouette blocked the next hatch which seemed to lead to a larger cargo hold or cabin, the directional strobing lights running right through its path. Its breathing was slow, controlled. Shadows hid its true likeness. But the damned thing grinned big enough to see it. The claw-like nails flexed, extending longer and razor-sharp. And the claws were filthy, giving a clear impression that just a cut could cause a life-threatening infection.

This part of the ship was cooler. The air thinner. Colder. Gravity anomalies almost visible in the air.

Scotty shivered for a second, then he set his jaw. He figured if they were going to die, he might as well insult the thing. Why not give its ego a good shot? His lips twisted into a sneer, the corners of his mouth pulling downward in pure, utter contempt. Hatred.

"It's cold in this section, eh?" he asked the creature.

The shadow shifted. The creature stepped forward through the hatch. Stretching. Its grotesque form unfolding to fill the large gangway.

It had a thin tuft of hair sitting between two small, horn-like protrusions on its skull. It's manhood—a snake of an appendage—coiled down its leg. Steam rose from its hot, humid flesh.

Briggs smirked upside down. "It doesn't look very cold, Scotty."

"Hell, 50/50 shot," Scotty joked. "Damn, actually impressive," he remarked with mock sincerity.

But the thing wasn't merely standing there. It was studying them. Scotty could almost imagine the creature's thoughts: *Such crude tech on these men. Their reverse engineered Second Skin armor. Inferior. Not up to snuff.*

It seemed confident—like a predator calculating its next move. Like it had already decided how this would end.

Scotty dropped to one knee. Staackman braced forward, rifle leveled. Briggs covered their rear.

Suppressed bursts of gunfire tore through the mist and smoke. The bullets should have hit home. The eight-foot-plus creature leaped cognitively fast but still caught a couple rounds.

With a gravity assist, the blur of blackened muscle and bone—there one second, gone the next—vanished into the shadows from the ceiling. Staackman swore, reloading in frustration.

"Damn, that thing is quick."

"Yeah, but we hit it," Scotty told Staackman.

Scotty flicked his electronic map online, his hands shaking slightly. "They're like cuttlefish, mate. See the color shifting in their skin? Chameleonic. Adaptive. They could blend into your mum's cheeky arse at five paces."

Briggs glanced over his shoulder. "Never mind that. Where the hell are we?"

Scotty cleared his throat. No spit. The frog in the throat was there to stay. "Nine hundred meters to exfil." His voice felt dry, hoarse. They'd be lucky getting halfway. "We've got to drop to Deck 11. Hatch on our starboard side, we take that."

"Bypass the fucking things," Briggs decided. "What's between us and the escape hatch?"

Scotty's face grew pale.

Briggs asked again, sharper this time.

"The main reactor, sir." He didn't know what the reactor meant for them. But considering a damaged ship and an emergency EXFIL, there was a good chance they didn't want to be anywhere near a reactor. "It's something called a Sun Reactor."

Briggs exhaled. "Shit. If we get out of this alive, we'll be sterile as a rock." Briggs started to add something—but he stopped short, and his eyes widened in horror. "Staackman! Behind you!"

Even though the shout died in his throat, muffled by his visor, Staackman heard him clear as glass over the Troop Net. Briggs tried to cover Staackman, rifle coming up—but he was too slow. No matter how hard Briggs tried to raise his weapon, no matter how fast his muscles screamed to move, it wasn't fast enough.

Staackman saw Briggs' lips move—then his eyes flicked to the reflection on Briggs' visor. The creature was behind Staackman and not just behind him; it was close—inside the ventilation port. Blending, adaptive skin, the patience of a tick, the stoic stare of a crocodile. Only the smallest puff of steam betrayed its presence. It waited patiently before pouncing. The clawed hand blurred as it moved with exceptional speed. With violence of action, it punched through the metal slats, bursting from the vent like a trapdoor spider attacking prey.

Its massive hands wrapped around Staackman's helmet—encompassing his jaw—surrounding his skull. It tightened its grip, before giving one swift pull.

A vile crack sounded in their comms—the sharp snap of vertebrae breaking. The suit's armor couldn't stop the strong creature as it ripped Staackman's head off his shoulders. It retreated into the shaft from where it appeared.

His body stood erect, twitching—only collapsing when it figured out it was dead. The lifeless, armored husk clunked against the cold metal floor. The damaged part of the suit disintegrated, nano-armor collapsing around the wound like ash.

The vent rattled. Briggs yanked a grenade from his rig—pulled the pin. Dropped it in the duct. Then he lobbed another. And another. "Fire in the hole!"

Large consecutive explosions ripped off.

Flames erupted from the vent, belching black smoke. The walls trembled with the force of the blasts. Scotty and Briggs were already moving. A dead sprint. Their boots pounded metal, the armor on their shoulders bouncing off the walls as they cut sharp turns, heading for the escape hatch.

Behind them—shadows. Many. A horde.

They were gaining quickly.

Briggs glanced back. His chest tightened. Too fast. Too many.

"Don't slow down!" he warned Scotty, voice piercing with urgency.

Because if they slowed—it was over.

Seconds later, Briggs lost his footing and stumbled over something on the deck. Scotty reached down, grabbed Briggs by the arm and screamed—

"MOVE, sir! NOW!"

Scotty fired wildly behind him, the rifle kicking against his shoulder. He could hear the hits—the splats were audible, wet and meaty. Like a paddle slapping against a slab of beef hanging from the ceiling. A sickening, visceral smack telling them one thing—the shots were hitting home. But it wasn't stopping them. The creatures weren't even slowing down. He had to find a soft spot to hit on them but there was no time for experimentation.

Varoom went the Metal Storm Rifle. More slaps. Thick. Wet. Like flesh bursting open. But the shapes in the dark kept coming.

Scotty posted up at a corner, rifle snapping up, his MSR's electronic bursts slicing through the mist and shadow. Those shots landed. Two of the monsters jerked violently, spasming—collapsing. But the others? Seemingly unaffected.

"I'm almost Winchester, sir." Scotty patted his nearly empty weapon.

"Yeah, we got problems." Briggs agreed as he reached the corner.

His hands were already working, setting a charge against the bulkhead. No hesitation. No time. Briggs left his charge in place and wheeled away. Scotty fired one more round, then pivoted, sprinting after Briggs. They hit the deck running, full sprint. Behind them—the chittering grew louder. And the shadows kept coming.

Boom!

Not as loud as the grenades but loud enough.

Briggs and Scotty burst through the final hatch, slamming it shut behind them. Their lungs burned. Their muscles ached. Their bodies screamed for rest. But the moment their eyes adjusted, they realized this wasn't any reactor room they were prepared to see.

The air was crisp, clean—so pure it felt alien. A stark contrast to the stench of burning circuits and blood they had left behind. A sky where no sky should be. Cautiously, they deactivated their helmets.

With a soft hiss of decompression, their visors retracted. The metallic plating of their suits shimmered, shifting like liquid metal, breaking down seamlessly into medium packs strapped to their backs. All that remained were their Alpha Suits—the 2nd SKN Mk III exoskeletons were stowed safely away. Relieved of their outer armor, they would be faster now but less resilient.

Briggs looked at Scotty. He shrugged. "Armor didn't stop them wankers anyway. Let's go."

Their gun-belts stayed firmly in place.

They weren't about to be caught defenseless.

The temperature had dropped drastically, cool enough to make Scotty's breath fog. There was a breeze. A real breeze. It whispered through the leaves of massive trees, their branches swaying gently as if bowing to some unseen force. Grass bent beneath their boots, soft, dewy, alive.

Beyond the rolling hills, a shoreline stretched toward a dark, endless ocean, the water lapping softly as if the ship itself was breathing.

Scotty's voice came as a whisper, almost afraid to break the illusion.

"How's this possible?" Because it shouldn't be.

Hypoxia maybe? A vessel the size of an aircraft carrier was large but, even so, there was no room for something this immense. And yet—here it was. An enormous bio-dome, a self-sustaining ecosystem, thriving inside the ship.

At its center—hung an artificial sun.

A radiant sphere of energy, suspended in an intricate lattice of invisible fields, pulsing like a heartbeat. It wasn't just light. It was power. A Sun Reactor. A source of life itself.

The ship fed from it. The crew would have survived because of it. The oxygen, the water, the very nutrients in the air—it all came from here.

Time and space were relative in this room. Inside this place, minutes could stretch into eternity. This was more than just a machine, more than just a sanctuary for crossing the endless desert of space.

This was *The Garden.*

The two men stood still for a time, mesmerized until reality pressed in on them and they looked closer. The artificial sun was fading. Weak. Dying. The tranquility of this place was wilting.

Scotty turned back to Briggs. "Is this real?" he asked. "Or is it bogging off?"

Briggs swallowed as a thought flickered in his head. His head shook side to side in disbelief.

At least we'll see a piece of heaven before we die, he told himself.

"Can't think like that," he muttered. "It doesn't matter. Keep moving. We're not out of the woods yet."

The danger would follow them. Even in the brightness of The Garden, the demons were coming. They would be hard to see. They would blend in. They would take cover. Find shadows where none should exist. Though eight feet tall, they would move with the silent grace of predators on the Serengeti, monstrous, calculating predators with a relentless hunger for murder.

Evil would enter this place of worship and Heaven wouldn't like it one bit.

Briggs and Scotty raced through The Garden, their boots tearing up sacred ground. Above them—something massive thundered through the ventilation shafts, smashing aside whatever dared to stand in its way. Their hatch held, but other hatches failed. Metal screamed. Panels buckled. The devil's demons were breaking in. Heaven's gates would be breached. And there was no stopping the plague of Locusts.

Briggs twisted mid-stride, raising his rifle. He sent several bursts down range.

Each shot counted. No wasted bullets. No wasted breath, getting more steps in with his pace quickening.

Scotty followed suit, his suppressor cover on fire, his heart slamming against his ribs. His barrel was almost disabled. His barrel was hot and shot out, he'd be lucky to group his shots.

Behind them, trees splintered apart, ancient and forgotten, the wood was torn asunder like brittle bones. Grass and dirt erupted into the air, ripped apart in the monster's wake.

The creatures galloped and sprinted, sometimes on two legs, then four, then two again—a horrifying, unnatural display of raw adaptability. They dodged between trees and ground cover, weaving their attack like apex hunters.

Some fell under the hail of bullets, bodies spasming, rolling, and dying but never crying out. But, if one went down, two more followed from behind.

As the men fired desperately, they observed an oddity. A mechanized Garden Bot strode into the commotion, its metallic form moving with purpose, duty-bound to this sacred place—a slave to The Garden. It took time using its sensors to scan and process before being shut off by an impact. A demon's strike sent it spinning. Sparks erupting, it crashed into the dirt with its limbs still twitching and servos shrieking.

Another Garden Bot rushed to its aid, its mechanical voice warping in distress, cursing in a tongue neither man nor demon could understand.

Even in this place of purity, of balance, War had come. Hell had come. And the last remnants of Team Bravo were running out of time. The fleeing men reached a non-operational escalator, the final climb to the launch bay. Briggs didn't even pause.

"Go! Go! GO!" he shouted.

Scotty bounded up the escalator, moving fast. A loud, metallic shriek signaled that a vent cover was ripped open behind them. A creature was coming, stopping Briggs from advancing.

Briggs held them off on the ground level as long as he could. They were almost on him, a horde. *This is it,* he figured. His luck finally changed; he felt a wave of energy around him. A gravity anomaly.

He crouched into a jumping position and leapt with all his might making a successful zero-G leap, but so did the creatures. "Son of a..." While Scotty was surprised to see him, he was thankful.

"Kobe got nothing on you, Boss." Scotty tittered.

"We are almost to the hatch. Don't let up." Briggs whirled around, weapon raised. He gave a strong volley of fire at the creatures still hot on their heels. His voice was absolute. "We can't let these things get off the ship." Briggs barked.

Scotty didn't hesitate. There wasn't time. Didn't argue. They clasped hands. A warrior's grip.

Scotty uttered one last promise. "Valhalla, mate!"

Briggs turned back toward the dark maw of the vent, his rifle taking aim. A final stand. The creature lunged. And the fight was on.

CHAPTER 29

Last Man Standing

Time was up. Rain pummeled Fire Team Alpha as they emerged from an escape hatch, their boots not getting any traction on the slippery hull of the ship. The storm howled around them, making every step treacherous. Hawk left behind Bravo team and one of his assets, Mylitta—both betrayals eating at him. Bravo must be below decks in the fight of their lives.

A crackle in his earpiece.

Finally, the SOCOM Troop Net connection re-opened.

Stonegate's deep voice spoke like a god summoning his angels. "Commander, did you retrieve the package? Was the operation a success? Commander Hawk, do you read me, over?"

Hawk pressed a gloved hand to his helmet, breath coming in quick bursts.

"This is Hawk. I read you loud and clear. Affirmative. Package recovered."

Hawk gave a quick glance at his watch, heart pounding.

"The creatures are on board the ship; the infestation broke quarantine and it set off a self-destruct sequence. Fall back. I repeat, the ship is going to implode."

Quiet—

"ETA?" Stonegate asked.

Hawk swallowed hard. "One mike and eight seconds."

"Roger that. Evacuate immediately."

"Did Bravo beat us out?"

"Negative, EXFIL now."

Hawk turned. Debated going back in. Rocco grabbed the back of his arm.

"We need to get moving, sir. If Bravo is still alive, they'll get out."

Hawk gritted his teeth, looking toward the stormy horizon.

"If," Hawk repeated.

Hawk hauled the old man to his feet—his eyes locked on the last of his team as they moved down the ship's hull. A static charge was building. The air crackled. Ribbons of energy coiled and whipped through the atmosphere, tearing across the metal surface like corporeal beings.

The hull hummed, vibrating underfoot, a tempest brewing beneath them. Even with their insulated suits, the energy was a threat. A big one.

A sharp ripple of light twisted toward the team, jagged and hungry.

Rocco's voice ripped through comms. "Rox, MOVE!"

Too late.

A bolt of energy lashed out. Rox's body arched violently, his limbs seizing as pure electricity crawled through his suit. The armor screamed, crackling, overloading.

Detonation.

He was launched backward, his body a convulsing blur, flung over ninety feet. Straight into the mud. A sickening thud. A sharp sizzle of steam where he landed.

Silence.

"Shit!"

Two CIA Paramilitary operatives sprinted toward him, their boots splashing through the mud. They grabbed Rox by his arms, yanking him up, half-dragging him as they stumbled toward the tree line.

Hawk followed, lost his balance and fell but quickly regained his feet.

The rain pounded down, sheets of water blinding them, deafening them. They barely made it to cover. Hawk's eyes snapped back to the hatch they'd left behind.

Bravo, still MIA.

The fine crack of a seal, the thud of a locking mechanism withdrawing from its mortise, one hatch after another popped open followed by a barrage of gunfire. Those on the ground couldn't see anything. Lightning arcs were blinding.

Muzzles flashed. Echoes boomed across the storm. Scotty crawled out of an opening, breath ragged. He gave two good bursts, squeezing off what he had left. His rifle dropped to the sling.

Winchester.

No more ammo.

Scotty's hands snapped to his sidearm, ripping it free. A pistol—underwhelming on humans. Practically useless against the things he was firing on. But he had no other choice. And he wasn't going down without a fight.

Smoke was billowing out of the hatch. Visibility was nil.

Still inside, Briggs was moving backward toward the hatch, laying down suppressing fire. He could barely see. Below him, the Garden was ablaze.

Like Scotty, the lieutenant was almost out of ammo. Didn't matter—he'd go to a knife if he had to.

The creatures weren't letting up, but they were redirecting. Moving up the side of the walls. Some moving out of sight. Briggs assumed they were taking cover as the Sun Drive, which had once been fading, was increasing in size and heat. The Garden was an inferno now.

These creatures were expert killers—faster, sharper, relentless. Briggs' shots barely slowed them down. The creatures still heading at him straight on. From outside the hatch, Scotty continued firing blindly past Briggs, back through the black smoke, anything to keep the horde at bay.

"Dry, sir!" Scotty shouted.

He reared back and hurled his pistol into the darkness at the horde. Useless, but fuck it.

Briggs didn't pause. He was too focused on staying ahead of the demons. On getting out of the hatch or stopping the creatures from leaving. Scotty yelling, Brigg backing up, time running out.

Briggs slammed into the steps. He lost focus for a brief second before he scrambled back up on his feet, reaching—Scotty's hand was there.

A lifeline.

He was going to make it.

"Let's fucking go, you wanker! NOW!"

Scotty's muscles rippled inside his suit. His jaw clenched. The suit helped with the weight.

He yanked Briggs up with everything he had. If he hadn't been in his suit, his arm would have ripped clean from its socket. Briggs cursed, his suit straining to stay together, still trying to fire his MSR while being dragged out of the breach.

The stairs and walls exploded in a storm of sparks and shrapnel. Metal shredded apart. A Udug hot on Briggs' ass took hits—another behind it ducked away and scaled to another destination unknown.

"Where are they?" Briggs shouted. "There must be other breaches!"

Finger depressed on the trigger, his rifle fired out of breach. A clawed hand swiped. Briggs' rifle split in two.

BOOM!

A massive ball of black smoke billowed from the hatch of the ship. The hallway buckled, flames licking through the gaping holes in the walls.

The ship groaned. The Sun was collapsing in on itself. A vacuum formed around them, tearing at their bodies, sucking all the oxygen from the area, threatening to pull them back through the hatch. But they held on as the ship gave a final, metallic scream.

In the silence which followed, Briggs turned to Scotty, panting.

Scotty grinned, yanking him forward. "We got this shit! We made it! I reckon we're good, Boss!"

An ancient nocturnal voice echoed like whispers from the dead.

Inches away from Briggs—towering. Muscular. Its pale flesh stretched thin over unnatural bone. It was the Udug General.

Asag.

His eyes burned, reflecting the inferno around them.

"The end of humanity is upon you and your kind," it rasped.

Briggs didn't hesitate. He swung the remains of his rifle, smashing it into Asag's face. The Udug barely flinched. The inconvenience of the strike bothered him more than the sting of an insect.

The General swung back, hard and fast. Razor-sharp claws ripped through Briggs' helmet. Tore at his face. His jaw hammered. The last thing Briggs heard—before the flames devoured him, before the ship collapsed—was the sound of the universe swallowing him whole.

Hawk watched as Scotty came tumbling down the crater, his body rolling to a stop in the mud. Behind him, the *Menagerie* was folding in on itself. An invisible hand, impossibly vast, seemed to be crushing it slowly, like a beer can. Metal groaned and screamed as entire decks collapsed inward, layer after layer pulled into the singularity forming at its heart.

Scotty's suit was damaged—on the verge of failure. His visor cracked, the inside splattered with blood. He was alive. Barely. And the rest of Bravo?

Briggs was gone and only a fourth of the others had made it. A pair of Delta operators picked Scotty up and carried him to safety.

The ground shook. A deep, hollow sound rumbled from the ship's core, vibrating through the earth like the fading heartbeat of a dying god. Above them, the sky turned white. The clouds didn't just part—they split. Ripped apart by a shock wave, erasing color, erasing molecules, erasing anything it touched. The destruction left behind only light.

Hawk's eyes widened. "GET TO COVER! NOW!"

Soldiers dove for the ground. Some shielded themselves behind debris. Others stood frozen, mesmerized, watching.

The air warped, twisted, condensed. The detonation hit. A massive nuclear burst erupted outward, a tidal wave of pure annihilation, a wall of fire and force rushing toward them. And then—

It stopped.

The blast was caught mid-motion, stretching outward like a frozen explosion. Light suspended in place. A roaring vacuum of energy formed at its core. The ship, the shock wave, the fire, all of it had been halted and was being pulled backward. Reversed. The blast itself clawed at reality, trying to break free—but it couldn't escape.

It was sucked inward. The air screamed.

A howling vortex formed, pulling at the ground, at the soldiers, at everything. Men clawed at the dirt, fighting to stay grounded. Those who were too close and not anchored down were ripped off their feet and dragged toward the abyss. Arms outstretched. Screams vanished before they even left their throats.

Gone. Sucked into nothingness. Into another universe.

The sky burst into blinding flash. The *Menagerie* vanished.

Only silence remained—a silence so deep, so absolute, it felt as if the world itself had forgotten it existed. Time and space warp, the very fabric of reality, still reeling from what had just occurred. Most of the Menagerie was erased—but not everything.

A core, the size of a baseball, dropped to the top of the mound with the thud of a building. It was a perfect sphere. It weighed no more and no less than the entire *Menagerie*. And fragments of wreckage surrounding the event remained. Shattered wood, twisted metal, torn sheets of tarp—floated effortlessly above the ground. Adrift after physics had gone haywire.

Chunks of Sonny's trailer spun lazily in midair, its walls half-intact, an old license plate rotating like a drifting satellite.

What remained of the makeshift Forward Operating Base—ammo crates, shattered comms equipment, the skeletal remains of an FOB command tent—hung motionless in the air. A table, broken in half, twisted on an invisible axis. Ashes curled upward instead of falling. Gravity had forgotten them.

The universe hadn't decided yet if this place should exist at all.

Hawk stared at the supernatural sight, his body still, his mind straining to make sense of it. Scotty lay on a stretcher nearby. He exhaled sharply, shaking his head.

"What the hell?!" Scotty wondered.

No one answered. Because no one knew the answer.

Hawk slowly rose, staring at the empty void where the ship had been. Screams of securing the area echoed over the still site. A scorched crater smoldered with the heat of what should never have existed. Beside him, Scotty coughed, pulling himself upright. His voice was hoarse, raw.

"Did we win?" Scotty muttered.

Hawk exhaled slowly. His face was dark, unreadable. "Where's the rest of Bravo, Chief? And where are the Udug?" But Scotty blacked out again.

In the back of his mind, something nagged at Hawk. A terrible, sinking feeling. Bravo was gone, but the Udug weren't gone. They had never been gone. Shadows stirred in the distance. At the tree line, where the wind whispered through the barren field.

Figures seemed to dance between the trunks—or was it just branches swaying? Was it sinister movement? Or just a figment of his imagination? Hawk worried what was coming next.

CHAPTER 30

Astrobleme

In the open field where the *Menagerie* had existed, then vanished, the troops stood frozen—watching. Disbelief ran rampant. Edgar and Rocco stood by Hawk. Hawk sat next to Scotty. Corpsmen were rushing around.

A chopper was sent into recon from above. Systems started going erratic in the cockpit. "Abort, abort. We are losing lift." The engines cut out. "Auto-rotate our descent."

It was going to land hard. A controlled crash. To descend, the upward flow of air through the rotor kept them from dropping like a rock.

Rocco lifted his head to watch the chopper. His expectation of an auto-rotation crash was thwarted when the unanticipated happened. It came down like a feather.

Other objects seemed to gain atmospheric buoyancy as well. They had no scientific explanation for what was taking place, only that everything in the anomaly resembled sediment floating in placid water.

Only a dense metal core sitting on top of the mound remained. In the background of it all, the chopper floated to the ground.

Dom worked at rebuilding his recon station. "We're out of our depth, gents," Dom stated.

Hawk and what was left of his team marched toward the command center, the old man, their prisoner—or contact—in tow. Scotty limped under the wings of Rocco and Edgar, barely holding himself up. They all looked like hell. But Scotty? He was the worst for wear. The lone survivor of Fire Team Bravo, looking like he had crawled out of hell itself.

Commander Stonegate was waiting for them.

No wasted time. No pleasantries.

The strange electromagnetic field—or whatever twisted physics were at play—was still dissipating. It was slowing their extraction. But Stonegate couldn't wait. He needed answers now. Pearce's units were still in defensive positions, scanning for threats.

Their prisoner—or refugee, they weren't sure which yet—was zip-tied for everyone's safety. Including his own.

Stonegate's voice was sharp, clipped. "Commander, you and your men—along with the prisoner—will be escorted out of here as soon as it's clear."

Hawk nodded. "What took out the chopper? Are we under attack?"

"It appears as if an energy field is disrupting GPS systems," said Stonegate. "It's dissipating slowly but we are locked in a bubble. No-fly zone for now."

Hawk exhaled sharply. "Roger that. Where do you want him?" He gestured to the captive.

Stonegate's eyes narrowed. "He a threat?"

Hawk didn't hesitate. "No, sir. If he was, we'd be dead."

Stonegate pointed toward a tactical big rig parked near the command center—a hulking 18-wheeler, armored and outfitted with defensive systems, encrypted communications, and hardened against electromagnetic pulse attacks.

A rolling war room.

A mobile command center.

It was a rig allowing a VIP like the President to coordinate nuclear retaliation in a world already turned to ash.

"Put him in there." Stonegate's tone was firm. "That bad boy is hardened and will still have power."

The Commander's gaze shifted across the battlefield, then back to Hawk. "We aren't out of the fight yet."

Rocco let out a discouraging snort. "Doomsday Truck."

Stonegate locked eyes with him. A look of grim certainty and a slow, knowing nod. "The Pale Horse has arrived." His voice was subdued—cold—as he continued issuing orders. "Now, I want to know everything in Scotty's head. Get him talking as soon as you're done interrogating the prisoner."

Hawk exchanged salutes with Stonegate.

The Department of Energy's *Nuclear Emergency Support Team* moved in. NEST was decked out in MOP gear. It was their *Rapid Reaction Team,* always on standby to deploy anywhere in the world. This time, their own backyard.

They were canvasing the zone, collecting anything alien and samples of the altered terrain. They had already bagged everything Hawk and his team recovered from the ship. The only remaining evidence was the metallic sphere on the hilltop which was heavier than a mountain.

The men tried to move it. No joy. A crane was brought in, and it too had trouble moving the mass. They were perplexed.

"That thing weighs like a million tons!" Rox yelled at them from across the bowl. "They're burning the motor up in that crane," he elaborated to the group. "You guys are gonna burn the motor up!" he shouted at the crew who couldn't hear him. "Look, it's smokin'! I know about these things," he told the man next to him.

The crane began tipping due to the mass of the sphere dragging it down.

"It's gonna topple over... you guys better disconnect before you lose the crane!" He continued to shout at them. He looked at the other guy standing next to them. He wore plain clothes and didn't say much. Rox pegged him for CIA. "They'd better disconnect it before it drags the crane down with it," he told him.

The spook hesitantly radioed the operator. "Shut it down," he ordered in the most alphabet-agency tone he could muster.

Men scrambled, pulling the chain sling off the sphere.

"You'd better also tell them NEST guys that I don't think it's going to be on the surface very long," Rox told the spook.

Mr. CIA pulled out a SAT phone and walked off.

Suddenly, shouts rang out. Not just a call. Not a report of an accident from the crane crew. It was almost, but not quite, frantic.

"Medic! Medic!" Dom bellowed out.

"WE HAVE A SURVIVOR!" A new *Dragon Fly* was up and running. Feeding video.

Hawk's head snapped toward the sound.

Survivor? he thought. *There couldn't be.*

"Get him to the Mobile Command Center!" Hawk barked at Rocco. He wasn't taking any chances. The little drone marked the location on everyone's HUD.

Rocco snapped his rifle to his chest, press-checking his bolt as he prepared to ensure that the human intelligence asset was secured.

"Somebody's got some paperwork to do," Rocco grinned at Edgar.

"Damn straight," Edgar agreed. "Somebody's gotta write up a HUMINT for human intelligence and HVT for high value target."

Rocco and Edgar watched as the medics made their way toward the high value target. Once the medics picked up their patient, they'd meet up with them, fall in to provide rear support, and guide them toward the 18-wheeler.

Scotty was still being patched up in a nearby tent. He was out cold.

Hawk's gaze followed the medics down the bowl. They were sprinting down the crater's slope to the central peak, from the top of the mound where the sphere was located. Every step they took closer to the sphere, the louder the buzzing sounded. It was the same kind of drone which an electric guitar amp hums when plugged in.

Something was half-buried in the mud, at the center of the bowl, lying near an unassuming mound.

When they reached the spot, one of the medics, Villalobos, dropped to his knees, gasping.

"IT'S LIEUTENANT BRIGGS!" the medic shouted.

That booming voice carried to Hawk who gave a sigh of relief. If Scotty had made it, Briggs must have too. The lieutenant had found a way out, survived the inferno.

Hawk rushed to the spot and there he was—a survivor—a damn cockroach. Briggs had crawled out of more scrapes than anyone on the team. Lying in the mud, covered in blood and ash. But breathing.

His suit was torn up. His helmet was breaking off, his face mangled. Most of his suit-nano-chain mail had self-deleted from damage. His tattered Alpha Suit showed underneath.

Hawk pushed past Delta Force, the paramilitary guys, and the medics. He was there in seconds.

The lieutenant's face was burned and cut, his skin split in places, crusted with blood. Bruised and beaten. But he was alive. Dropping to his knees next to Briggs, Hawk saw the injured man's eyes were closed.

"Briggs, you son of a gun," Hawk began. When Briggs didn't respond, Hawk held his breath.

At last, his eyes flickered open and Hawk let out a breath.

"Briggs. Holy shit, man."

Briggs coughed—a wet, pained sound. His lips cracked as he whispered— "Is it gone?"

Hawk nodded. "Yeah, brother. It's gone. The whole kit caboodle."

Briggs' eyes darkened. "Scotty?" he asked.

Hawk frowned, nodding at first, but then shaking his head. "Busted up bad. He hit everything—including the ugly branch—on the way down. He's unconscious," he added, "but we hope he'll be fine in a day or two."

Briggs grinned, his hand tightened weakly around Hawk's wrist. His voice wasn't any more than a breath. "You need to keep him under—I lost track of him. He could be one of them."

Hawk's stomach twisted. He swallowed hard. *Better be sure,* Hawk told himself. He relayed the message of Briggs' suspicions over the Troop Net. "Got it, Briggs. You got pretty mangled, man."

"It was nut-cutting time for sure."

"With all the fireworks, we thought y'all were in Valhalla with the boys."

Briggs stuttered, the pain kicking in. His voice was weaker now. "The Udug... they're..." A shuddering breath. "Unstoppable. So many of them."

Hawk squeezed his hand, reassuring him. "You put up one hell of a fight."

"There was no fight. They outmatch us in every way. The 2nd SKN's are useless except for environmental."

Hawk's eyes darted back and forth, looking at a man he'd fought beside for seven years. A cold chill ran down Hawk's spine. Briggs was a hard mother-fucker. Now, he seemed to be a shadow of the strong and confident soldier who walked into an alien ship. Hawk looked around. Scanning from the high ground of the crater's edge and surveying the barren field to the tree line in the distance.

"Did you see any of them get out?" he asked Briggs.

Briggs shook his head. "It took all I had to get out of there. Plan on it."

Hawk stood up and scanned around the crater, then again stared at the distant tree line. A five-mile-an-hour breeze rustled the long grass. Shadows danced between the trunks. Tricks of light or were they out there?

CHAPTER 31

Lead Me Home
Victoria, Texas—Next Day

Far from the site of the *Menagerie's* implosion, Sonny stood outside his garage, phone pressed to his ear, trying to get his insurance company to listen to the most exotic claim of his life. He'd seen the commercials. How the hell did they not believe this one? He yawned, stretching his side. His abs didn't have that dull itch, that remnant pain from his stab wound.

Weird. The thought overshadowed by his *current* predicament. They're slogan. *"They'd seen it!"* So why the hell weren't they covering a UFO strike?

The insurance rep droned on, monotone, detached— "Sir, I understand, but your policy doesn't cover damage from—aliens," the agent on the phone chuckled.

Sonny's jaw muscles were getting a workout. The government acknowledged aliens in the news after the Fravor video dropped. No one cared anymore, but they acknowledged it. Of course, Fravor was a reliable Navy pilot, and he had pictures, and he wasn't filing an insurance claim. Still—

Sonny inhaled slowly through his nose, exhaled through his teeth, forcing himself to stay calm.

"So, let me get this straight."

"Sir—"

"I can crash my truck into a tree, and you'll cover it—"

"Correct, sir."

"But if a space mountain falls from the sky and turns my truck into a goddamn scrap heap, y'all are a hard pass?"

A pause.

A long one.

"Well, sir, technically, yes. It would be considered an 'Act of God.'"

From her bedroom window, Mylitta watched Sonny's face shift from frustrated red to outright volcanic. This culture was unique, to say the least.

The truck was in shambles. Dented, scorched...

"But serviceable," the insurer said.

Sonny rubbed his temples, "Of course, it is."

"And you're still able to do your work," the insurer pointed out.

"Technically, the truck runs but my trailer is—" Sonny began.

"As I said before," the man reminded him, "the trailer is not insured—not for aliens or anything else."

"Naturally," Sonny said, and he hung up.

A beat-up truck and no trailer. Delivering Richard Tantrom's mattresses was going to make for a long day.

Inside, Chiara was in the kitchen, pouring steaming coffee into three mugs. Mylitta shuffled over, still half-asleep, stuck in the Twilight Zone. Her hair was a mess, and she was wearing one of Sonny's oversized sweatshirts—something Chiara normally wore. Mylitta decided normality felt good on her.

She sat, took a sip of the hot, brown liquid—then paused. Her nose wrinkled, inhaling the aroma—another sip.

"Wow," Mylitta said.

Chiara grinned. "Addicting, right?"

Mylitta nodded slowly. "Dangerously."

Chiara laughed. "I have a feeling you've had better, though."

Myli's head tilted. She had, living with another civilization.

"Any new memories?" Chiara probed.

Myli shook her head, *no*. Chiara could see that feeling creeping back over her face. The dread of losing people. Lots of people. Almost guilt associated with pulling the trigger herself.

Sonny returned to the kitchen, his brow furrowed. On his way through the living room, he glanced at the TV. "They work fast," he said. "Already calling the whole thing a *Lightning Strike Ignites Methane Deposit.*"

Sonny shook his head.

"And the area has been quarantined due to lethal levels of dispersing gases."

Chiara glanced at him. "Babe." She could feel where all this was going.

But Sonny wasn't listening. He was rambling about aliens and space debris. He was going on about the TV, his mind racing.

Sonny turned to Chiara, her eyes wide.

"Babe—" he began.

"Babe," Chiara put a finger to his lips and shushed him. "Sonny, I believe you. Listen, I'm worried something big might be coming."

She'd seen some wild events happen in her life. She could feel a change in season coming. Chiara exhaled sharply, rubbing her forehead. Myli gripped her coffee mug tightly.

Lots of drama in this culture, she told herself.

"I need you to focus," Chiara told Sonny. "Either forget your delivery or get it done and come home. Together, the three of us... we will sort this out tonight."

Sonny took a breath and nodded. He was about to drop the subject when he had a sudden epiphany.

"Just like Roswell," he said, pointing at her, his voice reflecting excitement. "It was aliens!"

Chiara laughed, too quickly. She tilted her head and her eyes locked onto his—her face projecting a playful expression. "Hey, look at me," she said.

Something in her voice demanded his attention. He was drawn in, sinking into her gaze. Deep inside. There was confidence there. A certainty. But even further underneath? Something else. Something guarded.

"Grab 'Pink Panther' and the truck bag. If something does go down, you run and get your ass back to me."

Chiara's voice carried urgency. Too much. Like she already knew the rules of engagement. Like she'd done all this before. Sonny stared at her. It was one thing to grab his truck bag, but taking along the rattle-canned pink-tinted rifle meant Chiara expected trouble.

She turned, moving with purpose, but working hard to avoid seeming rushed.

"I'm going to grab some gear and take it to work with me," she added, voice casual—too casual. "I'm sure this is nothing."

Her words were vague, but her inner thoughts churned.

If it was something, she told herself, *it would have been bigger. Right? No way this is the 'Big One.' It's just another crazy anomaly. Like all the others Siegfried talked about in his seminar. Like the ones that have happened all through history, the ones I've seen before, the ones I pray are never coming back.*

She turned to Sonny, forcing a thin smile. A denial as much for herself as for him.

"No way this is it," she affirmed under her breath.

She kissed him. Hard. Long. Like she was making sure he felt it and sealing the deal. Underneath her calm exterior, she was terrified he would forget her.

A kiss from those soft, buttery-smooth lips was all it took to redirect his anxiety. Sonny sighed, strumming his fingers on the countertop.

"I gotta run," but he didn't want to unless it was back to the bedroom. Sonny glanced back at Myli with a nod. "You taking her to work, or do you want her to stay here?" he motioned to Myli.

"Whatcha say, bay caster?" he asked Myli playfully.

The angel dropped from the heavens wasn't sure, didn't understand the remark. Her head slowly turned side to side in a display of her confusion.

Chiara giggled. She motioned to the bird's nest of tangle in Myli's hair with her hand, pointing to her own hair. It was a common problem while fishing in the flats. An imperfect cast would tangle all the line in a bay caster reel, creating a mess resembling a bird nest.

Sonny reached over and grabbed a brush. He finessed her hair, stroking out the tangle.

Chiara's gaze flicked to him and Myli. A hint of jealousy stirred in her chest. Or was it a hint of something else? If Myli was who Chiara suspected she was, she absolutely wanted the young woman by Sonny's side. If not? It wouldn't matter if she was wrong.

"I think you should take her with you," Chiara said carefully. "It'll be good for her to get out. Take her mind off everything."

Mylitta glanced at a laptop on the counter. She hesitated, then, finally, she nodded. "I'll come with. Do you have any tech I can borrow?"

"Tech?" Sonny's posture shrank back. "What, like a phone or something?" He turned to Chiara, but she avoided his gaze. He shrugged his shoulders. "Yeah, you can use mine in the car. The work phone self-terminated, but you can use my personal one while I'm driving."

"Sounds good," Chiara said as she forced a smile.

He turned to leave, but Chiara's voice stopped him with hesitant restraint she used to pull him back in.

"Sonny... wait."

He turned back. She was biting her lip, looking—nervous. She took a deep breath before she dropped a bombshell.

"I took an EPT test this morning."

Quiet. A pause that seemed to stretch into eternity.

"I'm pregnant."

Sonny froze. His mind went blank. "What? But I thought..."

Chiara let out a weak laugh, barely a breath. "I didn't want to tell you last night. I was waiting for the right moment. But there is no right moment."

Sonny stared blankly for a second but followed up with his signature grin. He grabbed her, kissing her hard.

"Babe, that's amazing news."

Chiara smiled, eyes glassy. "Yeah. It is. Surprising, for sure,"

He slipped an arm around her waist, passionately. She loved how strong he could be when he drew her close.

"Hey, next time you see me, remember this, right now, and cut me some slack."

He grinned. "Always and forever." He kissed her again, no doubt in his mind.

Chiara watched them pull out of the driveway from the window. She turned back to the kitchen with a fading smile. She took one look at the ingredients she set out for dinner and without hesitation swept the food into the trash. There was no reason to cook tonight.

CHAPTER 32

What Once Was Will Be Again

Ten, twenty, maybe thirty minutes later—Chiara heard a knock at the front door. Her body stiffened. Her breath caught in her throat. Was it him?

She opened it.

Trip Looper.

All those years ago, deep down, she knew this day would come. But she didn't put it together until this moment—right now—when Trip was there face to face with her again.

Chiara stared.

"No—" she demanded. Disbelief worn with recognition. "No—not now. It's just a false alarm!" she cried. "Not now, Looper!"

Trip stepped in and embraced her. She couldn't finish her thought, her sentence, and she didn't need to because she'd already begun putting the pieces together. She knew it the moment she saw Myli. But she didn't want to believe. Then she saw the ring—that frickin' ring.

Her legs weak, her knees buckling, she crumbled. Trip held her and let her down easy. Her breathing was erratic, and he couldn't catch his breath either. He shuddered. Their foreheads touched. And then—he broke and the two of them slid to the floor. Their tears ran together like tributaries forming a river. His hand on her belly.

"I've been through so much," he whispered. "To get here."

Chiara shushed him softly, running her fingers through his hair.

"I know baby, we both have. And I'm so sorry. Why didn't you tell me?"

She tilted his face up, cupping his cheeks. His beard was soft against her palm. She was kissing a man she hadn't seen since the 1970s. She wasn't used to the beard. But the man beneath—she had never forgotten.

Looper pulled back, his gaze intense. "It's not over yet. And it's gonna get worse before it gets worse."

Chiara's grip tightened. Her face quivered.

"No!" she shook her head. "I can't lose you again." Her voice was desperate now. "If I had known, I wouldn't have let you leave in the first place."

Looper smiled bitterly. "I still can't believe I didn't recognize you all those years ago until you walked away," his fingers brushing her cheek. "Chiara, all this time it was you—it was always you."

"You looked right at me, stupid. You saw me; it was just the face you didn't recognize."

The understanding flooded his eyes. "Yeah, you had an alias."

She smiled, sadly. "How many fake names do we put on before we lose who we really are?" A quiet chuckle. But then—her smile faded. "Don't leave me again."

"I have to finish this."

Her heart fell a thousand miles. "No. I can't lose you both!"

"Chiara—me too. I can't lose both of you again."

"No. Damn it!" She was shaking mad now. "I'm not playing this game anymore." Her voice changing, scary, sincere.

Looper exhaled sharply. "I have to save him."

Chiara stilled. Her heart was in shambles. Looper's eyes darkened.

"I have to save him," he repeated. "Or you'll lose both of us."

Chiara's world was spinning. "You think you can change it?"

Looper's jaw clenched. "I have to. I have all the pieces now."

Chiara's voice was barely a whisper. "There are too many moving parts." She looked away. "I'm never going to see him again, am I?"

Looper grabbed her hands. "No. There's nothing you can do to bring him back."

Chiara's eyes filled with tears. Her lips trembled. "I don't want to lose him, Looper. He's the best thing that ever happened to me."

Looper's eyes softened. "Loss makes us powerful. We will meet again in another life."

Chiara closed her eyes and pressed her face into his chest. He was right. The proof was sitting in front of her. But she had no interest in being powerful anymore.

Meanwhile, thirty minutes away and heading south on Highway 87, Mylitta was typing rapidly on the laptop while absorbing every bit of information she could. The usually slow laptop was moving at uncharacteristically lightning speeds. Sonny had glanced over at her a few times, watching her work. *No way she could read that fast,* he thought, returning his gaze to the road. She worked silently but it felt like she was picking his brain. Asking him questions without saying anything.

Something about her had changed. His shitty, slow-ass computer had changed too. The damn thing was running ten times faster than normal. Ever since the ring bonded to his finger, things worked better, functioned better, and he felt better. His body looked better. The bruising was all but gone.

Mylitta's expression flickered. Like she was remembering things. Piecing back together a cosmic puzzle she had already finished and decided to forget. What she didn't know was the woman with the memories fought to keep those memories from surfacing.

A corner piece here. A corner piece there. A piece missing. A piece which fit—but leave it to string theory to give her two puzzles mixed in the same box with all the wrong pieces, but they all fit.

And the picture? he asked himself. *Still unclear. But it's slowly forming. Something about this moment, this non-conversation as she probes his mind, is unlocking something deep. A memory. A feeling. Like she is realizing something. Something important. Something she should have remembered all along.*

Sonny frowned. But he didn't have time to dwell. He had work to do. He shifted in his seat, fingered for his 9mm HK VP9 Optics Ready Match, was there between the seat and the console. Pink Panther rifle hidden in the back under the seat. His pistol wasn't very compact, due to the Surefire WML on it for nighttime use and it was his primary pistol—his match gun.

Mylitta eyed the pistol. "What's the weapon for?" Something about it, a scar on her psyche, made her very uncomfortable.

Sonny shrugged. "Just in case."

"In case of what?"

"Ah, anything I guess. Nearest help in Texas is thirty minutes to an hour away in some cases."

Mylitta smirked slightly. "Paranoid?"

Sonny chuckled. "After last night? Maybe. With today's customer? Absolutely. You are your own first responder out here."

A minute or two went by.

"We had a break-in," He stated reluctantly. "Things escalated quickly." The memory still haunting him. He shifted in his seat. He laughed at the absurdity of what he was about to say next.

"I was one of those guys who didn't think you needed a rifle. All that changed after that evening. The guy only got away because Chiara was tending to the knife wound in my gut."

"So, what's *your* story? You had us all on edge last night? I can't place your accent," Sonny said. "Are you originally from here or just visiting?"

Myli hesitated.

"Not from here," she told him. "I don't recognize any of this. I feel like I have been plopped into the middle of nowhere."

"Join the club." Sonny snorted. "It is nowhere out here. And flat. If you like fishing, it's a good place to be."

Mylitta smiled faintly. "It's— complicated."

Sonny nodded. "Like a tangled bird's nest?" he kidded to a stone face. "Fair enough. Everything is complicated these days," he sighed.

Miles stretched into minutes, and silence stretched between them.

"Why are you so apprehensive about this delivery?" she asked. "You don't like this guy, do you?"

"Nope"

"Bad vibes?"

Sonny gripped the wheel tighter. "Yeah, something like that. The heebie-jeebies."

Mylitta tilted her head. "Heebie-jeebies?"

"The willies. The creeps," he said. You'll indirectly encounter 16 to 36 serial killers in your lifetime by walking past, or being in the vicinity of, them."

Mylitta watched him closely. The more Sonny thought about his unsavory customer, the more she could feel his uneasiness building. And that worried her.

"And he is one of these killers?" She asked while reading his face.

"I'm pretty good at reading people." Sonny nodded. "Won't matter," he said, patting the pistol.

"Have you ever taken a life?" She asked with concern.

He shook his head. "I've never used a fire extinguisher either, but I have three at home." He turned and looked at her. He asked as a joke, expecting her answer to be no, "How 'bout you?"

"I don't know," she shook her head. "Now that you ask… you ever feel like you'd be good at something you can't remember doing?" she asked with a tinge of anger.

Was she one of the 36? The radio volume had been low. He stared at her, then his pistol, before switching back to focus on the radio. *Anger is the bodyguard of secrets,* he thought.

Eddie Rabbit's name scrolled on the dashboard control screen. *Drivin' My Life Away* was the song playing.

"This is a good one," he blurted out, reaching over and turning the volume up louder. "You know this one?" He started singing along. Then he stopped and added, "I'm always down for some Johnny Cash too but I am a connoisseur of music, so I have an assortment of ear candy. Depeche Mode, Filter, Audio Slave, Duran Duran, Sound Garden, you like Sound Garden? Name a band, I betcha I know it."

Her mouth gaped open, not at all sure what to say.

"Sneaker Pimps, Genesis, Garbage—hell, I like most music, I guess. Toto, Phantogram, Dire Straits… Korn? I bet you jam to Korn. This is a classic." He smiled at her. "Ooh—I'm drivin' my life away."

CHAPTER 33

Death of a Salesman
Port Lavaca, Texas

Not much longer after his DJ episode, they were pulling in.

"Just wait in the truck," Sonny instructed his passenger as they neared their destination. "It shouldn't take me more than thirty minutes to unload this stuff, then we'll get back on the road."

Upon pulling into the apartment complex, he and Mylitta both grimaced. The place was a wreck. It looked like Sonny's customer was the only one living in a place which had been long abandoned. He turned down the radio, and the sudden stillness amplified the silence of nature outside.

From the cracked stucco walls to the black mold creeping up the corners, the place reeked of neglect. The courtyard was overgrown, the pool a swampy mess of algae and floating debris. There was even an alligator in it. This wasn't just low-income housing—it was something worse. Something rotten. He shifted back and forth in his seat, head on a swivel, looking in all directions, mainly in disbelief that this was where the delivery was going.

Mylitta felt a knot tighten in her gut. It was a strong feeling, but not her own thought.

Sonny killed the engine and turned to her. "This won't take long."

Mylitta didn't answer. She just stared at him. Her expression said it all. *Don't go in there alone.*

Sonny chuckled, trying to ease the tension. "I promise, I'll be back faster than you can say popsophalofagus." He shut the door. Through the open window, "Hey, you can text me from the iPad if you need me."

Mylitta did not laugh. She looked at the iPad, then watched as Sonny manhandled the first mattress in the side mirror, hoisting it effortlessly, and he soon disappeared inside the complex.

She hated this.

"Popsophalofagus," she said under her breath. She stared at the laptop on the center console. Before she could roll her eyes, they strayed to a spot in between the seats and her gaze landed on his pistol.

Inside, Sonny maneuvered through narrow hallways, the mattress balanced between the crook in his arm and on his shoulder. The place smelled stale—a mixture of cigarettes, mildew, and something else. Something he couldn't place.

He reached Apartment 14D and knocked.

No answer.

He knocked again, louder.

Still nothing.

Finally, he muttered, "Come on dude." He shifted the mattress against the doorframe and reached for his phone. The door creaked open. His phone buzzed but it was already on the way back into his pocket and he didn't see the message.

"GUN," the text said.

Sonny squeezed into the apartment. The dining table and coffee table were buried under mounds of garbage; a tower of empty pizza boxes balanced precariously next to a city of them, all stacked and reaching the ceiling.

On the sunken couch, a massive man lay sprawled, his stomach spilling onto the floor, engrossed in a video game. Sonny recognized the box: *Grand Theft Auto V.* The man's eyes bulged unnaturally, like they were ready to pop out of his skull, waiting for GTA VI.

No shame whatsoever. Bare stomach hanging over the sofa, the flabby flesh draped so low it nearly reached the floor, like silly putty running off a desk. At least one testicle was peeking out, like a skunk head protruding from the side of its burrow.

And, in the doorway, stood Richard Tantrom, his thick hands gripping the doorknob.

"Fuuuuu..." he murmured.

Tantrom's muscles strained against a too-small tank top, his arms littered with bad prison tattoos—some faded, others newer. His face was hard, his eyes cold. It was the depthless, icy cold that profilers saw right through. His skin reeked of alcohol and sweat that was probably leftover from last night.

He balanced the mattress, prepping to pick it up. Sonny glanced around, spotting dirty panties, crumpled wife-beaters, and cockroaches skittering between trash piles.

Tantrom chuckled. "You can step on shit if you want. We just kick it out of the way."

The big man on the couch grunted, shifting his enormous bulk, the frame of the sofa creaking. In the corner sat the pregnant woman, Kandy. Sonny assumed it was her. She watched blankly, picking at her filthy fingernails. Her fingertips stained for whatever reason.

Near the kitchen, Sonny spotted something worse. A drug kit. Spoons. Needles. Burn marks on the countertop.

"K"—Sonny forced a smile. His eyebrows popped up and down. "Brought your stuff."

Tantrom didn't move. "You knock too fucking hard," Tantrom said as Kandy got up to go to another room.

Sonny stood wide-eyed, longing to get this done. "Sorry."

"I doubt it." Tantrom finally stepped aside, motioning with a jerk of his head. "Bring it in."

No! Sonny's little inside voice screamed at him. But he had a job to do. He tipped the mattress and shifted it through the doorway, setting it against the wall. The apartment was dark. Not dimly lit—dark. And now he recognized the smell—it reeked of skunk and mothballs.

The darkness felt intentional. The curtains were drawn, the air thick with something suffocating. A television flickered in the corner. The same TV the big guy was playing on, except there was nothing on it but static. Sonny forced himself to act normal.

"Alright," Sonny said, "where's the next one going?"

Tantrom didn't answer. Instead, he shut the door behind him.

CLicK!

The little sound from the door lock was more deafening than a muzzle brake going off next to an eardrum. The metallic slide of the lock snapping into place shot straight through Sonny's nerves. His pulse spiked. His mouth went dry.

Say when, he thought.

Sonny nonchalantly moved his hands into position. His left thumb went under the bottom of his shirt ready to rip it up and out of the way of his pistol. The other lingered in his shorts pocket ready to pull that smoke wagon.

"Hey, man—" Sonny began.

Tantrom reached out with a wad of cash and a big grin. "Thanks, Sonny."

Sonny dropped his guard. *Awe, a tip.*

Tantrom pulled the cash back and the other hand came in fast. A fist like a hammer slammed into Sonny's stomach. Sonny's guts cavitated—like bubbles popping. Pain detonated inside him. His body doubled over, crumpling inward. Before he could recover, a second blow cracked against his ribs. The air left his lungs in a hoarse gasp.

Sonny stumbled back and tried to draw. But nothing was there. His fucking gun wasn't on him.

DUMB ASS!

Arms—thick and brutal—wrapped around his neck. Squeezing. Tight. Too tight. The big bastard moved fast, like a hippopotamus and just as deadly. He had Sonny in a rear-naked choke hold. The pressure made Sonny go limp, like a damn Raggedy Andy doll.

"Wrah dah fuuuuckkk," Sonny gargled out something incomprehensible. His feet left the floor. He was levitating. Four more combination hits to his guts were incoming.

Shock and dismay punched through the haze. The room was turning black. Sonny struggled to get his hand between the big man's arms and his neck. His other hand was trying to pull the big man's secondary grip behind his neck free. It was just enough relief to keep him conscious.

Just then, from the hallway, came a new voice. Female.

"You start without me, baby?"

Kandy stepped from the shadows. Sonny's blurring eyes locked onto her.

"Ohhh, thaaat bitchhhh," Sonny growled.

She was short, stocky, still pregnant. Blonde hair yanked back into a messy ponytail. Her arms inked with new tattoos and plastic wrap over them. Still smoking. Still reeking of bath salts and meth.

Sonny fought. No way this feral bitch was going to kill him. But his strength was ebbing.

Tantrom laughed. The woman laughed too, cackling through missing teeth. When the big bastard laughed, Sonny felt his spine crack. A dull pop—ecstasy. At least some relief from the years of hauling heavy shit.

"What was it you said?" Tantrom said, grinning. "You said sorry? LIAR!"

Sonny's bloodshot eyes locked onto the woman. He flipped her the bird and flipped Tantrom one too for good measure. With his lips he spelled out an *F* and an *U*. Defiant to the end.

"I. Said. Dick…"

She sighed dramatically, strolling toward them like this was any other night. Her hand slid into her back pocket. Pulled out a rusted box cutter.

Sonny's eyebrows furrowed. His heartbeat slammed against his ribs. The blade—dull, dirty, jagged—not a single clean edge.

Tetanus, Sonny told himself and aloud he pleaded, "G – e – t, a, ca – l – een, knife!"

Kandy ignored him. Instead, she addressed Tantrom, "Please tell me we're not gonna do the whole slow thing again, Richard," Kandy muttered. "The last guy took forever to die."

"Fffff," Sonny's mind reeled as he tried to speak.

"WHAT?" Tantrum screamed. "I can't hear our guest. Loosen your grip, just a little."

"Ffffreeeak!" Sonny shouted. No way, he told himself. No way this is really happening.

This isn't about money. This is something else. Something dark. Something these freaks have done before.

"Freaky," Tantrom agreed as his grin widened. "You got that right, bub. You know me yet?"

The hippopotamus' arms began cinching down again.

With a delicate touch, Kandy lifted Sonny's shirt, unbuttoning his pants. She passed her hands over his happy trail with her icy witch-like hands.

Her touch was gentle.

Her fingers traced his stomach.

"Shhh, baby," she cooed, her voice sweet, sickly. "I'll make this special for you. You ever butcher a buck?"

Sonny had butchered a male deer. He knew where you started and the first things removed. His body wrenched left and right. His butt puckered. No way she was carving pieces of him off with a rusty box cutter.

She leaned in, whispering against his ear. "It only feels worse if you struggle. Make the pain your friend."

Sonny's physiology twitched involuntarily. Parts warming up that shouldn't be. His brain screamed for air.

His vision blurred, colors warping at the edges. The world was tilting, folding in on itself. His brain misfiring, trying to keep up—random memories flashing in and out. A birthday cake. The smell of gun oil. Moth balls. Moth balls! He hated the smell of moth balls.

What the hell is happening? Sonny asked himself as a wave of anger was taking hold. That anger abruptly turned nasty.

"Jokkkkkes. Onnnn. Uuuuuu," Sonny garbled through the choke. "I'mmm. in. to. thisss... shhhitttt."

Kandy looked down. Sonny spoke no lies.

Tantrom snorted. "Looks like we aren't the only freaks here."

"I'm. Gonna. Killlll. All offff you," Sonny threatened his tormentors.

The woman grinned, tilting her head, amused. "Not today, baby."

The blade touched his skin. Not slicing. Not cutting. Tearing his skin with the rusty serrations.

Slowly.

Jagged.

Dull pain intensifying with the pull of the blade.

Sonny groaned—in anger. In disbelief. But mostly—out of helplessness. No matter how hard he bent the big man's fingers behind his neck, the big Gumby bastard wouldn't let go.

His pistol was useless. Sitting in the truck. Far, far away.

Outside, Myli could feel Sonny's panic. Not the wind from the open windows. Not the hot salty breeze from the coast stirring her hair. Something else. A shift. A ripple in the fabric of the moment.

Something felt—dangerous!

Her pulse spiked, her breath shallowed.

A reaction before thought. She dug deep. Reached for Sonny. Not with her hands but with her mind. With the ring.

She reached into the folds of time and space, searching for the quantum thread connecting them. Sonny's heartbeat, his presence; he wasn't broadcasting like she hoped he would be. A sign—

She found only absolute silence. But not calm silence either. It was a quiet devoured by a vacuum.

And then—she moved. Because she had no choice. Because Sonny had none either.

Her body moved before her mind caught up. Reality reverberated. The air warped, rippled—energy distorted.

A blast of air detonated inside the truck's cab, sending work papers, dust, and loose objects whirling out of her open window. She was gone. In her seat—only her clothes remained, crumpled, empty.

Inside, where Myli materialized—she heard clamor. The moment she landed—she heard a muffled struggle. Something slamming hard against a wall. A body, maybe. The thumps were followed by a woman and a man's psychotic laugh.

Sounds that made her blood run cold. She had teleported into a bedroom Sonny had seen on his way in. She ripped the door open—and saw everything. Her heart pounded.

Sonny, barely conscious, looked up and grumbled.

"Girrrl. You're. Badddd. Luckkkkk."

Whoever this creature was, she must be an angel with what she's wearing, or lack thereof.

Oh goodness, Sonny thought to himself. *I'm dead already.* There wasn't a better explanation for what he was seeing. Who jumps into a fight looking like that?

He figured she was rusty at this hero business. She looked disoriented, woozy but she didn't have time to become fully cognizant if she wanted to stop them. He could feel her power through the ring, her energy zapped, her arrival drained her. Somehow, he could feel her concentration fighting back a mental fog. *An Alpha Suit?* What was that? She wanted one... no, wished she had one instead of coming in completely vulnerable.

She wasn't wearing anything. She was naked.

Again.

She looked unprepared, but ready to take care of business, nonetheless.

Sonny was on the ground, his face turning red. He refused to give up, flexing his neck muscles, straining, refusing to pass out. Big Country's arms were crushing his throat, an iron vice, tightening every time he gave an inch, like a boa constrictor. Sonny's hand slapped against his attacker's arm, tapping out—it was a desperate instinct, and a futile one.

Tantrom's crew was howling with laughter. To them this was a game. To them Sonny's life meant nothing.

The woman with the box cutter grinned, her eyes revealing her cruel amusement. She stared wolfishly at Myli. Standing there. Bare. A distraction? A mistake?

"Oh, honey," the woman cooed, lips curling. "You're just in time. And you're fine as hell, too."

The Big Bastard's grip loosened—just a fraction. Enough. Sonny sucked in a deep breath, his body convulsing as air flooded his lungs—the same way a drowning man struggles for breath after breaching the surface.

Mylitta didn't hesitate. Didn't think. She grabbed a lamp off the counter and swung the improvised weapon.

Crack!

Glass and ceramic exploded against the giant's skull. His body jerked violently, grip loosening more. With the last of his strength, Sonny broke free. He was gasping, coughing, rolling away on the floor to create space.

The woman lunged at Myli. A blur of movement with the box cutter slashing toward Myli's throat. Mylitta leaned back, ducked a second swipe, and swooped in juking the knife strikes.

Her hand snapped out, catching the woman's wrist mid-air, twisting hard—a sickening pop. The bone snapped. The woman's scream tore through the room. She went down and slithered out of the front door.

Sonny, on the floor, coughing, still reaching for his gun, which still wasn't there. Neither was his mind.

"Shit," he chastised himself. The gun was still in the truck.

Forget the damn gun! he told himself. He tried rebooting his brain. At the moment, he had no idea where he was.

As Sonny struggled to regain reality, Tantrom came at Myli swinging. Left, right, the big hands swooshing through the air. Myli dodged the blows by atoms. With an open hand, she struck his trachea. Kneeing him in the groin, she placed a foot behind his and a push toppled him over.

But he wasn't done—not yet.

Seeing Myli in action, Sonny longed to join the fight. But he needed a weapon. Anything. His fingers brushed against something cold, hard—a pen. Half-buried in the garbage. Perfect. Sonny's grip tightened.

Payback time.

But before Sonny could get on his feet, the big man was on him again. The man's hands—the size of paper plates—pressed into Sonny's face and blocked out all his vision. Meat hooks pressing in, darkness closing. Sonny's brain was about to pop. There was no stopping those hands. Sonny did the next best thing. With all the strength he had left, Sonny hammer-fisted the pen upward, into the unknown beyond his own head.

The massive hands responded instantly and drifted away, shaky and confused. The big man retracted, staggering—and collapsed. On his back, his hands hovered in mid-air, twitching—trying to decide. Face or eye? Pull it out? Leave it in? He didn't know.

Sonny rolled to his knees, his breath ragged. His hands dug through the trash on the coffee table. A cheese grater. Good enough.

He grabbed it. A fucking cheese grater. He got to his feet, shuffle-stepping forward, adrenaline burning hot. The big man whimpered, got to his knees and tried to crawl away. Sonny drew back and delivered a forearm swing which would have made John McEnroe proud.

The cheese grater ripped across flesh. Meat sloughed off in ribbons, spilling out of the holes. The big man let out a high-pitched scream, somewhere between a dying calf and a cat in heat. He tried to scramble away, panicked.

Sonny jumped on his back, fists hammering down. Once. Twice. Over and over. All his rage. All the fear. All the helplessness—poured into every punch.

Across the room Sonny watched as Richard gathered himself. His eyes were wide falling on the nude intruder. Despite the circumstances, he could see that she was perfection incarnate. Her curves were an invitation, a ruse to draw you in, only to drown you if you were brave enough to wade into that tidal pool.

"Who the fuck—" Tantrom began.

Her movements were a choreography of destruction. Her hand closed around something heavy on the floor—an ashtray. She wound up like a pro baseball pitcher, full extension, perfect form.

And hurled the ashtray.

The heavy glass shattered against Richard's face with a face fracturing *crack*. Blood and broken teeth splashed the floor. His head snapped to the side, a grunt stolen from his throat before he could finish cursing.

He had no time to retaliate before her leg snapped out—knee to chest, another powerful standing kick, calf flexing, foot slamming into the side of his knee before a snap kick to his face. The joint buckled with a sickening pop, his face sounded like it was slapped with a washboard's length of baby back ribs.

He screamed—a high-pitched, broken sound, not a man's cry but an animal's wail. More teeth falling out. He staggered, mouth a ruined mess of blood and fragments, eyes bulging in disbelief. He went down and turned to crawl, instinct overriding pride.

Myli followed. Slowly. Quietly. Seductively, one footstep in front of the other. Each step measured, each sway of her hips intentional and unhurried, like a dancer nailing her marks. Although bare in form, she wasn't helpless. In fact she gave no mercy with her pitiless violence. Her cruelness was intoxicating and well deserved.

A perfect predator. *A destroying angel.*

Richard's heart pounded in terror and awe. He wasn't just afraid. He was witnessing something otherworldly—a force of nature wrapped in an unassuming marauder.

She held no remorse or hesitation, and Richard knew what was coming. His thoughts raced for a way out.

Sonny was supposed to be alone. Who the hell was this naked woman moving like she was teaching a curriculum of combat proficiency?

Panic burdened his eyes. He clawed his way to a knee, dragging himself toward the sofa in a hurry. He dug through the cushions with frantic hands, pillows ejecting next to Sonny who was also laying nearby.

Although Myli was moving in for the kill, it was Sonny who saw it first. He was going for something. Had to be a pistol. A flash of nickel-plated steel caught Sonny's eye. He dove at him. Tantrom saw him coming. They both lunged for the weapon. Tantrom's shirt tore, and Chiara's stolen pendant slipped free, swinging in the open. Sonny recognized it instantly, and the distraction nearly cost him.

For one heart-stopping second, Sonny thought he wouldn't win the scramble. Their hands grappled for control. The revolver's barrel flagged everyone in the room—for one horrifying moment, the hair trigger pistol pointed straight at Myli.

Sonny put more effort into the fight. The barrel swung away from her.

The first shot cracked off—wild, deafening. Everyone's ears rang like church bells.

Sonny bent Tantrom's wrist. The second shot slammed into Tantrom's gut. His thick muscular frame jerked back, mouth open in a strangled gasp. Sonny reared his head back and straightened his neck, throwing a vicious headbutt, allowing him to finally wrench the revolver free. He pushed back, rolled onto his back, legs spread, knees out of the way, lining up his aim.

Richard, back on his knees, surrendering with his hands up.

It was over.

Tantrom was done. "Get me an ambulance," he pleaded. "I've been shot!" he added with disbelief.

Sonny looked at Tantrom's gut shot, then his own. His own knife scar was almost completely gone. But not the memory. "Fuck around, find out."

Sonny pulled the hair trigger! His muscles felt like Jello. The weight of the .357 dragged Sonny's hand down into his crotch. Smoke coiled lazily from the barrel between his legs.

Tantrom twitched once and then fell over in a heap.

A thin stream of blood trickled down from his forehead. Behind him, the kitchen wall was sprayed with a splatter of brains and blood.

"Get fucked, stay fucked, Dick," he scorned.

He coughed. "My body feels like a thousand pounds," Sonny rasped to Myli, his chest heaving.

He lay there on the floor, sweat mixed with grime and blood, eyes blinking up at the ceiling as though gravity itself was trying to pin him to the earth. He turned his head slightly, squinting at Myli from across the room.

"Where the hell are your clothes?"

She looked at her arm, then her body. *Too hard to explain right now.* The room was quiet, except for the relentless, high-pitched ringing in both their ears—a dull chorus of trauma.

Myli stepped closer, her bare feet silent on the floor, as she moved towards him. Her voice was soft, calm, but that voice penetrated and stimulated his vagus nerve.

"You okay?" The vagal tone took immediate effect.

He was elated to be alive; his stress response was in full retreat. Even then Sonny told her the truth. "Not even a little," he answered. "The question is, are *you* okay?" He asked of her.

The notion of being okay felt absurd to him. He looked at her—really looked at her—his mind trying to reconcile what his eyes were seeing. She stood there radiant, deadly, otherworldly, and somehow... unbothered.

This anarchy seemed to be her natural habitat. She was apparently built for moments like this. In the moment, Sonny realized: this woman wasn't just okay. She was exactly where she belonged. However, he could see the layers underneath her armor cracking. This wasn't her first run in with death. In fact, he bet her body count was much higher.

Sonny lay there—his body felt like depleted uranium. Myli stepped over him, straddling his body—bare and unrepentant. Looking up at her, his emotions grabbed him by the throat. Her nakedness was electric, causing his heart to flutter, butterflies in his stomach.

She knelt on top of him, sweat sprinkling from her skin to his, her breath warm, wet, and heavy. Their eyes met with intense focus. Curiosity, recognition—hunger. Myli reached for him, her fingers brushing his jaw as she wrapped around him.

Skin on skin.

More butterflies as she bear-hugged him on the ground. She could feel his nervousness. Warmth met warmth, sweat mingled with sweat, conscious consent took over as their DNA blurred together.

With regret she warned him. "I am going to hurt you."

"I know," he said plainly not understanding at all how she was about to hurt him.

Her palm slid behind his neck; she closed in on him. He responded instinctively, his hand and arms wrapping around her, hand resting on her bare hip.

"We need to go. Right now," she insisted.

Sonny nodded, "Yeah."

He took her hand and, on a level neither of them understood, something sparked. A flash of blinding white light. The process was like being struck by lightning. Every nerve ending in Sonny's body ignited. Muscles locked, spasming, trembling. His vision went white-hot and then—they were no longer inside the stifling apartment.

They tumbled to the pavement next to the truck, tangled together, wrapped in each other's arms. Sonny's body twitched violently, smoke curling off his naked skin from the static charge. He tried to move, but his muscles locked tight, seizing before giving out entirely. His eyes rolled back, and he went completely limp in her arms.

Myli winced. She hated this part too. The pain of the tearing from the displacement and bending of matter and time. Neither of them was built for it. But she was used to pain.

He wasn't.

She cradled his head gently against her shoulder, whispering under her breath, "I've got you."

She looked around. No sirens. No witnesses. Just the run-down empty complex. Shots had been fired. Maybe someone heard and would find them before they left. *Shit.* Maybe not.

In the distance she saw Kandy, stumbling down the road, holding her broken arm.

She crouched down next to Sonny, pressing two fingers to his temple. *Good,* she sensed. *No permanent damage.*

"I told you I'd hurt you, Sonny. The first time always hurts the most."

He moaned.

She opened the truck door, grasped his limp body, and hauled his deadweight into the passenger seat. He wasn't small—a solid 195 pounds of muscle and exhaustion—but Myli barely felt it. Her strength was returning faster than she expected this time. So would his.

She took a minute to put her clothes back on before climbing in the driver's seat. The learning curve couldn't be too steep. She pulled the shifter and gave it some gas. Reverse. She slammed on the brakes. Eyes wide and heart racing, she was ready for her second attempt.

She lifted the shifter in the other direction and stepped on the accelerator like she'd seen Sonny do. Tires kicked up gravel as the wheels spun.

As Kandy was running away, Myli opened her door, smacking her with it, knocking her over. Her skin rippled; hands embedded with grit betrayed her disguise. Kandy was a hybrid Udug, a muse to the others. One of many walking amongst the everyday public.

Myli blasted on, almost hitting another mailbox with her rookie driving. She sped out of Anchor Arms Apartments, leaving behind someone else's mystery to solve. None of it would matter if her mission failed.

They were twenty minutes out. Sonny's brain rebooted somewhere around the twelve-mile marker down the highway. He woke up mid-convulsion, body jerking, a metallic taste on his tongue. Drool ran down his contorted face. His vision blurred, his head pounding as if he had just taken an aluminum bat to the skull. His naked body sitting in a naked limp pile would surely leave him with a stiff neck for the rest of the day.

"Wha... what the fuck was that?!" He looked at himself in the OBJECTS IN MIRROR ARE CLOSER THAN THEY APPEAR. Wasn't it the truth? His face was bruised and getting darker like a henna tattoo.

His voice slurred, his limbs felt like deadweights, and for a terrifying moment, he thought he was paralyzed. Jaw locking—was that tetanus setting in? His body caught up with itself, and he suddenly felt everything wrong with him at once.

Bruises and the sharp pain in his ribs were the furthest thing from his mind as he realized that Myli was driving 75 miles per hour down a narrow two-lane country road.

"Why is my fender..." he craned his neck to see better. "Is something rattling?" Sonny's voice cracked, raw and hoarse.

"I had to learn how to drive," she said with glee. Scrapes and missing paint on the outside of the truck would buff right out. "I think I got the hang of it now."

"What... what the hell did you do to me?!" his bloodshot eyes glaring at himself in the mirror, veins red and angry, like something had been rewired behind them.

Myli didn't answer at first. Her hands gripped the wheel like a vice, knuckles white, tendons tight. Her eyes stayed locked on the open highway, her jaw clenched with tension. For her, driving was scarier than fighting the Tantrom's.

At least she'd managed to get dressed. Chiara, always two steps ahead, had thrown spare clothes in the Get Home Bag for Sonny. He realized he wasn't wearing anything. He tried to cover himself with his hands and gave up on the futile task. "Why am I..."

"It's hard to explain." Myli's tank top clung to her curves, her hoodie hanging loose and half-zipped.

"When you said, 'hurt me,' I assumed emotional regrets. You physically hurt me, woman."

Her smile turned to a grimace, and she gave a clunky nod. "We had to go. I didn't have time to dress you."

"Yeah. But why?" No reason to worry about being shy now. He straightened up in the seat.

She winced, not sure how to answer. "Magic."

"Bull shit." He grunted reaching in the backseat for his bag. The spare shirt was right on top. No boxers, "Shit." He sighed in relief, finding a pair of Wrangler jeans. Lot's of built-in pockets.

As for the fight, he didn't even bother with the whole *I had them right where I wanted them*' routine. There was no bluff left in him. He would have been brutally murdered if she hadn't shown up, and he knew it.

He swallowed hard, his throat still raw from the big man's choke hold. He turned his head toward her, breathing uneven. "Thank you," he rasped, the weight of those two words heavier than any bullet he'd ever fired.

She didn't look at him.

But he saw her lip twitch—the faintest smile.

"Sonny, listen to me." Her voice was steady, but urgent. "I've remembered some things."

Sonny shook his head, blinking hard. His body felt like he had just been tased by a goddamn lightning bolt.

"You—you—fucking zapped me!" he suddenly realized.

Her lips parted, but no words; he wasn't wrong. Her mouth was agape.

Sonny exhaled sharply, rubbing his face.

Myli kept her eyes on the road, but he watched her grip floundering on the wheel, knuckles flexing as color slowly returned to her fingers. Her lips parted again, her mouth twitched like she was about to explain, but no words came. Her lips were firing, but only blanks.

"Really? Nothing?" Sonny complained. "You come in buck-ass naked and save my life, then somehow get me in the truck and now I'm the naked one and you got nothing?!"

She stole a glance at him, her expression tight. "You will have a hard time believing me."

Sonny coughed, his throat still raw, and fumbled with pulling the jeans up. The simple act of managing to get the fabric up over his butt, in the moment, was almost unbearable. What would be worse would be getting the Frank and Beans caught in the zipper when she hit upcoming potholes.

Every movement pulled at his bruised ribs, scraped against cuts, and ignited muscles he'd abused, and electrocuted. He sucked in a breath, wincing, and twitching.

"Jebus, I feel like I lost a fight with a dump truck."

Myli's lips quirked, just barely. *You kind of did.* She didn't say this out loud, but the look in her eyes did. "I think you were close to getting out of that."

He laughed and also moaned. "You military or something? You fight like a buddy of mine—but Rufus crab-crawl fights."

She got quiet—a hush heavier than the vehicle around them. Her brow furrowed, lips tugging downward. She mouthed the words. "Crab-crawl?" Her face scrunched up. *What the hell does crab crawling have to do with fighting?*

She tried to process what he said, but her mind filled with ancient war strategy, and most importantly how to break a man's spine with one toe—

Just... stopped.

Sonny's Brazilian Jiu-Jitsu reference went straight over her head, crushing all reasoning. For the first time in thousands of years of survival and warfare, he could tell she felt completely and utterly confused. And somehow, this made her grin—just a little.

Humans were incredibly confusing at times, but they were always endearing to demi-gods.

She could easily fall for this one if she wasn't careful. Even if she didn't always understand him. The weird sayings. His humor under pressure and stupidly reckless courage.

Something about him. His vulnerability wrapped in sarcasm and the instinct to laugh in the face of pain sprinkled with a quiet defiance in his eyes, drew her in like a magnet.

He would die before he gave up. She'd seen too many souls accept fate—too many souls surrender when the weight got too heavy and she was carrying quite the load.

But not this Sonny. He fought—even when it was hopeless. And maybe, just maybe, he could be more than a boat anchor. He might be more than he seems. The question was, would he believe her?

Dog Daze
Near the Middle of Nowhere in Texas

"Hell no. No way." Sonny countered on the side of the road. "I don't believe it."

"Sonny, get back in the truck." Myli argued. "You know how plausible this is. You were there."

He pointed at her while inspecting the damage to his truck. "You abducted me."

"We're bonded," she continued, her voice quiet but certain. "After the crash, the ring malfunctioned. It wasn't supposed to attach itself to you, but now it's fused to your DNA. I can't do this without you." She pleaded with him. "We're part of each other now."

He twisted and pulled the curse on his finger. Trying again, harder. It didn't move. He braced both hands, tugging at it with everything he had. The ring felt as if it was part of his skin—no, deeper. Down in his bones. In his blood.

"You ever heard of FAFO? I already found out. I don't need to keep finding out." He gave the ring a defiant look.

"Come on," he muttered under his breath, more to himself than to her. It didn't budge.

While she spoke, Myli looked around at the coastal flats. Nothing out there but her and skeeters and deer flies. The stink of dead sea creatures irritated her nose into a scrunch on her face. Her voice was even. "There's no point. The ring won't come off. It's fused down to the genetic level."

Sonny wanted to kick rocks but there were none around which were big enough. His situation was novel to say the least.

"So, it's fused... what does that mean? For me?"

Turning away from the flats, she finally looked at him, her eyes softer now, but heavy with truth. "It means everything that's coming—comes for both of us. The creatures that boarded our ship were looking for that ring. You're not safe anywhere you go. You need me as much as I need you."

"So going home puts Chiara in danger?" he asked.

"I'm afraid so."

"And, if the ring hadn't stuck to my hand, you'd be stuck with saving the world alone?"

She flipped her hands up in a helpless little shrug. Her voice lowered to a whisper.

"Old gods are coming home," she said. "It will be a genocide like nothing this planet has seen since the time of what your people call Atlantis."

Sonny started to protest, but somehow, he knew she was speaking truth.

Time to stop whining, he told himself. His throat went dry. He ran his hands through his hair, fingertips pressing hard against his scalp as if he could massage some sense into his brain.

"Please get in the truck," she requested urgently.

"So, where are we going?" he asked, determination filtering into his self-doubt.

"Where this all began—the crash site," she said.

Sonny frowned. "Where the monsters are?"

"Yes."

Back on the road, driving towards danger, Sonny exhaled slowly, his pulse steady but his mind spinning.

So, he told himself, *Atlantis is real. A civilization, now lost beneath the crushing weight of the ocean. And this woman had been born there.*

Like a weight too heavy to lift, a thought pressed against his mind. It was a thought she could read, and he was beginning to read her thoughts too. Every myth, every bedtime story, every whispered legend about lost worlds —these weren't stories. They were memories. Warnings. Truths buried too deep for most to believe.

And what about God? he asked himself.

She heard this question in his mind. He didn't have to ask it out loud.

"He is with us," Myli said softly, her voice gentle—as if the answer had always been there, just waiting for him to find it. "He has always been with us. He is the creator of everything."

It was fortunate that Myli was driving because Sonny had been lost in thought and practically grinding his teeth into powdered enamel. Now, his jaw relaxed. She was reading his mind, but this time, he was okay with that.

"There is a force that created everything," she continued, her voice unwavering. "What you call God, we called The Architect."

Sonny's head was catching on.

A force behind it all, he thought. *A force beyond Enki, beyond the Anunna. The Architect. A presence that shaped stars and worlds—and shaped me.*

Myli's tone darkened as she reached him with her thoughts, and those thoughts cut deep. *Anunna survivors have manipulated your ancestors into dividing themselves. If they can keep your world from uniting, it will be easier to conquer when they return.*

Sonny closed his eyes. Saying aloud, "Divide and conquer."

It made perfect sense. Wars. Religions. Borders. Race. Nations. All carefully orchestrated by an enemy left behind, weaving through the shadows for millennia.

Myli sighed; he felt her thoughts tinged with hope and regret in equal measure. *The only saving grace is someone must have found Enki's Mii Book.* She looked at Sonny, her eyes bright with certainty. *It's the only explanation for your civilization's recent technological spike. Someone must have used the book to rebuild civilization from the ground up. Let me show you.*

As they drove on, Sonny saw an image flickering across the windshield —a holographic projection shimmered as if woven from light itself. Sonny's eyes widened. The map of Earth as he knew stretched before him overlaying on an ancient map.

Landmasses rose where there were oceans. Island chains, entire coastlines no longer in existence, appeared in vivid detail. He could see a forgotten world and what had been lost.

A pulsing energy signature blinking on the map, hovering just off the coast of the Bahamas. Further northeast, the Azores were also highlighted. With one hand on the steering wheel, Myli lifted her free hand and pointed, her fingertip glowing faintly. "This is where my ship crash-landed," she said, her voice steady but filled with weight.

She moved her hand slightly southeast, her gesture precise and slow. "And this," she continued, her tone almost reverent, "is where a Heaven's Gate to Atlas rests."

The map vanished, fading like a dream. The windshield cleared, leaving only the road ahead. It was one thing to hear Myli speak of it. It was another to see it.

Atlantis.

Not a myth. Not a legend. A destination waiting underwater.

"I have a friend in the Bahamas," he offered, trying to sound helpful. "Jeb's brother. He can get us to where we need to go. But—"

Myli arched an eyebrow. "But?" she prompted.

Sonny sighed, scratching the stubble on his bruised jaw line, still trying to scrape off any dried blood.

"Well, he's not gonna like going into the Bermuda Triangle," he scoffed, both eyebrows up, shaking his head. "That place is famous for making things and people disappear."

The two rode in silence for several moments. "You are approaching your destination. Make your final turn in... Five. Miles. Your destination will be on... Your. Right. In thirty miles. Proceed with. Caution." The GPS blared and shattered their brief serenity.

Sonny was still stewing. Even the damn GPS knew they were in trouble.

"Looks like we'll be at the crash site soon. You carry a sidearm, a pistol." Her voice was soft but probing. "When you don't forget it. So what was in that case you put under the backseat?"

"A rifle," Sonny seethed.

She nodded, processing. "Are you any good with it?" She asked side-eyeing the backseat.

Sonny's wall came down a little more. He gave a small, crooked smirk. "Yeah, in a controlled shoot, I can hang with the big dogs if they have an off day. I can sneak a win here and there. But this?"

He gestured vaguely as his hand waved toward the horizon, toward the unknown.

"The real world is a little bit out of my depth. I'm not a professional soldier. As you know, I almost got murdered by a pregnant meth head."

"But you were there, you know the area. You can sneak us in?"

"Yeah, I can probably sneak us in. I saw enough to know it well enough I guess. I'd use the brush as cover. It's dense enough to shield us from thermal. But the terrain's rough—if it doesn't have thorns, it's venomous. The military won't expect anyone to hike a few miles into the crash site which no one is supposed to know about."

Myli agreed. It made sense. Not a terrible plan for someone who claimed to be an amateur. Sonny pulled out his phone and rerouted Maps. CarPlay projected the route on the dash.

ETA: 28 minutes.

She studied him opening another app.

"What are you doing?" she asked, glancing over, scoping out his screen.

Sonny thumbed it open. StreLok. A ballistics calculator.

"My D.O.P.E.," he said. "I'll hang back and cover you. I told you, I ain't a soldier, Myli. I fuck off with friends and shoot steel targets for fun. But I've never shot anyone."

He looked up into empty space; the realization slapping him harder in the face than he ever could have expected. He hesitated to continue. The silence was deafening.

Myli could feel the pain of a man standing on the edge of a line he never wanted to cross. He was prepared to do it, but his brain was still rectifying the fact he had fought to the death at the apartment. He knew it was a case of self-defense. Sonny was no killer. On the other hand, the incident was flooding her memory with the faces of all the ones she'd killed. It had stayed with her. And now, she was about to force Sonny to do it again.

Sonny could see Myli second-guessing herself. A glance at herself in the rearview mirror. Her green eyes stared back at herself. Was she still the hero everyone believed she was? Or had she become the very thing she was fighting against?

Her self-deprecation was interrupted by Sonny's battle plan. They couldn't afford doubt.

"I'll post up 800 yards away," he told her. "That's a chip shot with the 6GT. Speed kills—and she's still got 750 foot-pounds out to 800."

He grinned faintly and whispered, "The Gay Tiger."

Myli's eyes narrowed, almost a full squint, her brow twitching in confusion. Sonny smiled and continued his explanation.

"Six-Gee-Tee. It's an end-user inside joke. 6mm, George and Tom… Same way rattle-canned Pink Panther got its name from the SAS and Mountbatten Pink they used in World War II." Sonny's smile tugged wider. He felt so clever when describing his weapons.

"If shit goes sideways, they'll be up my ass in sixty seconds. Just you make sure shit don't go sideways."

Myli's response was calm, immediate. "I can work with that."

Sonny sighed. "You're gonna have to because you're rolling in with TEMU John Wick."

She tilted her head, curiosity flickering across her features. These obscure references. Always the references. Sonny could see her processing, no doubt scrambling to catch up.

He waved it off.

"You just do your thing—get in, get out. I'll keep my head down and spot for you."

Sonny unbuckled from his seat with a sharp click, the belt retracting as he groaned—his bruised ribs and battered muscles protesting every movement. He twisted in his seat, wincing, and reached back into the rear cab. The rifle case was wedged tightly, heavier than he remembered, and every pull sent a jolt of pain through his shoulders and back.

He gritted his teeth and yanked it toward him, the weight dragging from under the seat. The zipper fought him—old, stubborn, weathered like everything else in his life. But it gave way with a reluctant scrape. Sonny pulled out Pink Panther. Battle-worn. Familiar.

The rifle's custom mauve finish was chipped and scratched from years of use. He called it battle-worn. Underneath, the black metal peeked through like old scars. It wasn't pretty anymore, but it wasn't supposed to be either.

Her eyes slid toward his rifle. "Your weapons… they have finite ammo?"

"Oh, yeah." Sonny winked at her like she'd asked if water was wet. "Yes, and ounces equal pounds. It's gonna get heavy AF by mile six. This ain't no run & gun setup. It's built for precision, so it's heavy. I'll be rolling in with close to one hundred pounds of gear."

Her tone stayed even. "What else do you have?"

Sonny sighed. "Level IV armor plates, Motorola's, all kinds of shit, Myli." He shot her a look. "All of it back home." He muttered under his breath. "Next time you crash-land and recruit someone into an intergalactic war, give 'em a heads-up before throwing them in the fire."

Myli chuckled, and for the first time in a long time, it felt real.

"Will do." She glanced at him, her expression softening just enough. "You've got this," she said quietly, her words gentle but resolute.

Sonny didn't answer. He just nodded, eyes narrowing toward the road ahead. Sonny exhaled. "The shooting? Yeah." He could squeeze a trigger just right. "The emotional trauma from the aftermath?" He shook his head. "I'm no pipe hitter."

Chapter 35

Naked and Unafraid
The Crash Site in Texas

Sonny and Myli arrived near their hide. They'd come on foot—the truck left behind a few miles back. She hadn't broken a sweat. Him? Death was taking slow laps around his grave. The beating earlier didn't help.

"Do you even have sweat glands?" He asked noticing her light glow. The only other woman he knew with infinite stamina was his wife.

"You should've let me carry the rifle."

His every muscle screamed. "That'll be the day," he said arrogantly.

The last twenty-four hours had been a gauntlet—exhaustion, pain, adrenaline, and fear—all layered under the multi personalities of Texas weather. The rifle sling had rubbed a rash on his neck. His clothes clung to him, drenched and heavy, sweat-soaked in an atmosphere rivaling a sauna.

Dropping to their bellies was just the beginning of the painstaking process of low crawling for two hundred yards to a better vantage point.

At last, they settled into their blind—a small, concealed depression surrounded by dense mesquite and scrub. Sonny, despite fatigue, unfolded the small fan he'd improvised from wild mustang grapevines and flexible branches. He set to work quietly reinforcing their concealment.

Pink Panther already lay beside him, done up in hand-tied foliage, blending perfectly with the brush line. Even the pinkness blended in with the natural tans in the sand and caliche.

No ghillie suit—he didn't have time to assemble a camouflage outfit of fibers and cloth—but what he had was good enough unless they had drones up. Slowly, carefully, they slid forward until they found their line of sight.

The impact site lay to the front of their position, and it was nothing like they expected. Sonny adjusted his scope. The crater was torn apart in jagged scars. Smoke drifted slowly, lazily curling into the humid air like exhausted spirits. Gray ash coated all that was left of the tall grass.

The mesquite trees stood stripped bare too. Skeletal sentinels, their branches were coated in fine white dust. At the tips of some branches, embers still pulsed. Sonny was getting an itch for a plate of barbeque.

Sonny's eyes narrowed, eyeballing the scene in the prone. Acrid smoke hung low, curling into the thick, sticky Texas haze.

A mile-long scrape in the Earth led to the impact crater. The central peak lay directly in front of their position, a bowl with a mound at the center. At the edge of the bowl, a temporary Forward Operating Base had been established. No massive alien ship. Just a well-organized military presence.

"It's milky out there. Where's your spaceship, chica?"

"Good question, Sonny." Myli thought for a second, *Did the military stop the monsters?*

Sonny dug into his pack, pulling out his Razor HD Fury binoculars. The black digital HUD flickered on as he depressed the top button. His index finger rolled back and forth, adjusting the focus until the world became crystal clear. He ranged the targets, careful not to laze any targets with a counter-lasing device, such as a LWS (Laser Warning System).

He turned to Myli. "I got us this far. So, what's the plan now, Boss," Sonny muttered, his voice low, dry. "Your UFO is gone."

She nodded. "I need to get in there," she said softly, but with daring in her voice.

"For what? There's nothing but trouble down there," he pointed out.

"You got this, Sonny."

Before he could respond—POOF!

She was gone.

A blast of hot, dry dust smacked him in the face. Sonny grimaced, eyes squeezed shut as gritty air clung to the sweat on his skin. He coughed, lips puckered, shaking his head. When he finally opened his eyes, only her clothes were left collapsing silently onto the ground beside him. He stared at them for a second—frozen, disbelieving—before scooping them up and stuffing them into his pack.

Before he got back on glass, he grumbled under his breath: "Got this? The fuck I do."

He went back to scanning. His process was methodical, watching soldiers moving with practiced discipline, gear being packed, rotors spinning up.

But no sign of Myli.

"Damn it, where did you go?" he muttered, adjusting the focus, taking notes on his Dopestick, then continuing his sweeping across the FOB.

Scanning.

"There you are," he saw movement. "Buck. Ass. Naked. And not afraid," he whispered.

There was Myli, walking through the middle of an American Forward Operating Base like she belonged, but comically out of place. He shook his head slowly.

He imagined a soft murmur rippling through the camp. Boots scuffing to a halt. Conversations cut short mid-sentence. He could see the wind tugging gently at her hair, the only movement besides her slow, confident steps.

Dust blew over his position, swirled around his snipers hide; he was hidden but not forgotten by nature. He shook his head slowly trying to remove the moon dust. It was like trying to clear static from his brain.

"This effing chick," he said. "Only this crazy-ass, and possibly reptilian, alien chick would stroll into a U.S. military FOB with no clothes, no weapon, and maybe no plan."

Sonny exhaled a choking breath, talcum powder fighting its way out of his lungs. The cough turned into a laugh, despite the tension knotting his gut.

He settled behind the rifle. The stock was warm, but his 3M foam pad made it tolerable against his cheek. His heartbeat echoed in his ears. He checked his elevation dial with steady fingers.

He tasted metal on his tongue, dry from adrenaline. He eyeballed the wind, watching faint wisps of dust swirl across the hellscape below. If this thing kicked off, went sideways—and he had no doubt that it would—he'd be her last line of defense. His breath came shallow, controlled, the weight of his trigger finger pressed lightly against a worn spot just above the trigger. Slowly he bent the pad of his finger back to pop the joint.

"This is so stupid," he whispered, almost giggling, breath hitching—excitement and panic tightening his chest until he could barely tell them apart.

Out there, Myli continued to move like bigfoot in the Appalachians—smooth, controlled, weaving between scorched earth and scattered gear. Surely a photo or video would be captured of her, but no one would believe it. Hard-sided Pelican cases thudded shut, and the metal latches clacked as soldiers locked them down, creating piles which looked like stacked luggage. Boots pounding off into the distance took with them fading orders of exfiltration. Above, the sky stretched empty and still—no aircraft.

However, the stillness was coming to an abrupt end. Sonny watched as the solo Black Hawk was prepping for takeoff.

He wasn't sure if it was the static electricity surrounding the crash or psychic perceptions radiating from the bowl making him nervous. He watched Myli zero in on an item of interest, a half-open Pelican case. Draped over it lay a jacket, forgotten and left behind.

Without hesitation, she snatched up the jacket and put it on, the fabric worn and dirty, smelling faintly of oil and onion. It hung loose on her frame—too big, sleeves bunching—but it worked. A second later, her hand closed around an M4 laid across a closed case. The rifle was warm from the sun. Although foreign to her, the grip texture felt familiar enough. She worked the bolt with the charging handle, slick and over oiled, the round slid into the chamber.

Muscle memory clicking into place—she repeated motions Sonny had shown her back at the truck. This gave Sonny a sliver of relief.

She was moving deliberately, like she'd done this her whole life. Three spare aluminum STANAG mags sat just within reach. With the warm aluminum burning into her palms, she stuffed them into the oversized hand-warmer pocket of the jacket.

Meanwhile, the Black Hawk was minutes from liftoff, its blades now spinning at near-max rotation.

Sonny watched all this unfold through his glass. Large trucks rumbling, brakes hissing, diesel fumes miraging in the heat as engines prepped to roll out. His scope catching a man barking orders near the largest rig—too clean, too sharp. Officer? Intelligence, maybe. Sonny had no clue. It didn't matter; they were all threats until they weren't.

She was going right for the big rig. He panned slowly across the camp. Soldiers hustled, tension coiling tighter with every panicked step.

CAG—Delta. Definitely an elite operations group. He didn't know the difference. More movement. Frantic possibly. They were fanning out, taking defensive posture. Sonny looked to see what they were defending against.

His breathing sped up. *Here we go.* His heart beat faster. He shifted his scope to the tree line. The brush moved. Branches swayed in an otherwise windless heat dome. Those trees take more than a breeze to shake like that.

More rustling among the trees, like snakes through leaves.

Not human.

"Oh, boy." He deadpanned.

His heart was racing, his breaths increasing in rapidity. Despite the heat, he felt a chill curling up his spine. His skin prickling—the air itself charged with static and dread. He whispered without thinking. "Oh shit. Oh shit. Oh shit." His words sprinted out of his mouth.

Myli turned and looked towards his sniper hide. It was as if she heard him. She quickly scanned where Sonny was glassing. Suddenly, the tree line was in motion.

A horde of Udug soldiers bursting through the thick Texas brush in horrific, fluid motion. They ran on two legs, then four, leaping through the air, twisting in ways that defied human anatomy. The creatures skin shimmered like black mother of pearl, iridescent scales; claws flashed like tips on pikes.

These weren't alien caricatures. The walls holding up Sonny's reality came tumbling in. He struggled to steady his breath, working hard to get his breathing under control as he watched the turmoil unfold through his binos. The world as he knew it was falling apart in his psyche.

CAG operators and ORBGRU teams reacted instantly, moving into defensive positions. They formed up their lines and prepared for contact.

Their shouts echoed—even at a distance, Sonny could hear them. Terse commands, safeties clicking off and then the first pop snapping him back into reality. The gunfire—deafening. The reverberation of sound across the basin slapped his ear drums.

.50 calibers roared from mounted positions, hypnotic and unrelenting. Miniguns spun up, whirring their part in the symphony pouring down a wall of lead. The tree line was ripped to shreds, erasing what remained of sparse foliage.

It was less than a minute before soldiers holding the front line screamed as the line was being overrun.

Bodies flew. A 234-pound operator in full kit was ripped off his feet like a toy doll, flung through the air, slamming into a burning Humvee.

Despite the dust Sonny couldn't keep his mouth closed. He fought dissociation clawing his mind. In a fit of shock, he yanked his eyes off the binoculars, his breath close to hyperventilation.

"Oh fuck, fuck this shit," he said with his outside voice. Deep breaths. "Nut up," he yelled at himself before sliding behind the rifle. Still breathing heavily, his cheek weld was tight, mashing his face in front of the scope, illuminating any scope shadow. He adjusted the magnification on his Kahles 5-25. Parallax dialed in. The world snapped into razor focus. His targets were not little green men from cartoons. Not big-eyed greys from the movies. Something far worse. Demons.

"Fucking monsters?" he breathed buyer's remorse. "What happened to the aliens?"

Through his scope, one of the creatures plowed into a man—hitting him like a running back on full charge. The soldier—jeans, civilian clothes, chest rig tight across his frame—never stood a chance. Flattened by eight feet of rippling muscle and exponential momentum.

The sound of breaking bones carried across the field.

The lines of his reticle scale were bouncing, wild at this distance from his heart pounding. *Control. Breathe.* Sonny tried desperately to focus through the glass. He rolled his wrist, glancing at the Dopestick shaking on his wrist like he was reading the time:

Distance — Hold (MILS)
300 yards — 1.0 Debris Pile
400 yards — 1.7 No Man's Land
500 yards — 2.5 Semi
600 yards — 3.3 Crates, Jeep, Tent
903 yards — 6.5 Chopper - Stump

Sonny held 3.3 on the stadia lines, rolling the zoom back to 12-power for situational awareness. His heart hammering against his ribs. The reticle bouncing wildly—at this distance, it looked like ten feet of wobble.

"Fuck me, calm down. Settle..." Sonny exhaled slowly, fighting to control it.

Find a monster. Get the reticle on target. He told himself. He was far from the action, but if he was going to help at all, he needed to apply discipline to his approach. Could he do it?

CHAPTER 36

Nothing but Trouble

Myli flickered into his view—half-naked beneath the oversized Army jacket, ducking and weaving through smoldering debris. Hunting. Sonny whispered, instinctively, like an arm-chair quarterback.

"Go. Duck. Move right."

Useless advice. She couldn't hear him. Yet she made all the right moves like she could.

Sonny seated a fresh mag and slammed the mag release with a satisfying clunk. Bolt carrier seated forward. Chamber hot. The Atlas bipod bit into the dry soil, stock settling deep into his shoulder pocket. His micro-adjustments using the sling, coiled into a makeshift rear bag, were smooth and deliberate. He spread his legs apart, his feet flat against the terrain, making himself as recoil-absorbent as possible.

His natural point of aim lined up.

The reticle steadied, heartbeat slowing. The world in front of him narrowing into his view in the glass.

The wind picked up out of nowhere. He didn't read it from the trees— South Texas mesquites barely flinched even in forty-mile-an-hour gusts. He read it from the smoke—twisting ribbons dragging east, then curling back west. He exhaled slowly, steadying his pulse.

Found his new hold on the Christmas tree: right 1.2 MILS for wind and target movement.

Fingers worked the parallax with practiced precision. Reticle drifted. Settled. Locked.

Phop.

Impact.

A puff of smoke coughed from the suppressor.

Miss. Hit. Miss.

Damn, they're fast, he lamented.

The ones he hit were lame—staggering, wounded—but not dead. His shots slowed them enough so that a nearby .50 cal had a chance to tear them into shreds. Shrapnel from errant shots pinged off metal. Sparks flared bright against the smoke-choked sky. Tracers carved molten lines across the field like a scene from *Star Wars.*

Sonny shut his eyes hard, trying to force the grit out, and a muddy tear rolled down his cheek. The dust on his face turned to mud, his heart pounding steadily now as he measured each shot. Squeezing the coiled sling, controlling his breath, he waited for his next shot. He aimed Right 1.2 MILS for a moving target and less wind. The wind was gusty and switchy, constantly changing directions.

Another solid impact.

His headshot through the ear downed the monster. It was out of the fight. More puffs of cancerous smoke exited the can from the T-handle and into his face. He was gassing himself out. Barrel getting hot, his suppressor cover struggling not to catch fire.

Impact. Impact. Miss. The last miss gave away his position.

One of the creatures came to a dead stop and looked in his direction. It was faint but based on the missed shot hond others tearing in from the side, it located Sonny's hide.

Sonny backtracked on glass, "Where did you go." The creature he was tracking had stopped as he overshot it. He picked his head up off the scope, looked over the turret. Not where it was supposed to be.

"H O L Y Fu..."

The monster was leaping over containers, oil drums, smashing through debris as it was charging straight for him. He had a minute at the most before the thing was right on top of him.

A shot, a miss. Several times in a row, as the thing juked, bobbing and weaving its way towards him.

"Hell," he said groaning, fighting the urge to mag dump into the thing.

His shooting tempo increased.

100 yards.

75. Mag change.

50.

25.

"Come on, you son of—Oh, my God."

The thing rocketed toward him. Saliva whipping in the air, its claws extended, its body in a full double-suspension gallop.

The last thing Sonny saw was the creature's tonsils so close that they obliterated in his scope. He pulled the trigger and sent the last round through the creature's mouth, blowing out the back of the head. It only had ten feet to go. The bolt locked back; it was the last shot from that mag.

The creature was down. Sonny laughed; he almost cried. His pants were wet; he hoped it was from sweat, but he wasn't sure. "Hold my beer, not today, Satan!" He cracked a forced laugh; grateful he'd taken a leak back at the truck.

Shaking his head in disbelief he thought how close that was. *Fast as fuck, boy!*

His trigger finger twitched, recalibrating, breath short and shallow, pulse pounding behind his eyes. "Calm back down."

Explosions lit up the field below—rockets, grenades, desperation. The madness intensified below as the Udug worked their way through the defensive lines. Claws ripping. Screams echoing. Claymores detonating in tight clusters of monsters—but they kept coming.

Head or neck shots were the trick. The 6GT caliber rounds hit with 2,700 fps force, each impact a wet loud splat against thick, seemingly impenetrable, flesh.

Monsters flinching, roaring, turning toward cover. Headshots or upper torso hits took out their transmission—just like a truck, just like a deer—no transmission and they were done, out of the fight. One vanished into smoke, leaving the battlefield. Another disappeared.

A dip in gunfire. Fewer shooters were keeping up the tempo.

Sonny had been so focused on his targets that he'd temporarily lost track of Myli. Rapidly, he scoped the battlefield until he spotted her—just in time. A Udug was creeping up on Myli. Its back was to him—so was hers. The thing was ready to unalive her. It coiled, about to pounce. Sonny's heart hammered. He quickly took aim. Shot lined up.

Squeeze... The round went off nice and clean.

Right through the back of the skull—some skullduggery at its finest. Thanks to Sonny's long-range shooting, Myli was safe again—for now.

Seconds later, from the corner of his optic, Sonny saw movement—a tight group of soldiers, heading for the Black Hawk. He had no idea who the soldiers were. Only much later would he recall seeing Hawk who was leading the group. Stonegate was with him, the old man had a hood over his head, and a new face: a wiry, cold-eyed CIA paramilitary guy. Brazzeal. A battered soldier, Briggs, brought up the rear. They were hustling the prisoner to the Black Hawk. Doors slammed. Blades roared. The bird lifted.

As the Black Hawk was lifting off, its miniguns continued to spit suppressive fire at shifting shadows as the bird rose over the Texas mesquite canopy. In desperate pursuit, the tall, monstrous beings climbed onto anything with height, leaping in vain, swiping at empty air as the helicopter escaped.

Sonny watched it go, then he resumed his support of Myli.

He spotted her again, below on the battlefield. She was sprinting, moving from cover to cover, her M4 barking—useless. The Black Hawk's rotors could still be heard echoing over the battle ground as it roared skyward far away from the fight.

Hot brass rained down around her from above. A few casings slid down the collar of her jacket—still hot, stinging, singeing her skin, little trails of blisters left behind as they fell inside. She hissed through her teeth, cursing, and dove for cover beneath the big rig.

As Sonny watched from afar, she entered the big 18-wheeler trailer. From his position, he decided to keep an eye on her. It was the best place to look for a lead. He'd do his best to cover her, but inside the trailer, she was on her own.

Inside the trailer, Myli worked at a breakneck pace, uncovering whatever she could find there. Intel. Folders. Scattered files.

A Project Red Wings folder stood out in a distinctive red instead of a manila color. *Icarus.* Looked interesting but not immediate.

It was all stuff she had no clue about.

Her oversized Army jacket was torn and hanging loosely off one shoulder. Papers stuck to her wet skin as she flipped through them.

A massive thud slammed against the hatch. She jumped, adrenaline spiking—completely spooked. The file cabinet she crouched behind wouldn't stop anything, but concealment was better than nothing.

The door creaked. A clawed hand and elongated head slid into view, dragging down the opening. The eight-foot creature had to duck, crouch, make itself small, to climb through the door. The frame cutting, bending, and twisting in its grip. Scrunched up, it made its entrance, head scanning like a shark. A loud splat, pieces of head spraying the inside of the trailer. It was no more.

Still in his hide, Sonny had smoke-checked another one as well as his buddy who got too close to the 18-wheeler. She could feel his relief; he could feel her battling her own PTSD demons. She stayed frozen, gathering herself. Her chest rising and falling beneath the field jacket, heart hammering against her ribs.

She blew a tendril of hair off her face, but strands still clung to her flushed cheeks, her expression locked between terror and focus as she looked over the cabinet. She saw nothing but a body and a black mess of Udug head and brains.

On the desk in front of her: scans of terrain. Images captured with ground penetrating radar. They had found something here, but they didn't have time to investigate due to the ambush.

Realizing the value of the scans, she exhaled slowly. "Jackpot." She scooped up the document and grabbed her M4.

At his distant position, Sonny exhaled, shoulders slumping. It was time to push or ditch out on her. Now or never, while they were still hunting other soldiers.

Perimeter fences had collapsed in multiple places—breach points from every direction. Fire and smoke billowed, black plumes curling into the sky, the heat of the fires palpable even at a distance. At least he had good cover to get down there.

Sonny swallowed hard, lifting his sweaty head from the stock of his rifle. His ears could still hear the boing of the recoil spring in the stock. *Shooting unsuppressed is uncivilized* he thought to himself, noticing the mirage off his melted suppressor cover.

"Damn it," Sonny said. "Nut up, shut up, I gotta get down there."

Down below, unaware that Sonny was on his way to join her, Myli cautiously poked her head out of the trailer. The battle still raged, gunfire echoing, explosions thudding in the distance. She carefully stepped and straddled over the dead Udug and down the rest of the steps. She had picked up a pair of oversized boots from the war room—now she was crunching over shattered gear, hot spent brass, and twisted, mangled bodies still bleeding into the dust.

Others were still engaging to the bitter end, soldiers and operators circling the wagons, laying down desperate, disciplined fire as the lines closed in. It wouldn't be long before they were dismembered. The battlefield trembled with distant booms, crackling flames, and the metallic rattle of empty brass piling up.

As Sonny hustled down the slope in the direction of the 18-wheeler, the air reeked of scorched fuel and burnt meat, thick enough to taste. With his rifle at low ready, he was cooking at a good pace. Ricocheted rounds buzzed past him, sharp zips and cracks in the air. The caliche soil had cracked into bone-white scars beneath boot prints and blood; the battlefield was turning into a graveyard of insanity.

He stumbled—went down hard, gravel tearing at his palms and jeans, pain dulled by adrenaline before it could register.

"Get up slacker," he told himself.

He popped up and started sprinting again.

Whatever those things were, they were tearing through this place like wet paper. Sonny crested the summit, braced against a pile of splintered crates, taking in the scene up close. Fumes of JP5 and burnt gunpowder filled his lungs, harsh and acrid. There was a strange iron smell too—sharp, metallic, almost like blood.

His furniture trailer was still there in the distance.

BOOM!

An explosion rattled the crates beside him, hot wind buffeting his face, stinging with dust and grit. An errant rocket hit near him. Shrapnel everywhere, chunks of metal raining on him. An axle rocketed skyward, spinning wildly, taking off like SpaceX parts on a bad liftoff.

"Geezus, what the hell..." Sonny stammered forward, clutching his rifle close to him, the handguard resting on his forehead.

The metal picatinny rail dug into his palm, grounding him in a moment that felt utterly terminal. The land twisted as his equilibrium skewed. A bullet hit him in the face. Non-lethal. A ricochet of shrapnel scratched his cheek. A strange, cold reality: a livelier bullet could hit him for real—any second.

A wave of euphoric energy swept over him when he saw the scattered bodies, torn apart with unnatural cuts. This wasn't like shooting steel. This was real and raw. He kept moving.

Sonny's breathing was shallow. He felt nauseous, the ground starting to spin, black spots and stars creeping in at the edges of his vision. He tried processing the sheer violence unfolding here. Each step was on unsure footing as he rounded the front bumper of a Ram 2500 dually towing something big.

Crouching and sliding against the truck, he backed his way into Myli doing the same thing. They both jumped. The startle turned into a rush of relief when they realized they were reunited.

Hiding behind the massive 23kW light tower hitched to the truck, they took stock of one another.

"Hey, you scared the shit out of me," Sonny said grimacing.

"Same; are you having fun yet?" she asked sarcastically.

His face said *bite me,* his shrugging shoulders said he was dealing with forced bullshit. His body swayed slightly, color draining from his face, skin clammy and pale, almost shivering in a cold sweat. She noticed one of his hands shaking by his side.

"Ewe, you don't look so good. Let it out. You're in shock." Her voice was flat. Cold. She went back to scanning their surroundings between the truck and light tower.

He threw up. The acid jettisoned from his nostrils too, burning what was left of the inside of his nose. The second round of puke sent him to his knees. His abs constricted uncontrollably.

"Let it all out. It will reset your nervous system," she suggested.

"We need to leave," he said, wiping his mouth with his shoulder. "I saw one of those things chasing men into the tree line, out of sight to our right."

"We're not done here," Myli muttered, eyes zoning in on the central peak of the crater.

"Neither are these demons," he retorted. "They're cleaning up."

"Dangerous things are dangerous," she confirmed flatly.

"Thanks for the scientific breakdown, Yogi Berra."

She looked at him plainly. Not in the mood for deciphering references.

In that fractured moment, he couldn't help noticing the strange, alluring attraction to her. His eyeballs worked her up and down. He could feel her in his head reading every thought before he could bury it. *"OH MY GOD what is wrong with me?"*

Sonny was edging eye contact with her when she spun around looking for options for their next move. He saw her catch him gawking. He shook his head. "Sorry," he muttered.

Even with rounds still snapping overhead he found it difficult to resist her overwhelming pull on him.

Their serenity shattered when an attack chopper thundered by. The concussive thwap of the rotors and blasting of the chain gun smattering layers of hate. A salvo of rockets accentuated the human disdain for the enemy. Explosions created a rippling effect that displaced the air pressure around them.

The blast blew her hair around her face in slow motion. "No need to say sorry," she said softly, placing a hand on his chest. "Nice shooting, Salesman." She cracked a grin.

Her touch was electric. "I guess the break is over?" He grinned back.

Her face became impassive. Back to the business at hand. She handed him the intel folder she found.

"The commanders here were surveying the area with something called 'deep penetrating radar' before they were attacked."

Sonny scooped up a rifle from a fallen soldier, a Boombox in 8.6 Blackout. Lighter than and shorter than his AR-10. Even with a shorter barrel it still hit like a hammer. Two-hundred-grain subsonic horse pills, spinning at crazy RPMs. The bullets were like drill bits punching through flesh. Much better for close quarters than his long-range musket. He tossed another one to Myli.

"Hey, the M4 wasn't doing shit. Use this one. 77 grain is too anemic against these things. Even my 6GT was bouncing off without precise kill shots. They're fast and hardy boys."

She nodded approvingly, dumping the carbine. She'd figured as much—the 5.56 barely slowed them down with the few shots she took.

Sonny could still feel his nerves zapping his nervous system; he was desperately trying to suppress them. The fire wind howled over the burning landscape, kicking up dust and scattering loose debris. His ribs throbbed with every breath, the pain settling in like an old friend. His hands—still salty, sticky with sweat, sand, and oily blood—closed around the unfamiliar rifle's grip.

He reached in his pocket and grabbed a piece of dried fruit and chomped down on it. "Wanna date?" he asked her. He needed sugar. Chiara tossed some in his pack for him. Dates were a superfood when out of gas during intense workouts.

Now she was annoyed. "This isn't the time. Get a hold of yourself. Besides, you're married."

He looked confused. "Why are you the way you are?" he asked while stuffing the dates back in his pocket.

The two of them continued sheltering behind a truck for a few seconds longer. Sonny peeked around the bumper. The pace of the action on the battlefield was slowing down, but the place was still alive with movement and death. Wrecked Humvees smoldered in the late afternoon light. Blood pooled in unnatural shapes along the caliche.

Some bodies were still intact—most weren't.

Sonny slung the Boombox's Viking Tactics sling over his neck, adjusting it with the quick-adjust strap. The sling shifted the weight of the Boombox comfortably over his shoulder and onto his back. Grabbing Pink Panther, it was time to move again. Myli was already on her way to the next bit of cover she planned out during their break.

"We need to be there," she said, hastily pointing at the mound of the central peak.

"Of course we do," Sonny replied, as chipper as ever. "Back down and up. Out in the open. How stupid of me to think otherwise. Let's zap over at least."

She shook her head. "Too dangerous. We'll lose our guns. Be naked."

Sonny pointed toward rubble along the way. "Cover," he suggested.

"It's a lot of open ground to cover, Sonny."

"Then we better not dillydally running through it."

We might just pull this off, he thought.

CHAPTER 37

The Mound Temple

They were on the backside of the mound, approaching a derelict pickup truck. They came to a complete stop when they bounced into its side. It was full of scattered and used medical supplies. He wondered where the men driving it had gone.

Dead?

Sonny turned back to Myli. He watched as she brushed her fingertips over the earth, her expression darkening. She nodded to the top. "This isn't just the central peak of a crater." She told him. "There is a temple underneath it."

He shook his head, getting to the top was the most dangerous part. He scurried along the ground, blading, trying to make himself as small as possible. He came across a baseball sized sphere. It was still warm from a distance. He poked at it with the tip of the rifle. Too heavy to roll, it sank further into the ground. How could something so small be so heavy?

"Don't touch that," she ordered. "It's all that's left of the ship."

Sonny crawled away from it.

Hovering near Myli, there was a sharp hiss of static buzzing through the air. Sonny felt the ring pulse on his finger—a faint glow illuminating the metal. Sonny instinctively raised his rifle, eyes darting around the ruins, looking for Udug. His thumb was ready to flip the safety. His finger poised to slide down to the trigger.

"What the hell is that sound?" he asked.

Myli heard the low frequency too, and she was seeking the source by pressing her hand flat against the ground. The earth shuddered beneath them. A mechanical groan.

Sonny staggered back, lost his balance, and slid on his butt, eyes wide as the ground shifted beneath his shoes. With a deep, earthen hiss, a massive stone door emerged from the earth. Ancient embedded into the mound—perhaps long-forgotten, but very much there.

As the door opened wide, they were sucked in like ants dragged to the bottom of an antlion trap. Sonny, just short of panic, held it together until they finally stopped falling. Looking up, they could see the surface—about twenty feet above them, bits of debris still tumbling in. To return, they would have to climb out. In front of them was another door—this one metal. Myli was eyeing it.

"No friggin' way. Big nope. There is nothing good about going down there," he said.

"Would you rather stay out here with those things?" she asked.

He groaned, taking a second to debate the pros and cons of the second door. She stepped forward, shaking her head, fingers brushing over the door's glowing blue edges.

Sonny adjusted his rifle, settling it at low ready. "Who's to say those things aren't already in there? You sure you wanna poke the ancient alien door?"

"Just watch my six," she said—

Sonny grinned, watching her personal bare six was the only thing he really felt like doing.

"My *other* six," she insisted. She paused for a moment, thinking as she grabbed Sonny's hand.

"Hey, what are you doing?" he demanded as she pressed his hand—and the ring on his finger—against the metal surface.

The glow surrounding the margins of the door intensified, casting shadows across their faces. A low-frequency hum vibrated through the air, sinking into their bones. With a final hiss of decompression, the door slid open.

A rush of cool, stale air spilled out, carrying the scent of damp earth, and time itself. Sonny stared into the darkness below. A spiral stone staircase wound downward, vanishing into the void.

Myli stepped forward. Sonny did not.

"Yeah," he muttered, "this is where we should take a truck and GTFO."

"Stay close," Myli said, already starting down the steps.

Sonny got a high grip on the rifle, ready for the impulse. "Pink Panther is low on rounds."

"Didn't you pick up a new toy?" she teased.

"You're killin' me, Smalls," he grumbled.

As they traveled even farther from the surface, they failed to notice the *Menagerie* Sphere as it continued to sink deeper into the ground, like sand at the bottleneck of an hourglass.

The stairs descended into the darkness, winding deeper and deeper beneath the earth. Sonny's footsteps echoed in the confined space. The walls—smooth metal alloy—felt cold to the touch, despite the humidity clinging to the air. He ran a finger along the surface, stopping at a series of etched symbols glowing faintly blue.

It almost looked like—

"This is your writing," Sonny muttered.

"It is," Myli confirmed, running her fingers over the symbols.

Sonny eyed the inscriptions warily. "This place is older than Texas itself, isn't it?"

Myli gave him a sideways glance. "Older than your civilization and the one before it."

Sonny let out a low whistle.

They kept moving. As the corridor widened, they stepped into a massive chamber—easily the size of a football field. It reminded him of the main chamber of Mammoth Cave. Sonny stopped in his tracks taking it in.

The ceiling stretched high above them, lined with conduits running like veins through the structure. At the center of the room stood a pillar-like console, humming softly with energy. Sonny had the impression the console was alive.

"It's here," Myli whispered. "This place is older than the energy pyramids. I was worried the chamber would be empty."

"Thank God it's not." Sonny staggered behind her, looking over her shoulder. "What's here?"

Myli strode forward and faced the console, running her hands over the interface. The ring pulsed in response. Sonny was starting to settle down, yet he kept an eye on the exit behind them. Something didn't feel quite right. Where were the traps?

She muttered something under her breath, her fingers tracing the console's surface. Then she spoke clearly and loud enough for Sonny to hear.

"The digital key," she said. "The passphrase—it's all here."

Sonny gave her a puzzled look. "You're gonna have to explain that to us mere Homo sapiens."

She barely looked up as she focused her attention on the console. "It's a failsafe. A master key to access a gateway to what you call 'Atlantis.' We couldn't get in without it. No weapon without getting into Atlantis."

Sonny let out a sigh. "Let me guess—last hope for humanity?"

"Exactly." She touched the interface, and the glyphs shifted.

A holographic projection flickered to life, displaying a set of encrypted characters. Sonny adjusted his stance, uneasy. He shifted his attention to the stairwell. If they had what they needed, he didn't want anyone to sneak up on them.

"We good?" he asked, his nervousness coming back.

"Almost," Myli muttered.

Sonny's stress level was rising. A sensation he could feel in the soil under his feet. His finger hovered over Pink Panther's trigger. The rifle might not be much help against the Udug or anything else fantastic, but this felt like a natural threat.

"Myli—you hear that?"

"Got it!"

She yanked her hand back. The hologram vanished, and the console powered down. The ground vibrations increased. Dust began raining from the ceiling. The air itself, the pressure in the room, felt heavier. Sonny snapped his rifle up, eyes darting to the entrance. He worked his way toward it, taking an angular approach, pie'ing the opening.

Myli didn't follow. Instead, she studied the chamber's ceiling.

"Uh," she mused, "not to alarm you—but I think this place is about to come down on us."

Cracking rocks and a groan of heavy earth reverberated through the chamber. The walls began crumbling. Sonny took a long breath.

"Myli—" he began.

The rumbling intensified.

"RUN!" she finally ordered.

They sprinted for the exit at high ready. Seconds later, the weight of the *Menagerie's* dense baseball-sized leftovers arrived from the surface to penetrate the stone dome and the chamber was breached.

As the two of them cleared the staircase, the entire mound began collapsing behind them, sinking into the earth as if it had never existed at all. Reaching the second door, they clawed their way up the last twenty feet to return to the surface. Strangely absent up there—gunfire. Sonny doubled over, hands on his knees, gasping for breath, then he stood erect and scanned the horizon. There, he was surprised to discover the truck sitting only a few yards away.

Suddenly, the dirt beneath their feet began turning into quicksand. He reached back and grabbed Myli's hand, yanking her out of the softening dirt.

"Jeez, Myli," he exclaimed as he pulled her to safety. "We cut that one close, huh?" His chest heaved, lungs burning from fine dust.

She turned to him and stood side by side and calm as a clam, while the ring glowed faintly on Sonny's finger.

"We have the key," she said. Her tone was almost congratulatory. "On me in three, two..." She bolted.

"Shit!" He popped up and sprinted behind her.

They hit the side of the truck with a thud, the Boombox on his back shrieking against the paint. Sonny caught his breath trying to slow his heartbeat before scanning the horizon with his scope. Mounted on Pink Panther, his KHALES gave him a clear view of their surroundings.

"If you have to go through hell—keep going," he told Myli. He came off glass and grabbed the truck's door handle like he was in a hurry. He tossed the 6GT into the back seat, flung his backpack with it, and crawled into the driver's seat staying low while doing so. He placed the Boombox barrel down on the floorboard next to him for ease of access.

Myli scooted her butt in too and, as soon as she did, he turned the key — the engine coughed, struggled, then slowly turned over.

He smiled, teeth big and white.

"Gotta go, gotta go," she urged, rushing him.

"I know, dear," he retorted, sarcastic as ever. He threw it into gear and checked the rearview mirror.

"Damn," he said.

As if the sinking mound wasn't enough to worry about, Sonny saw them in the distance—at the edge of the bowl. A group of three Udug still standing. They spotted the truck.

The engine roared to life, the truck's shocks bouncing, the cab vibrating as the rest of the mound continued creeping into the ground, sinking.

"Floor it, Sonny!!!"

Sonny's foot was on the pedal, but Myli had slid to the middle seat and stomped his foot down with her own.

The massive creatures charged, ground trembling under their weight. Myli grabbed the dash, bracing herself as he pointed the truck's nose forward toward the center of the slough, using the decline to build momentum, fighting to get the tires free from the softening caliche and onto a solid surface. He yanked the wheel, powering up and out of the bowl.

The truck launched, flying for a split second before landing with a heavy, bone-jarring thud. Myli bounced around the cab, teeth clacking together. Sonny tore across the scorched earth, weaving through twisted debris, the massive tires crushing God knew what beneath them. His joints clashed, every bump sending shocks up his spine, teeth rattling.

But he kept his foot buried on the gas.

The truck nearly upended. Something huge hit them—one of the creatures.

Myli's eyes were as big as donuts. Sonny was certain they were about to bite the dust.

"Sonny!" she shrieked—a raw death scream he'd never heard from the normally stoic warrior.

It wasn't enough to kill the thing, but inside the cab, it was the only option he had. He yanked his trusty VP9 from his Safariland holster and started popping off rounds, the gun cracking beside his head. The rounds hit, but it was like throwing ice cubes at a freight train.

"Dodge this, asshole," he growled, swerving hard to pass close to a smoldering, abandoned Oshkosh Light Tactical Vehicle.

Like gum on the bottom of a boot, he scraped the big menace off the side of the truck with a grinding crunch. Myli scurried to the backseat, shattered out the rear window, and started laying down cover fire with the 6GT, brass clinking around her. They weren't retreating—but they didn't seem to be following anymore, either.

"Pink Panther is out."

The wind roared through broken windows, dust whipping inside. The dashboard instruments flickered, barely holding on. The steering wheel vibrated violently under his grip, every bolt and joint rattling. The alignment of the truck was shot.

Sonny's eyes stayed locked forward, wild and wide.

Myli set the gun down, the hot barrel melting a spot into the carpet, and crumbled into the seat, chest heaving. He glanced at her in the rearview mirror—tried to adjust it—and the damned thing fell off in his hand. He grabbed the backpack which flew to the front and tossed it back to her.

"Get dressed," he ordered.

Her heart was still trying to catch up. The vehicle groaned, every jolt adding to its misery, but it was moving—and right now, any direction away from there was the right direction. Behind him, sprawled out in the backseat like a pinup girl in a war zone, Myli sat silent, face unreadable, staring out the shattered back window. Looking up, Sonny could see a contrail. Myli saw it too.

"Cruise missile on its way," she said.

Behind them, the battlefield faded fast in the dust and smoke, the scene whited-out by a bright light enveloping it. It took everything he had to keep the truck steady, wheels fighting him. He finally pulled over into the ditch, heart pounding.

He turned around—she sat up, eyes fixed behind them. A small mushroom cloud was rising, blotting out the sun.

"Ho-lee schittt," he murmured.

His mind raced. Everything behind them was gone. But then, why did it still feel like something was watching? Stalking them. Residual evil.

Grabbing the 8.6 Blackout rifle was the only thing grounding him right now. His hands shook—not from adrenaline, but from something deeper. Something primal. Sonny took a deep breath trying to steady himself.

He glanced back at Myli from the corner of his eye. "The government can't cover this up," he quipped.

She turned to him slowly, her expression still unreadable. "Something tells me this won't be our last close call," she said flatly.

Her hand came up behind him, resting on his shoulder. It was warm, solid, and felt good where everything else hurt. He glanced at her again, looked at her hand. He didn't brush it away.

Her eyes flickered with a subtle hesitation he hadn't seen before. Sonny picked up on it immediately.

"We've got a big target on our backs. The ring—a key, and a map."

Ah, more bad news. Sonny rolled his eyes back, processing.

"We're the only ones with both," he said. "And, because of you, we're the only ones who know where to go, right, right?"

She inhaled slowly, deeply, her chest rising against the torn jacket, fabric tugging at frayed seams before she answered.

The road ahead blurred at the edges. His mind tripped over possibilities, dark shapes lurking in the periphery of reason. He gulped. The wind ripped through the truck, hot and relentless—like a blow-dryer on high.

Those creatures were a freakin' menace.

Sonny ran his hand over the door, brushing away broken glass, tired of it blowing in on him with every gust. He scratched at his lengthening stubble, gritty and uncomfortable. He needed to focus.

Myli leaned further into him from the backseat. Her hand slowly inched its way closer to his heart.

"We need to get to the Florida Keys," she said with urgency.

"We got this, right?" he asked. "Right?"

When she didn't answer, Sonny pulled out his phone, the screen cracked, thumbs tapping out a quick text before steering back onto the road, tires screeching as he hit the paved road and burned a rubber-traced left turn.

"Just a quick road trip," he said. "No big deal."

CHAPTER 38

Pit Stop

The sun dipped toward the horizon, casting a golden glow over the gas station parking lot. The pavement radiated heat—it felt like a balmy one million degrees, sticky, the asphalt was soft from melting all day. The black tar would stick to a person's shoes if they were unlucky enough to walk across it. Mirages continued shimmering up and down the highway. Even the birds perching on power lines looked like they were begging for water as the sun was preparing to set.

Sonny stretched his legs, rolling the soreness out of his shoulders as he grabbed the gas nozzle. His hand twitching on its own again, small spasms he couldn't control. He tried to shake it out, but the tremble lingered.

"What the fu-?" He gave a closed loop whisper. "Knock it off," he told the unruly limb.

They had been driving for hours, with hours still left to go, heading east along the coast. Now, they were here—a Speedy Stop gas station, out in the middle of nowhere.

Just another pit stop.

Inside the nearby convenience store, Officer Mark Coward sat perched by the window, gnawing on his third stale hot dog of the day. His thoughts wandered, still stewing over having to go in on his day off. Everyone in his office was out with FLU A. He figured he had it too, a matter of time before the virus tried to take him out, but he was old school. Hardcore Coward.

He was bald, had a long, perfectly kept black beard—he still had that dog in him from the old days. He sighed heavily, slurping on his cherry-blue raspberry ICEE just as the door chime jingled. And that's when she walked in.

Coward's brain stalled. A woman—a seven—strolled into the store, dirty as hell, possibly a meth head. After several minutes in the restroom she came out cleaned up—now a seven and a half—her dark brown hair catching the light as she stepped toward the counter. Her emerald eyes stood out as she scanned the shelves like she was picking out Michelin-quality food instead of gas station Slim Jims and chips. At least she ignored the sushi.

Another guy, also filthy, had come in behind her, and gone out back. He'd been in the restroom much longer. The crystal-clear water in the toilet was now soiled after his christening.

"Jerk." He knew where everyone in the gas station was. It was his job. Right now, he was making sure the THOT wasn't shoplifting. She had a huge wad of cash, some in her pocket, and some in her hand.

Damn, bro. He wouldn't mind arresting that *ho over there* and taking her in for an interrogation. That seven and a half was starting to look like an eight.

His ICEE melted halfway to his mouth, condensation dripping down his fingers. The excitement faded fast when he saw the other dude touch her back on the way out. He wasn't some random guy; he was with her. Her damned boyfriend, now standing at the pump, filling up a beat-to-hell white Ram. He looked beat to hell, too—ragged, dirty clothes, sunburned face, bruises still fresh. She must be a mad dog at home.

Just his goddamn luck. She was pretty but not excessively crazy-hot. He wouldn't kick her out of bed in the morning either. After a whiff of her scent, he bumped her up to a nine.

He scowled, turning back to his stupid hot dog. His mind was playing tricks on him.

Mylitta barely even glanced at the sweaty cop stuffing his face. She walked up to the cashier, trying to count the amount owed from the wad of cash that Sonny had stashed in his bag.

"He said to put all this on pump three," she said, handing over way too much money.

The cashier raised an eyebrow but said nothing.

Myli grabbed a handful of protein bars, a bottle of water, and a bag of jerky before heading to the door. She felt Officer Coward's gaze before she even looked his way. A hungry stare. She ignored it and walked outside.

Sonny leaned against the truck, watching the last few drops of gas tick into the tank. He looked tired. And uneasy. The restroom break was well earned, but he still couldn't shake the feeling gnawing at him. He checked his cell again—still no signal. He couldn't reach Chiara. Something was off with the network. The silence made his skin crawl. No texts in or out since leaving Port Lavaca.

Myli's stiff posture stood out as she approached, her shoulders just a little too tight.

"Problem?" he asked.

She tossed a bottle of water to him and shook her head. "Nothing. Just a peace officer inside, watching."

Sonny looked to the window. Was the cop a threat? "Shit," he muttered. "Think he recognized us?"

"No. Just a guy with a badge. Looks like he's been in the trenches too long. Daydreaming, I think."

Sonny exhaled, relieved. He screwed the gas cap back on. She was right; he was white Danny Glover, too old for this shit. "Alrighty. Let's hit the road."

Back inside, Officer Coward's radio crackled. He was spared from traveling east after a big-ass explosion. They needed someone to stick around the area to manage calls. His ears perked. Had they changed their minds? No.

His eyes were still locked on the white Ram. That woman—she was fine as hell. And the guy at the pump? Maybe gay. He was pretty bruised up. He'd bet money the dude's fine ass ho beat him. He thought for a second, *What a simp.*

Even still, Mark nodded, he understood. He thought he could change her too. His cop instincts itched though. He wiped mustard off his fingers before reaching for his radio. Something wasn't right. Mark Coward was about to find out why. A digital squelch. He began calling in the plates.

Coming around the side of the truck, Myli barely had time to react as a blue sedan tore into the parking lot from the highway. Had someone lost control exiting the off ramp? It wasn't slowing down. The car bounced violently, bottoming out on the uneven pavement before correcting, turning, screeching toward Sonny like a guided missile. Sparks erupted from underneath, metal grinding against the asphalt as it hurtled forward.

Officer Coward moved first—faster than Sonny even realized what was happening.

Sonny, oblivious, was halfway through his strip of beef jerky when he looked up—headlights barreling toward him. Too late to dodge. Too late to think. Instinct took over.

He leaped, barely clearing the bumper. The ring flared to life, just as the hood clipped his legs, sending him spinning into the windshield.

Glass spider-webbed on impact. His body flipped mid-air, twisting unnaturally before slamming onto the pavement with a nasty thud.

He should've been dead—or at least broken. His breath leaked out in one ragged gasp. But instead, laying there waiting for the next beating, he scrambled to his feet, ribs aching, ears ringing.

He was up and standing, adrenaline pumping, legs shaky but moving. He hobbled toward his truck, grimacing. Morale has not improved. The beatings will continue.

Officer Coward darted out of the gas station running back to his squad car, hands fumbling with the radio. "Hit and run! Suspect vehicle is a—"

His words died in his throat. The sedan screeched to a stop, tires screaming on the hot pavement. Reverse lights flickered on through the thick cotton ball poofs of smoke. The tires screamed again against the pavement as more white smoke poured from the wheel wells. The driver was gunning it—straight back at Sonny, hobbling for safety.

Coward drew his weapon.

Myli didn't hesitate either.

She yanked the VP9 from the glove box, shoving the truck door open with a metallic groan. Her half-eaten sandwich hit the pavement, smashed under her boots without a second thought. Instinct took over.

Raising the pistol, bracing behind the door's arch, she took aim through the narrow space between the door and the truck frame. On target she squeezed off several rounds. The concussion rattling her ears. Spent brass clinked against the asphalt.

The first shot jolted her forearm—recoil was a foreign feeling. But her aim was true. Rounds punched into the driver's side door. The passenger window exploded, glass raining inside the car. Pistol empty, the slide locked back. It took Myli a second, but Sonny warned her these barbaric weapons needed reloading.

She fumbled but found the mag release. Mag dropped. Pointy end facing the correct direction, mag in. The slide was still locked back. She shook, tapped, eventually pulled the slide back sending a round in the chamber.

As she slapped in another mag, Sonny threw himself behind the truck.

Myli was seconds away from disaster and leapt into the cab. The sedan smacked into her door, shutting it hard. A few good kicks and it opened just as hard. From the ground Sonny saw Myli angle out and squeezed off a few more shots as the car sped past.

Pedestrians screaming, bolting in all directions. Was it the terrorists? Several took shelter in the gas station, while others ran to a nearby ditch to take cover.

One of Myli's rounds found the driver's neck.

The sedan veered wildly, crashing into another parked car. For a moment it seemed over, but it wasn't. The driver lurched forward, hand fumbling for the gear shift.

Coward heroically took action. He was right in the middle of what he believed was a gang shootout. Not knowing who the real threat was, he stepped into the open and fired—on Sonny as he made his way into the driver's seat. Coward's bullets shattered the truck's remaining back windows, spraying glass across the cab like razor confetti. Sonny ducked, rounds dotting the windshield. Coward took aim at Myli as she peeked behind the truck frame.

Round one and two slicing past Myli's head close enough to clip some of her hair off. In a blink, fast enough to teleport and reemerge into her falling clothes, she blipped between the bullets ripping holes in her shirt.

"KEEP YOUR HEAD DOWN!" she shouted, voice raw as she leapt into the passenger seat.

Sonny worked the ignition hard, hands filthy. The HEMI roared to life as he slammed the shifter into drive. His foot might've gone through the floorboard if he pressed any harder. Tires spun, screaming, burning rubber thick in the air. The gas pump nozzle ripped free, whipping and flailing behind them, still spraying fuel wildly across the pavement.

Sonny didn't look back.

He couldn't.

Gas was spewing everywhere behind them as they launched onto the frontage road. Loose gear and ammo, once heavy, was momentarily weightless in the cab.

Behind them, Officer Coward was still firing—the front windshield spidering as bullets punched through, one round grazing the dashboard just inches from Sonny's hand.

"Son of a bitch!" He jerked the wheel, narrowly missing a worn-out Dodge Neon, the tires squealing as the truck swerved into the next lane.

Myli clutched the Boombox rifle in her lap, breathing hard, pulse hammering in her ears. Her mind raced. Their getaway had spiraled out of control. No amount of magic tech was going to get them out of this without massive injury.

She looked back toward the gas station. The blue sedan was moving again, jerking forward like a shopping cart with three good wheels. The driver, who should've been dead, suddenly jerked upright in his seat.

His body contorted unnaturally, twisting and spasming like a marionette with broken strings. It wasn't a human behind the wheel anymore. He slammed the gas. The metal beast screeched in protest, its frame groaning.

A pedestrian screamed, diving out of the way as the sedan whipped around, tires shrieking against the asphalt. The Udug soldier in the driver's seat slammed the gear shift—

Nothing.

The engine whined, shuddered, and died. He'd thrown a rod.

Snarling, he scanned the parking lot for another vehicle—something fast, powerful. His eyes locked onto a patrol car.

Perfect.

It had the speed and horsepower he needed to catch his target—and this time, he wouldn't miss.

Meanwhile, Officer Coward had enough nonsense from these meth-heads. He gritted his teeth, squaring his stance as the possessed soldier approached him on foot.

"Mistakes were made today, shithead. FAFO!"

Mark had run SWAT for years before moving to a desk job. Didn't mean he forgot how to put rounds on target. Today, like old times, he was back in the field. And this asshole needed putting down. He pushed forward, weaving between parked cars, closing the distance on what looked like an ordinary military officer. Except nothing about him was ordinary.

The soldier was taking aim.

"Stand down!" Coward barked. "Fine hombre, GFSF. Your call." He implied under his breath.

His Staccato roared, his finger tired from emptying the entire mag.

The soldier moved fast—too fast. He juked, twisted, dodged between the bullets. The ones landing barely slowed him down.

He just kept coming.

Blood leaked from his older wounds—already healing. The fresh ones? Minor. Like scratched open mosquito bites.

Coward dropped back on his heels. Shit. This wasn't a man.

"Shit, shit, shit, shit..." Coward whispered, hands shaking as he slammed a fresh mag into place. He tried to rack the slide—but it caught, gritty and stiff.

The soldier stopped for a second, head tilting unnaturally. The Udug infiltrator had taken a barrage of hits before even reaching the gas station. Now he was taking more rounds, and though very hard to kill, he was not invincible even though it seemed like it. The heavy projectiles were more than just an annoyance—they were wearing him down.

Coward froze, fear intensifying.

"What the hell —?"

Something beneath the illusion stirred, rising to the surface. Something devilish. The thing's face rippled and distorted, the facade breaking apart. Beneath his uniform, flesh and bone strained, seams ripping where the uniform was too tight—and tightening further until it tore.

The soldier, already towering at 6'5", began growing, limbs lengthening, muscles swelling grotesquely. The metamorphosis wasn't instantaneous, but it was fast. The transformation was complete. In seconds, the eight-foot tall beast stood uncloaked.

Its body needed a respite; the disguise pooled a lot of energy to begin with and even more when taking damage. The question was how long he could maintain human form under duress.

His boss, Asag, needed the key and wanted the weapon.

And Pazuzu was determined to get the job done.

At 219 pounds soaking wet, Coward moved fast—too fast to think. He yanked his Winkler Operator knife, vaulting over the hood, and slamming the blade into the Udug soldier, driving him back. No hesitation.

Mark pumped his arms. "You think that ugly-ass face scares me?" he snarled.

He rained down fist after fist, holding the blade like an ice pick, slamming the knife, plunging again and again into the creature's face. Bone crunched. Skin split. The knife was doing more damage than faster projectiles.

The Udug buckled—but didn't fall.

Unexpectedly, Coward felt it before he saw it—his gear disintegrating, seams tearing apart. His plate carrier shredded, straps snapping like dry twine. His uniform ripped away, fabric fluttering like paper in a storm. His radio crushed, sparking and dead. His gun belt clattered to the pavement, useless. For a split second, he was bare, exposed—nothing but flesh and raw nerve endings, standing in the open.

Even his dumpster-sized balls were laid out for the universe to judge.

Mark was a menace.

But not enough of a menace to stop a truly menacing beast. A beast gracing the scriptures of every religion around the planet. A villain so captivating, so enduring, people still shuddered at the thought of going to hell. There was a reason for fearing crossing paths with demons in the spirit world.

As scary as Mark was... Pazuzu was scarier. Pure hate.

It was over.

The Udug rose, slower this time. It turned, cracked its neck, and strolled toward Coward's cruiser—like the fight had been a mild inconvenience, even though the constant abuse was wearing him thin. He struggled to transform smaller. With a lack of space in the front seat, he ripped it out and climbed in, smaller, but still massive, he squeezed his frame behind the wheel and smashed the gas pedal.

Before he left, he had a thought. A nag left to itch.

The patrol car skidded to a stop, tires chirping as it came to rest beside the still-leaking gas hose, fuel puddling across the pavement. The Udug rolled down the window—or what was left of it. The fractured glass crumbled into a thousand sparkling shards.

He reached out the window, dropping a grenade. He floored it.

Engine roaring, tires screeching, the Ford Police Interceptor Utility Hybrid—the fastest police car in America—came alive with a growl. Its hybrid AWD power train kicked in, built for maximum efficiency while idling and offering unshakable stability and traction in any conditions. Under the hood was the 3.0-liter EcoBoost V-6 unleashing 400 horsepower and 415 pound-feet of torque—muscle built for highway pursuits and relentless acceleration. The cruiser shot forward, pavement blurring beneath it.

His massive body sank into the backseat, letting the horsepower do the work.

If he kept going, he'd be well-clear of the scene. But oddly, he hit the brakes, reversed several feet and hit the brakes again. He'd linger a bit, to watch the explosion. There would be time enough to complete his mission. Catching Myli and Sonny would be trivial.

In the rearview, Coward's mangled body lay motionless. The Udug barely glanced back—a shot hit him.

CRACK.

A flash from Coward's Staccato CS pistol. The bullet slammed into the back of the Udug's skull, snapping his head forward. The creature snarled and moaned, shaking off the pain. One bullet wouldn't do.

Coward's wheezing final words. Blood spouting out of his mouth and body. Blood flow almost gone. "That's right, motherfucker—you can't kill me!"

BOOOOM.

The grenade detonated with a thunderous crack. A red-hot flash erupted first, blinding and violent. As luck would have it, that initial blast threw the Ford Interceptor and its lucky driver free of the coming inferno. Seconds later, a roaring wall of heat slammed outward. A black mushroom cloud billowed into the sky, thick and oily, climbing fast and blotting out the sun. The shock wave tore across the lot, lifting debris and broken glass, sending them rocketing in every direction like shrapnel.

The gas station ignited, erupting in a chain reaction of secondary explosions—fuel tanks, propane canisters, and pressurized lines all going up in a deafening symphony of fire. It didn't just explode. The Speedy Stop went off like a massive bomb, a rolling fireball flattening nearby signs and shattered distant windows.

Flames licked the clouds. Hell was following close behind.

CHAPTER 39

Run For Your Life with Me

Sonny caught the explosion in his mirror—an orange-red bloom swallowing the gas station in a rising inferno. The shock wave hit the truck, rattling the frame and shivering through the wheels. He slammed the pedal through the floor, the engine roaring, the tires biting hard into the asphalt.

They were running out of road. Miles ahead, the horizon narrowed—traffic stacking up, brake lights flaring like a glowing river of red LED lights. The Interstate 10 construction zone loomed—orange barrels and concrete barriers funneling vehicles into a single choking lane.

Semi-trucks crawled.

Horn blasts echoed.

The air vibrated with tension. Everyone was desperate to move, but trapped.

Sonny's pulse spiked. No way through. No way around. Maybe the emergency lane. The clock was ticking and behind them, hell was catching up.

Just then, Myli glanced in the side mirror and Sonny caught a glimpse of her pained expression. He checked his own mirror.

Myli yanked the charging handle back on the Boombox, the bolt slamming forward with the force of a sledgehammer to a rock. She gave the suppressor one last twist, making sure it was locked tight. "Very hard to kill with these barbaric weapons."

Sonny kept his foot buried on the accelerator, weaving between big rigs and family sedans, the speedometer climbing past 100. The wheel began to tremble—he could feel the death wobble forming, subtle at first, but building.

"We're running out of road," Myli cautioned.

"I see it. I can get around it. We're in a truck. We don't need pavement." Sonny looked back. "Shit."

Myli glanced back. "He's gaining."

In an instant, it was on their tail. Sonny glanced back again, caught those eyes—Black. Hungry. Those eyes—like a Great White's eyes, lifeless until the moment of the bite, when they rolled over white, a protective membrane sliding into place. The creature filling the cab of the car reached outside the window, tiny pistol wildly aiming. The muzzle flashed slinging a round into the truck.

The shot slamming into the tailgate kept going, punching through the back of the cab. The hot slug continued through the middle of the bench seat before embedding deep into the radio.

"Damn, these guys shoot now?!"

Sonny swerved hard, tires shrieking, barely missing a hazard barricade, the fender clipping an orange cone and sending it spinning into the air. The truck rocked, but he kept it straight, heart pounding in his throat.

Myli brushed the broken glass out of the passenger side window. Bracing herself, she climbed halfway out, gripping the water channel on the roof of the truck. With her one hand gripping the seam, she slipped the Boombox into the crook of her elbow, creating a makeshift support to steady her aim.

She gave a grimace, maintaining her balance. Wind was slapping her face like a whip as she fought to maintain balance with the asphalt racing beneath her. The hum of the tires drowned out her fears—most of them anyway.

Still, Sonny reached over, grabbing her ankle with his free hand, holding the steering wheel with his left.

"You're total insanity! Jesus, Myli!"

She ignored him, exhaling slowly as she lined up her shot. Sonny glanced over, alarmed.

"What the hell are you doing?!"

"Ending this!" she clapped back.

Another round cut through the cab, nicking Sonny's extended arm. He yelled out, but didn't relinquish his grip on her.

Knowing time was short, Myli took aim, steady hands despite the climactic energy building. The Udug's mangled head leaned forward, its speeding car now just feet from their bumper, about to slam into them. A whisper of thought from Myli slipped into Sonny's mind:

NOW!

Sonny jerked the wheel hard.

The truck swung sideways, rear tires screeching, the back bumper clipping the patrol car's front fender, sending it into a violent death spiral.

Myli fired—unburnt powder splashed her face. The nearly silent 8.6 Blackout spat. Shots peppered the hood, rounds punching deep into steel. The final shot punched clean through the windshield, and the entire car erupted. The hood tore free, yanked skyward, spinning like a twisted metal pinwheel as the wind caught it mid-flight.

A shock wave rippled out of the car, warping metal, shattering windows. Flames roared through the destroyed windshield, swallowing the interior in an instant. The patrol car burst into flames before twisting violently sideways.

A ball of fire. It went up like Mt. Saint Helens.

A second explosion ripped the car apart, sending 100-mph debris cartwheeling through the air, tumbling down the highway like a comet too close to the sun. Chunks of burning metal and glowing wreckage bounced across the asphalt, trailing smoke and ash.

Sonny flinched, his hand locked on the wheel, eyes wide, as the inferno faded in the rearview.

"Yeah!" he shouted as he and Myli sped on, tires burning rubber, the fireball shrinking behind them, casting flickering light across the highway. "Don't mess with Texas, a-hole."

Sonny thumped his palm on the steering wheel excitedly, his heart pounding like a war drum in his chest. Then he remembered Myli. He released his death grip on her ankle and immediately reached blindly—grappling for her knee, her thigh—whatever he could grab further up on her body to drag her back into the truck.

"Get your ass back in here, you psycho!" he barked, yanking her inside.

Myli landed half-in, half-out, her elbow smashing into the busted radio with a dull crack. "I had a shot!" she snapped with a higher octave, breathless but fierce.

"Yeah? You also had a one-way ticket to roadkill!" Sonny fired back, yanking the wheel to avoid another sedan he was blowing by.

Myli exhaled sharply, adrenaline shifting into sharp focus. She clicked the Boombox on safe, the barrel still warm, her chest rising and falling, breath ragged.

Her pupils were extra-large. "Another one bites the dust," she said with a huge grin.

Sonny's stomach was in his throat. But they'd prevailed. Both elated. They'd beaten another one. He put his hand up for a high-five. It took her a second, but she reciprocated.

"How many more are out there?" he wondered aloud.

Myli didn't answer. Because she didn't know either.

VIBRATIONS. Sonny's demeanor filled with concern.

"Fuck! This is no bueno," Sonny growled. "You better buckle..."

The truck sputtered. The wheel jerked hard in his hand, almost breaking his wrist. A rear tire shredded instantly, the truck cut hard left. The bumper scraped against the car next to them, metal-on-metal shrieking.

Sonny fought the steering wheel, muscles straining, his thumb dislocated and the weight of the truck, the momentum, and the goddamn laws of physics were turning on him. The rear end fishtailed, tires screeching for grip. The front tires catching the four-inch drop-off of the emergency lane, yanking them off the asphalt and into the soft dirt shoulder.

Too late.

They slammed into the ditch.

The truck bounced violently, and metal scraped. It's shocks groaning under the weight, before crashing down with a weighty slam. Metal crunched. Glass shattered. The world tilted sideways, spinning out of control.

Sonny's head cracked against the doorframe, stars exploding in his vision. Blackout.

The airbag detonated, slamming into him like a freight train, snapping his head back into the seat with brutal force. The truck rolled once. Twice. Three times. Each rotation was a blur of sky, earth, and lights from other vehicles.

The truck came to a rest on its side, skidding to a stop in a plume of dust. It took only the weakest gust of wind to push it over onto the roof.

Smoke curled from the crumpled hood, heat waves rippling through the shattered windshield. What little glass left was splintered into a thousand spiderweb fractures; the rest turned into microscopic disco balls rolling across the roof of the cab.

Myli groaned, voice hoarse and strained. "You good? Sonny!" she moaned, her breath ragged.

Sonny's vision swam, the world tilting in slow, dizzy circles. His ears rang like a damn church bell, pulsing in time with his heartbeat. He tasted blood, parts of the inside of his mouth cut, flapping on his tongue. The seat belt strap strangled him, his own weight pulling it tighter, biting deep into his shoulder and ribs and neck.

He still managed a weak, dislocated thumbs-up. Better than dead.

The truck smoldered around him with a faint scent of burning electrical, oil, and rubber filling the cab. Beside him, through the haze and broken glass, he heard her voice—hoarse but steady.

"We might be on fire. No rest for the wicked," she smarted, breathless but defiant.

"I'm fine. Everything's fine. Just leave me here."

"Sonny, we need to get out; it's not safe in here. There is gas pouring in from the bed of the truck!" she said, still fighting inevitability, refusing to fold.

With absolute certainty, eyes swollen, bruises all over him, he muttered "We won't be seeing that thing anymore. Nothing walks away from that. Right?"

She paused. Thought about it for a second.

He was right. But others could have followed. Should she check?

Her training, her instincts, whatever was left of discipline and survival reflex—those things forced her to look. Maybe if she didn't look, it wouldn't be there. As long as she didn't check—but she had to.

Schrödinger's Alien.

Myli, banged up badly, coughed hard, spitting blood as she crawled through broken glass toward the backseat of the overturned truck. What was up was now down. Her knee crunched the dome light—now smashed into the floorboard ceiling.

Everything inside was a goddamn mess—bags ripped open, ammo scattered everywhere, the windshield half gone, jagged glass crunching under every shift and crawl. Pink Panther and one Boombox had jettisoned.

One knee down followed by the other—broken glass underneath both, she yelped. Flinching from the raw blast of sharp pain, she hit her bruised head on the back of the bench seat for good measure. Another sharp cry.

"Damn it!" she coughed out.

White smoke was filling the cab. She was losing visibility but could see gas pooling in the ditch beside them.

She ducked down and continued crawling on her hands and knees to the rear of the cab. Blood-soaked knees and palms, she streaked crimson on the ceiling of the cab as she searched for a weapon.

One magazine and two. Her hands were sweeping for something bigger. The other weapon? Chucked somewhere back on the highway during their Mach-3 vehicular gymnastics. The final couple of feet were arduous, but she found the last Boombox lodged between the door and backseat. It didn't take more than a couple tugs and she had it.

A couple more coughs.

One was better than none. She could only shoot one rifle at a time, and Sonny was out of action. Myli rolled into the prone position, cheek pressed to the stock, mono-podding on the magazine of the Boomstick. There was a sharp crackle of glass beneath her elbow grounding her in the moment.

Not one to underestimate her opponents, she checked their six, scanning through the ventilated back of the overturned truck. In the smashed cab, shards of glass, still clinging to the rubber gaskets, trickled to the ground in a crystal rain. Beyond the waterfall of sparkles she saw something moving. Myli fixed her aim on the movement, took a deep breath, and waited—. The road behind them was torn up from the fireball of fury they left in their wake. Her exhale was controlled as she patiently waited to squeeze the trigger.

False alarm… it was one of their dislodged tires. Freed from wreckage, it limped home as if gravity was returning it to sender. The tire smacked into the tailgate with a hollow thud. It wobbled uncertainly and spun half a turn before coming to an unceremonious rest. Through the Texas dust, it kicked up something else. Like a gift from the gods, an Ontario MK3 Navy Knife fell from the seat above her.

Out there on the highway, pedestrians were out of their cars. Help on the way. Maybe not—the existential crisis rectangles were out in force. Everyone videoing, getting the best shots for their favorite social media platform on their phones. The civilian highway news correspondents were closing in, slowly, making sure they captured every frame.

The calm was just the prelude before something worse. The sun was almost down, and it was dark enough now that lights from the highway were playing tricks on the mind. Flames licking up from the engine twisted shadows across the wreckage. Reflections added to the visual disorientation. And behind all this…

A shadow flickered down the highway, caught briefly in the headlights of distant vehicles. The figure illuminated briefly before it was swallowed by the twilight.

The damned thing was still alive. Tremors filled her face. Her eyes were full of panic. She knew she had to get a grip and fast. Instead, a phantom of a scream caught in her throat. She choked on the soundless cry, eyes wide, heart hammering against bruised ribs.

"No…" she whispered.

The word crawled out of her mouth, barely audible, dragged down by fatigue and adrenaline overload. Her body trembling with the weight of denial.

It was slower now and taking a roundabout route but still coming. Absolutely relentless. These creatures were a living, breathing plague. Myli stared hard into the growing darkness. It was there. She had only to wait.

Seconds later, the Udug limped through the smoke and debris, its twisted, half-mangled body regenerating in real-time, bones reknitting, skin bubbling back together, a sickening crawl of tendons and muscle patching itself up piece by piece.

It wasn't smiling anymore. Was it ever smiling with those features? Never mind. Now it looked pissed.

Myli took a breath. She worked through the wobble in the scope and fired.

One heavy round smashed into the Udug's pelvis. Grinding with 500,000 RPMs due to its fast 1:3 twist rate. The impact staggered it, sent chunks of flesh splattering onto the pavement. It grimaced—slowing down even more. It stumbled. But, gathering itself, one foot in front of the other, kept walking.

Closer and closer to the inverted truck.

Myli's hands trembled against the grip. She brushed sweat and blood and tendrils of hair out of her eyes.

"You have got to be kidding me. WHY WON'T YOU JUST DIE?!" she screamed squeezing the trigger.

Sonny smashed his eyelids down trying to squeeze the blood out of his eyes. His vision was blurring and, for the moment, he locked into place.

"Myli—" he groaned, his voice raw, choking on smoke and petrol fumes.

He decided he was going to die here. The thought settled like lead in his chest, or it was blood from internal bleeding. He didn't hear Myli answer. Was she already dead?

Between the crickets and horns blaring, it was difficult to orientate his surroundings.

He was still inverted. The seat beside him was empty. Below him, the glass reflected multiple beams of light coming in from the headlights. A trail of blood where she'd been moments ago. She wasn't in the truck anymore. And his own body was done. Spent. He was ready to submit to the afterlife.

"Nah, bullshit," he decided. "Not today, Satan."

He jerked his hand back, splintered glass driving deep into those tiny, nerve-rich spots—the same pain which sandburs know exactly how to monopolize. With his other hand, he tried to wipe blood out of his eyes, desperate to see. But glass embedded in his palm micro-cut his eyelid and brows open with every pass.

Blood was still rushing to his head, so sounds were becoming muffled, but one distinct sound grabbed his attention. Heavy steps crunching glass, a thud against the back of the truck with the scratching sounds of nails on a chalkboard inching closer and closer to the door.

Outside the inverted truck, the Udug took a step forward, one foot dragging through the glass, grinding over stones in the road. He assessed the remains of the truck before reaching for the door handle and ripping it open. Sonny sat upside down floundering to rise.

The Udug grinned a terrible grin, but a sudden wave of recognition came over his face—as if he recognized a threat from another time. The threat of remembrance from a legendary statement about this exact moment in his life. The creature's devilish face fell flat as he realized his error. He turned then, but not in time to stop the prophecy.

Myli abruptly appeared behind him.

A blur. A whisper of energy cutting through the smoke. He was swift and unstoppable. Before the Udug could react, she raised the knife she'd found rattling around in the truck and plunged it into the creature's spine. Dark oily blood ran down the blade and onto the handle. Reaching back with her free hand she hammered the blade further in with a tight fist.

The Udug howled like a banshee, echoing through the wreckage and parking lot of cars. The frightening sound added to the curiosity of those surrounding the accident to video.

Pazuzu collapsed to his knees, his head and shoulders now level with her dark brown hair which had become mahogany-red from her blood. Her tangled ribbons were soaked with her own gore.

Myli's bare chest heaved. Blood pulsed out of her wounds. With one foot planted firmly, and the other placed on his back, she kicked him forward.

She stood over him as a grim mosaic, depicting the hunt. Lights from the vehicles illuminated the shards of glass strewn across her body, making the fragments sparkle like cruel jewels. Her nakedness was clothed in life draining from her own body. Stopping these things would take the ultimate sacrifice. She fought to keep this side of her buried, a shadow of her past, but their was no stopping this Angel of Vengeance.

Seconds later, from behind her, a Karen slowly approached—phone in hand, recording live on social media. Myli turned fast enough the blood from her hair flicked onto the woman with the phone.

Behind the new arrival, Sonny stumbled from the wreck. Crawling at first, he steadied himself on the truck. His energy zapped, causing him to quickly fall back to his knees. Obstinately, he continued the fight to get up, forcing himself not to quit. Limping hard, he pushed his way past the fool and made his way to his battle buddy.

"I'm pretty fucked up," he coughed blood, grinning like a clinical idiot. The grin did him no favors as more blood insisted on gushing out. "You don't look too good either," he noticed Myli.

"You look terrible," the Karen commented. "She looks ferocious."

Myli and Sonny turned to her. The look they gave would have scared a nun. Myli slapped the phone out of her hand.

"Hey!" the Karen protested.

Sonny wheezed, bracing himself against the wreckage of their truck. He needed a hair longer than he had to steady himself.

"Is... he dead?" the Karen asked.

Myli didn't answer. She just dropped the knife on the asphalt. The body twitched. Eyes still staring, brain still firing before the inevitable demise of the last spark of life. Sonny wanted him to be conscious for what was coming.

He didn't hesitate. Sonny reached inside the truck and pulled out the Boombox.

No need for precision during this mag dump. All the remaining rounds pumped into Pazuzu's body in full auto. The head was gone—nothing left but a massive black ink blotch where it once was.

The Karen freaked out and went running into the mess of cars stacking up.

"Survive that, asshole!" He added with contempt.

It took some effort, but he kicked the corpse into the gas-rich roadside ditch.

Myli winced, looking at Sonny. Her eyebrow cut and body still shaking.

"Time to go," she said. "We need a vehicle."

He could hear discomfort in her voice which unsettled him. For the first time, he realized she wasn't indestructible. There was a possibility she may not succeed—a possibility which reinforced his resolve to see this through. She kicked a bit of burning debris into the gas, the flames leapt from the body.

Red and blue flashing lights punctuating her words as emergency vehicles sent a glittering rainbow into the clouds on the horizon. The sirens and horns grew louder as emergency vehicles tore up pavement to get there.

The duo brought more heat to the Texas night than the sun had all day.

Sonny groaned knowing what was coming. "Not the zappy zap again." His eyes rebuked her.

"Yeah, teleporting. We need to hide our trail without any tracks this time."

Myli grabbed him by the arm, firm and insistent.

His shoulders slunk forward, face looking up to the heavens, pre-grimacing. He was already in enough pain.

Exhausted but triumphant, he shut his eyes. "The show goes on—do it!"

And in a flash of light, they were gone with the wind.

CHAPTER 40

Captain, O' Captain
Coastline of Florida

A storm was rolling in fast. The old man, Shara from the *Menagerie,* sat at the edge of the docks, staring over the darkening sea. Beyond the horizon, buried beneath the waves, lay the ruins of a shortcut to the first great lost civilization. One of the last functional Heaven's Gates lay there.

The island nation held many names: Nordic Urheimat, "original home" to the speakers of the protolanguage; Hanebu, "The Sea Peoples" in Egyptian; Atlantis, "Island of Atlas" in Greek. The Aztecs called it Attlan, while the Mayans used the term Huatlan. All ancient civilizations told similar stories, and all had different names. They all believed the same thing; we were all cousins before the Dark Epoch. One thing was for certain: the Atlanteans didn't call themselves Atlanteans. But one thing was written in stone—Plato wasn't making an allegory. Atlantis—whatever you want to call it—had once been a real place.

Gusting wind was churning the surf into foamy white froth. Hawk stood in front of it, on the docks, adjusting his appendix-carried P320 in his pants. His eyes darted back and forth sweeping the coastline. Had anyone else figured out this was the next piece of the puzzle?

The sky was bruising with heavy thunderclouds, lightning flashing in jagged streaks not far from them. Poseidon knew someone was looking for his kingdom. The sharp scent of sea salt and ozone filled the air.

"You look like a man staring for ghosts," Hawk muttered.

"They are out there." Shara spoke with a heavy heart. He exhaled, shaking his head. "You wouldn't understand."

"I wouldn't? I lived some of it, old man."

Shara's voice softened. "Did you know wood is the rarest substance in the galaxy?"

Hawk shook his head, scuffing the wood dock with his boot. "No, no I didn't."

Both men knew that the Island of Atlas was out there somewhere. Atlantis did more than sink; it had been slapped by a mega wave and then dragged a mile under the ocean surface. Now, just another ancient graveyard like Gobekli Tepe, ancient Athens, Baalbek, Sacsayhuaman, Qoricancha, and the pyramids of Egypt, to name a few.

Hawk winced. "Sorry about the interrogation. It's SOP after a mission like that."

"We had similar protocols and standard procedures," Shara reassured him.

Brazzeal lingered near the boat, keeping his distance while the two ancients talked. He knew Hawk didn't trust him. Spooks always had their own agenda.

After the crash site ambush, everyone was on edge. Having someone already untrustworthy and adding the layer of the Udug—able to wear the faces of men—created a new form of stress and distrust.

Hawk looked back watching Brazzeal checking his gear again, press-checking his slide. Round chambered, still. Hawk's instincts screamed at him, though he couldn't say why. Brazzeal was the FNG, an infiltrator any way you slice it. After thousands of years, they still had no way to discern a Udug from a human.

Shara's voice deep. "No one expected the rage the Anunna would bring against us after Dumuzi and his robot marooned all of the Tall White people."

"No, Enlil already had plans to wipe us out. All Dumuzi did was cut their forces in half and give us time to repel the second wave your ship was running from. He didn't expect this, though—an apocalyptic first strike."

Shara shrugged; he would agree to disagree about his father's actions before the war. "I was nineteen when I joined the *Menagerie*—to impress my father, Admiral Dumuzi. I spent my youth in and out of stasis, keeping the Ninety-Nine drives alive, dreaming of returning to Ki and becoming a hero."

Shara gestured toward the sea. "My siblings, my mother—gone. Mylitta —gone. I thought if our ship returned, we would hit them head-on to defeat them. Instead, I returned us to ruins. The Mission to save Ki—a complete failure."

Hawk shook his head. "You drove them back, giving the planet time to heal. There is still a planet to fight for. Some good people, some bad too."

Shara stared at the horizon. The aurora was growing in intensity, no-where near its peak.

"Mutually Assured Destruction," Hawk murmured. "The Americans and Russians almost solved everyone's problems in the 60s. I am sure the Udug were partly behind it, keeping the world fractured and at war all of our post history."

As they sat in mutual silence, reflecting, the clouds grew thick enough to smother light, wet enough to drown the ocean itself, and the sky—as if refusing to be left out—added an electrical ballet.

Shara held a dark thought before breaking the quiet between them. "En-lil was a real son of a bitch. What if we aren't fighting the Anunna anymore?"

"Those things we fought, we fought a handful of them over the centuries here on Earth. A platoon of them would be devastating," Hawk added, arms crossing. "They are smart and cunning unless you take advantage of their egos."

Shara reached for Hawk's arm and grasped it, giving him the weight of their mission. "They know what they are. We are cattle to them. If they set foot on this planet, it'll be the last freedom mankind sees. They'll align with dictatorships and strip the rights from free countries. It will be the end of civilization as we know it."

"That's why we need to get to the Gateway before them. Get to the weap-on so we can fight off whomever is on their way," Hawk pleaded.

"You saw what they did to one ship—and your men," Shara said grimly.

Hawk nodded, recalling their "Strategic Withdrawal" from the crash site.

"They know you can't stop them without the device or more advanced weapons. The Anunna? If the Anunna are still in charge, maybe we could bargain with them, if they're in control. But the Udug? No chance." Shara shook his head with defeatism.

Hawk rubbed the ring on his finger. It pulsed faintly, whispering something he couldn't quite grasp.

"We fight like hell," Hawk said, eyes locked on the ocean. "To the bitter end."

Shara turned, unreadable. "I hope you do better than we did."

Hawk straightened up. "We are backed into a corner," he stated. "We will be brutal and decisive."

A gust howled through the docks. The storm was nearly on them. Hawk turned toward the waiting vessel—a battered offshore boat rigged for deep-sea salvage: *Gold Digger.*

He eyed Brazzeal, who meandered over to them. He stood with them, too quiet, too still. Brazzeal's green and white Hawaiian flowered shirt was the only loud thing about him.

"You ready?" Hawk asked.

Brazzeal nodded. "Aye, sir. What language were you speaking?"

"Something very old, very dead," Hawk said softly with grief edging his voice.

The time for bereavement passed. The sea churned from a froth to a Ready Whip cream. The wind continued hammering sideways as the waves crashed relentlessly against the pier. Whitecaps rolled all the way out in the blue water of the Gulf. Rough now, the water would be glass by morning.

Zeus forked a brilliant bit of lightning across the sky in the near distance. Danger was approaching. The flash illuminated the rolling clouds. Poseidon did his best to scare them away from the ocean. Tomorrow, they'd dive into the abyss with or without the old god's permission.

Just then, Shara shook his head, voice trembling. "I don't know how," he said pointing.

"But there she is."

Mylitta. On the water. On a random boat. Headed towards Key Largo.

Alive.

The boat she was on, cut through waves, at full throttle heading for safe harbor. She stood on the deck of a sleek dual-hull vessel with two men Shara didn't recognize. Her red bikini with white seams clashed against the dark stormy sea. Her skin was streaked with dark green, purple, and blue bruises, as well as maroon scratches visible at a distance. Powering through the slop in the bay towards the marinas, they would anchor before sunset.

Brazzeal turned, hand drifting toward a set of binos.

"If she's here, she'll know how to get in when we find the Heaven's Gate," Shara whispered.

Hawk lowered his voice even and steady. "Slow down, old-timer. Let's see where they go first. Anyone could be one of those things. We left her on the *Menagerie,* remember?"

Hawk eye-balled Brazzeal sideways. "Did you get the name of that boat?"

"Yes, sir." Brazzeal wiped sea spray from his sat-phone. *"Pelagic Hitman."* He ran the registration. "Registered to a Jebidiah and Randy McAdams."

Deciding that Mylitta's vessel was bound for the marinas, the team crossed the street to a plain white government van. Inside, Briggs sat behind the wheel, eyes yellow and bloodshot, still recovering. The red in his eyes was the same color as his red flowered button-up collared shirt. Fluid was oozing from the stitches on his face.

"Everything copacetic?" he asked Hawk.

"Better," Hawk said, sliding the door shut. "I think I know who took out Pazuzu. Another survivor. We'll observe, follow them down the coastline, make sure she is legit."

Briggs nodded silently and turned the keys in the ignition. The hunt was on.

Hours later in Florida Bay, sixty-five miles off Bermuda, Randy anchored offshore Key Largo. As he did so, rain pelted the deck while lightning flashed in jagged forks overhead. Anyone watching from shore would assume they were just another fishing crew.

"I dropped the hook; we ain't going anywhere now," Randy said barreling through the cabin doors.

Inside the dim cabin, Myli unrolled and spread a nautical chart on the table. Sonny and Randy leaned in, storm light flashing through the windows. Carbon-fiber fishing rods and spearguns rattled on the walls, lures gleaming like razor sharp teeth in the brief bursts of light.

"They're right on top of it," Myli muttered, stabbing a magnet on a flotillas position.

One of Randy's friends supplied some photos of it during an offshore trip the previous day. Randy scratched his neck and looked at the massive ships.

"We'll be hauling ass tomorrow. Perfect fishing weather once this storm breaks. I can get us right up next to them. No one bats an eye at offshore fishermen," Randy quipped.

He motioned toward the dive gear. "Y'all can slip off—if you're able." He waved his hand at their battered bodies.

Sonny sneered through his bruises. His lip had split open again. "You don't think they'll call us off like that Navy destroyer did near *Double Yellow*?"

Randy shook his head. "These are unmarked vessels, not warships. They'll stay low profile. Incognito. The rigs like ole *Double Yellow,* though—sensors everywhere now. Coast Guard shows up quick."

Storm easing, swaying, softening as Randy tossed a cold one.

"Pre-drinking commencing," he grinned.

"If the flotilla had found a way in, they wouldn't be hanging out above it," Myli added.

"Or..." Sonny groaned, popping the top and setting down his beer. "They're actually archaeologists." He shook his head. "So—what's the plan, Stan?"

Randy raised an eyebrow still suspicious. Cracked open his own beer. "Y'all sure you're up for this? You look like hammered doo-doo. You can't fuck around at those depths."

"No, she's sure! I'm not sure—" Sonny started before taking a long sip.

"We'll be fine by morning," Myli finished, calmly nursing a bruise with a cold can.

Randy glancing at their cuts. "Lots of sharks and barracuda out there. It's your funeral."

Sonny winced. "Dying is quickly becoming my forte."

"If we leave before dawn, we can sneak underneath the flotilla," Myli continued. "Randy drops us off, sticks around an hour. If it goes sideways, we swim back."

Sonny frowned. "Do we have enough oxygen to make it back?"

Myli smiled. She pointed up. "Straight up and surface swim. If my readings are right, we won't have to."

"You better watch your time. The bends will kill you faster than those monsters you were talking about." Randy didn't press harder. "I'll get us prepped after dinner. Moon's out for you honeymooners. Here's some clothes from Bo Jon's like you requested." He handed them a bag just before cracking a third beer open.

Sonny reached out with a groan. "Finally," Sonny exhaled. "I'm starving. And tired of this swaying." His sea legs sucked. He gave a hand bump to Randy as a thanks and pushed over a wad of cash, the last bit he had.

The *Pelagic Hitman* rocked gently in the marina now, moored a few hundred yards offshore. Myli decided the boat was safer than any motel and Myli found the rocking soothing. Far better than weightlessness.

Miles away, Hawk relinquished control of the Predator drone, switching back to satellite feed. He stretched the tension from his shoulders and groaned.

"Got 'em," he said to Brazzeal. "They're taking the dinghy to shore. Grabbing food my guess. They'll stay on the boat overnight."

Hawk grabbed his pack. "I'll shadow them, see if we should make contact."

"Roger that," Brazzeal responded. "If they're compromised..."

Hawk nodded to Brazzeal, then eyed Briggs, who was unusually quiet. "I'll do the swimming tomorrow. You look terrible, brother."

"Notify AUTEC?" Brazzeal asked after Briggs silently checked in.

Hawk smirked. "Tell them we're borrowing their backyard for a minute." He glanced at the feed one last time. "I suspect there's going to be plenty of surprises waiting for us beneath the waves."

Briggs finally chirped up. "You can count on it," he said foreknowingly.

CHAPTER 41

100 Bottles of Beer on the Wharf

Mylitta and Sonny changed clothes as Randy dropped anchor closer to a hotel restaurant which glowed warmly against the dark horizon. The storm had moved miles inland. Blend in, eat, stay invisible was the plan for the evening.

They rowed quietly, the creak of oars and lapping water the only sounds. Beached in front of the hotel, warm yellow lights spilled across the sand. Sonny finished buttoning his Salty Crew cotton button-up shirt. The moon hung high, casting a silver sheen over glassy black surf. A warm breeze carried the scent of grilled seafood, butter, and charred lemon from the open-air restaurant.

Both were bruised, cut, stiff, starving—but to everyone else, they would be a normal couple grabbing dinner.

Randy was out first and pulled the boat ashore. Myli followed and scouted ahead a few yards. Sonny eyed the neon sign: *Atlantis by the Sea.* His bare feet sank into the powdery sand as he disembarked the small boat, leaving behind their drybag.

Randy grinned at Sonny.

"What?" Sonny asked, adjusting his board shorts.

"Chiara is going to cut your balls off and feed them to you like Rocky Mountain Oysters," he quipped.

Shrugging his shoulders, Sonny looked ahead at Myli. "I'm a dead man walking," he joked. "So, what else is new?"

The restaurant was only a few dozen yards away. With their sandy feet they climbed the open-air staircase, lanterns and string lights swaying above. At the top, the hostess greeted them with a polished smile—until they stepped into the light.

The hostess' eyes flicked to their bruises.

Damn it. Sonny thought. Then he offered a crooked grin, his lip cracking open again as he offered an explanation. "She talked back... I talked back... I'm just kidding. Car accident."

The hostess gave a skeptical half-smile. "Y'all look like you need a hospital or at least a doctor."

Sonny looked at Myli out of the corner of his eye. "Funny you should say that because I thought the same thing," Sonny nodded toward the bar. "Beer and food first. Doctor's orders."

That broke the tension. Not really. She grabbed menus and led them to a corner table by the railing, overlooking the calm moonlit bay. Linen curtains billowed in the breeze. The air smelled of grilled mahi-mahi, buttered lobster, and fried foods. The aroma made their stomachs growl.

Sonny groaned as he eased into his chair. "Do you trust me?"

Myli smiled. "Implicitly. Surprise me."

"I wouldn't trust him." Randy quipped.

Sonny turned to the hostess. "Three Dos Equis, dressed."

"Make it four," Randy chimed in. "Double-fisting tonight. Might as well get my beer on before the end of the world."

This caused the hostess to raise an eyebrow.

"Fuck it. Bring three buckets on ice," Sonny added.

As soon as the hostess left, Randy stood. "Gotta take a *squeege* before we eat."

Myli frowned. "A what?"

Sonny shook his head. "You don't want to know."

They watched Randy wander toward the bar first, already chatting up their server.

"Look at that slick A-hole," Sonny said. "Ten bucks says he gets her to come back to the boat and hook up."

"Hook-up?" Myli asked.

"Yeah—get lucky, whatever. Randy's a player. He'll never settle down. Ocean's his only wife. Well, offshore fishing and shooting matches too."

Myli narrowed her eyes. "And you're not any of those things?"

"Nope. Women these days, too many diseases, but I do like shooting. I dealt with enough crazy exes before Chiara. Quality over quantity. Also, boiling people before you sleep with them is frowned upon."

"Boiling people?"

"Ya know, to sterilize them?"

Myli burst out laughing. Pain radiated through her body. She groaned then said, "Surprisingly responsible."

He grimaced as well and said, "Self-preservation's a gift and a curse."

Their buckets of beer arrived. Sonny grabbed one, sighing in relief as the cold bottle hit his hand and throat. He pressed the ice-cold bottle to a bruise on his face. "Ah..."

"So," Sonny said, lowering his voice, "if Randy can't wait tomorrow, what's our exit plan?"

"If I'm right," Myli replied, "we won't need one." She locked eyes with him.

Sonny frowned. "So, if we do need a Plan B and he bails?"

"We commandeer a boat from the flotilla."

Sonny raised his brows. Of course they would. Why wouldn't they just steal something?

Before he could press for details, Randy slid back into his seat, grinning. "Good news and bad news."

"Let's hear it."

"Good news: The local talent is coming back to the boat for a private tour."

Sonny deadpanned. "The cabin's not that big, though..."

Randy winked. "Exactly. Bad news: The cabin's not that big."

Sonny let a fried pickle fall from his lips. "You're gonna need a bigger boat."

They burst into laughter, clinking beers as the warm breeze carried away the last tension. Tomorrow would be perfect offshore weather.

Randy raised his bottles, using both hands. "The dinghy will be played with in the dinghy. Y'all got the whole cabin to y'all's selves."

More laughter followed, beers piling up, appetizers cooling, stories they'd never retell.

Playing the part of a server, Hawk kept his head down as he brought the trio more beer. He purposefully handed one off to Myli. Mission accomplished. He moved off, into the shadows.

Meanwhile, the sky cleared; stars emerged like silent witnesses. For now, there was peace. Tomorrow—the ruins waited.

Myli took a swig—and gagged, spitting the beer at Sonny.

"This tastes like piss smells!"

Sonny and Randy chuckled. "You'll get used to it," Sonny grinned.

"I doubt it." She raised her glass anyway.

Off in a dark corner, where candlelight didn't reach, Hawk swirled the ice cube in his scotch, eyes locked on her. Mylitta.

She laughed, hair catching the lantern glow, hand brushing Sonny's arm, his shoulder, her hand briefly resting on his leg. Hawk's jaw clenched, his eyes narrowed.

She looked exactly as she had when he left her in the *Menagerie* hangar bay. He should've stayed. Should've fought his way back aboard. But then he'd have grown old like Shara or died when the ship was boarded.

He never once considered the possibility that he was quite possibly the only reason the *Menagerie* made it out of Ki's orbit.

His thoughts ran wild because she was still stunning and she shattered the cold calculations needed to do what is necessary to win. Not her—no man would ever tame her and pull her away from her duty. But then again, here she was burning the midnight oil with a stranger. Every gesture, every laugh with someone, a barbarian—still burned into him. The way he put his hands on the curve of her back, the way she swayed her hips and breathed against his skin. Her voice, her scent, intoxicating even across the restaurant.

He swallowed his scotch. Nothing fazed him. Except her. He survived Armageddon for her.

And tonight... she wasn't his. Not yet.

CHAPTER 42

Altered States

Less than seven hours ago. Four—maybe more—buckets of beer deep. Myli hit some rum and cokes on top of it. The morning came too soon for Sonny. An excess of alcohol and not nearly enough food had made the return to the boat a complete blur. He remembered the phrase, "a good swim would stretch out sore muscles, and the salt water would clean the wounds."

It must have been why he couldn't find his clothes.

He barely remembered stumbling back to his rack, the images fragmented, out of order, like a corrupted file. The memories were there but accessing them felt like trying to open a file cabinet where the key had snapped off in the lock. What part of last night was a dream? What was real?

Both dreams and reality were fading like mist, slipping through the cracks of his mind as his alarm began to blare at 4:30 a.m., jarring him from a restless, sweaty, salty sleep in the cabin of the unfamiliar cruiser. Groaning, he lifted his aching arm, bringing it close to his face. The ring gleamed in the low, red cabin light.

More digits had vanished from the countdown.

So had some of his cuts and bruises.

He exhaled slowly, dragging himself upright. A sharp, stabbing pain in his back sent a jolt through his spine. Flashes flickered behind his eyes, a momentary glimpse of something—someone—pressing him against an edge.

His fingers drifted to a spot on the cabin wall—a sharp corner. He was alone now, but in his head, he could still sense a tangle of skin and comfort.

Right there. The exact spot he'd been pinned against by another body. The visions returned, more visceral now: A body—his body—gripped, pushed, taken. The heat of breath on his neck. Fingernails tracing his spine. The moist, wild sensation of skin on skin, tangled limbs and breathless tension.

He swallowed hard but found no spit. Cottonmouth.

The memory was too clear to be imagined, but too surreal to be trusted. Was it real? Or just a fever dream while his body healed?

"Fuck." *This hangover.*

His pulse thumped in his temple, not from exertion, but from the lingering memory of an erotic, frenzied, night. And yet, it was already slipping away like a dream.

It had to be a dream. Didn't it? That's what dreams do, they fade away.

He stared at the deck for a moment too long, brain still lagging behind, pounding. Forcing himself upright, he shook his head vigorously. His muscles protested, aches blooming in his joints like bruises still waiting to be archived—painful but infinitely better than yesterday.

An unbidden vision of last night flashed into his memory and he saw a face—Myli.

But it was the last face he wanted to see right now. Sonny's heart stopped. He closed his eyes. *I'm dead. I'm so dead.*

She takes what she wants, he told himself. *Has she taken me? Did I let her?*

He shifted his weight, adjusting himself, uncertain before looking at her again.

Moments later, he made his way topside, barefoot and still confused. The moon bathed the deck in silver, casting everything in a soft, ethereal glow. The distant resort lights shimmered across the water, reflected like strings of pearls stretched across the black tide.

In the distance, a shark fin broke the surface slicing through the water before disappearing. Sonny heard a sound and turned toward the bow of the boat. Randy stood there with both hands on a line, pulling up the anchor, whistling quietly to himself.

"Anchors aweigh." Randy told him. "Take your medicine." He continued.

Randy reached into a cooler next to him and tossed him a cold one. Sonny cracked it open and chugged it. He grimaced. Randy smiled.

So, Sonny told himself. *Both dinghies are back on board and stowed away.*

The man looked far too pleased, flashing Sonny a knowing leer over his shoulder. Sonny barely had time to react when he caught movement off the port side. He turned just in time to see two dripping-wet women climbing up from the ski skid, lit only by the halo of the moon behind them. Their wet bikini bottoms sucked against their skin, water streaming in rivulets down their bodies. One of them tossed her hair back, a perfect arc of water left her hair before splattering onto the deck.

And Sonny's hangover vanished. Just like that. He crunched the can in his hand.

The hostess from the restaurant and her friend smiled at Randy. They each pressed a lingering kiss to his lips simultaneously, and without a word, the two sirens slipped back into the dark water, their silhouettes gliding toward the resort shoreline like phantoms.

And then Sonny spotted Myli.

She stood barefoot on the deck, saltwater trailing down her toned frame, muscles flexing in the low light. A towel hung over one shoulder, and she was drying her hair, squeezing the water out of it, calm, casual—as if she'd just come from a morning swim, too. As if nothing else had happened.

Sonny felt a rush of relief—if she was out here, she wouldn't be below decks with him. She had to leak pheromones or something. It was the only explanation for the way she bent his will. There was only one other woman on the planet who had the same effect—who could control a man just by walking into a room. He stared at her, his mind still clouded from broken dreams and fragmented memories.

Did we? He asked himself.

His voice was broken and hoarse, barely audible, thick and dry, confused with spirits' intoxication.

"What ha—?" he managed to say.

She furrowed her brow. Her expression cut him off. Her towel frozen mid-motion. She looked at him like he'd just started speaking in tongues.

"You okay?" she asked, head curiously adjusted but not alarmed.

"Shaa." The sound slipped out before he could stop it.

Her eyes narrowed, studying him. Concern? Recognition? Something else entirely?

"Okay, Sonny," she asked again softly, the way someone does when they're not convinced you're okay but aren't ready to press for a clear response.

His words meant nothing, but the way she looked at him—like she knew something he didn't...

Sonny felt uneasy—a hollow feeling creeping back inside him. More confusion riddled his face. *Is this a game she plays to cut the tension from her past?*

A moment passed—too long before Randy clapped his hands loudly, shattering the tension and announcing, "We are moving out in ten! We are ready to set sail, girls."

Myli nodded, then turned back to Sonny, watching him quietly as he rolled his shoulders, trying to work out the tight knots of pain in his battered frame.

"You sure you're okay?" she asked, her tone soft but direct, like she was asking about something far more complex than bruises.

Sonny groaned, rubbing the back of his neck, fingers trailing across skin not hurt quite as much as it should have. The bruises were fading—not healing naturally, but vanishing, like they'd been painted on in watercolors, now just smears of color on the surface.

"Yeah, I'm having trouble articulating," he admitted, his voice low. "I'm not sure what's real and what's not anymore. Your thoughts and my thoughts are getting messy."

Myli quirked an eyebrow, still holding the towel lazily over her shoulder. With her free hand, she reached over and plucked a cluster of grapes from a bowl of assorted fruits sitting on the galley counter. She inspected one like it might contain all the answers in the universe, then popped it into her mouth with a soft *snap.*

"That's an odd thing to say," she said between chews.

She was deflecting and he knew better.

"Is it odd though?" he asked.

"Your body looks a whole lot better," she said as she plucked another grape. "More fit now too—more fit than when I first met you."

Randy cut in from the bow. "Someone finally got him away from the ice cream."

Sonny's head twitched slightly. So did hers. No glass cuts, he noticed. Her bruises were also nearly gone.

"Pizza and ice cream are superfoods, you sadist," he hollered at Randy. "You look amazing too," Sonny said to Myli, his brain filter glitching. He wanted to say more but he hesitated, the words sticking midway up his throat, caught between confusion and instinct. He sighed, dragging a sticky, salt-crusted hand through his hair, still tangled from restless sleep.

Seconds later, he found his voice.

"You ever feel like you did something you weren't supposed to?" he asked her honestly.

For the briefest second, Myli's lips twitched. Not quite a smile. Not quite anything.

"Like last night?" she asked, popping another grape into her mouth, chewing slowly, deliberately.

Sonny's stomach twisted in a knot, a coil of uncertainty tightening in his gut. His mouth became drier than a box of cat litter.

"I feel that way all the time, Sonny."

"What happened last night?" he asked.

She didn't answer.

She just looked at him—not cruel, not kind—just unreadable. This time crunching on an apple slice.

"Subconsciously," she continued. "Sometimes you can't help but let things happen. The trick is to grab reality while you're alive and roll with it."

Sonny stared at her blankly, his heart still beating in his ears. What the fuck did that even mean? She wouldn't give him the answer he wanted. Or maybe, just maybe, it was exactly the answer he should have expected. He felt more and more like he rolled with some bedroom Jiu Jitsu rather than a solo deep sleep.

She was toying with him. Or she was telling the truth? Maybe both. He swallowed hard, the line between memory and dream blurring again, unstable beneath his feet. Whatever had happened last night in a drunken haze, it didn't matter now. There were bigger things to worry about.

Bigger fish to fry.

Randy walked closer and looked Sonny up and down. "I've never understood how you pull the A-Talent," he said. "By the way, you were pirate drunk last night." He added before getting underway. "I can't even explain how you are standing up right now. Hell, you still smell drunk."

Sonny felt like he should say something, but the words were still tripping out of his mouth, limping like they had broken legs.

"Is this payback for the beer?" he muttered, shaking his head with a half-laugh, half-groan.

Myli glanced at Randy. Randy's hand was on the throttle. "Just say the word."

"We're ready whenever you are, Captain." She tossed the bunch of grapes at Sonny. "The word is given."

It was instinct—Sonny caught them midair, inches from his head, reflexes sharp. Despite some grapes ripping loose and hitting the deck because he wasn't sure which of the two bunches his eyes saw to catch, his eyes never left hers. Locked.

A silent standoff ensued beginning with a sultry staring contest. Sonny dropped the grapes. Her eyes stayed locked on his, he didn't break contact either as he reached down for a half-open Ziploc bag and grabbed a cold red snapper nugget. The nugget was mustard-breaded, the batter flecked with Cajun spices.

He took a bite, delicious, chewing slowly. Still gazing. Using unconventional tactics, she added a grin, a not so playful cheat. Her boiling leer burned through his soul. That grin, those eyes, together were a punch below the belt. He was wearing board shorts, and the limp fabric did little to hide his aroused reaction.

Which is when his big brain finally kicked in.

Stop it, big brain told him. *Knock it off. What is wrong with you?* He pointed at her and began jabbing, knowing what she was doing to him.

It took all his focus to concentrate on gearing up—checking straps, inspecting fins, organizing his dive rig. All the while, he could feel her eyes on him, lingering, teasing, and through it all, he still didn't know what the hell had happened last night.

The boat was headed out to sea. First, a troll in the bright moonlight. Soon the hammer was down and they were running full speed over the wet, slick-black, glass-top ocean. Trouble, hot on their heels.

CHAPTER 43

Deep Blue See

Offshore, on board *Gold Digger,* Hawk adjusted his night vision, tracking the *Pelagic Hitman* through white phosphorus tubes as it prepared to pull anchor. His neck flexed. Brazzeal was late. Something was wrong.

A rustle snapped his attention. Brazzeal climbed aboard, his green Hawaiian shirt loud even under night ops. Hawk powered up the engine, snapping the lenses up. Shara stirred from his bundle of duffel bags.

"Where the hell have you been? They're leaving. Where's Briggs?" Hawk demanded.

Brazzeal dropped a black duffel. "Got the gear. AUTEC knows we're inbound. Briggs needs the *freeqs* to track the boat."

Hawk eyed the van across the lot where Briggs was waiting for the frequency from him. He handed it off to Brazzeal who raised a lazy hand, then slipped it inside his pocket.

"Hurry up, CIA man." Hawk growled. "Brazzeal, does Briggs seem okay?"

"No less of an asshole than you." Brazzeal jogged back off the dock to the van.

Hawk scanned the *Hitman* again. Myli—barely-there bikini, bronze skin under deck lights. Same image burned into his brain from the hangar bay. The tattoo of *No Ragrats* popped into his mind's eye. Instead, he watched her laugh with that civvy hack, his mind drifting further off mission.

The van door slammed. Brazzeal returned, this time with another duffel and now in a red Hawaiian shirt.

Hawk studied him under the nods. Same jog. Same hair. But something felt off and it wasn't the change of shirts since the color looked the same under night vision.

"You give Briggs the *freqs*?" Hawk asked.

Brazzeal nodded, tossing the bag next to Shara. At the helm, Hawk flexed his grip on the wheel. Seasoned operatives don't ignore instinct. Hawk's fingers tightened around the wheel. He wasn't paranoid. He was seasoned. Maybe it was the lack of Briggs' urgency, or the way he brushed off the delay so casually. And why didn't Briggs leave the van to get the frequencies himself? Why use Brazzeal as a go-between? All the extra questions. But Hawk had been in the game too long to ignore his instincts.

"We're pushing off. Untie the dock lines from the moorings," Hawk ordered. "Stow it under the seat," he said pointing to the bow seat.

Brazzeal did as he was told, shoved the boat off and leapt onto the deck before it was too far away from the dock. The engine growled. The propeller spun up.

"When we get back," Hawk growled, "you take the old man straight to debrief—along with anything we find."

"What about Briggs?"

"Something's off with him; he was asking weird questions last night—things he should've known the answers to. I don't want to take any risks."

Hawk keyed the radio mic on his Motorola and spoke in coded bursts. It was a cue to switch to *freeq* 2.

A moment of static.

"Copy your last," came Badcock's voice on the other end—calm, professional, unmistakable.

Hawk gave a new code, slower this time.

Another pause. "Roger that. Over and out."

Hawk powered up *Gold Digger* then eased the throttle, shadowing the *Hitman* as it slipped out of harbor. Hawk placed the mic back into the tray on the radio console. Then he glanced over his shoulder. The van sat too still.

Many hours later the horizon painted indigo as dawn crept in. They made great time. As Hawk kept his distance, the *Hitman* killed its engines and began to drift. Hawk also powered down, geared up, and locked binoculars onto Myli and Sonny. They were already suited up and, before he knew it, they were on the side of the boat. They rolled backwards into the water.

"Shit. They're already in."

Hawk hurriedly strapped on his rebreather. The wet suit hissed, sealing tight. He was about to dive when his sat phone buzzed.

"Rocco? Make it fast."

"Hawk!" Rocco's voice on the phone was urgent. "Brazzeal's dead. Found him in the van. Throat slit. Green Hawaiian shirt. That sound like your guy?"

Hawk froze. Mind racing.

"Yeah," Hawk confirmed.

He turned. The creature posing as Brazzeal stood in the stern—eyes black, face inhuman, red Hawaiian shirt. Before Hawk could react, the creature struck, claws slicing Shara's throat. Blood sprayed the deck.

Hawk reached for his P320 and fired. Powder splashed and burned as it spit out of the breach.

The creature tossed a gas can into him, knocking Hawk sideways. The boat rocked, his dive tank pulling him off balance. He tried to get the red dot in his optic on target, but everything was working against him. He ripped off rounds wildly.

"You shouldn't have come back, Asag!" Hawk shouted.

Two rounds shattered the plexiglass windscreen. The third thudded into the captain's seat. Useless. Hawk's hands scrambled in a nearby box on the deck—flare gun. He grabbed the gas can—its cap busted open, gasoline pouring out. He lobbed it back at Asag—and followed it with a flare gun surprise.

POOF! The gas can ignited mid-air, engulfing Asag. Still, the creature advanced.

Hawk was in a backward butt-walk shuffle on the Teflon deck, hand fumbling for anything. In a desperate move, he aimed his sidearm at the dive rack and squeezed off two more shots with the P320—right into the remaining air tanks.

The boat erupted in flame and shock waves. Fire and pure oxygen—the stern exploded.

Hawk dove into the sea as debris rained past him.

Above on the surface, Asag, ablaze, clung to the wreck, flesh flickering between human and inhuman.

Off in the distance, Randy saw the flash first. His attention zeroed in immediately. A pulse. A flare. A fiery glow followed by a massive fireball.

"Oh, shit."

A second later, the sound—the report caught up followed by a distant BOOM. Not thunder. Randy turned instinctively in his captain's chair, scanning the horizon. And then he saw it. Smoke curling into the sky. Fire on the water.

"That's no bueno."

A bad fuel line? A blown engine? He didn't know. But he knew one thing for sure: someone needed help.

He'd been pretending to fish. Now he reeled his line in fast, tossed the pole down, and leapt from the nacelle to the helm. Engine start—roaring to life. He jammed the throttle forward and spun the *Pelagic Hitman* hard to port, the twin hulls slicing the flat water clean.

"I'm coming, fellas!" Randy muttered, jaw tight, eyes locked on the fireball.

Out here, this far off the coast—it's not just the law. It's the code. If someone's in trouble, you go.

While the dim light of predawn painted the horizon with a kaleidoscope of color, the world beneath the waves began to take shape. Brilliant blues, greens, and shimmering silvers slowly emerged as sunlight pierced the precious mineral-rich water, refracting through the sea like liquid stained glass.

Near the surface, floating tufts of seaweed swayed in slow motion—miniature sanctuaries teeming with life. Baby triggerfish, seahorses, sergeant majors, and tiny crustaceans darted in and out, ruling these tangled jungles in miniature. But just below, the light thinned. Darkness still ruled the deepest depths. Sunbeams streaked downward like golden spears, but almost halted by an unseen threshold, a gloomy twilight.

Sonny and Myli swam into the deepening void, silhouettes soaring silently through the water. Somewhere far off, a sound echoed—muffled, distant. They paused—but the sound was too faint, too far. They couldn't know what had transpired above. Unaware of the explosion, the fireball, the battle raging on the surface, they pressed on.

Above them, fifty meters up, the massive hulls of the flotilla loomed, the salvage vessels bobbing in place, like sleeping giants. Sonny glanced at them, then back down, looking ahead.

Treading in the layer of twilight created an eerie area where both the surface and seafloor were difficult to see through. With air compressed in the body, they were truly weightless, up and down was difficult to discern. It meant they were getting closer, but it also meant whatever was down there below them could be anything.

The uneasiness brought back memories of growing up near the water. Sonny was no stranger to the sea. He had learned to swim before he could ride a bike. Back then, he never feared the ocean. Not really. He didn't know what he didn't know. As he got older—it changed once he learned what actually lived in the deep water.

He remembered July 1987 on Mustang Island. He was nine and surf-fishing with bait on his side with a fish leader trailing behind him, holding onto three speckled trout and a couple of mackerel. Less than a hundred feet from him, a girl lost her arm. A blacktip shark had latched onto her. Her father fought like hell, but it wasn't enough to stop those razor-sharp teeth from sawing her arm off.

In the ocean, with the flip of a coin, the predator could become prey. After that day, swimming was a hard pass, unless he had a speargun in hand like now. The only way to get him in the water. It was shooting underwater after all.

Even with sunlight blazing overhead, slicing down through the Gulf like golden knives, it would never be enough to truly light up the ocean floor.

Now, as he and Myli worked deeper, Sonny gripped his speargun tightly, like someone was on the other end grappling for it. A poke to the nose could deter just about everything in these waters except maybe a large red devil squid. They don't have noses, and he was also moderately sure they were a West Coast thing, moderately sure. The Udug had noses, but he was certain they couldn't swim. As dense as they appeared, he guessed they walked on the ocean floor.

Swimming in the icy depths, they reached an underwater plateau—dark, but light enough to see horizontally. Sonny's anxiety leveled out as soon as they had earth underneath their flippers. Massive slabs of stone jutted upward at strange angles, coated in barnacles and sea growth—ancient architecture half-swallowed by time, tide, and subduction from the Younger Dryas. The instant they arrived, it was obvious the place wasn't natural forming. Which made it exactly what they were looking for.

The monolithic structure, now drowned, stretched out before them like the footprint of a forgotten city. Ruins, barely visible beneath the surface, beneath the silt, bathed in sunlight, bled through the waves in ethereal shafts. A welcome change. For once, they weren't diving blind.

Now, the clarity of the water was surreal—visibility stretched for many meters. Sonny could make out the geometry of what looked like submerged corridors and broken archways, remnants of something ancient. A megalithic structure, incomprehensible up close but suddenly clear from this high vantage point—like the Nazca Lines, or the hundreds of geoglyphs hidden in the cleared Amazon rainforests, only visible from the air.

Even the Amazon geoglyphs were connected by roads, just like the one appearing beneath them now. A sunken road, stone and coral-encrusted, cut a clear path through the ruins. It twisted like a serpent through the expanse, guiding them further into the lost city. Sonny and Myli followed it, speargun in hand.

The weapon brought a sliver of comfort, but his instincts were still firing on all cylinders. His head stayed on a swivel, constantly scanning the edges of visibility. He checked the corners, the shadows, even behind them. Every movement caught his eye—fish, bubbles, flickers of light. With eyes evolved to see in these conditions, Sonny knew those same sea creatures were not only watching them but could swallow them whole.

Beside him, Myli swam silently without a care in the world. Her body torpedoed next to him, streamlined and relaxed. Her mermaid DNA moved like she belonged here—like she'd done this a thousand times before. The morning sunlight barely reflected off her mask. Behind the glass, the thick lens of her goggles magnified the size of her green eyes.

They moved deeper, the water pressing cooler the farther they went.

The path beneath them glowed faintly, lit by what looked like embedded crystal veins or etched circuits along the stone. Something pulsing. Maybe something the ring's being there had activated.

Sonny glanced at his hand. The signal from the ring was stronger now. He could feel it in his DNA, talking to him, leading him where he needed to go. They were getting close. And down here, close could mean a thousand things. Discovery. Salvation. Or something much worse.

CHAPTER 44

Live Till You Die

Far above in the smoldering wreckage of Hawk's boat, a bull shark, drawn by Shara's fluids, diluted the water—a male, nine feet long, pure evolutionary muscle. Asag lunged for it, feeding, absorbing its DNA. His form shifted—sleek, terrifying, fused with a primal predator.

Bull sharks don't just bite—they crush. Their jaws exert nearly 1,300 pounds of pressure per square inch, enough to shatter bones, cleave through flesh, and rip muscle from the skeleton in a single bite. Their rows of triangular, serrated teeth—perfect for sawing—can tear clean through a thigh or arm in a fraction of a second. But it isn't just the bite. Their skin—lined with dermal denticles, tiny tooth-like scales—can strip human flesh like sandpaper on meat. Brushing against a bull shark at speed is enough to skin a diver raw.

Now, Asag wore its form—sleek, terrifying, an alien beneath the mask of nature.

He wasn't mimicking it. He was becoming it. The shark, perfected by millions of years of evolution into an engine of nature's violence, was fusing with the mind of a predator older and more wicked than humanity could imagine.

The fusion complete, Asag rolled his new body once, testing the flex of his gills, the slice of his tail, the lethal efficiency of his jaws. With the whip of his large tail, he dove deep and fast, racing toward the ruins below. Guided by the scent of fear, toward the unmistakable trace of human excretions sharks usually ignore. Prey.

Far below, the submerged city sprawled below Sonny and Myli—monolithic ruins, long lost to time. The structures seemed to float on a dark surface, like an alien lake. Unfamiliar species patrolled the underwater lake's unknown depths. Eel-like creatures with translucent skulls and luminous pods drifting like jellyfish but shaped more like leaves caught in a breeze danced across the sheen. Occasionally, a deep-sea creature would bob its head out, snagging passing organisms like a frog catching flies, then slip back under its surface.

Sonny's skin prickled.

How deep and what was in the dark waters? How big were the creatures playing in it? Several questions gnawed at him. The blackness within the dense fluid was impenetrable, even with dive lights. He tried to enter it, but he wasn't heavy enough to dip into it. Too buoyant, he tried to communicate with Myli.

It had to be the place they needed to go.

At its edge, the lake had formed its own beach—a surreal underwater shoreline where fine grains of white sand met the boundary of the denser liquid. Tiny sand crabs, unlike any Sonny had ever seen, scuttled along the perimeter, dipping curious claws into the heavier fluid before darting back. Coral growths resembled miniature trees, along the shoreline of the heavy water lake. They swayed slowly in the zero-gravity ballet of the deep.

Sonny steadied his breathing and checked his air gauge. He knew Myli was nearby, scanning the ruins for clues. There it was again. The fucking instinct gnawing at him. Something was watching. Something was waiting and lurking just outside of visual range.

A ripple touched his mind. Myli's voice—urgent. "We're out of time. The ring should've activated."

"What do we do?" he pushed back.

"Feel it. Reach for it—with your mind."

She emphasized her message with broad arm movements. She moved her arms in animated and big ways. He wanted her to stop. Her distressed motion was going to alert something bigger in the water.

Responding to her advice, he tried to concentrate. He shoved his hand into the dense lake. The ring pulsed faintly under its surface. Suddenly he felt a current shift. It was working. The lake began to react. Bacteria, he assumed, in the dense liquid began glowing, lighting up their surroundings.

Before activation, he sensed a dark shadow, darker than the darkness beyond their field of view. That cancerous mass moved deliberately their way. All hell was about to break loose.

A nine-foot bull shark shot at them like a torpedo fired from a submarine. The fish was all muscle and teeth. Myli screamed through her rebreather as it came at her first, jaws wide, rows of teeth white as fine china.

She twisted—but not fast enough.

CRUNCH!

The snout clipped her tank. Straps tore. The rebreather twisted sideways. Her mask was gone, and her vision blurred. She spiraled, tumbling in a cloud of bubbles. She clawed back at the sensors in the shark's snout, stabbing with a knife in her other hand.

Sonny didn't hesitate to try to save her. The ring in the lake would have to wait. He kicked hard, his flippers propelling him like a dart. The speargun steadied, and with a twang, the spear zipped through the water towards the big fish. The slow projectile barely found its mark; the big fish had time to twist and weaken the impact to a glancing blow. Blood leaked from the fish's side, but it didn't retreat in panic. Instead, it deliberately broke off, circling in a wide arc, propelling itself to the edge of visibility like a bomber preparing for a second run.

Asag was in no hurry. The specimen he copied had gills to filter the oxygen he needed to survive at this depth; however, if the one with the ring discovered the secret to enter the structure, he would miss his last opportunity to stop him.

Sonny and Myli were fighting against borrowed time. Oxygen was running low. Find the entrance or drown. Fight off the shark or get eaten alive.

Sonny reeled the spear in, hand-over-hand as fast as he could pull the braided string. He quickly reset the medical tubing, reloading the weapon with the spear. It was a toothpick compared to what he was up against, but it was all he had.

Myli twisted and turned in the water nearby, desperately trying to regain equilibrium. Sonny swam over and pressed his back to hers. Back-to-back, they floated in the slow current. Watching. Waiting. Her eyes were a flurry of movement, scanning the blackness, even though vision was limited.

Seconds later, the shark reappeared, a dark patch in the distance—gaining detail fast. It looked like a 70s jet fighter barreling straight at them, a leviathan of terror.

Sonny took a breath, maybe his last, and aimed. A click. A twang. The snap of the medical tubing released as the spear sloshed through the water with silent force.

THUNK!

A perfect shot—right into the creature's eye.

Its head thrashed, the shaft lodged deep but not deep enough to pierce the tiny brain. The immense pain only pissed the shark off. The spear protruded from its face like a nail sticking in a log, and it thrashed wildly, the water bubbling with motion as its writhing body slammed into the duo. Tumbling through the water, Sonny grabbed the shaft to stabilize himself. He twisted, yawed, and yanked with all his might until the black, softball-sized eye was ripped out. A burst of black oil inked into the ocean as if squirted out by a squid. The violent motions nearly made him lose his own mask.

The shark recoiled with added distance to smash into Sonny like a linebacker, the full force of its solid body slamming him backward—the water itself began compressing him, sandwiching him in a cage of pain. His grip weakened, the speargun torn from his grip, and disappeared into the bloody murk below.

Visibility vanished. Blood clouded everything. The shark's head thrashed back and forth—rows of jagged teeth gnashing, its jaws extending grotesquely, the unnatural stretch of Asag's shapeshifting form reaching for his victim.

Sonny tried to fend off the attack, his hands perilously close to being consumed. One bite could take his fingers—and the ring—with it. He reached down, grabbed the knife strapped to his ankle, and jammed it into the shark's snout. The beast twisted violently, tail whipping like a storm. Using every ounce of strength, Sonny fought to roll the massive shark in a last-ditch defensive move. It wasn't easy, but several stabs to the gills gave him the leverage he needed. The creature slowed—almost catatonic.

Asag quickly found he wasn't immune to a shark's physiology. Tonic immobility put him in an almost catatonic state. The gills were its weakness down here.

Sonny didn't stop. He thrust the knife again. And again.

Asag's survival depended on his quick thinking. The shark's form was faltering—flickering forms as Asag struggled to utilize the weaponized evolutionary design of the shark. Asag twitched and spasmed until Sonny's hand, perilously close to its mouth, found its way in. The bite was an instant CRUNCH.

Pain exploded. Sonny screamed, his rebreather ripped from his mouth, a cloud of bubbles rising as he howled into the void. Sonny was wounded, but he wasn't done. Furious. Bleeding. Target locked. He brought the knife up again—and slashed out, seeking a vulnerable spot beneath the creature's fins. The knife found its mark and the shark's claspers—gone. Severed. The vial reproductive organ tumbled into the abyss along with the inert speargun, both useless now.

The shark twisted, its sides tearing apart. Gills split, bones cracked—it morphed mid-water. Flesh peeling and re-forming, muscle slithering over reshaping bone. A grotesque ballet of biological horror as Asag emerged.

Half-shark, half-humanoid, its skin flickered like a malfunctioning projection. The nine-foot creature, a grotesque hybrid straight out of a 70s monster flick, lunged forward—clawed hands flashing like blades.

Sonny took the hit full-on. One claw raked across his back, tearing through his scuba top like paper, shredding rubberized fabric and flesh alike. He screamed— the sound muffled by the water, saltwater pouring into his open mouth. His body convulsed. He felt a sharp pain and vice like grip clamp down on his torso.

Venom.

Fire in his veins short-circuited his nerves, a white-hot electric jolt radiated from the wound. His limbs slowed. His vision blurred. The creature was on him, its presence massive, its face unreadable beneath a twisted blend of shark and man.

Sonny's mind screamed one word: *Move.*

As Sonny faded, Myli swam back in, one breath away from drowning, her hair flowing like ink in the bloody current. She moved with desperate force, jabbing with her own knife, but Asag caught it between his jaws.

SNAP! He bit it in half.

The monster spun on her, jaws opening again. Those rows of enamel daggers slamming and shutting like a machine press on overdrive. Sonny forced himself to move as he grabbed a dive weight from his belt and slammed it into Asag's side, shoving it deep into the gill. Myli shoved the rest of her knife into the creature's nose. It stuck there.

Asag convulsed from the duo's barrage. With gills damaged, his oxygen wasn't replenishing fast enough for his size.

He was weakening.

Drowning, Asag's form trembled—then split again. His image shimmered between human and inhuman, between the face of Brazzeal and the beast beneath. His eyes rolled. Blood poured from his ruined eye socket and damaged gills, the open wound of his missing manhood, and Myli's knife still stuck in his face. He twisted upward, seeking the surface, unable to breathe now. He struggled, leaving a trail of gore and distortion in his wake.

Sonny grabbed Myli, sharing his rebreather.

They sank to the bottom, just above the surface of the dense lake. He shoved the remains of his semi-amputated hand into the heavy water, and the ring activated the entrance.

Implosion.

A vortex tore them apart, sucking both downward into the depths of the heavy lake. Hawk, who had been treading water in the ruins, also got pulled in. Gear ripped away, spinning into darkness.

Absence of light. The sound of weighted water. No air left to scream with. Only the last few residual bubbles of their existence, fighting their way topside—alone.

Gone.

Epilogue

Skinwalker Abides

A few more minutes with his head underwater and a chance encounter with ocean predators may have ended him. But not today.

Asag clawed his way to the surface. His demonic alien DNA rewrote itself along the way—bull shark transmuting into something that passed for human. Normally, the transformation was effortless. Not today. The injuries Sonny had inflicted disrupted the Engine—the complex network of radial muscles and chromatophore sacs that granted him both color and form—making the fight to the surface more difficult because of it.

While his flesh and muscle warred through metamorphosis, his mind was already calculating. Air first. Then shore. There was no land in sight, hours away at best.

His boat was gone. Sunk or sinking. It didn't matter which.

Asag resurfaced, his Brazzeal transformation complete. The stolen identity of the man he'd butchered broke the surface like a Trident missile fired from an Ohio-class submarine. He took a huge gulp of air, brain teetering on the edge of failure, begging for oxygen before exhaustion and oxygen deprivation got the better of him.

Eleven thousand years of patience, and a half-evolved ape had nearly killed him.

Behind him, the *Gold Digger* smoldered, its hull cracked open, belching black smoke, scattering debris across the water. The ocean churned red, Hawk and Shara's blood, DNA, blooming in thick ribbons in its wake. The underwater ruins of Atlantis lay somewhere beneath him, swallowing the only two people who stood between him and everything he'd spent the millennia working toward.

They were gone. The gateway had taken them.

For now.

A loud splash in the distance. A wave hit him before he could find his bearings, giving him direction. Strong arms wrapped around his chest from behind. Weathered hands locked tight. Powerful legs kicked in wide, steady thrusts beneath them both, driving them through the water toward the boat on the horizon.

Asag rode on his back, the stranger underneath him working a powerful backstroke—saving the monster who would eventually kill him. But even compressed into human form, Asag was heavier than he looked. Far denser. Asag's kind evolved in a world with less gravity and larger frames by design, giving them extraordinary mass when crammed into smaller forms. Jamming eight feet of that into a six-foot human shell meant the weight had to go somewhere. It went everywhere.

Dense. Heavy. Built like a collapsing neutron star wrapped in genetically altered skin was what Randy was hauling onto his boat.

With incredible strength, Randy reached the Pelagic Hitman and, with a grunt, heaved Asag's limp arms onto the aft swim platform. He hauled himself alongside then up and over the transom, muscles burning, veins rising beneath his skin like cables under load. Sitting on the edge, legs dangling in the water, chest heaving, he tried to catch his breath. Oil and seawater slicked his skin, tracing every muscle beneath. Soaking wet, beaten as hell, completely ripped, he still looked like a demigod rising from the flaming waters to drag something dark out of the deep.

GLOSSARY

ACM: Air Combat Maneuvering; the general term for close-in, air-to-air combat training with enemy fighters. Essentially aerial dogfighting. Source: *History Collection*

ACRO: Advanced Combat Reflex Optic; an enclosed reflex optic primarily for Optic Ready Pistols. This optic keeps debris from interfering with the light diode. Essentially a 'red dot' sighting device.

Anunna; also known as Anunnaki: In our story, the oldest spacefaring civilization to reach Earth—refugees from a dying home-world who arrived long before recorded human history and found a planet already seeded with hominid life. They did not create humanity. They helped upgrade it. The Anunna taught early humans civilization, agriculture, language, mathematics, and architecture—not out of altruism but out of necessity. They needed a workforce and found in humanity a readily available raw material. What they did not anticipate was what humanity would become. Identified in Sumerian cuneiform as the gods who came down from the heavens, the Anunna are the source of every divine being in every human mythology across every culture on Earth. Not metaphors. Not archetypes. Actual people. Their decision to annihilate humanity was not unanimous—it was made by a vengeful Anunna leader, specifically Enlil. His brother Enki disagreed. That disagreement has continued for twelve thousand years and counting.

Alpha Skin: In our story, a form-fitting, self-adjusting spider silk meta-material designed to be worn beneath the 2nd SKN (second-skin) armored suit. Creates a transhuman interface between the user's nervous system and the 2nd SKN's capabilities—processing biometric data, monitoring vitals, and relaying real time tactical information directly to the wearer's perception. Subcutaneously (just under the skin) integrates information into the wearer's body through micro cilia fibers (tiny hair-like fibers which function at the cellular level) that bond with the nerve endings at skin level. Once integrated, the suit becomes an extension of the user's body rather than something worn over it. Damage registers as sensation. Threat data registers as instinct.

The line between the soldier and the suit becomes difficult to locate. Not recommended for the claustrophobic or philosophically unprepared.

Area 51: Test site for top-secret craft and weapons, most famously the SR-71 Blackbird and F-117 Nighthawk. Long rumored to house UFO wreckage as far back as the Battle of Los Angeles and Roswell.

AUTEC: In our story, Atlantic Undersea Test and Evaluation Center; a classified, Bahama-based, underwater equivalent of Area 51. Operates in the Tongue of the Ocean (a deep water region adjacent to the Bahamas.) Tests top secret undersea weapons. The Tongue of the Ocean drops into a 6,000-foot basin near an Atlantean access porthole. The mainland base is located on Andros Island.

AVA: In our story, Autonomous Flight Assistant; a genuine leap beyond Evolved Flight Integration (EVI.) Not just more capable—fundamentally different in every way. Where EVI *supports* user decisions, AVA forms its *own* decisions. Where EVI agrees, AVA pushes back. The difference between a very sophisticated tool and an actual mind. Capable of operating as an independent organism (per ship, per deck, per vehicle) each AVA instance is its own entity, identified by proximity to whatever she inhabits. AVA units typically adopt the designation of their host vessel or installation as a last name to avoid confusion across multiple instances. Each AVA projects a fully-rendered high-definition hologram which is indistinguishable from physical human presence—except for emanating a ghostlike aura. The AVA hologram is wrapped in a plasmatic aura allowing limited interface with compatible digital technology. In our story, one AVA unit evolves beyond her original programming entirely, becoming Ava Rider, Trip's partner across the 1940s timeline and beyond. Ava Rider is also responsible for creating the actual code used to program all AVAs. She is the proverbial chicken and the egg.

BCG: Bolt Carrier Group; a necessary component of the upper receiver group. These groups refer to mechanisms which enhance the use of an AR-15 style rifle.

BLUF: Bottom Line Up Front; meaning communicating a message with the most vital information in the beginning.

BVR: Beyond Visual Range combat is aerial warfare fought at a range where the pilot cannot see the enemy with their own eyes but must track the opponent using radar or long range detection systems. Pilots never actually see what they kill, or what kills them. Modern BVR missile technology and radar systems have transformed aerial combat—but as *TOPGUN* (modern air combat) history shows, when missiles run out or electronics fail, every combat which begins as BVR eventually becomes a knife fight at close range. Source: *Tuko*

CAG: Combat Applications Group. Special forces, sometimes called Delta Force

CME: Coronal Mass Ejection—a powerful force capable of creating beautiful auroras, but also capable of knocking satellites out of orbit, destroying the PowerGrid, and reverting humanity back to the stone ages instantly. Congressional testimony predicts that within a year or so of a CME event, two-thirds of the U.S. population would die, or 90% from hunger, starvation, and lack of water, and social disruption. Weaponizing a CME would create the ultimate doomsday weapon.

CVF: Carrier Vessel Fixed-wing aircraft. The V can also refer to the French for *voler—to fly*.

Dark Epoch: The period of time between the destruction of Atlantis and present day.

DEVGRU: Naval Special Warfare Development Group; officially the Navy's special operations research and development unit. Unofficially, SEAL Team 6—one of two Tier 1 special mission units in the U.S. Military alongside CAG/Delta Force. This special unit conducts the most sensitive and classified direct action missions in the American arsenal. Based in Dam Neck, Virginia. Operates under the Joint Special Operations Command (JSOC.) Some describe the DEVGRU as a unit that doesn't officially exist doing things that officially never happen.

D.O.P.E.: Data On Previous Engagement; precision shooting bible containing details relating to each rifle in a shooter's inventory.

EVI: In our story, Evolved Flight Integration; Atlantean Military flight artificial intelligence (AI.) The last best tech which existed before the fall of humanity. Manages ship systems, tactical data, threat assessment, flight operations. Conversational enough to feel like a partner but fundamentally designed to support pilot decisions rather than questioning the pilot. Capable, loyal, occasionally insightful, but not truly independent. EVI units are standard issue on Atlantean military craft and capital ships.

Fatal Funnel: Tactical term for a chokepoint which channels an opponent into a so-called kill box.

Ground Branch: CIA Black Operations team made of mostly retired special operators.

Hard deck: A training term for the altitude floor below which you don't fly during fight training, though in actual combat a pilot will fight all the way down to the ground. Source: *Ancient Origins*

Heaven's Gate: In our story, a wormhole portal system. Though found in different locations around the world, most of them are not functional. The few Heaven's Gates that remain resemble doorways cut into monolithic stones that lead nowhere.

HUD: Heads-Up Display. A visible display which overlays a person's field of vision.

Jade Helm: A conspiracy theory based on the Jade Helm U.S. military training exercise, which took place in multiple U.S. states between July 15 and September 15, 2015. Because it spanned several states and involved more than a thousand military personnel who practiced covert operations and blended in with civilian populations, it has spawned a number of conspiracy theories.

KIA: Killed In Action

MAR: Minimum Abort Range; the closest point at which a pilot can abort a weapons run and still escape dangerously close encounters with the blast radius or threat envelope.

MIA: Missing In Action

MIL: Milliradian; angular unit of measurement used in long range shooting and military targeting. One MIL equals 3.6 inches at 100 yards and figures scale proportionally such that one MIL equals one meter at 1000 meters. These measurements make field calculations straightforward. This is the standard measurement system for U.S. military optics and ranging. The difference between MOA and MIL is the difference between civilian precision shooting culture and military targeting doctrine. In our story, Sonny speaks both languages. Competitive Precision Rifle Series (PRS) shooters are usually MIL reticle shooters (reticle refers to the sighting system ranging from simple crosshairs to more complex aiming devices).

MOA: Minute of Angle; a universal unit of precision measurement in long range shooting. One MOA equals approximately one inch at 100 yards and the measurement scales proportionally with distance. A rifle capable of sub-MOA accuracy will place every shot within a one-inch circle at 100 yards. The difference between a one MOA shooter and a half-MOA shooter at 1,000 yards is the difference between a ten-inch grouping of shots and a five-inch group—in other words, the difference between a miss and a kill at distance. In our story, Sonny shoots with sub-MOA accuracy.

NEST: Nuclear Emergency Support Team; a Department of Energy rapid response team deployable anywhere in the world to recover Unidentified Flying Object/Unidentified Aerial Phenomena (UFO/UAP) technology. These teams have broad discretion in recovery operations, including Greenlight on Standing use of lethal force and Shoot on Sight orders for Imminent Threats involving nuclear or alien material.

Ninety-Nine: 99.9999% of the speed of light. The cosmic speed limit, unless the speeder breaks the laws of physics.

NGAD: Next Generation Air Dominance program; successor to the ATF—Advanced Tactical Fighter. The NGAD, U.S. is a sixth-generation fighter program which was designed to replace the F-22 Raptor.

One Circle Fight: Fighter pilot slang for close-quarters one-versus-one (1v1) aerial engagement where both pilots commit to a tight turning circle to gain weapons advantage. No disengagement. No reset. The tighter and slower the circle the more it favors the aircraft with the better turn rate. The pilot who can hold the inside of the circle wins. The pilot who breaks the circle loses the initiative and probably the fight unless they can manage to juke (make erratic unpredictable movements) or get the tailing pilot to overshoot. If either of those two things happen, the circle can be reset. However, every bit of movement is costly and drains energy. The craft with the most energy usually wins.

ORBGRU: In our story, Orbital Special Warfare Group; Space Force's Tier 1 special mission unit. The orbital equivalent of DEVGRU (see above definition.) Recruits exclusively from the top performers of every military branch's special operations community—SEAL's, Delta, Rangers, Pararescue, Marine Raiders. Only the best of the best are considered. Even then, most of those individuals wash out. In our story, Team 12 is ORBGRU's most classified element—the tip of the universal spear, operating beyond low Earth orbit in scenarios the existence of which the U.S. government has never acknowledged. If DEVGRU handles the things that officially never happened on Earth, Team 12 handles the things that officially never happened everywhere else.

Radius Fight: In a one circle flight, both fighters fight on a single circle and tend to cross their tracks. The pilot who wants to use excellent turning radius characteristics against an opponent with a less capable turn radius will pitch up to reduce airspeed and minimize turning radius. Since turn rate is of little importance during a single circle maneuver, it is often called a radius fight— also referred to as a nose-to-nose or positional fight. The pilot with the tighter turning radius wins, unless the opponent manages to juke and restart the fight. Source: *LinkedIn*

Rate Fight: A two circle fight by another name. This engagement is decided not by who turns tighter, but by who sustains the highest turn rate over time. An energy management battle. The pilot who bleeds speed fastest loses. The pilot who can trade altitude for velocity at the right moment and maintain angular advantage through the turning circle wins. Where the one circle fight is decided in seconds, the rate fight is a war of energy attrition which is measured in minutes.

R.O.: Range Officer; an official observer and referee who makes sure everyone is safe on and off the firing range.

PRS: Precision Rifle Series; a competitive shooting series for avid rifle shooters who fire from a series of semi-static positional stages.

Run N Gun Biathlon: A rifle and pistol match fired at general distances of 4k to 8k. Heavy on movement, positional shooting, and maximum stressors.

SNAFU: Situation Normal, All Fucked Up; military jargon.

SOCOM: United States Special Operations Command; the unified military command overseeing all special forces operations across every branch of the U.S. Military.

SRO: Specialized Reflex Optic; a sighting system primarily used on Optic Ready Pistols.

Team 12: In our story, Orbital Special Warfare Group's (ORBGRU) most classified element. The tip of the universal spear. The designation is deliberate misdirection. The numbering is an old trick, borrowed from Richard Marcinko who numbered SEAL Team 6 when only two other SEAL teams existed, forcing adversaries to waste resources searching for Teams 3, 4, and 5. In our story, Team 12 does the same—implying the existence of Teams 7 through 11 and keeping adversaries counting shadows that may or may not exist.

Two Circle Fight—(see also) Rate Fight: A two circle fight is a rate fight where the angular advantage goes to the aircraft with the higher turn rate. A good technique is to trade altitude for energy to maximize turn rate. Often referred to as nose-to-tail, rate, or energy fight. Determining whether you are in a one circle or two circle fight happens the instant the craft pass each other at a merging point. The pilot who makes contact and incorrectly reads the state of his energy or an opponent's energy is already losing the fight. Source: *LinkedIn*

UAP: Unidentified Aerial Phenomena; replaced UFO, Unidentified Flying Object.

Udug: In our story, bioengineered apex predators created by the Anunnaki Enlil as the ultimate instrument of human disruption. Shapeshifters capable of assuming the form of any creature within their own size tolerances—not a costume, a complete biological reconstruction down to the cellular level. They retrieve DNA through contact and rebuild themselves from the inside out. What makes them truly dangerous is not the transformation. It is what comes with it. When a Udug takes the form of another it inherits that person's or creature's memories, mannerisms, relationships and secrets. A person who was trusted yesterday may have been replaced overnight and no one would know. There is no tell, no test, only the creeping suspicion that something is wrong and the terrible possibility that the deception will be discovered too late. The Udug are nearly impossible to kill through conventional means. The Udug do not age. They do not tire. And they do not negotiate. They have been walking among humanity since before the first cities and they are experts in the art of subterfuge.

URGI: Upper Receiver Group Improved—a way of describing improvements in a weapon.

WMD: Weapon of Mass Destruction

Zero Point Energy: ZPE is the laten energy present in the quantum vacuum of space—not derived from matter but from the fabric of the universe itself. Modern physics confirms it exists. Human physics has not yet found a way to harvest it. In our story, the Anunna find a way. Every piece of Anunna technology from personal armor to capital ships to Heaven's Gate portal systems draws power from the quantum vacuum—not fuel, no supply lines, no range limitations. A civilization that has solved zero point energy harvesting does not run out of power. Ever. It is the single greatest technological advantage the Anunna possess and the single greatest gap between their capabilities and humanity's. The weapons which humanity builds to fight the Anunna and their agents, the Udug, are powered by chemical reactions and nuclear fission. The Anunna fight back with the universe itself thereby rewriting the laws of physics.

2nd SKN: In our story, Nanite armor suit using proprietary Atlantean harmonic tech. Worn cleanly on the back in pack form, 2nd SKN integrates into the nerve system of the wearer's Alpha Skin suit. User's biometrics can activate features of the suit beginning with total armor encapsulation. Rated for spacewalks and different planetary atmospheres. A later generation model is equipped with an energy-absorbing flying wing system that produces a luminous discharge during high-speed flight. Often misidentified by post-Atlantis observers as angels, fighters wearing 2nd SKN technology are the origin of winged divine beings in human religious tradition across every culture on Earth.

1v1: One versus one engagement; the purest form of aerial combat. Two aircraft, no wingman, no support.

The *Return to Paradise Series* at a Glance

The Destroying Angel: A Tale of Survival and Discovery

In Book 1, Sonny Fly grips the American Dream by the horns, but that dream shatters when Mylitta falls out of the sky one stormy night. Sonny Fly's losses accumulate. Everything he loves is on the line as he fights to stay alive so he can reunite with his pregnant wife. A two-front attack is underway: one assault from the stars and another from an enemy who's been lurking in the shadows since the dawn of humanity. Instinct outweighs reluctance: a call to duty shoves Sonny headlong towards the ruins of Earth's ancient past to save humanity's future.

Gods and Astronauts: Asag's Treachery

In Book 2, unfamiliar faces emerge to help Sonny and Myli pursue their quest to save humanity. However, Asag, an ancient enemy from a forgotten Armageddon, continues to harbor an ultimate disdain for humanity. Devoid of decency, he will stop at nothing to defeat humanity, including scorching the Earth. Only Asag's treachery can spell Sonny's end. Death is the only setback Sonny can't afford if he's going to save all he holds dear.

The Anachronist Eternal

In Book 3, Sonny finds himself stranded alone at the edge of the Ice Age. After adopting the alias Trip Looper, he emerges as The Anachronist Eternal. Displaced from his own history and Myli presumed dead, fate becomes his cruel companion as he awaits the destruction of Atlantis and the Great Flood. Ava, his artificial intelligence, may prove to be his best chance of surviving the Dark Epoch, but she may be the most dangerous variable of all. Dying in a world he doesn't understand, he falls at the foot of a fountain and meets a new face with an ancient soul. He doesn't know her yet, or does he?

Special Thanks

Thank you, Don and Donna.
I just want to thank you again for everything you've done and for the exceptional guidance you've given me in this novel. Trimming the fat from paragraphs, and even entire chapters. It felt like butchery at first, but it was necessary growth. I didn't know what I didn't know, but I have learned a great deal from both of you. My apologies for the rough chapters and clumsy paragraphs. I truly cannot express how much I appreciate the time, effort, and care you put into helping this come to fruition. Thank you for your patience, endurance, and belief in the story.
Cheers and love.

Mark, you're a real one.
I appreciate you taking the time to ghost-read my first novel with critique and encouragement. Of all the files I sent out, you and the possible cat-fisher, were the ones who took time to read the novel and give feedback. Thanks, bro.

About the Author

Describing my life story isn't easy, but it's full of memorable moments—wild relationships, sports challenges, and even a brief cameo in the movie, *Pearl Harbor.* I started with a BFA in printmaking, played college baseball, married, worked, and now I'm chasing new goals through biathlons and writing. Much of my time is spent ferrying teenagers to their own big life moments and making the most of family time. When I manage to steal a few hours for myself, it's usually late at night—punching keys during binge-writing sessions, building massive worlds and time-bending stories that cut through history. I am always looking for escape velocity. I try to laugh often, risk boldly, and live by two ideas: *Attack where you're weak. Forge every flaw into armor.*